MISS MASSACRE'S GUIDE
TO
MURDER AND VENGEANCE

by

Michael Paul
GONZALEZ

Miss Massacre's Guide to Murder and Vengeance - Author's Preferred Edition
c. 2018 ThunderDome Press
ISBN: 978-0-692-06217-3

Design and Typesetting by Michael Paul Gonzalez

Cover by Michael Paul Gonzalez
(images acquired through license with Shutterstock)

This book will be released in electronic format, but its primary goal in design is to remind the reader of the simple pleasure of holding the printed work in hand. It's small enough to take with you to spread the word far and wide: the paper book is not dead.
Show it. Share it. Help it survive.

Inspired by
Sigourney Weaver, Geena Davis, Uma Thurman,
Cynthia Rothrock, Charlize Theron, Michelle Rodriguez
and every woman who has spilled righteous blood on screen

and

Joanna Jędrzejczyk, Angela Hill, Rose Namajunas,
Ronda Rousey, Shana Baszler, Julie Kedzie, Gina Carano
and every woman who has ever stepped bravely into a combat arena

Dedicated to
Zenon Gonzalez-Lopez and Olga Gonzalez
Aleksandra Bienkowska
Carl Gonzalez
Ollie

Victorious warriors win first and then go to war,
while defeated warriors go to war first and then seek to win.

--Sun Tzu

Do not take revenge, my dear friends, but leave room for God's wrath,
for it is written: "It is mine to avenge; I will repay," says the Lord.

--Romans 12:19

"Death is too easy for you, bitch! I want you to suffer!"

--Pam Grier, Foxy Brown

Sometimes the heroine has to write her own happy ending. I read that once, on a gift card or something, and it really stuck with me. I'm chasing mine by shooting people in the head. Building incendiary devices. Slitting throats and poisoning people. Probably a happy ending would require me being alive at the end. Disney won't be putting this story to film, so I guess it doesn't matter.

Once upon a time, this city was postcard-perfect. Now it's known for two things: constant rain and an unusually high murder rate. Dry spells here are few and far between. The weather's doing its part for the city's reputation and I'm doing mine. Thunderstorms are a boon to business; shopping malls, movie theaters, anywhere people can get out of their house and still stay inside.

For a crazy lady with a rifle, it makes everyday work a chore.

It's filthy up here. Those dry times during the day, that's when moss grows and birds crap and pollution settles down to earth. The rooftops are steep, coated with grime both natural and man-made. The moss clings to the gutters, sewage and stink seep across the gargoyles. Just add water, and it's an instant rotten, sludgy mess.

I'm up to my nose in it, loving every minute. Because I have a purpose. Because this is how things have to be. My forearms burn from the climb, but I won't stop. I was a housewife. I wouldn't hurt a fly. And here I am trying to paint a sidewalk with a man's brains. It's easy to do what you think you can't. You just close your eyes and think of other things. Find a reason. Make one up if you have to. I have ten of them.

Our city was founded long ago by some European devotee who wanted to bring a little piece of the old country with him to America. So the buildings are large, looming, Gothic-Teutonic-Franco-Hispania-buy-a-postcard-and-show-people-where-you-visited. That's the center of the city. The little nucleus from which the great beast spawned. The good part of it is the tiled roofs, which make my climb a little easier. I can punch into the tiny overlap of each shingle for finger holds. And the patterns on the roof, the contrast of dry tiles and wet, terra cotta and tin, help with my camouflage.

The bad part is the angles. This city resisted sprawl, so buildings grew up before the city grew out. We haven't had the fortune of a disastrous fire to gut the town so a more sensible plan could be implemented. I should work on that.

Right here, where I need to punch a small hole in a big head, the streets are narrow and poorly lit. I suppose I wanted to start with a challenge. See if I was up to this whole thing. If I can get the shot off without taking a ride on the roof-grime express to the concrete, I'll consider this a rousing success.

I pull myself over an apex and begin my unsteady descent to the gutter. In planning, I had envisioned myself methodically lowering my body. In doing, my fingers slip and the world lurches sideways. Visions of gore-splattered pancakes dance through my mind as the edge of the roof races up to meet me. Then pain, glorious pain, the kind of pain that meant I was still alive as my body turns sideways and wraps around a gargoyle at the roof's edge at thirty miles an hour. My leg takes the force first, then my ribs. That impact would have snapped my shins like dry kindling. Lucky for me I took them off and left them higher up on the roof. The small things, right? I watch the rainwater cascade down my thigh stump and into the alley as it dangles over the ledge. The pain is indescribable, phantom fire where my foot once was, genuine throbbing agony at the base of my thigh. It feels like it's bleeding, but it always feels like that when I bang it on something.

I slam the hatch closed on the panic welling in my mind, the visions of my own mortality. Almost dead isn't dead. What the hell, this isn't the kind of thing you live to tell about anyway.

Just move and think of other things.

The wind kicks up and the skies let loose a downpour with no warning, sending the denizens of the city scattering like rats in a sewer flood as Vasili's limousine pulls up to the curb by Vincenzo's Ristorante.

Thinking about killing him makes it easier to ignore how easy a mistake up here will kill me.

I watch the sea of ritzy umbrellas bob towards doors below me, hooded heads ducking for cover under canvas overhangs. Soon enough, the

Michael Paul Gonzalez

sidewalk is completely empty. I have a clear view of the tail end of his car through my scope: the rain sluicing down its sides, the two big goons moving to his door, watching both sides of the street without thinking to look up.

I wrap a weightlifting strap around my right wrist, running it through the mouth of a study-looking gargoyle. My left arm tenses as I pull the rifle in tight to my shoulder. My thigh stumps rest on a narrow concrete ledge.

A bit of advice if you're planning to blow someone's head off: find the simplest way possible. I didn't, but it means the trajectory of this bullet will be harder to trace. An able-bodied man wouldn't be able to set up shop here on this three-inch piece of concrete. The right tools also help. This is not the place for a full-on, long-barreled tank-puncher. This gun is custom, more of an overgrown pistol with a light hunting scope. Easy to carry, easy to conceal, easy to fire.

Now, the trust fall. I lean forward. More, and more, and still more, until gravity takes my stomach over the edge. I wince at the brief zero-G experience. The strap shifts in the gargoyle's mouth, then snaps tight as I dangle forward. My right hand is instant pins and needles from the strap digging in. I'll need to make this quick. Ignore the rain that running down the back of my collar. Breathe. I just have to see this through like it's routine, like I've done this a million times before. Maybe I have, who knows?

Scoping in, architecture presents a new challenge. There's a gutter pipe that obscures where I think Vasili's head will be when he stands up. Change to a heart shot instead? I don't want to risk it. I want him to see his final thoughts as they spill from the hole I put in the front of his head and paint the sidewalk.

Vasili's goons grunt a few words to each other and open his door. My finger tightens on the trigger, then eases as two pieces of arm candy shimmy onto the sidewalk and jiggle into the restaurant to save their hairstyles. Any true marksman will tell you that you don't pull a trigger, you squeeze. I know this, so those two pneumatic blondes will live to leech off another man.

Vasili makes his grand entrance. He's small, wiry, not the type of man who looks like a killer, but I know better. He's got that slightly unhinged look in his eyes; not the coal-pit stare of a serial killer, watery eyes that shiver with nervous energy. He kills from a distance, never sees his targets up close. But he's done his fair share. Counting down, he's number ten on my list. Not that there are any numbers higher than ten.

Here is where I should say my memory is not that great, due to prolonged use of recreational pharmaceuticals and severe physical and emotional trauma. I'm working through things. I know all the buzzwords. There are things that I don't remember. I'm pretty sure that there was only one other guy who didn't make the list that preceded Vasili into Hell. Or maybe I've got more notches on my belt than an Oklahoma gunslinger.

The point is, I've done it before, and I plan to do it again until it's done. Ten more times, starting tonight. Starting right now.

Vasili is feeling boisterous tonight. He grabs one goon by the shoulder, doing that street-hug thing where guys will make as much arm and shoulder contact as possible while simultaneously slugging each other in a rough and manly way. It says they care, but not, you know, *care*.

How should I do this one? This fucking gutter pipe is killing me.

Head? Heart? Head? Neck? Knees, then head?

A shot anywhere other than the vitals is wasted. If I had a bow and arrow I'd have the satisfaction of watching Vasili run until he bled himself out, a shaft jutting from his kidney. Fun to imagine, but not as fun as what's actually coming.

The simple path is always the best, but I like to give voice to the demons in my head. I like to let them savor slow and painful ways to do a person. It lets me focus on being methodical.

Good hunting sense says it's a heart shot. But I'm not a good hunter. I'm a great hunter.

Vasili will not have the time to wonder what has happened to him. He won't have time to suffer. He's a bit player in my story, and he doesn't deserve anything better. The empty space I leave in his skull will send a message.

Lightning cracks the sky and I begin to count the seconds. The storm is moving away, and at last check was about four miles.

Four…

I make a final decision that the gutterpipe is old rusted iron, and no real problem for my steel-jacketed long-range round. And then, lucky me, he steps back to say something to the driver, and he's in the clear.

Three…

My sights dance in a large circle around his head, to his chest, his head, then his neck, his head, his jaw, and finally I've got my spot dancing on the base of his skull.

It's almost as if he's begging for it.

Two…

I squeeze the trigger a fraction of a second before a thunderclap hits. To anyone in the restaurant, it looks like Vasili has slipped on the sidewalk, comically stumbling into his thugs' arms. The beautiful people inside are too busy with their meals to see the details: the hole at the base of his skull, the blood that stains the car and the sidewalk and rushes and rinses towards the gutters, the second henchman heaving his guts into the street because a stray piece of skull and brain hit him in the lip.

That's all I need to see. Just enough to make sure he's dead. No time to get misty about these new beginnings. No sense being greedy. Greedy people get caught, and I have nine more people to visit.

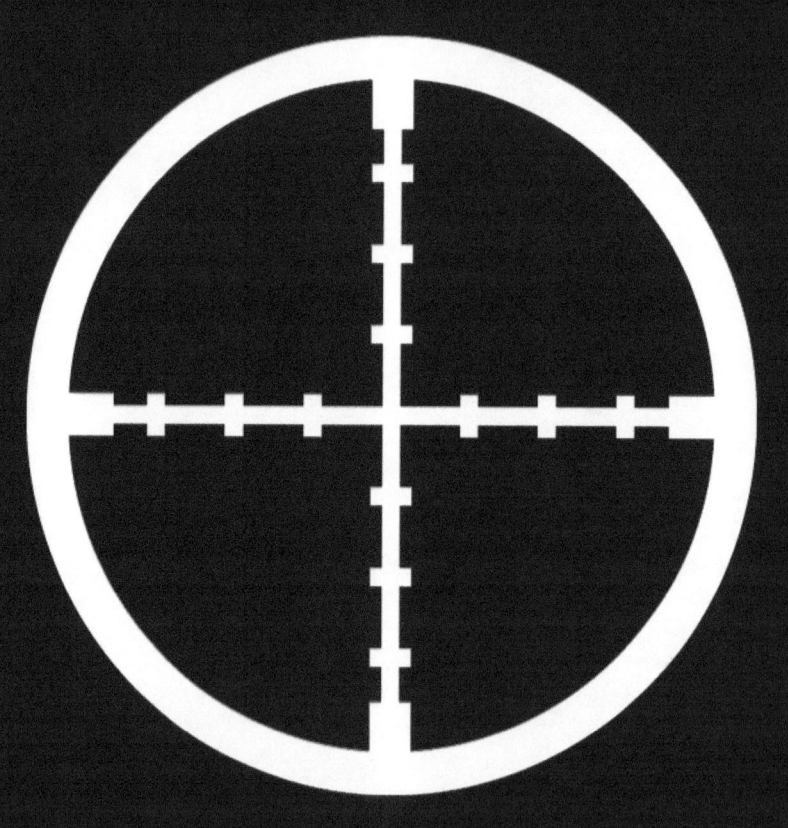

PART ONE

Making a List
and Checking it Twice...

Everything was a blur after the adrenaline from the kill wore off. It made the climb back up easier. I was bolstered by the shouts of Vasili's men, screams from the public. I lit the way to the top with my smile.

That light went out as soon as I got up top. I had a tarp set up on the roof to keep my getaway gear dry, like I had drilled a thousand times, but something got to me. I was sloppy in my prep. It was the whole idea of the list. Making a kill list is easy enough, but when you're on the doorstep of punching the first hole in the ticket, well, that's another story.

I was like a kid rushing to meet Santa Claus. So excited about getting the job done that I didn't think about what I'd be coming back to. I rushed. Forgot to tie off one of the support ropes for the tarp. It wasn't tight enough, it started collecting water, sagged, broke. Sent gallons of water rushing over my climbing legs and everything else I had stored up there. Not what I wanted to see after such a clean shot.

I bought one of those little powder-blue pillboxes at the pharmacists, the kind old people use to separate their daily doses of tabs and pills and whatever to keep their feeble hearts beating. I'd drawn a smiley face on it, the way my daughter used to when she'd leave me a note. I didn't have pictures of her anymore, but I could replicated that crooked happy face blindfolded. The pillbox was a listing ship in a small puddle in my shooter's nest, ready to crest the edge and ride a mini waterfall off the roof. I snag it, staring at the two little Sharpie-eyes in the lopsided circle.

I see her face. This was her face. The joy part. She loved me.

Right? Didn't she?

The box has fourteen slots, M-F AM/PM style. I cut the walls out of four of them on one side to make a long tray for needle storage. The other compartments hold one small glass vial each. A limit and a promise. One hit to pre-game each hit. It helps me focus. I can't remember much about the people I'm going after until I go under with the needle. And even then, if I try to remember more than one step up the list, the images become too intense and my heart feels like it will explode. And that's when the drug is doing what it should.

It's called Clearwater, a derivative mix of oxycontin and morphine, cut with some other basement chemical. Mother's Little Helper, and it's goooood. It's also expensive. So I have to ration. Half a hit, kill a fucker, finish the hit. Sometimes it's three-quarters before. Sometimes the whole thing. How long have I been doing this?

Finishing the little syringe I started right now would be pretty nice, but with my heart pounding the way it is... I shouldn't do it. I tell myself *don't do it* as I'm taking the cap off the bottle. *Don't you fucking do it, don't fill that needle, don't flick it, don't test it, don't scratch your vein you whiny little unhinged shit!* Even numbed by the cold rain, I feel the tip of the needle burning at my arm, licking it hot and lusty like a tiger over fresh prey.

But I stop myself. Focus on the list. The idea of finding the rest of these people, I imagine it's the same way I used to feel about the idea of meeting a boy band when I was younger. So much excitement and energy focused on one moment, and then you meet your heroes and you want to kill them. That was another life. That was my life before. I tell myself anticipation is a much stronger drug, a much harder pull. The next kill will be better than what's in this syringe.

I put the loaded needle back in my kit, put the vial I pulled from the slot marked *S.S.-9*. I punch a small hole in the tray slot labeled *V-10* with my field knife, then I retrieve the spent shell from the little bag I taped over the ejection port of my gun. I go to put the shell where vial V10 used to be. A job well done.

It doesn't fit.

I try it a different way, but there's no way to close the shell in there.

I put a lot of thought into this. This was supposed to be symbolic of—I mean, each slot, could fit all kinds of small trophies. Pulled teeth. Gore-soaked garrotes. Poison quills. Remembrances of meetings past.

Now it's just back to being a stash box. Maybe that's a sign that I shouldn't be leaving evidence.

I jam the box in my backpack, which is soaked, ten extra pounds of water weight to haul down the side of the building. If I had legs, I'd kick myself. I planned and trained for weeks, and didn't think to tie a solid knot. Check, double-check, and check again. The Mantra.

I'm not good at this. I used to be.

I slide over to my climbing legs, shaking the water off. Under the best of circumstances, prosthetic legs are not easy to put on. Mine are modified to come on and off quickly. They rely on friction and pressure clamps to stay in place. The inside of each one is like a Slip 'n Slide, full of water and squirming like a toddler. It makes them uncomfortable. They'll probably twist around while I'm trying to climb back to the ground. No way I have enough left in me to make it down using just my arms.

The solution is simple. I can't spend the night on the roof, so I pull my legs on, sling my rifle on my back, shoulder my pack, and I start the descent.

It's wet, slippery, and scary as hell. The bricks feel like wet glass. Everything hold was so easy to find on the way up. When you can't see them beneath you, it cuts your speed.

A mental note: if I survive this I need to get a book on rope climbing.

Thirty feet up, I shake my right arm to get some feeling back in my fingers, and the rifle slips off my shoulder. It happens.

I spread my legs to try and stop the rifle from going below my waist. It wraps around my body and butts me in the crotch before sliding lower. In my past life, I would have wondered about the Freudian nature of such a thing. Now, I'm too busy trying not to fall. The rifle strap catches the foot of my left leg and wrenches the prosthetic around, giving me an Indian Burn as the leg swings out and away. The rifle is about to pendulum back into my right leg. If it hits, I'll have to hope there's a soft patch in the concrete down there.

I hold my breath, death grip the wall like it's my enemy's testicles, and use my free hand to bat at the release on my leg. The weight of the weapon overcomes friction and the leg releases. I watch my only means of defense and half of my locomotion tumble into the blackness of the alley.

It takes everything I have to get my hand wedged back into the wall. My heart thunders in my chest loud enough to drown the noise of the storm. I hope my falling debris wasn't too loud. Last thing I need is attention. Actually, the last thing I need is to fall.

But hey, at least I'm lighter now.

But in the midst of all of this thinking I've scuttled my way to a drainage pipe. I say a little prayer of thanks for the distraction, followed by another thankful prayer that the rifle didn't go off when it landed. I guess that's a Hollywood cliché, but I've got shit luck with these kinds of things. It would all be so meaningful if I knew who I was praying to. I shimmy down the pipe, cursing under my breath as my fingers are sliced to shit from rusted iron and sharp bricks behind the pipe flay my knuckles.

Sirens.

I stop about twenty feet off the ground. Public hits like this one, the cops move a lot faster, especially when there's an upscale crowd involved. Chances are, they'll fan out pretty quickly to establish a crime scene and find witnesses. Cleaning up after a murder, the

Michael Paul Gonzalez

cops see everyone, homeless or not. Up here, almost level with the downspouts and small gargoyles, I fit right in. I'm just a small, legless lump, a stone beast meant to keep bad spirits away from the building. Walkie-talkie chatter echoes off the alley walls. Someone coughing. Someone rooting through my stuff by the dumpster.

Glancing across the alley, I see a pale version of myself reflected in a window. Missing one prosthetic, I look like a tortured Barbie doll. Skinny leg pointing the wrong way, clothes tattered. It's not like I can dive down and chase after whoever might be going through my stuff. I have things stashed throughout the alley. I have a good set of walking legs down there, a warm overcoat, even a thermos of coffee. I just need to get there, put myself together, walk back to my van.

I hope it's just a homeless guy. He's taking his time. I pray it's just a nosy street punk. Can't be a cop. They always have a friend nearby and they never shut up. Move the fuck on, nothing to see here.

I had to pull the bag-lady routine to get here, using a wheelchair and pushing a shopping cart to carry my goods. It was loud and obnoxious, but people don't see the homeless. I used to be a crusader about that kind of thing. Does it count as exploiting the homeless if pretending to be one makes your job easier? Shopping carts are fabulous war wagons. Couple of blankets to cover my "junk": my assortment of legs, some food, and my current prize possession – the rifle case. It's a fabulous red attaché I found in my van, gold closures, alligator hide, nice. I can't remember what I used to keep in it, but a little foam and some ingenuity made it the perfect stash case when I broke my equipment down. It's the only vanity I allow myself. Which makes me even angrier, because everything I brought is down there, every option I have to get out of here, whether on wheels or wobbling legs, some fucker's rooting through it. All I can do is hang here and try to think of a plan, hoping it comes to me before my grip strength leaves.

Wish in one hand, hold a wall in the other and see which hand gets tired first. My fingertips rip down the brick like a match on a starter strip and I fall into an open dumpster, into the embrace of warm decay. My remaining leg strikes the dumpster on the way in, the sound tolling like a funeral bell for a good minute. A whole person would have been in real trouble had they taken that fall. I think about how many bones the impact with the dumpster would have shattered and it almost makes me wistful.

Still hurts. Something could still be broken. I don't have time to figure it out. If someone's out there waiting to pop me, I might as well meet them halfway. I pull myself up to the edge of the dumpster. The alley seems clear, but I know better than to trust my eyes. I drop over the edge, go flat, flopping and snaking my way across the alley floor to my shopping cart. The wagon lays on its side like a dead beast, its innards picked clean.

No walking legs. No running legs. No case for the rifle. Not that it matters, because I don't see the rifle either. And at the end of the alley, my wheelchair is gone. Thank god I kept the keys to the van in my pocket. Now, how to get there?

I pull myself up and teeter slightly on my one good leg before smacking down to the pavement. My other leg lays by my face, not much the worse for the tumble. Its empty socket stares at me, accusing me, cursing me for letting it drop. I pull it back on and stagger to my tiny spike-feet.

Where's my rifle?

My thighs are cold. Hope that's not from blood loss. I shiver and the phantom pains come. I miss my feet. I can feel them, freezing, stinging. I look down and see the little spike-ends of my climbing legs in a puddle. Cold feet. Now *that* makes me happy. The buzz dies when I try to move my toes. They're moving, all ten of them, but they should feel wet and they don't. Ghosts.

I'll have to walk out of here on these modified legs. They're really only designed for me to rest my weight on while I'm going up a vertical surface. They have a little bit of spring to give me a boost. But they make me about a foot and a half shorter than I should be. I totter down the alley like a drunken dwarf dancing in the rain. I can't do it. But I have to do it.

My van is half a mile down the street. It would be faster to swing on my hands and stumps. Half a mile on my shredded hands to save a few minutes. I should go. I'm still pissed that someone took my stuff. I can find them.

And then what?

The rain picks up. That gives me some cover, masks my noise. It does the same for anyone else who may be following me. I try to keep my head on a swivel, but I'm already standing on two swivels. Snapping my gaze to one side could throw me off balance.

I dive into some trash piles, rooting around in the garbage and filth until I find an old blanket. This'll work. I steady myself on a trashcan and create a makeshift toga to cover my stainless steel gams. The street at the end of the alley pulses red and blue, voices on top of voices.

I stumble, and I flop, and I catch myself on the walls, and I stop every five feet to bend over to catch my breath. None of it is an act.

The glamorous life of a professional killer. Well, pro implies I'm getting paid, so… amateur. Funny how that word has become derogatory. It means *doing it for the love*. I'll never work a day in my life.

The rain wave passes, easing enough that people start to come out to gawk at the crime scene. Rich people are voracious spectators. They love crime scenes, car crashes, anything that reminds them that something happened where money and power would make no difference. Or maybe they like to see other people suffer, I don't know.

I don't care. I jostle along, my troubles inching slowly behind me. Fifty feet away from my van, right around the time when I really start to feel like I've made it, right when my thighs feel like someone is dipping them in acid and I can barely breathe, a car drives by. The headlights are off and the windows are tinted, so I can't count how many people are inside.

They don't honk. The window rolls down in the back and there's a sharp crack, just a little louder than the rain hitting the pavement.

It's one of my walking legs, bent up like a pretzel.

Somebody was sending me a warning that could have come from a Dick Tracy comic. All I was missing was the yellow coat and hat.

Am I scared? No.

Angry? I would say no, but I just spent the evening climbing up a building so I could kill someone. Any good therapist would say I have issues.

What I am is several hundred dollars in the hole. Vengeance killing isn't a cash-flow business. Like any starving artist, everything I do comes from the heart. No sense getting mad. I can't chase the guy down. I'll just have to hope number nine has some cash in her wallet.

I was keeping my head down. Totally off radar with everything I did and bought. Nobody was supposed to know this was starting tonight.

And yet.

What a night. Why does anybody bother making plans? Shit like this always happens.

Someone knows I'm coming, and they're telling me they're ready. The problem is, this isn't a video game. I'm not running to the right until I get to the final boss battle. I arranged the list so that I wouldn't necessarily have to work harder as I progressed. This could be a message from number one or number seven, or maybe just someone who's angry they didn't get to kill Vasili first.

I need to find nine people whose only connection is that they're all part of one horrific night in my life. I was classic, white-bred, Middle America. My inner feminist cringes to hear me say it, but a housewife's greatest treasure is her home and her family. It goes with the job description. They stole it from me.

My whole life turned upside down in two heartbeats. I don't remember much of what happened. Just that my husband and daughter are both dead, and I was supposed to die too. Who has time for details? Not me.

My list, they're all connected, in the criminal sense of the word. But not to each other. They run in the dark spaces between the walls of the city. They feed on the people society throws out. Drug addicts, sex addicts, the asylum inmates freed by the lack of tax-dollar support. All of these people who grind up the city's human refuse and get rich.

One of them apparently knows somebody strong enough to bend airplane-grade aluminum poles with their bare hands. Looking at the rain-spattered metal and plastic, I start to wish for phantom pains. Somebody broke my leg. I want to feel it. *Really* feel it. I feel it in my heart.

I didn't budget for this level of catastrophe. I can't remember my name, let alone my bank account number. Waking up into this new life, finding my house trashed, all I could do was scrape together money, things to pawn, and then get on with things. My life ended when my family died. This is penalty time. I just need to stay on the field long enough to get some good shots off. The worst they can do is kill me and send me back to my family. And if none of them can manage to do that, I'll take care of it myself when I'm satisfied everything's done.

Prosthetic legs aren't cheap. Sure, you can get them in almost every city. They're not that hard to find. It's like buying shoes. Some people don't care what kind of shoes they wear. Some people are picky for whatever reason. Fashion. Comfort. Quality.

It's not like I'm Bruce Wayne. I'm not stockpiling these things in a cave beneath a mansion. I keep all of my legs under a tarp in the back of my van.

Me, I want reliability, and you don't get that just anywhere. I have one dealer. His legs don't stand up to what I put them through for very long. But they do stand up. Or run. Or climb. Whichever design I ask for. Unfortunately, his shop was hundreds of miles from here. Actually, it's just across town. When you don't have legs, every measure of distance is a matter of semantics.

In my past life, I had a lot of shoes. A lot.

We live and learn.

Now, all I have to stand on is climbing legs. It all sounds so optimistic. I'm sure if society wasn't so disgusted by mass murder, my story could be a movie of the week.

News at ten, movie at eleven: "Legs of Steel: Climbing Toward Hope."

Then there's the matter of my rifle. Sure, I can get a new one from the same guy that does my legs. But you lose enough unregistered weaponry and it will make any dealer nervous. Something could come back on them.

I have three guns left in the van. I could go rob a store to get money for some new equipment. With these dwarfy climbing appendages for a smash-and-grab robbery, I don't have a leg to stand on. (In my past life, I found jokes about handicapped people offensive.) I'd have to walk in and put a slug in the cashier's leg, take what I need and get out.

Thirty feet from my van and I'm passing by the front of an electronics store. A wall of TVs behind the glass, all of them on different City News reports. At least fifteen faces stare at me. Women too mannish to make it to the big-time cable news networks. Men with those weird big square heads and side-part George Jetson hairdos. Pasty face-lifted puppets who tell us things for our own good. The little headline over their shoulder, silhouettes with turbans superimposed over different phrases:

City under invasion.

Or...

City Under Siege?

Or...

Terror in the City.

These three-word combinations the result of hours of back-room closed meetings with ad and network execs. Then the real artistry starts. The video packages roll:

Shadowy figures. Slow-motion shots of Sikh men buying groceries or talking on cell phones. Black men hanging out on street corners or in parking lots. Poor white trash in hunter's safety orange jackets putting gas in their trucks or conversing over meals. Subtle hints: this is your enemy. Be on the lookout for this.

Then the money shot, live, thirty yards from the yellow tape surrounding Vincenzo's. Vasili's lumpy mess covered with a black body-bag while the police scour for spent shells, witnesses, leads. This is all about me. All of a sudden I love the news.

This is America the Scared. *Nobody* likes people with guns now, not even the gun nuts. The news eats it up. Every crime is now committed by a disgruntled black man, a disgruntled Arab (but only if mass murder or explosives are involved), or a disgruntled white man.

Closed-captioned frightened suburbanites are claiming to have spotted me just before the shootings. The media eats it up. Be on the lookout for a terrorist. A dark man. A swarthy man. They keep looking for answers half a world away. *He's* got dark skin. *He's* probably ex-military.

Nobody sees a woman. Just fine with me.

Half of the killings that flash by on the screen are just random gang activity. But it's what I'm doing, and where I'm doing it, that's making the difference. It's gotten over the sanctified walls of suburbia. The upper-class is involved, that odd threshold where death moves from inconvenient to important, random death to tragic loss. The chief of police is up there, vowing to get the man responsible, promising more patrols to keep the peace. That means pulling one or two more black-and-whites out of poor neighborhoods and rolling them through already-safe communities to keep up appearances. Increased security doesn't make people feel safer. It's the *illusion* of increased security that cows them.

It does make me think about a strategic shift. Here I am thinking politics when I should be thinking ratings. One more high-profile kill will really thin out the police presence in the seedier parts of town, and I'll be able to make a lot more noise before anyone comes running.

The story wraps up, and how do they follow all of this death and destruction?

A formerly (and still mostly) paralyzed celebrity is showing the world he can move his finger. Who cares? I can still feel it when I move my feet. I can still feel my toes twitch. I just don't have the dead weight to drag around. If I were him, I'd focus that finger until it was good and strong. Strong enough to pull a trigger. Go find that car that broadsided you. Go nail that horse that bucked you. Don't sit back and take anything, ever again.

I don't know what I would do if I was trapped in a chair. Don't know how I'd calm myself. Well, actually, I *do* know. It's in a bottle in my backpack.

When I was confined to a hospital bed, when they were still cauterizing nerves and blood vessels, and feeding me with a drip bag, I made a new friend. We'll call her Mrs. Morphine. She came to visit me with the push of a button. Nerves don't die easy. They make sure your whole body knows that you're never going to feel again. They flare in panic, they send jolts of electricity screaming through your bones, trying to find the doorways and passages that have disappeared. But my new friend, she would wash down my veins and make everything cool and blue and murky.

I had a little trouble shaking her when I left the hospital. Then I met her bigger, stronger uncle, Mr. Clearwater. He's like one of those bad sexual affairs. He still comes around, but I only want him there when things get really rough. And sometimes they still do. When I feel like someone is boring into my spine with a rusted file, I ride Mr. Clearwater. He *really* likes me, and I've been having a hard time telling him no lately. I've got at least nine more dates to make, and I feel like he's the only thing that might get me through.

Nerves. Just nerves.

I catch my breath. Now the screens are showing a picture of Charles Baldacci, last month's target. Loving tributes from family members. It's obvious some of them didn't really know him. They just wanted to be on TV. They should send me a thank you card.

Was he a criminal? Did he just have a bad reputation? I know the truth. I don't know why the media isn't showing any of this. They're acting like he's just a loving family man in the right place at the wrong time. A good, bullet-riddled Samaritan. His blood is in the gutter. His memory should be too. Why should he get the lead on city news? When everything happened to me, I only got one piece. One little five-minute story that didn't rate.

Woman with no legs learns to walk.

Brave woman pays the price for testifying.

After me came a five-parter on animals who could play sports. They spent two nights on the annual Air Show. I got five minutes. The parties responsible for my condition should not be so lucky.

Getting out of the hospital, running the gauntlet of microphones and cameras. And the questions. All of the stupid questions. They knew I couldn't talk, and yet.

"If you could speak to your attackers, what would you say?"

"Are you afraid?"

"How does this make you feel as a woman?"

And on and on and on.

The answers are:

I am speaking to my attackers one at a time, just like Wyatt Earp.

Am I afraid? I've always been afraid, but not of the things you'd think.

And as a woman, I feel pretty, oh so pretty.

Where did I leave my keys?

III

Oprah's on TV, giving one of those weak high-fives to some chunky woman, and I'm *there*, so there, saying "you go girl", and blubbering right along with them.

Positive change today.

Make my life right.

This happens sometimes. If I stay out late, if the memories are too painful, I get a heavy thumb on the syringe and get these weird dreams. Flashbacks of that other life, that faraway time.

The house has deep-pile carpet. The curtains are an embarrassing homemade job that was inspired by one of those crafty TV women. Sort of a sash on a gnarled branch that arcs over my window. Bringing the outside in. To make my house warm. To bring nature to my place of living, so that I won't have to go out and experience nature to *experience nature*.

I have legs though.

Glorious, long legs. Legs that are more Jayne Mansfield than Mama Cass. The kind of legs that keep people interested. When I get like this, I spend a lot of time looking at my legs. Why not? Enjoy them while I think I have them.

The living room is a tastefully done, well-decorated museum of trinkets and knick-knacks. Not too gaudy. Sort of a museum of nearly art. Mass-produced, hand-crafted, collectible things that may rise in value or depreciate over time. A collection that is different from a million other households in America only in the way I choose to arrange it.

Oprah keeps talking. I keep listening. Something about men. I can't understand what she's saying anymore.

Then she comes in.

My daughter, not Oprah.

At least I think that's who she is. This girl. She smiles at me for a while, and then she sits next to me. I think she's asking questions.

I feel my face drift into a honey-warm smile at the sight of her, feel that connection, that protective instinct, the desire to know everything about her, to marvel at all she's done. A couple of bad trips ago, I got this rancid fire in my stomach when I saw her, and I knew it was because she's gone now. And I knew, looking into her eyes, that I would do anything for her. That's when the list was born.

She's still talking. Her face melts into a mask of despair when I don't answer. She's repeating something. Shaking me.

"Not again. Not again."

That's what it sounds like, but I'm not sure. She's looking over her shoulder for something. The door is still open. A shape ghosts into the living room. Dark, shadowy.

I wish my alarm clock would go off. I can't even remember where I went to sleep. If I'm in my van, I'm going to have a stiff neck. I don't actually have an alarm clock. I don't even remember how I got into this. Why do people have to die? Why did anyone have to die?

This girl is crying now, her cheeks shiny and wet, and she's pounding on my chest. Pounding and pounding. Slapping me. Shaking me. All in slow motion. I'm trying to tell her to stop, but I can't even form a syllable in between her peppering blows.

So I shout to myself in the dream. Tell myself to wake up. And the kid climbs off me, staring at me. The more I scream, the more freaked out she gets. I even feel like Oprah would tell me to shut up.

The shadow at the door creeps into the edge of the room, male, female, I don't know. Pushing past her, moving for me. Closer and closer, stretching out, coming straight at my face.

All I want is to open my eyes before it reaches me.

This was just supposed to be a small enlightenment. Clearwater should have been painting pictures of Susan Schrader in my head, but it's fucking with like it always does.

The dark shape has palmed my face, fingers forcing my mouth apart, grabbing my tongue, pushing into my throat. It's funny, the things you try to forget, they never let you go.

I'm choking on it, burnt copper and singed wood. I can't breathe. I need to wake up. The shadow is the taste of everything I've ever done wrong, and I just need to get a breath in to scream and wake--

IV

There are nine people left on my list. I've been reading it over and over while sitting in a puddle of my own sleep-sweat outside of my van on the sidewalk, in broad daylight. Parked in the suburbs. The sun had just come up and I was lucky that no early-morning joggers saw me and tried to help, or worse, called for help. I need an intervention. Instead I climbed inside my van and tried to figure out where to go next.

You'd be surprised, if you really sat down and thought about it, how many people are responsible for a single act of violence. And I don't mean that in the psychobabble, I had a bad childhood, Daddy-loved-the-bottle-more-than-me-so-now-I-must-kill kind of way.

I'm staring at number nine. Picturing her face, remembering everything I can about her. Why I hate her enough to kill her. Do I? Can I? Those are memories I can inject when the time comes. In the meantime, I need to plan. No repeat performances of last night's post-game show.

There are some things that come naturally to me. The shooting, I've always known. It used to be such a great thing. Relaxing with a rifle and a loved one. The most hardened NRA member would weep at the beauty of my idea of a perfect date. I just don't remember who it was I used to go with. My husband. Sure. But that's pretty ethereal.

I need a name.

What's new to me? The logistics. Planning. Moving. Stealth. Sabotage. Vital points. How to kill with a gun. A knife. Your bare hands. How to improvise a blunt-force object. There are so many books that teach you how to do these things. I've read most of them. If I make it out of this, I'll compile them all into a handy guide. *The Happy Homemaker's Handbook for Homicide. Miss Massacre's Guide to Murder and Vengeance.*

Today, I'm going to buy a Boy Scout's field manual. There are knots after knots after knots in there. I will learn new and better ways to climb. Better ways to secure things. I will not lose another item.

It's all a growing experience. Learning to climb, learning to move again...that was my favorite media quote: "One life has finished for her. And now, like an infant, she must learn to eat, to move, to walk...to live again. Back to you, Jane." Fuck you, Brad.

The media gave no shits about me. They painted me as a fighter, a story that would make people at home sit up and root for me while their own lives fell apart. I was a pawn for their ratings. What stung the most though, is that they were right. I had to start completely from scratch. First came breathing without assistance. Then came eating, which will never be the same again. Then walking, crawling, communication.

After the basics of life returned to me, I started to read up on detective work, sniping, hand-to-hand combat, and interrogation techniques of the world's elite forces. I mean the really good ones: Spetsnatz, SAS, Delta Force. To learn about them is to learn about humanity, and an easy way to lose all hope for a brighter future. You think about what SEALs and German GSG-9 forces do to preserve peace and you know peace will never exist. In a chicken-or-egg way, the presence of such men guarantees violence eternal. It all just fit so nicely into my brain. Each of these books was like reading a favorite fairy tale. I knew all of the characters, knew the ending, and just read for the joy of it.

Once I was out of the hospital, my life became about digging. Rummaging through records and files and photos. Trying to remember what happened to me, which I think I've got down, and trying to remember who was responsible for it.

There are details I'm still shaky on. My husband. I remember snippets of our life together. Not who he was, or what he did. But he was handsome. I don't think we fought much. Maybe we hardly saw each other at all. My daughter. Where I used to live. Which hospital I was in. But then there were all of the missing pieces, little black marks across my brain that drove me insane. Did I have friends? What kind of wife had I been? What was my husband's name? My daughter's? Mine? The more I thought about that, the more my brain kept feeding me images of who put me there.

So I made a list.

I remembered their names, mostly. Some of them were shadows and vague memories. I remembered some locations. From there, I talked to people who knew people, and I was on the move. Nobody thought to ask why. Apparently I had been quite the social butterfly on the underground circuit. Everyone thought I was tracking down a fix. And I was, but I got information too. People were scared of me, and not just because of how my face looked.

So the mind was willing, but what about the body? I could shoot. Could I fight?

Practice. I found a few homeless people, drunks. I didn't kill them, just tested myself to see if I could throw a hard punch, or even just strike a person in cold blood. It got easier with each one. I learned to grapple, found ways to fight that worked more on leverage and grip than power and momentum.

Then, I met Charles Baldacci. The details here are fuzzy, too. He was trying to break up my practice with a strung-out junkie in a courtyard. She was a bleeder and a screamer. Not that I was going to do anything more than scare the hell out of her. Maybe get her to quit, to become all of the things I couldn't. I had my gun out. Just to convince her. A little nudge. But Baldacci saw us and yelled, and without thinking, I just turned and fired. Quick-draw style. I didn't even know I had it in me.

Thirty feet away, a hip shot with a revolver.

Right between the eyes, literally.

Luckily for me, the junkie, who was in shock, went nuts. She ran over to his body, babbling from withdrawal and nerves and who knew what else. I put her down with another shot. Just to see if I could, I guess. I'm not proud of this, any of it. I have a job I need to do.

The cops wrote it off as a drug deal gone bad. It was two less roaches in the motel. This was a step towards making sure nobody else close to me got hurt again. I stepped on that little voice that told me that this was wrong, that everyone I cared about was long gone. But anytime it ate at me, I could always inject my cares away.

The bad bile of these memories is burning me. I pull a vial out. Syringe between my fingers like a fancy cigarette, free hand dancing in my pockets for something to tie off. The national Clearwater boom started right here in our humble city when an ambitious piece of trash named Shakes was on a bender. He was working for a hustler named Caligula who, at the time, was going by Pompidou. Pompidou was playing hypodermic darts and Shakes was his board. Stuck seven different needles in his chest, Demerol, morphine, chased it with a couple of oxycontin pills, a little nicotine, you name it. Shakes was a resilient lab rat. He said it was close to the best high he'd ever had.

Close wasn't good enough for the ambitious fucker named Dr. Robert Fortescu, and he refined the formula into what we know as Clearwater. Word has it that the Doctor and some of the higher-ups in the other drug cults are working on a chewable soft tab form. Higher, faster, and no track marks.

Just thinking of that sordid history makes me hungry for a jolt. So I take a tiny taste, a few drips in the lower lip. Junkies call it Three Tears. A trio of little droplets that kind of does a drive-by on your heart, makes you think some amazing high is coming, but it never does. Still, the adrenaline starts to flow, my head floods, and I can focus.

My hand stops looking for a tie off. The burn of memories, the hate and shame and fear of what I know and don't know, slowly recedes.

Time to get down to business. The list.

The ten, I knew for sure, were the prime players. I wish I could just buy a box of bullets and speed through this, but it's dirty work fumigating a city. Slow and steady and methodical. Can't have stragglers running away to breed new colonies.

Right now, the list looks like this:

10. Vasili

9. Susan Schrader

8. Grace Brooks

7. Shakes

6. Caligula

5. Delia Sugar

4. Hooded Jack (?)

3. Dr. Robert Fortescu

2. Veronica Madden

1. ???

It's a mighty big river. And now I've taken the first step with Vasili, forged into those raging waters. And there's no turning back. Delays will lead to lost opportunities, and one opportunity lost means the whole thing is a bust. The faster I get through this, the sooner I get to die. I knew the first time I helped someone take their last breath that my lifespan would shorten with each life taken.

The underworld is a small community. People talk to people about other people. Shakes. Caligula. I'll see them soon enough. And I know they're connected. You have to stack these things carefully. I need all of the information flowing to me, and I need everyone downstream to remain blissfully unaware that I'm sailing.

Number nine. Now.

By the time I set up for the evening, I've read the Boy Scout Manual back to front, front to back. Shaded in the little symbols on the page as I finished. Were I many years younger and male, I could be a Wolf Scout. I'm just satisfied that the knots I've used can hold my weight, and the makeshift pulleys I've made will help me down. Plus, I can use a compass, fold an American flag properly, and identify poison oak. I'm a regular Davy Crockett. My gear will stay dry in the future.

Moot point, as tonight's festivities are indoors. Time to kill a lawyer.

***

Around nine PM, I lay back in my webbing hammock, like Michelangelo painting the Sistine Chapel, me and my list, me and my gun, the finger of God reaching out to take back what he gave. Even God makes mistakes.

I'm tied in to the ceiling, using some fire-sprinkler pipe to take my weight. When the time comes, I'll roll over and shift to the nylon cords I strung through the cement crossbeams, and I'll be facing my target. Hell of a climb. I've been here since about six o'clock. I rolled by the parking garage in full homeless mode at about around five, staking the place out before making my move.

I just had to wait for a large enough SUV to exit, blocking the parking attendant's view. Then I coasted around the corner, hustled down the ramp, and rounded another corner. After five, most civilians are out of an office building. I had a window of about thirty to forty minutes while all of the office staff inside cleaned up and shut down for the day. I got into position in a corner and waited until quarter to six, then I made my move.

I found the crossbeams I needed. I found the inclines just like the paper said. I made the climb up in just under eight minutes. When I practiced for this, I made it in three. Nerves. But I got up here, and thank God the copper piping held me. Now it's just a matter of waiting.

What I'm looking for is a flutter by the door. A little trick I learned by watching the others leave. There are three sets of doors leading to this garage. Air doesn't circulate too well if they're all closed. When someone opens the second set of doors on their way into the garage, the paper shreds I stacked on the floor will be disturbed by a breeze that blows under the crack in the last door.

I have two pistols tonight. Fully-loaded. Laser sights so I don't make an embarrassing miss at close range.

I'm expecting three people. Susan Schrader will be coming, followed closely by a personal assistant or two. My right hand is for her, my left hand is for them.

My right hand holds the good stuff, cross-tops, steel-jacketed hollow-point rounds. The kind that will leave a dime-sized hole on one side of her body and a softball-sized hole on the other. My left hand holds the rubber bullets. Little high-velocity jelly-rubber projectiles that are playfully marketed as "less-than-lethal ammunition". Just a nice solid dose of pain for the peons.

The paper on the floor flutters a bit, then explodes out in a whirling sea. Susan, hard worker that she is, isn't wearing her high heels tonight. I should have heard her coming. Last one out of the building. She's earned a little comfort, right?

I'll give her comfort. I'd rather give her fury, an angry speech that will make her realize that tonight, she doesn't get to drive her Audi back to her penthouse. *Tonight, you punch out for good.* I don't know, some dramatic thing like that.

When I planned this out in my head, I always envisioned stalking over my target, forcing them to look at my body. I would ask them:

Do you see what you did? Do you know who I am?

But it all seems like wasted time and wasted energy. It's much better their final bit of oxygen is used up making their brain spin through the Rolodex in their mind, searching for answers: was it this person or that one? This wrong revenged or that hungry criminal bidding for more power? Better they shouldn't know.

Or maybe I'm still too chicken to talk. It's not easy for me. Other people can speak without thinking. Insert politician joke here. But for me, speech is work, and damn hard work at that.

I can hear them talking out in the hallway.

-Did you remember your papers, someone asks.

-Let me check.

-Did you call your husband?

-I'll call from the car. Can I relax? Can I have a minute to my own thoughts? I'm going home to eight more hours of paperwork. You've got, what? Two hours of social media while you fall asleep bingeing shows online?

Susan, Susan. So shrill.

I understand how hard you've been working. Who you've been helping to put back on the streets. Whose cries you've ignored in your quest to line your pockets. You deserve a break today. I'd like to start with your spine.

Someone's hand is on the door. A jingle of keys, then a beep as they pass their access card over the sensor. The lock clangs over and the door opens.

It took hours to set this up, and I have less than thirty seconds to finish it. Everything has to happen fast. Fast fast fast.

I stiffen my right arm, hoping I've profiled the woman correctly. She's got her PAs pretty whipped. She'll be the first one through the door. She's neurotic. She walks too fast and too stiff in her high heels. Problem is, tonight she's barefoot. She might be able to sprint. That said, she's overloaded, carrying her heels in one hand, holding them by the straps, checking her cell phone for messages and trying to get keys out of her purse.

She's under me. Right under me.

But the damn PAs haven't come in yet. Susan hasn't moved far enough from the door to allow them passage. Not that they would dare to walk in front of their mistress.

Can't take her down until I can take them down. Once they get inside, the magnetic lock on the doorway seals. Only someone with a keycard can open it, and the only people with keycards are bosses like Susan. So everyone has to be inside the garage where they can't run back for help. Plus, I need time to get away. A lot of time. I've got my harnesses rigged in so I can drop to the floor quick after the kill. Then I have to get over to them and get their phones, this by crawling with my arms.

Susan finds her keys and now she's moving like someone lit her rear end on fire. This is horrible. I can take her now, but I'll have to get the others at the same time. Two shots, two different directions, then a cleanup.

I focus and take a breath. I look at the PAs and pick the quicker-looking one. I look at Susan and lock my right arm. I close my eyes, and when I open them, I squeeze. Sight-acquire-fire.

I watch the PA go down in a heap, gasping for breath and hands scrambling at her exploded shirt.

Susan is bent at a funny angle over the trunk of her car, a huge burgundy blossom spreading across the side of her blouse. The second PA, God bless his helpful little soul, goes rushing right over to her. He's patting her, calling her name, getting fingerprints all over her. Not that I'm reading into any of this, but he's shaking her by the butt as he asks if she's all right. I think he's taking what he can get.

My left arm stiffens and I squeeze, nailing him right between the shoulder blades. He gets a lot more of Susan as he collapses over her doggie-style and then falls to the floor, pulling her down on top of him.

For a minute, there is no noise. The peons twitch a little bit, but you couldn't call it moving. Jelly sacks hurt a lot. If you've never been hit with one before, you're going to think you're dying. You'll feel like your guts exploded. Hell, even if you *have* been shot with one before, you won't be whistling Dixie. They're both in shock. They don't know what to do next, and thankfully, they're blind to anything that doesn't involve their immediate safety.

I ratchet my way down from the ceiling, stopping just above the ground to release myself. My waist pack snags one of the nylon cables, twisting it off. I make a move to catch the pack, but it's falling too fast. And then, so am I.

It's in slow motion, so even though it's only about three feet, it feels like an eternity. My legs begin to kick, feet pointing to the ground and pinwheeling, body trying to right itself. Except I don't have feet, which means the stump of my right thigh jams into the concrete first, causing pain like I haven't felt in some time. I almost black out.

Paranoia sets in, and adrenaline follows. I roll over, tap the stump to check for blood: it's dry. One quick look at Susan: still dead. Time to clear out the evidence.

My waist pack is burst open like the spilled guts of a suicide diver: my keys, some spare change, things that I can't leave lying around for evidence. I scramble to get them up as fast as I can.

Mercifully, the rope harness I rigged up behaves itself. Another simple knot, learned from my new favorite book before I got up to the ceiling, is easily shaken loose. The nylon cords slide down from the support beams and I stuff them in my pack.

I pull myself over to Susan and watch her pupils dilate. She frowns at me. , not sure if it's recognition, but then she lets go. She's gone.

The PA paws at her from below, struggling for breath. Security probably would have gotten a kick out of this video in the morning. But their recorder is in the parking booth, which will be my last stop on the way out. The attendant left for home a couple of hours ago. After all, nobody can get into or out of the garage after seven o'clock without the gate opener. Everything looked perfectly safe on his last security sweep. He walked his route and left, and never looked up to see me.

Susan spasms, letting out a strange huuuuh sound, which happens every once in a while with fresh corpses. It jolts me, reminds me of where I am, and how much pain I'm in from that fall. Every time I extend my right arm, there's a shock like a rusty nail lodged in my shoulder socket. My right thigh feels like it's on a low boil. White spots flare in my eyes and my mouth tastes like copper. I need to get out of here.

Susan spasms again, this time a multiple burst of short, staccato *huh-huh-huhs*. It doesn't scare me. People do this when they die. Few people know about it because Hollywood doesn't show it. Muscles twitch and dilate, including the diaphragm, so the lungs can pull in minimal air, rush it over perfectly relaxed vocal cords, and you get a nice little dead man's laugh.

I watch, hoping to see some kind of spark leave her, a black mist escape from her mouth.

A series of images flashes across my brain.

A courtroom. A woman, crying. Another woman watching, stern faced. Vasili, smiling. Somewhere else, blood. A lot of blood and sound, and I should be doing something to stop what's happening, should at least try to...and in the courtroom again, I'm crying, not me. Not me. Not guilty. Not guilty. Not...

Someone *is* crying here. Someone is sobbing. Susan? Did I miss a vital?

"Where...where?"

It's one of the PAs.

She's rolling on the ground, clutching her stomach

I had been aiming for her shoulder. Sloppy work, but down is down, I guess. Better her than me.

What will she tell the media? She *will* talk to the media, they all do. I'm not going to ask her not to, because that's going to make me look even worse.

I should say something. Your boss. There are things about your boss you don't know. She's bad. She's a very bad woman.

I don't say anything. Instead, I gather up their scattered cell phones.

"Where...my book...why...I left in the..."

She's in shock. She can't even see me. She doesn't know who I am. She never will. She gasps for breath, reaching her hands down to her stomach, bringing them to her face, checking for blood again and again. A bruise, I want to tell her. All it will leave is a big ugly bruise, and most of us would be thankful for that.

She closes her eyes, convinced she's going to die. She keeps breathing and breathing. Susan's blood has trickled over, so I move before it laps against me. The police will see the blood, and they will question this poor girl just out of college. They will accuse, they will prod, but eventually, they will figure out she had nothing to do with it. I will be far away by then.

The PA opens her eyes again and her hand hits Susan's blood. When she sees it, she'll think it's hers, and that will be just enough to trigger a surge for a life-saving scream.

I go to the corner of the garage, where my flatbed cart full of raggedy blankets waits for me. The rope shifts around in my backpack, clinking against the little clear bottle inside, and I hear it talking to me.

Feeling bad, huh? You're not going to make it out of here without me.

Shut up.

You're going to pass out. They're going to find you. You need me.

Like I have time to shoot up.

Drink me.

What am I, fucking Alice?

It takes everything I've got to lift myself up six inches and flop onto the flatbed roller. I pull the filthy blankets around me, the camouflage of being just another hungry mouth on the street. I huddle inside the dirty warmth, safe on my wheels. I slap at the floor with my hands, propelling myself towards the garage exit. I think the bottle is going to win when I get back to the van. My shoulder hurts way too much to be anything less than a sprain.

I swallow the pain and I hustle, pushing harder, telling myself that the bottle didn't win tonight. I will have earned it. I'm not addicted. I'm in pain and it helps me.

After stopping to nab the security tapes and smash the monitor and cash register, I move to the street entrance. It takes a little bit of doing to get around the tire spikes at the exit. When I finish, I'm out of breath. I want a place to rest. I want my van. I want a bed. I want my old life.

I stop at the curb as the pain wins the battle against my resolve, emptying my guts into the parking lot. Homeless people do this sometimes, and if people see, they'll turn away. The plan survives, I tell myself. Just keep on puking.

The street is empty. Or almost.

There's that damn car again.

Sitting across the way. I stare at the driver's-side windows, obsidian mirrors blinding me to the truth. The car takes off like a shot. Nothing thrown at me this time. No cryptic messages. This message was loud and clear. I am being watched and they want me to know it.

This is getting old. Maybe I should find a new hobby.

It starts to rain, loud and heavy enough to cover the PA's screaming.

Brown sedan. I think it was brown. Could be dark gray. Four doors. Didn't catch the license plate.

I'm actually glad the car was there. The adrenaline brings me back up, dulls the siren song of the Clearwater vial in my backpack.

I make my way back to my van, the sound of rain hitting my roof, each drip matching the ragged breath in my lungs. The wet streets absorb the headlights and there's not much in the way of ambient light. It's just one big, smeary twenty-minute jaunt. I know the route so well I could do it with my eyes closed.

The next time I blink, I'm in the library, my staging ground. Somewhere between driving and realizing where I am, I parked my van – hopefully – and slept a little. You can learn about anything here. Makes and models of cars, for instance. Helpful tips on hunting. If you like learning how to kill, the Library of Congress suggests *Gray's Anatomy, Archery for Beginners, Rifle Hunting the NRA Way, Perky Patty's Perfect Guide to Pulverizing Household Pests.* Books that detail the weakest parts of the human anatomy, best spots for kill shots, helpful household products that make great poisons, that sort of thing.

The main branch of the library is attached to the records

department of City Hall. I can look up anything about buildings: when they were built, why, the architecture style, ventilation systems, unused hallways.

The architecture of City Central is incredible. It's a ridiculously huge complex, laid out (as the name suggests) near the center of the city, all domes and sandstone and brick and green gutters and bas relief. Magnificent. I could climb this building with just my arms, there's so much carving and stonework. The library is here, City Hall, the County Seat, DMV, BLM, you name the letters, they have an office here.

I love the library. I hate being rushed. I don't know who's following me, but if their intention was to mess up my plans by making me rethink my plans, it's working.

Frances, my contact behind the desk, thinks I'm a graduate student. He greets me with a smile every day, runs about as fast as his chubby legs will carry him if I need something. I think Frances likes me. I don't like Frances, but I don't hate him either. He feels sorry for me because I have no legs. He feels bad for me because of my hairline. He told me once that he could see through the scars on my face, that underneath was a radiant flower.

He actually said radiant flower.

He touched my cheek when he said it, and I haven't been quite as nice to Frances since. He's lucky I didn't dislocate his fingers and sprain his wrist, but honestly, I was just shocked that another person would want to touch me. He's still professional towards me, still helps me as much as possible. But we both know a line has been crossed.

Frances is the kind of guy who'd really like the person I think I used to be. The lady who did arts and crafts and watched daytime TV. Somehow, Frances would be interested in these things, or at least say he was because he'd be afraid of losing me. Once I start to learn more about my past, I might talk to him a little more, just to see what kind of friends I used to make.

The museum tour of my mind is a full package deal, and if he sees one exhibit, he'll get nosy and want to see all of them. Letting Frances into the newer corners of the museum would scare him. I think he's the type of man who, if sufficiently provoked, would wet his pants. It may also lead him to make phone calls, to brag to his two or three good friends over their game of Mazes & Monsters at the coffeehouse. And maybe he'd call the cops. So I don't let Frances in.

Right now, he's bringing things up from the basement archives. He ran when he left, trying to impress me, I think. He told me about his diet. He's lost ten pounds in the last month, all from eating only one kind of sandwich, every meal, every day. Honestly, I think he's got one of those faces where it will never make a difference, all round and cheeky. His corduroy pants screamed as he scuffed away, like a three-hundred-pound cricket.

I asked him for the ground plans of three different parks on the outskirts of the city. I wanted original layouts, landscaping receipts, anything he could find. Frances has been working for at least a month on this. It's for my thesis paper, as far as he knows. I'm comparing and contrasting the city as it is now to how it was forty years ago. I'm exploring the impact of urbanization, poverty, and gang activity on underdeveloped commercial properties. Or something.

Loud metallic thumping starts up behind me, screeches and groans and cables and chains. The elevator is hauling Frances back to me. The doors rattle open. Frances tries to whistle as he approaches, but his breathing is labored. Frances doesn't enjoy walking.

"It's our lucky night!"

Our. So clingy, Frances. Let me go, let me be.

Frances sets down three musty rolls of blueprints. He hands me an old brown folder, bound with string, still warm from being held under his armpit. There are photos inside, neatly divided by decade, showing the progression of the parks.

"I don't know if you needed them, but I also found a great bunch of newspaper clippings from when they converted half of Bremmerton into a parking lot. A bunch of real nifty stuff. Did you know the soccer field used to be a natural amphitheater? All sorts of uproar from the citizens when they converted it, you know? Still holding on to the idea that art could win out over the suburbs. Like the city wasn't growing like...like a..."

Frances isn't good with metaphors.

"...big...city. Anyways, it gives you a good idea of what the people had on their minds."

I nod my head at Frances and bury myself in the photos. The grounds surrounding the soccer field. I had no idea it was built so perfectly. Tailor-made for my needs. It'll give me time to set up, time to get away, natural blinds. The acoustics. This is going to be poetry. Dangerous, too. I need to get a closer look at things. But...

Frances hangs by the table expectantly, shifting a little from foot to foot. He feigns interest in the photos. After a few minutes he pretends to look at the blueprints, running his fingers across certain lines, saying "hm" thoughtfully, hoping, begging me to ask a question.

I don't. Frances slinks into the shadows. I think he's pretending to reshelf some books, but I know he's watching me.

Hunters have remarkable patience. I can wait him out, pretend that there is a detail in one of these photos that is somehow crucial to my work. But I don't. I spend about three minutes on each photograph and jot a note on my notepad. If you're fascinated, other people will be too.

Unfortunately, Frances is in love. So he waits and shuffles and breathes and wheezes and sighs and clears his throat and moves and dusts and reads and looks out the window and brushes by the table three times to see if I need anything and goes back to re-shelving and begins the cycle over again and all of it lasts forty-five minutes.

Forty-five minutes.

I wanted to give Frances a hundred dollars. A hooker could have given him something for forty-five minutes that he needed, and I could have told him where to go to get the best deals. I feel bad wasting his time, and I feel bad that he's wasting my time. Finally, the elevator doors rattle open and Frances's breathing recedes down the open shaft.

I'm alone again.

Now I can get into the specifics.

Where are the highest trees? Where are the tallest bushes? How often is the area landscaped? Where are the service roads? What can you see from the most-traveled roads? The least? Is there a back door, a way few people enter? If you have no legs and have to run across open fields on artificial jogging legs, which path will give you the most cover and the fewest obstacles?

I have to make the park my home. I have to know everything about it, because the next job is going to be horribly public, and fairly dangerous.

Up until now, what I've done could be filed away as random acts of violence. An anomaly. Two in a row will probably bring new tags: *obsessed* or *focused*, a possible vigilante, a probable criminal warlord. This next one is going to be ugly. It's going to put me in the category of *brazen* or *crazed* or even *lunatic*, although I think they'll only use that on the tabloid news shows. It could even land me the big *M*. Monster.

But still, the hit has its upside and downside.

Positive: It'll be the last hit before I drop into the underworld. You start by nailing public figures. The kind of people who, when killed, elicit responses like, "I just don't see what anyone could have against him." The kind of people who are called *genuine citizens*, *caring individuals* and *pillars of the community*. You make it look like an organized hit. A family thing. Maybe one of the drug cults getting out of control. Anger the public. They yell enough, then the police feel like they have to act. So the cops roll into Red Light, or the wharfs, or the warehouse district, and they start busting heads. The criminals lay low, bunker down. *They stand still.* My kind of target. The cops don't stick around for long, but the beasts are slow to come back out of their caves.

Positive: This will make two women in a row. Again, that ghost of the feminist I was in my former life cringes. She would use words like *problematic* about my methods. I like being problematic. And later I'll get to be misandrist as hell and she'll love that.

This hit, though. Wives will focus on this. They will talk about it incessantly. On the phone, while their husbands listen. To their husbands over dinner. To their boyfriends. They won't feel safe going out at night. They'll gather and protest. The men will feel compelled to do the same, not in the name of justice, but as always, just to get the women to stop talking. It's all marketing, pure and simple. If anything will make cops start moving, it's the assassination of two prominent women in the community.

And best of all, it will cement the image of the killer in the press: he's a man with a grudge, a crazed misogynist, all of the hastily chosen talking-head experts will say. A religious fanatic, someone with an axe to grind. Someone who hates women.

Negative: This will be very public, and noting my past two performances, the fuck-up factor will be high.

Susan Schrader, last night's main course, was probably the second or third most popular female attorney in town, if such things as popular attorneys exist. If you made a list of the top ten lawyers, she'd be the only woman on there, near the bottom of course, damn glass ceiling. She has helped a lot of people get their lives back in court. One of her clients deserved life in jail, and she got him off with minimal time, and I can't have that.

That vision I had in the garage, the courtroom scene, had left a few solid facts. Susan Schrader defended Vasili in the court room. I think I was testifying because he tried to kill me. It had something to do with my husband, too. Susan, that bitch, didn't care. She just put Vasili in a shiny suit and stood up next to him with her Honorable Citizen paintbrush in one hand and her this-woman-is-hysterical-and-not-a-viable-witness brush in the other.

The bottle would be great now. I could try to bliss out and focus on that courtroom until the drug brings a vision of my past into the light. But now I need focus.

Focus.

Number Eight: Grace Brooks. A powerful woman, one who controls many different things by day and even more by night. When they syndicated her TV show, she took out a healthy life-insurance policy on everyone in her family. Rumor has it her husband tried to cash hers in early. He even added some additional accidental dismemberment riders to the policy. And then he found out that everything he knew about her was just the surface of a very deep, dark pond. He also found out she had a policy out on him, too. Not too huge, since she was already rich. She had connections, and they made it all look like a horrible act of gang violence. She's been the merry widow ever since. Her ratings are higher. She even established a charity fund for after-school programs *in his name.*

Ruthless businesswoman. Personable, yes. She gives to a lot of different charities. Her own empire, stretching far and wide across the land, and for the most part, perfectly legal. She's a bit of a recluse. Her shooting studio is located on her expansive ranch. She doesn't have to go anywhere for anything.

In fact, Grace Brooks only routinely sees daylight in public once a week in the late summer and early fall, and only for one thing.

Grace Brooks is a soccer mom.

A professional game would give me so many opportunities. So many different ways to get close. But a kid's game is too intimate. The no-legged lady puffing her way across the grass would be singled out in no time. Grass is hard for me, unless I've got my running legs on, and those make me the center of attention. They're big loopy things, sort of inverted question marks, loud when I move because of the way they spring back. So I have to do this one long distance and hope no one hears my springy serenade as I flee. I hate it.

Shooting three in a row. It feels cowardly. I know, the end results are all that matter, but killing at a distance doesn't really feel like killing at all. Part of me hungers to feel it, feel the breath leave someone's body, see the spark fade. It scares me, but I have to know. I have to know because it will open doors. And part of me knows it's another line to cross, another forward step that can never be retraced.

I want to get my hands dirty. I won't love it, but I'll need to get used to it. The next chunk of the list will be far more up close and personal. In the meantime, I need a new rifle. Progress is progress, no matter how you look at it.

Across the room, the clock strikes ten. I'll have to get copies of some of these maps to study later. That means talking to Frances again. A woman's got to do what she's got to do.

A flicker. A little bolt at the corner of my vision. I look out the window: nothing. This being City Hall, there are a lot of vermin here, both the literal and figurative kind. But whatever just moved across my sight was no mouse. No bug. Too bright and red. I wait for my pulse to slow down and go back to my studies. Every hair on my body is standing up, even the phantom hairs on my legs. If this is what I think it is, sudden movement probably won't help.

The drawback of the City Central is that the large government buildings are surrounded by the even more monstrous buildings of the downtown business strip and the Gothic Promenade Mall, like this grand old structure is ground zero of the population explosion. Good old urban sprawl. A shooter's best friend and worst enemy.

It's when I look down at the map that they make it obvious. A bright red dot, smack in the center of my paper. It moves, slowly, across the table and over my hands before climbing my chest and circling there for a while.

Somebody's got me sitting dead red.

You live by the sword, you die by the sword. If they were going to shoot, they would have pulled the trigger years ago. This is more of the same intimidation shit. They want me to know they know. So, a quick deduction tells me that it could be one of two things:

I have something or know something that they need.

Or...

They don't mind who I kill, as long as I don't get close to their boss.

I take my time rolling up the maps and laying them across my lap. I leave the books spread out, alongside Frances's extra efforts.

Now, here's a dilemma. Do I try to look tough and wheel my way to the elevator, turning my back on them? Or, do I back up, keep my eye on them and show them that I acknowledge their presence?

Either way, they're getting the finger before I leave.

I should be scared but I'm not. I don't feel much anymore. I'm not psychotic. This much I know. What I am doing is not a cry for help. What I am doing is not self-destruction. God knows I've had enough of that. I want to live. For at least another two weeks. It's about all I'll need. Then we'll see. I cherish my life. It is because I cherish my life that I'm doing any of this.

I have eight people left to live for, and I'm going to lose them all. They've taken half of me, and they'll have to fight for the rest. And I don't care how much it hurts or even if it kills me. I've lost any sense of hesitation I may have once had. And the thrill that comes with that, with riding the crest between life and death at any moment, it's delicious. It's better than sex or chocolate, and Lord knows those were my two legal vices in my other life. Now I only have one.

I am bringing justice.

God, that sounds pathetic, I know. I'm just angry. Just an angry woman looking to solve her problems. The truth is always far from poetic and never too exciting. But the stuff about the chocolate stands.

As much as I've tried to ignore it and keep working, the sniper is still waiting. Professional courtesy. I've glanced around enough to know this isn't a distraction. The only person trying to sneak up on me here is the size of a water buffalo and in love with me.

I could wait this out. I fell asleep here in the library once. The drawback, of course, is Frances. Last time, I woke up to his roundness towering above me, just folding his hands and staring. Staring at where my legs used to be. I'm a notoriously heavy sleeper. Could sleep through an earthquake. I actually did once. So who knows what else Frances might have done while I dozed? Who knows why he was folding his hands, why he was staring?

He probably wanted to touch them. So many people want to touch them, run their hands over the smoothness of each dome, feel the scars, the hard protrusion of what's left of my femur. It's not that some perversity might have taken place that bothers me. I've had enough indignity in my life that I can't be bothered with such things. It's the objectification.

Some handicapped people choose to call themselves "differently-abled." "Handi-capable." What a load. Only someone not permanently bound to a chair for life would think of something like that. Or someone fresh in the seat, trying to convince the world and themselves that nothing's changed, they just have to try harder now. They have nothing but time.

I make sure not to have that luxury. We're different all right. We get a very special gift. We get to be the center of attention everywhere we go. People either cater to our every whim, or they stare at us like we're going to explode or fall apart or hurt somebody.

Apparently, I'm not reacting enough for the shooter. The light on my chest starts to blink. They're picking spots. Hand. Chest. Hand. Neck. Re-sighting while the laser is off, turning the laser back on only to prove how accurate they are without it. Very nice. I fight hard to suppress my smile.

The elevator's coming again. Frances must have found something even niftier to bring me. I wonder if he'll see the light on my chest.

"Here's an extra map I found."

Jesus, he's breathing like a boiling teapot.

"It looks like there have been some changes to three of the north-side parks in the last four years, and plenty more changes on the way. There are four-dozen imported oaks near the soccer fields. They rolled them in here fully grown, huge right out of the forest. Our tax dollars at work. Geez, with all the crime here, you'd think they had better things to spend money on—"

I hold out my hand and Frances places the map there reverently, a page giving the queen her scepter. I use the map to point at some of the photos across the way, and of course, Frances pounces like a big eight-hundred-pound blob of a jungle cat. Perfect.

He moves in between the window and the elevator, and for once, I'm happy to have him close. Frances is my shield. My final proof the sniper was not out to kill me. Unless he was packing some kind of single-shot bolt action rifle, he could have taken Frances down and followed with a fast shot to the head. Sometimes, just the idea that with a motion of your finger you could change a life, is enough.

I look out the window, but the sniper has already capped his laser. He's not giving anything away.

I wheel back to the elevators quickly, motioning to Frances. I wave my copy card at him. He lumbers to the elevator, still taking up the whole aisle, probably with a red light dancing across the rolling hills of his back.

Frances squeezes into the elevator. The smell is horrid. All grease and old Bakelite and unwashed crevices of flesh. His heavy breathing almost outmatches the machinery. Even standing in an elevator is something of an effort for Frances.

As we begin to lower, I look towards the window and flip the bird. The red light dances across my middle finger and down to my heart. Somebody out there has a sharp eye. I'm below the floor before I can get a good look out the window.

Frances notices my finger and starts to laugh.

"Yeah, I hate research too. I had a hard paper to finish once, you know, before I decided to stop college..."

And on and on and wheeze and on and sweat and on and on...

By the time I get my copies and escape Frances, I almost hope the sniper is waiting outside to put one through my heart.

Let's go for a walk.

Why not?

I've got legs again, and damned if I'm not going to use them. Why shouldn't I cartwheel? Why shouldn't I wear the shortest shorts I can find?

These dreams are always so strange. I'm coated in makeup, choking through the smoke in a red room.

Not red.

The light is red.

The room is filthy...swarming with people. Everyone drinking...

It's a bar.

Okay. What am I doing in here?

Getting a lot of looks, that's one thing. People are aghast, if I may use such a word. The room rocks slightly, shifting as I walk. Like the floor is made of rubber, or maybe I've been drinking.

Everyone rushes towards me, a few of them holding towels,

napkins, anything. Reaching for my face.

A word is shouted: **NO.**

And now everyone hesitates. Towels half-outstretched. Posture hovering somewhere between fight or flight.

I didn't say it. Who said it?

Everything in the room is two-toned, either red light or shadow. I thought maybe my legs were dirty, but they're splotchy. Dark black splotches barely visible in the dimness. Maybe these aren't cutoffs I'm wearing. Maybe my pants were torn. I'm bleeding. I'm hurt.

But look at my legs! No cuts…where did the blood come from? How could I ever have taken these things for granted? God, I would spend all night rubbing them and squeezing the flesh, but this crowd gathering around me is already giving me strange looks. Every time I turn my head, there's a shower of droplets.

I push some of the people away. Blood and anger, do not touch me. There's a voice bellowing, I think it's saying *police*. Ah good, help is here. Or is it? Everyone starts to back away from me now. I should get out of here. I should sit down. But then again, I could bleed to death. Maybe I'm good to leave. Maybe I'm just wobbly drunk, okay enough to drive to the hospital.

What can I do?

There's a scuffle in the middle of the room. People tangled up. A man pushing his way free from a mob. He was fighting someone, and that someone is down and bleeding worse than me. The man's in pretty rough shape too. He calls out again, *police*, and instead of thinking, *good*, now I'm worried. Dread settles over me. Am I in trouble? He looks at me, and his eyes say a lot. There's anger there. Love, anger, release. He bolts, heading for the exit.

Something taps my foot. A bottle, the bottom half of a broken bottle, rolling on the floor. Was I holding that? Someone in here got sliced. Or maybe it was me.

A mass exodus, people are pushing and punching and

surging, all of them trying to block the door, to get that man. They're going to kill him. Dread. The man throws a couple of elbows, busts some noses, and hits the exit, flying out the door with a mass of angry people streaming after him.

The bar gets dead quiet. There's just me and a couple of other people. They look at me and they're scared. Is it because of how I look or because I want to kill them?

I want to kill them? Hardly seems worth the effort. Might as well go and see what's happening outside.

I sway through the door, leaving them behind me. The night air in the city is horrible when it's just finished raining. Rain brings the filth of the skies down to our level. And it's too damn humid; like trying to breathe tomato soup. I'm choking on it. My jaw feels like it's gone Picasso.

I take the steps one at a time, crumbling concrete lifting me slowly back to the alley. Underground bar...is this the kind of place I would have let my legs take me? I want to leave, but there's something happening out here that I have to see. Somebody is calling my name. Calling for help. Screaming.

Now there are other voices, orders, the man from the bar sounds like he's been pinned down.

Down a corridor of trash bags and dumpsters, homeless people and club kids waiting to get into the basement I just pushed out of... Kids, so young they shouldn't be here, not this late, not in this part of town. If any of them have noticed any of this, they're doing a good job of hiding it. Or rather, they know better than to notice what's happening.

At the end of the alley, a mound of people pulls away from the man from the bar, down on the ground. Someone's shaking something over him, a tin box. The smell of gasoline.

Thunder rips the sky and it starts to rain again. Washing me, making me pure. It's cold enough to make my face go numb, my lips buzzing. The water cascades strangely off my chin, like it's coming down a spout. It burns. It makes my chin feel like rubber. I touch my jaw and even with all of this rain, my fingers come back coated in blood. Something is stuck under my chin. At first I think it might be my necklace tangled up, but it's too big. Too round. And it hurts when I tug at it, whatever it is. But like any annoying scab, I have to pick at it. Grab it and pull. Like ripping out a Band-Aid.

Only it's glass. Lightning flashes, making it clear that what I'm holding is the top half of a broken bottle. Bits of my flesh stuck in some of the cracks, my blood soaking the label, and I'm worried that the last thing I'll smell is the hops and barley of this cheap swill.

Someone grabs me from behind and spins me and I fall. At the edge of the alley, the man creeps around the corner on all fours. I watch him retreat and my chest fills with air. The pelting of the rain swallows my scream. I gasp to scream again, and the rainwater is like acid on my tongue.

I hit the ground, and across the way there's a big white SUV, the rear door open, the faint silhouette of a girl there, green-skinned and rings around her eyes.

Pinkish water sluices down my front and my legs and I'm like a newborn. Covered in blood and screaming incomprehensibly at the world. My legs are clean. White, clean, shivering. New, so new. This is worth it. A new beginning. This is what I've waited all my life for.

The sky above me is blotted out with silhouettes. My eyes swim and the men towering above me look just like the downtown skyline from the balcony of the library. Tall, featureless, angry architecture. A blinding flash explodes at the far end of the alley. It's not lightning. Too orange, blue, red. Too small. Swirling like a tornado in the night wind. They're letting me watch this, they want me to see it. The pain in my jaw, my body, it's nothing compared to the implosion in my chest. My heart is breaking. I feel it tearing, beating, losing something that I can do nothing about.

Him.

And her.

One of the men holding me up twists my arm and says, "We should get you to a doctor."

No.

"You're going to the Doctor."

I tip my head back and scream some more, just to hear my own voice, I'm in control of this, this flashback, just a flashback, just a dream of something that happened a long time ago in a life far, far away and now I only have one recourse, one road to walk, one thing to do. Dreams are useless, flashbacks are nothing. What matters is primal.

Animal needs.

Territory.

Revenge.

What's mine is mine and my honor is mine and why won't the sky ever close over this city?

There's filth everywhere, even though the rain never stops, it never stops, never stops...

VII

I wake up screaming. Sucking breath, slapping at the walls, unsure of anything: where I am, who I am, what happened. Seconds turn into minutes, and nothing resolves. My left hand feels numb, fingers still loosely curled around a shiny vial. It's a little emptier now. As best as I can, I loosen the tubing with my right hand.

Looks like I backslid a little.

Another night in my van. One of these times, it's all going to catch up to me. Cops, creeps, someone is going to bust into this van and finish me. But at least it's not raining. The sky is overcast, full of clouds, a gray lumpy mass that looks like my mouth feels. I roll down my window and dangle the bottle by my fingertips. It would be so easy to let it drop.

You need me.

Do not.

You're going to get hurt.

I can handle it.

Go ahead and toss me.

I lift up my hand and let the bottle drop. Even still, my hand swoops down and tries to catch the bottle. It bounces once on the concrete, chipping but not breaking, and I still hear it.

You still have eight bottles left in your bag. You're not fooling anybody.

I'm fooling myself, and that's good enough. I still feel invincible.

I learn as I go.

Personally, I think I've gotten pretty good. I might botch the small details, but I get the desired result. The world is a happier place. So why am I so unhappy? Dealers, wife beaters, vandals. They shouldn't get news time. They should be the 8-point print in the police blotter, somewhere in the back of the paper where few dare to read. Their messy endings should be printed between foreclosure auctions and speeding tickets, name changes and domestic disturbances. But they're front page news. Just like me, and I plan to stay there. You only have to do one of two things: keep killing or get caught.

I'm driving towards the heart of the city, listening to the water hissing underneath my car, like one long ripping strip of newsprint. I'm a little giddy, the same rush of adrenaline that used to come at age eight on the way to the toy store. I need legs, so a meeting with my supplier is in order. I know he'll be a little disappointed in my performance, but not the results. He'll get me back on new feet again in no time.

If there is anyone left in the world I can call a friend, it's Joe. To the buying public, he's Joseph Colton Beckmann, owner of Surplus Military Warehouse. G.I. Joe to his friends. Joe is a disgruntled veteran who sells surplus military field supplies to the public, and military material of a more interesting manner to the people in the shadows. In his spare time, Joe is a craftsman of sorts. He has a lot of leftover airplane parts, sheet metal, pipes, tubes, wires, tires, glass and rivets.

Joe's hobby is making things. Things like cannons, and having watched him repair the back wall of his shop on numerous occasions, I can say that Joe is only improving in his skill. Joe, who hasn't seen his left leg since before I was born, also likes to craft different kinds of prosthetics.

Walkers. Runners. Climbers. Kickers.

He's working on a great set for me: one boot to plant, and one with a sharpened skate blade on the kicking leg.

It's not cheap. I know he's going out of his way for me. No HMO in the world would subsidize his work. But Joe is a philanthropist. If I need it, he can make it. Legs with concealed holsters. Legs with hidden compartments. Ceramic legs. We even tried PVC legs once, but they were noisy and brittle. What Joe truly has a surplus of is creativity.

And oh, you should hear Joe on his good days. He's a conspiracy nut. He knows every possible scenario. He's certain he'll die at the center of a massive plot, something that shakes the whole city. Doesn't like other people to talk. Loves to talk himself, as long as he doesn't think you're recording him.

You have to walk through two metal detectors to get into his store, and two more to reach his private workspace. But I get the red carpet treatment. Joe just smiles and lets me through. If I *don't* beep, he worries. He knows that if I'm missing metal, then I'm in trouble.

I've been parked outside of his shop for at least twenty minutes now, working on my story. How did I lose the legs? Or do I need a story? If someone makes something for you under the table, you have to guard it with your life. Joe doesn't need any evidence of his handiwork floating around. Someone finds a leg, the way the joint is made, maybe there's some similar parts to a bomb that went off somewhere. Anything that connects Joe to… well, anything, he's not going to be happy. Part of the trust is not losing stuff. That trust erodes a lot faster when you tell your gun dealer you lost a gun.

Shit.

I could go for pity. Pity legs would be free. Or deeply discounted. I'm not one to beg, but I need a way to get around like nobody's business. I'm going to have to swear that I'll track the rifle down. That I'll clean any trace of it. Nothing left to do but throw myself on the mercy of the court.

I drag myself to the back of my van and open the doors, staring out at the empty street. I drop my *pièce de résistance* to the ground, lowering myself into it a second later. It's low, but not too low for me to push the van door closed. I slap my way up the sidewalk, hoping the scuff marks on my hands will earn me some sympathy. Here I come in my little red wagon.

Joe melts the instant I come through the door. Whether it's from pity for me, or nostalgia from the Radio Flyer I'm using to get around, I don't know. Don't care, because I can tell I'll be walking out of here today. Joe and I, we have a system. Ever since the first day I came in, he's been able to communicate with me like nobody else. He sees the problem and he fixes it.

"Did I ever tell you why they fought the Gulf War? Did I tell you what that was all about?" Joe booms across the room.

I shrug. Not that it matters. This speech is going to continue either way. There's only one other shopper, some kid looking for a cheap backpack, a GreenPeace type who's nervous just being in this store. Joe's doing his best to make sure the kid leaves and doesn't come back. That kid might be the saving grace that stopped him from tearing me a new asshole the second he saw me.

"The Gulf War was not fought over oil, or land. The Gulf War…" Joe is winding up now, "THE GULF WAR was not fought for special interests, not for a bunch of ragheads in sand huts…" and he has the kid's attention, "and especially not for skinny pus-nutted no-load shitbag scrawny college pencil-pushing cockbreath son-of-a-bitches," (Joe was a Navy SEAL, and their eloquent manner of speech has never left him), "who want to buy backpacks designed for MEN who FIGHT AND BLEED for their country, and stick a bunch of happy whale stickers and pot-leaf patches all over the…okay, he's gone."

The kid actually left a trail of burnt rubber on the way out of the store. Behind his dark glasses, I know Joe is giving me a wink. "I've still got it." He hobbles over to me. "What happened to your legs?"

I shrug. I start to say something about the rifle, but stop myself. Never talk backroom goods in the front room. Joe shakes his head and staggers back behind the counter, the conspiracy train has been momentarily derailed.

He pulls aside the curtain that marks the line between legal and illegal, safe and sane, righteous and cowardly. Which side is which, is all a matter of personal politics. I roll through the front side of the store towards that curtain, past castoff boots, Army Butt Packs, cots, books (*Pimp Your MRE: Easy, Fast, and Deeeelicious!*) and other items that would be handy on any camping trip.

I always get a wave of nostalgia here. Every time is like the first time. I feel like I've lived here my whole life. I remember the first day I walked in, just looking for a tip on a more powerful weapon. Joe took one look at me, turned white as a sheet. There was nobody else in the store. He stuck a gun right in my face. I didn't even flinch. Probably because I was too scared to move. But he didn't shoot. His eyes were watery, black and deep, like he was looking into Hell. Then, he just nodded his head, told me he thought I was someone else, thought maybe he was having a flashback, and gave me the gun. Just like that. Brought me to the back, showed me what he could do with legs. I don't know if I believe in kindred spirits, but I know Joe's one of the good ones.

The metal detector behind the curtain goes crazy as always, and Joe glances up once, quickly, just to make sure it's only me coming through. Once I'm in, he bolts the front door with the push of a button, shutting down all exterior lights. The store is officially closed to civilian business.

Crossing over that curtain is one of my favorite trips. "It's like a different country back here, no passport necessary for any proud patriot," Joe would say. Out there is the equivalent of a yuppie camping store with higher-quality merchandise and lower prices. Out there is full of patches and pins that only crazy bitter vets and crazy bitter teenagers sew onto their jackets. Back here is purpose. Back here is where you only say things you mean. And you only buy things if you intend to use them. No questions asked, but help can be offered if desired.

I hand Joe a letter I wrote in the van, detailing what's happened so far with the list and what's happening next.

He stares at me, his eyes a little... off. He doesn't take the list, instead going behind a counter and returning with half of a gun. Half of my rifle.

I don't know what to do, so I try to say I'm sorry. I say *try* because I have a motherfucker of a time getting the letter S out without slobbering everywhere.

"It's clean now. Bought it off of a tweaker who found it in an alley. Know anything about that?"

I nod.

"Can it happen again?"

I shake my head no.

He stares at me. I stare at him. Alpha wolf bullshit. I have to give him some time to feel like he's laser etching a message into my skull, that it's received, and then lower my gaze.

He nods and hold his hand out for the list. I hand it over. Joe's been nothing but encouraging and helpful with my project. He never got to see the person that took his leg. I'm a bit of vicarious revenge fantasy for him. Every customer back here is connected to someone high up on a wanted list in some way, so he's got his finger on the pulse. He hates most of the people he sells to, but you gotta make money if you wanna eat, so he sells. I think I'm his way of balancing things out. He gets a kick out of having a hand in rearranging the hierarchy. Justice is dirty work. He's helped me plan through about number six so far.

Joe pulls out pipes, tape, padding, solder, butane. He's a rare bird in this business. He's the only Jewish gun nut I know, and he's not afraid of anything. Most of these types are armed to the gills, waiting for some mythical invasion, but Joe is calm. Prepared.

"I'm tired of those college pukes coming in here."

I nod.

"Bunch of shit. Guess what I found out?"

Joe falls into a working rhythm, and out come the conspiracies:

How the cold war has moved beyond militarism and is nearing an endgame in cyberspace and in boardrooms, and I tune him out as he rounds the bend into his most common thesis: that all of this is possible because an underground Druid sect has organized a twisted, inbred bloodline that has supplied all of our presidents since the Kennedy assassination in a plot to slowly drive us into poverty and socialism. Joe rolls into one speech after the other, and I row my little red wagon, drifting through the store, Pocahontas on a stainless-steel canoe on my favorite concrete river. Paranoid codewords drift by me like songbirds from the shores, Bilderberg, Zionism, radical Islamic whatever, white nationalist et ceteras. I take in the beauty of the aisles towering like steep canyons, the banks overflowing their with lethal bounty.

Acetylene. Gunpowder. Primers. Reloaders. Ball bearings. Barbed wire. Fun fun fun 'til her Daddy takes her femurs away.

"You been sleeping much lately?"

I shrug.

"You look like Hell. The news is just starting to pick up on Susan. Good stuff. Number eight now, right?"

I nod.

"You should get some rest first." Joe approaches me with two big cupped pieces of acrylic. "Let's hope you haven't lost too much weight. We don't have time to re-mold." Joe hoists me out of my wagon and sets me on a table. He pushes each cup over my thigh. A nice, snug fit.

"All right. Give me a minute to finish," Joe says.

Aside from my last two blackouts, I guess I haven't gotten a whole lot of sleep. I haven't eaten much either. I've been saving up for the next section of the list. There are so many things to buy. I hand Joe a map of the park and a list of questions, which he'll answer later in his familiar pencil scribble. Last minute details.

I've had some thoughts on the way over here. This is what my list says now:

10. ~~Vasili~~

9. ~~Susan Schrader~~

8. Grace Brooks – need camo webbing and barf bags.

7. Shakes – maybe sooner

6. Caligula

5. Delia Sugar

4. Hooded Jack (?) – Could be driver

3. Dr. Robert Fortescu – could afford black car

2. Veronica Madden – vehicle?

1. ???

Joe gives me a lot of quiet time. It's almost as enjoyable as the library. He's pretty excited about the middle of the list. Has all sorts of advice about collateral damage. He is of the opinion that I'll need explosives. He starts to share some ideas, but I'm too nervous to think about it. I'm focused on my first real public execution.

The idea of pulling this hit in front of a bunch of children sickens me. This is why I've added barf bags to my shopping list. I know I'm going to vomit. I know I'm going to have visions of the life that was, with its perfect house and weekend outings and beautiful daughter.

And another vision hits me.

Joe blurs out, replaced by a man in white.

Dr. Robert. Smiling over me. He's got a jar in one hand, and I can't see what's in it. He leans close to my ear, and his skin smells like sterile bedding.

He whispers, "First, do no harm."

He holds the jar up. The contents baffle me. I've seen it before, or something like it.

"Sometimes, you can never apologize enough. Know what this

is?"

He sloshes the jar in front of me, some faded lump of maroon and white and yellow floats in there.

"It's a bookend," he says. "Fancy, yes?"

I think I know what it is, but I don't know where it came from. I know what he's going to say. I only hope it's a lie.

"Such a shame when an older man comes along and steals your daughter's heart. What's a mother to do?"

He runs a finger down my chest, his nail scraping circles through my thin hospital gown right above my left breast.

"I'd like a matching set."

And he pushes down harder—

"HEY!"

Joe has me by the shoulders, shaking me a little. "Flashbacks are a bitch, huh?"

I look down, shake it off. Joe knows better than to push for details. He turns and walks off to his workbench.

My body shakes. To stop the bile rising in my throat at the memory of that jar, I get my mind back to work. She's gone. Can't bring her back. Can only make sure someone pays for it. Do I move the Doctor up? Take him sooner rather than later? No. Everything is arranged for a reason.

I tap my finger on the list. Dr. Robert.

"We'll get him. Just wait, we'll get him."

I slide my finger up to Veronica Madden.

"I've been looking," Joe says, "and she hasn't been seen in a while. I think she's gone. She shows her face again, I'll help you take care of her."

I tap my finger on her name harder. Not a good enough answer. I want her dead.

He rests his hand on mine and slides it higher on the list. Ever the military man, he's keeping me in line. Now. Brooks and new equipment.

This is why I've added camo webbing: I'm going to set up two sniper stands. The first will be where I'm not, and it will be covered in the webbing. None of the families should notice it until after the shooting has started. I'll rig some remote flash pops to simulate muzzle flare. The reverb from the rifle report should echo enough to have no discernable location. The visual clues should lead them in the wrong direction for a few minutes. The other stand will be where I do the shooting, pretty far from the field, and it should give me time to get away. That's a lot of *shoulds*.

Joe is back, this time with fully assembled legs attached to the acrylic cups. He pushes my thighs in, recreating me. One of the cups makes a farting sound as my leg pushes in and I stifle a laugh. These times are deadly serious with Joe.

"Rise," he says. "Rise and walk."

I hop off the table. Joe has been experimenting. The joints are springier. I don't wobble as much when I walk. This, I like. It's almost natural. I decide to be brave and try to pivot. I swing with my arms out, stopping after going around about a three-quarters turn.

Joe is crying. I smile at him.

"Walk," he says. "I gave your legs back. Walk."

I oblige him, walking around the aisles, pulling my wagon behind me. I can hear him shouting encouragement, not that I need it.

"Built-in sneakers. They flex like a false foot. But no more loose shoes or untied laces. What do you think?"

I nod my head. Joe puts his hands on my shoulders and we hobble slowly, our little ritual, towards the full-length mirror at the back of his storeroom.

There, my reflection surrounded by the castoff barrel of a Sherman tank, tattered flags and dusty boots, I feel beautiful.

Joe beams behind me, a proud father who has given birth to me for the umpteenth time. I smile, much as I hate it, and I force myself to look at my face.

I ignore the gap in my teeth where I lost an incisor and bicuspid. I tilt my head down to hide the blossoming pink flower of a scar that decorates my lower jaw. I can't do anything to conceal the fat sluggy scars that trace the length of my face. My hair is combed well enough to hide my bald spot. My eyes don't match. My skin is mottled and crazy-quilted. I try not to tighten my cheeks too much, because then the scars start to fold in on themselves and I look like a pumpkin three weeks after Halloween.

Joe is still bright and paternal.

I look at my legs, and he says, "Beautiful."

And just like every other time, I nod my head and start to cry, because I agree with him. I try to mumble my thanks to Joe, but of course I can't. I want to tell him how lovely I feel.

But there's the lip scar. The damaged mandible. The disfigured tongue.

I mumble anyway, and Joe stops me, thank God.

"I know," he says. "I know. I'm here to help."

Joe lowers a camo comforter over the mirror.

"Let's talk payment."

VIII

The security guard on duty in the lobby of the municipal building is bored to tears. He stares out at the sea of humanity filing in for jury duty, for marriage certificates, DBAs, with the same impassive corpse-like gaze. The few stragglers who try to get his attention fall silent, cowed by the weight of his blue-collar ennui. They shuffle into the corral, waiting to pass muster. I approach one of his friends off to the side and ask him a friendly question.

"Kargn nee hher, wha kine iggit?"

He keeps working. I could try asking him the time again, but I doubt he'd understand. And we are on a schedule, after all.

This is how I pay the bills. Joe's nice, but nice costs. He knows I'm broke, so he lets me pay in trade. It's a little nerve-wrenching, but I can take it. He gave me the equipment I needed. Now Joe has some material he needs to move, and he needs to move it fast.

There's a verdict expected to come down early this morning. Someone's walking out free, or possibly leaving the courtroom to start serving a nickel upstate. How they leave the courtroom doesn't matter. They will leave the building in a bodybag. I won't be around for any of that. I'm just a small cog in a big machine.

I'm delivering ammunition. Five bullets. Enough to get me

arrested or shot on sight if they search me, but we'll deal with that in a minute. The idea is that I am going to create a distraction as I go through the checkpoint. Someone else, whom I don't know, will drop off a specially made clip for a 9mm handgun, and they'll be a temporary home for these bullets, expanding rounds that cut through their targets like a buzzsaw. Joe explained to me how these were somehow in violation of the Geneva Convention, but that someone near and dear to "the cause" had need of them. Yet another person will be dropping off the gun itself. Or maybe that's been subdivided too, I don't know. Knowing's not my job today. Get in, deliver, get out.

So I'm strapped down with bullets, all hidden nicely inside of my legs. Joe will have plenty other operatives working here this morning, but we'll never see each other. Fail safes. When it's all said and done, there could be two or three fully assembled pistols in there. The odds of getting through and delivering Joe's verdict get higher with each person sent in.

I drop my purse on the floor, the rocks and cans inside popping out a nice harsh note that gets the door guy's attention. The guy watching the door shoots me his most menacing glare, but the sight of my face is enough to melt his icy heart. Actually, he looks like he's going to barf. I shuffle forward a few feet as the line moves.

The cacophony inside pours over me; I almost feel like I can see the sound. All of these conversations, poor saps scheduled for jury duty, everyone trading horror stories about what they had to give up to be here today. Wage slaves and white collars, unemployed, retired, grinders, slackers, everyone is briefly on equal footing. We must all be searched. We must all uphold our civic responsibilities.

I can do this. Easy. Sure. In Joe we trust.

My fingers brush lightly against my thigh, the ridges and valleys of the bullets, support straps of my legs, everything keeping me upright. Ahead of me, there's a wall of people, all of them stalled and steaming like a line of overheating cars on the freeway. They trickle through the narrow checkpoint, some of them pulled aside and wanded, some of them patted down. Some have to take their shoes off, rich and poor, they dump their wallets and coins in filthy plastic trays. They try to make small talk with the disgruntled workers in the line.

Nobody's having any fun here. Which is perfect for me. This is my stage, and I am ready to perform.

I get in line and I wait, shifting from side to side every once in a while to take the pressure off my hips. Moving forward two inches at a time until I get near the front of the line, where an angry looking lady who's wider than she is tall stands guard, directing traffic. Choosing who goes where. Everyone has their summons out along with their ID. Not me, because today I get to mess up on purpose. If it comes to it, I left my I.D. in the car, a passable fake that Joe gave me identifying me as "Martha Washington". It might come into play later, but I hope not. I have no idea where any of my real identification is, and I prefer it that way. Makes things easier. No trail to sweep up behind me.

In line two, there's a problem. Some idiot appears to have brought a tiny knife through security, which, he loudly protests, is purely decorative.

"What am I gonna do with this?," he says. "I couldn't cut butter with this thing. Government regulations, my ass! You should be pulling out the guys with -- look at the gangbangers like that guy over there. They're the trouble. You know it, I know it, everybody here knows it! It's not like *I'm* trying to shoot somebody. It's not like I brought a bomb."

At the last word, the amount of activity at checkpoint two triples. A policeman moves over to calm the man down, which only succeeds in agitating him. The wand lady steps over.

This guy is stealing my show. This is supposed to be *my* big moment. I glance at my watch. It's early still. Too many of these kinds of distractions could be bad. But maybe he was sent by Joe to buy me time, who knows? Maybe I'll still get to shine.

An older, chubby guy in a blue sweater, some kind of supervisor, he's floating around the whole scene, trying to direct traffic. "Next! Let's go!"

My line is officially stalled, and two spaces over, several of our county's best employees are fully engaged with an angry white man who's lost his sense of entitlement. Which means I'm being shunted over to gate three, toward a beefy guy with a white-walled buzzcut who looks like he took some time off from ramming his steel-toed boots up new recruits' asses to be here. This should do nicely.

I keep my eyes locked on Buzzcut, who after a quick glance at my features, has his eyes locked on the X-ray screening machine. Without looking, he gestures to the little stack of plastic trays.

"Keys," he says. Then adds, "Change."

I empty my pockets and wait for the tray to start going through the machine. Then I hobble forward. My mind is chanting a mantra at the machine, daring it to ignore me. And as I take my first step through the big square arch, I start to relax.

And then it's New Year's Eve right above my head. Bells and whistles and lights. I don't know whether I should feel like a terrorist or the millionth customer.

I look to gate two, where everyone involved in the ruckus has simultaneously stopped, their heads craning in my direction. The wand lady straightens, takes a half step towards me, but then stops as the angry white man starts to walk away, thinking he's free.

Are our government buildings secure? Yes. But are they understaffed? Severely.

Buzzcut is on his feet, waving the wand lady back to her frisking duties with Middle America. He jabs an angry finger, motioning me through the gate again. I step through and hit the jackpot, pyro and ballyhoo, and now Buzzcut makes a brisk motion for me to step through and to the side.

The guardian of the only other open gate sighs, shaking her head. The weight of the world is now officially on her shoulders. It's her versus the entire slovenly population of the city that was too stupid to duck out of jury duty, at least until me and the knife guy are removed.

Buzzcut reaches behind his back and produces a long black wand, holding it out stiffly at waist level, and all of the teachings of Dr. Freud run through my mind. He's coming for me, waving it around, coming to search my body and shut me down.

Wand me, you fucker, let's see what you've got.

He starts at my head, has me stick my arms straight out, which of course makes me shift a little and lose my balance. I teeter, then straighten up.

"Been drinking?" he asks, pushing my shoulder with the wand.

I teeter again. Keep it up, you fucker, you just wait until you see what I've got for you. It's going to destroy you.

I shake my head, offer him my best confused look.

Drinking? *Moi*? How dare you?

He wands me again, over my shoulders, around my waist and back, getting little positive hits at my belt buckle.

"Lift the front of your shirt please," he says, and not nicely, and not even in a sleazy-pervy way.

I, of course, act appalled again.

My shirt? Why? What are you getting at?

"Belt," I mumble, in a way that probably makes him think I'm sauced.

He starts to wand my hips and the sound moves from the little *beep-beep* to a positive death scream as he makes it to mid-thigh. He draws back and eyes me.

"Are you concealing any metal objects on your person, ma'am?"

Here's my confused look again, you fucker, just you wait. You see where your life is going after today.

He starts to pat down my legs and runs his hands over the irregular bumps around my thighs. He draws back quickly and wands me again, getting the same scream. His hand starts to go to his walkie-talkie, getting ready to hail security.

I muster some tears and reach down, squeezing just above the knee joint of my left leg. I slide the pantleg up and let him get a good look at my crusty old sock, bunched up there, before I raise the curtain higher and the show really begins.

Aircraft grade black pipe. I sniffle. I can see the hesitation starting to build in him. I push my hand deep into my pocket, finding the buckle and opening it, releasing my left leg. Hopping a little, I shake it loose and get my balance, sliding it out of my pants and holding it stiffly toward him.

He doesn't take it.

The whole place is quiet now. Even the angry white man has gone from crimson to pale, and all jaws are slowly returning from gaping to their full upright positions.

I drop the leg.

Adding a theatrical sob, I tug up my right pantleg and show him another pipe, arms flailing as I keep losing balance, screaming, "Is this what you need? Do you feel safe now?!" which nobody understands but everybody feels. I look for a place to sit down and throw the other leg off.

Hoping the whole time that I've done what I set out to do. Hoping that he feels wretched enough to stop me. He doesn't. He's waiting for it, I think.

But the wand lady struts over quickly, realizing that I'm causing a massive traffic backup and a potential security hazard just by being a distraction.

"Jesus Christ, Bill," she mutters under her breath.

Bill is shaken from his stupor. He blinks twice and then wands my left leg, lying on the floor before him.

"I'll be damned," he mutters.

"Sorry," he says, trying to smile and looking more like he bit into some rotten fruit.

I sniffle again and lean back on the wall with one hand,

motioning towards the wand lady, my hero, my savior, could she please bring me back my leg.

She picks it up, handling it at first like a dead snake, but then, seeing my face, she grips tighter to show me she's not afraid.

"Do you need some help, hon?" she asks. "A wheelchair to get to your floor? Where you headed today?"

"Yah," I say, shaking my voice and letting some drool fly. "Goory googy."

"Where?" she asks.

I lean on the wall, bunching my pants up and getting my thigh reconnected, hoping that all of this movement isn't going to shake the ammo loose inside my right leg.

I gesture at the rest of the line.

"Jury duty?" she asks. "I'll get a chair for you. You'll be sitting all day anyway." And she laughs, gives me a warm smile, and I try to return it, I do.

Bill leans in a little, whispering to my savior. Her eyes roll, and I know he's just asked her the million-dollar question. She shifts a little, then gets it out:

"I'm sorry about all of the confusion and inconvenience. We'll get you on your way as soon as we can. I just need to check your ID. Heightened security because of all of the activity lately."

And I let my face go slack for a half-second, then lightning quick, I slap at my pockets.

"Do you have your ID and summons? Those instructions were clearly indicated on the envelope and papers you would have gotten with your--"

"No!" I whimper, then whisper it again. It's a good word, one of the few I can still manage with ease. I keep slapping pockets, willing a couple of salty tears down my cheeks. I mime driving to the lady, and tell her I forgot everything in the car. All of the sympathy drains from her face. Now I'm just an ugly retard who can't do anything right.

As politely as possible, she tells me I can't enter the building without proper government-issued photo ID.

"Okay," I say, one of my easy words. "Okay, gut I gorra go."

I motion to the ladies' room, my final destination. I babble on and on of how Buzzcut scared me, I really need to go to the restroom, and maybe they'll be able to issue me a new summons upstairs, please help me I don't want to be humiliated. She starts to tell me there are restrooms at the coffee hut on the corner, and I go toddler on her. It's too far! Too far! I'm going to pee my pants!

And I break her. I win. She escorts me to the lobby bathroom, doesn't even ask if I need help in there. Tells me to make it fast but that I still need to get my papers from my car. So I make it fast. There's nobody else in the bathroom, so I hustle to the stall and detach my right leg, unscrewing a clever compartment near the thigh cup. I pull out a slim box of ammo wrapped in bubblewrap and lift the liner from the sanitary napkin box that sits next to the toilet. Deposit the ammo at the bottom of the box and replace the liner. Nobody's going to go digging for bullets under all of this spent biological ammunition. I have my leg back on in minutes and stand back up.

It would be nice now to have a little fun. Splash water all over the front of my pants, soaking them, go out screaming and trying to make them feel really bad. But I don't need attention anymore. My work is done. I do spritz a little water on my cheeks for a realistic after-tears look, and the show goes on.

The wand lady escorts me back through security to the lobby doors and I'm on my way. She apologizes again, gives me seven variations on "I'm sorry to inconvenience you but rules are rules." When I'm convinced that I'm alone in front of the building, I stop at a bank of fossilized payphones and drop a quick call downtown. Joe's voice answers, and our conversation is short and simple.

"Mm-hmm?" he asks.

"Mm-hmmm," I answer.

There's a brief pause.

"Thank you," he says.

I notice the angry American making his way out of the lobby. He's dialing on his cell phone. One of Joe's other lines rings in the background. He tells me, "later."

Fare thee well, fellow traveler.

I've earned my daily bread.

Now I've got a soccer game to catch.

Sunday! Sunday! Sunday!

Game Day!

I have a CD I listen to sometimes before a mission. A bad recording taken off of a TV broadcast, but it works just the same. It's one of those dramatic trumpet and drum numbers that comes before the football game starts. When they show athletes warming up and retired jocks overanalyze things until a simple game has escalated to a blood feud.

It's a matter of honor. It's about respect. It's for the love of the game. Cliché, sure. But man, it gets me going. Until I roll over and see the field.

I spent the night in my shooter's stand in a tree two hundred yards from the field. Way out of sight, out of mind. I drifted off to the sound of the breeze rustling the branches, the clouds scudding everywhere and offering no hint of sunshine, ever. I lay back between a couple of branches, nice and cozy.

I stared at the empty field until well after dark, picturing her, watching her move the way I'd seen her on TV. Thinking about where she'd walk, where she'd sit. She hates the public eye. She has to be somewhere safe. Somewhere her daughter can look at her for encouragement, but not somewhere that feels like she's sitting in a fishbowl. I spotted every place possible, walked them over and over. It's why I picked this tree. I've got a clear view of a spot removed from the stands with a good view of the field and quick access to the parking lot. As the night faded into dawn, I pictured a beautiful, quick, clean kill shot.

This morning, things are ugly. Kids everywhere. It's *Lord of the Flies* by Disney. All of these tiny tribes in their brightly colored uniforms. They're so proud of their cheap t-shirts, their horrible cutesy sponsored team names emblazoned on their backs.

Ace Lumber Lumberjacks.

North Street Coffee Buzzers.

A & L Siding Weatherbeaters.

These kids with their ratty uniforms are in awe of the professionals, the kids whose parents are paying for soccer more to get them out of the house for a few hours than anything else. The pros don't have sponsor names. They don't need sponsors. Just mascots. And they get the cool uniforms.

Wasps.

Polar Bears.

This should be a day when these working-class kids, these castoffs, get a moment they will remember. Handing some rich punks their asses.

I'm going to be sick.

What if Grace Brooks splatters? What if I hit her and it's not lethal and she runs? Runs across the field, grasps at children, screams at them as she dies? What if?

But there is no other time to do this. No other time that would be this easy. I'm not a Hollywood action star. I can't swagger into her private mansion, I can't disguise myself and get into her soirees.

It has to be now. It has to be now. It has to be...

Michael Paul Gonzalez

I grab the first bag from the neat stack I made by my rifle case. Nothing in the world seems smaller than the paper bag you're spilling your guts into. I feel it bulge in my hand, wet and steaming. The optimist in me sees the bag as half empty with more on the way. Dry heaves hit me and for a moment I'm afraid I'll tumble from my stand. I don't, but my rifle does. I catch the strap with my forearm, wincing as it bangs against the side of the tree. I haul it back up and examine it. I look at the scope. No scuffs. No harm, no foul. I might have knocked it out of alignment, which would be just my luck. I don't have time to re-sight, and I don't have time for Murphy's Law. Let him shit on me all he wants. I'll adjust.

I gently set the rifle down, wrapping the strap tight against my body. The heaves come again. I fill the bag up and fold it as best I can and leave it next to me, warm and foul-smelling. My hands do not shake. My eyes are still sharp. I can see through the kids. I can aim around anything.

I will teach Grace Brooks a lesson.

She hasn't arrived yet. I'm pretty sure this will be a case of her showing up one minute before the game starts and leaving one minute after her daughter rotates out for the last time.

The papers are going to have a field day with this one. Was it an obsessed fan? What kind of monster would commit murder in front of children? Was Grace Brooks really this madman's target? (I know they will say mad*man*.) And always the why, why, why? And the are, are, are?

Are we under siege?

Are terrorists involved?

Are your children safe?

The heaves come again and I start to fill up bag number two when I go dry. My stomach is in knots. I should go. I'm right at the edge of the platform. I can climb this tree while wearing my standard legs, no problem. So I will be able to walk out of the park. I could walk right now.

Maybe Grace Brooks can wait. Maybe there is a way to do this in private. Vasili was easy. Nobody liked him. And he was the catalyst. He turned me to ashes and I rose again.

Why are you trying to do this without me?

I'm fine.

But you could miss. The kids...

I'm focused. No vial. I just have to run the checklist, same as every time. Hip bone connected to the leg bone, and so on. I remember the night at the bar. Something to do with the man who ran off and got burned. They wanted me too. Why didn't they get me? Vasili was at the bar. Shit. Memory flood. I have to chase this. But I have to focus on the field. Was he the one that ratted me out? Should I have done him up close to get some info? Was Grace connected to this?

There are families here, the vial sings, *Look, here they come now!*

But what about my family? What about the people I lost?

You're jealous, jealous, jealous of all the happy families. Come on, just a little taste. Calm you right down.

It's too late. I want to take this one sober. I want to understand why I'm doing this.

What did Grace Brooks' daughter do that she deserves to see this?

My subconscious is hitting below the belt today. Grace Brooks' daughter will not see the shot. I will make sure of that. But Grace Brooks cannot be allowed to draw breath from this day on.

Any of the children could be my daughter. Running, happy, getting red cheeks and running back to me with sweat-damp heads, hair that I could tousle, hands to squeeze...any of them could have been my daughter, and that's why I have to do this.

Take her daughter too. She shouldn't have to live with the pain you're going to cause. She shouldn't see her mother suffer.

Michael Paul Gonzalez

Shut up. Shut up. Shut up!

There's a muffled honk, warbling and drunk, from the horizon. The ref just blew the starter horn and the game is under way.

And there she is.

I put a pillow over the voice in my head and hope that this time it suffocates. This would be so easy if I had lost my conscience with my legs.

Grace Brooks is wearing a dark scarf around her hair. She's looking relaxed in a cable-knit sweater and khaki pants (Brooks Fall collection, $779 MSRP), sitting on a small chair slightly removed from the rest of the parents, right where I hoped she'd be. She's got a couple of people next to her, assistants maybe.

If luck is on my side, her daughter will score a goal early. Grace smooths her hands over her pants and leans forward, her face dancing through each quadrant of my scope.

Just one goal, Susie or whatever your name is, and you can high five Mom and then run back to the field, not facing her, and this day will be over.

The air thickens and smells sweet and cold. Rain's coming. That's a good thing if it holds off until after the job is done. Grace felt it too. She's looking for an umbrella somewhere in the clutter of jackets and coolers and junk at her feet.

Grace Brooks, you should not have been so greedy. Import/exports of artisan furniture and handcrafted goods from third-world countries as a shadow operation to bring in drugs. All of the pieces are connected. Hip bone to leg bone. Grace's drugs to Vasili's guns to my family's death. There's a few blanks to fill in, but this is enough to justify my righteous anger. The jury has come to a decision. Your execution must be carried out before a rain delay hits.

She looks excited. Her little Haley or Ashley must be doing something good. I can't be bothered. A quick glance at the field: They're battling in front of the far net, a big mass of kids and dirt. Colors massing and writhing and wrestling, chasing a ball and laughing and screaming.

Execution will commence in five, four, three, two...what is Grace looking at?

One.

My finger is squeezing on its own. I feel the gun buck against my shoulder, the silencer taking away most of the sound, the breeze in the trees finishing the job. Everything is so slow. I feel like I'm watching the bullet. Like I am the bullet. Riding the bullet right for Grace's forehead.

What the hell is she looking at anyway?

No...

No, Haley.

No, Ashley.

Stephanie.

Whatever your name is.

What the hell are you doing there? What are you doing there? Why aren't you in the pile at the other end of the field? Did they sub you—

Things are speeding up. Betty-Ashley-Stephanie-Marcie spins, a lovely pirouette, a small spritz of red shooting from her shoulder.

No.

It doesn't happen this way.

I don't miss.

I never miss.

Do you have time for Murphy's Law now?

Oh shit.

Grace kneels over her daughter, unsure of what happened. Now she's rising up, her lungs filling, preparing to push the most primal of screams from her body.

I grip the rifle again. Which way did my shot go? Where was

the drift? I adjust. Please let this be right. Let this be right.

Exhale. Close eyes. Inhale and hold. Open eyes. Sight-acquire-fire. Squeeze. Slow squeeze and exhale. All in less than a second. Shot number two. This time I'm not riding the bullet. I'm on edge, ready to pull as many rounds as this takes to finish.

Grace Brooks gets a small bark out before the bullet passes through her throat.

Roll over Stephanie-Ashley-Jill, don't look at your mother.

I clean up my stand, shoveling my bags of bile and my bullets into a duffel, breaking the rifle down into its case. I drop the bag down and slide down the rough bark with my rifle shouldered. The world is heaving. I can't run in a straight line. Everything's gone carnival funhouse on me. I'm self-aware enough to know that this could be causing a scene, that I've forgotten something. The distraction. I push the remote for the flash pops in the decoy tree. They go off in rapid succession and a new round of screams comes as everyone hits the dirt.

I make it all the way to my van before the heaves hit me again. My stomach finds new things to lose. I feel like my very essence is gushing from my insides, scorching my throat like some blackened demon wrenching its way out of my mouth. I have to tell myself that somewhere in that puddle on the ground there is my heart.

I don't care, I don't care, I can't care.

Grace Brooks deserved what she got.

Ashley-Miranda-Katie is going to heal. Non-lethal shot.

But look what you've done... She wouldn't be suffering right now if you were humane...if you were a better shot...

The next wave of nausea rolls over me and I have to gun the motor of my van to cover the noise of my scream. I leave the park, one hand on the wheel, the other scrambling in my backpack for comfort, too shaky to grip the vial as a swarm of people move on the field.

Colors massing and writhing and wrestling and screaming

and screaming and screaming. Not for a ball. Not for a game. For Grace Brooks and her daughter.

For her daughter, please God, for her daughter.

No sleep tonight.

If I stop for a second, if I let exhaustion take me, it's going to be nasty. I can just imagine the things I'll see, little girls, all decked out in the colors of the rainbow, moving across little plastic green hills, and I've got to hit them with a rifle to win a prize. So I keep moving.

I'm all over the radio. Well, not me. The suspect. They're looking for a man, small and skinny, size-twelve shoes. I peppered the fake sniper stand and the ground around the tree with bootprints to throw them off my scent. The suspect may have been drunk or may have a previous war injury because his gait suggests a stiff-legged limp. I left a half-full can of beer I snagged off a sleeping homeless guy on the decoy stand, next to a copy of the Bible, the Qu'ran, and *Living with Grace Brooks* magazine.

But the main focus is on Deborah Marie Holden. "Brave Little Debbie", the newscasters dubbed her. And of course, as consolation, kind Samaritans from around the city have been sending in snack cakes.

Keep your strength up, Debbie.

These cakes aren't as sweet as you, Debbie.

Little Debbie.

Debbie, whose shoulder was vaporized by a steel-jacketed round from a high-powered rifle. What the hell was she thinking?

At any rate, the chief of police has sworn to apprehend the man responsible, which is just fine with me.

Grace Brooks died at the scene. They say Debbie went into shock the moment she got hit. I hope so. I hope she buries everything. And that she doesn't watch the amateur video snapped up by the news stations and replayed every half hour. That it took Grace five minutes to choke on her own blood. That it took half a dozen people to hold her back from her daughter. That in the end, she managed to squeeze Little Debbie's hand and share a final moment between mother and daughter, back to you in the studio, Bob.

I'm not happy with this turn of events. I want to get away, but there's no time outs here. Things are in motion. I started it. I have to finish it. I have to go into the city, deeper. Into its darkest heart, the abandoned warehouse district, home of the drug cults and the slum runners. Where the fiends and the misanthropes play.

This was the first hit not followed by an appearance from that dark car. Maybe Grace was sending it? If that was true, they would have seen me coming. I wouldn't have come close to making that hit.

I've done a fantastic job of ratcheting up police presence in the city. Everyone's batteningdown the hatches now. The first few hits got the underworld worried about a civil war. Now the cops are kicking in doors, looking for information on who killed America's Favorite Mom™.

It's my job now to get to number seven on the list before they do.

Shakes.

Shakes is a walking database. He spent the early part of his street career as a one-man focus group for new designer drugs. Messed him up a little. His spark plugs don't fire in the right order. Comical at first, fun to watch and listen to, but he's also unpredictable, dangerous. He's one of Doctor Robert's favorite boys, which makes him powerful by proxy.

He's going to help me shape the rest of my mission. Not of his own free will, of course. Persuasion will be required. He knows people higher up on the list. As the head of a lesser church in the warehouse district, he deals with everyone I need to know, directly and indirectly. He sends his people out with the goods. They come back with money and information. He works closely with a floating brothel ring – that's Delia Sugar's thing – which in turn works closely with the higher echelons on the list. One good turn deserves another.

I wish I had a partner for this. Not for backup. I just need a mouthpiece. Speaking is no longer my strong suit, and I'm not sure it ever was. I drool incessantly when I try to talk. My lips struggle for half a minute or more to form certain sounds. I'm positive my face scrunches up and makes me even harder to look at, because I've seen the way people find other things to look at when they converse with me.

I have so many questions for Shakes. How much was he paid to set me up? Who hired Vasili? Why was I attacked? Did he see what happened to my daughter? And why do I remember the name Hooded Jack?

And for every question I ask, I'll take a little piece of him until I get the answer I need. Shakes is going to lose his legs. And tongue, I think, as it seems fair. The faster and better he answers, the less his misery will be—

Something darts in front of my van and I swerve a little. I slam on the brakes and jump out of the door, the van still rocking on its springs.

There is wildlife in the city, hidden by the tall buildings and deep alleys. Creatures great and small who have been cut off from the woodlands, wandering the concrete jungle searching for food. It isn't unusual to see antelope migrating in the park fringes before sunrise. There's a reason the alleys smell like skunk and condemned buildings have become aviaries for many exotic breeds of birds.

I search the perimeter in the front of my car and see nothing. Behind me, barely visible in the glint of the taillights, twin golden reflections. My rifle is up and ready and I exhale and squeeze, and everything goes into slow motion with the explosion from my firearm.

A shape moves across the street. Bouncing. A little girl in a soccer uniform. I reach out to her and yell for her to get down. And the bullet passes right through her, striking whatever small creature I thought I saw back there. For five minutes, I'm afraid to move. Afraid to track my quarry because I think I'll have to step over a dead body.

But there is no body. Only a shopping bag with a neat hole in it, and ten yards further on, a dead fox. I use my forearm to wipe the tears from my eyes, hoping it will be enough to stop them from falling. I sling the rifle over my back and whip out my knife, trying to lose myself in the work of dressing this fox as fast as I can.

I hobble back to my van, leaving behind everything that was in the fox and a little that was in me as well. I need to clear my head. I can't handle Shakes on no sleep.

I pull over at a rest stop and pop a can of sterno, cracking the windows to let out the stench. I skin the fox as best as I can in the dark, and get to roasting. Eventually, the fox smells good enough to eat. As soon as I'm full, I stow my gear, lock the van down, and hide in the back, covering myself with as many blankets as I can find. Under the covers, alone with myself, it's like being with the worst enabler. My right arm is snaking some surgical tubing around my left. I don't even remember filling the syringe. I should probably get a new one. I can't stop myself. The tears start to come as the needle goes in.

The little pill box sits in front of me, three piercings and empty bottles under the labels V, S.S., and G.B. The bottle under "Sh" is in my fingers. I wonder what I'm going to see. Time to tear some more boards off the windows in my mind.

I spring up, the needle still in my arm, and close all of the windows while I have some strength. I don't want anyone to hear the screams when I wake up. I know they're coming. I know I'll have legs, but I don't know if it will be worth it.

I'm sorry Deborah Marie Holden.

So, so sorry.

Michael Paul Gonzalez

Dinner time.

I'm coming out of the kitchen with an armload of casserole, my shoulders burning, remind me of how long I've been working. I bring this cheesy steaming goodness into an empty dining room, a masterpiece in a deserted museum. I call out to my family.

Dinner time.

They don't answer. I scratch my chest under my shirt as I head for the door. In the living room, my daughter sits on the couch, slack, empty. Her eyes are hollow.

She's been crying.

I want to ask her what's wrong, but instead, I stand at the door and wave. She doesn't wave back. I motion to the kitchen. *It's dinner time.* She shakes her head, looking at the TV. She won't look me in the face.

"We ate," she says.

Well, you shouldn't have, I answer. I told her what time dinner was. I must have.

I ask her what she thinks of my legs. Partly to make her laugh, partly because I wonder what other people think. She shakes her head imperceptibly, ignoring me as only she can. I dance for her, just a short little jig, something that would embarrass the shit out of her in front of her friends.

Dinner, I ask.

She won't look.

Dinner time, I plead.

There's no answer.

You don't like my food?

She stands up and starts to leave the room. She picks up a dirty plate from the coffee table. "I'll do the dishes."

I grab her arm. It's dinner time, I scream at her. Where's your father?

"We ate, Mom! We ate! We ate! Three hours ago, it's midnight now. Learn how to handle your shit. Fuck!"

I don't think I've ever heard her snap this way before. She retreats up the stairs.

You don't want to spend time with...

Bang. Her bedroom door slams in my face. I rest my hand on the doorknob. I must have been making food for a reason.

Whenever something in our lives would go drastically wrong, my daughter would blame me. If I had been normal, maybe her Dad would have stuck with me. Maybe she'd be valedictorian now, instead of dead. Why can't I apologize, make things better?

I'd tell her, a woman shouldn't define herself by her husband. There are plenty of strong women out there, raising kids on their own, juggling work, making success out of apparent failure.

"Making curtains with your daughter is not a sign of success. Teaching me how to use greenery to make the living room warmer doesn't do shit for me, Mother."

It would if you tried.

"You're not Grace Brooks, Mom, and you never will be."

The hallway grows darker, a shift like a sudden cloud across the sun. Her door bursts open and she blows past me.

"I'm going out."

No. No no no no!

I'm screaming, stomping, pulling at her sleeve. Begging her not to.

"Don't touch me! Sooner or later, you'll have to get over this."

She jerks her hand free and jogs down the stairs, knowing I can't follow too quickly.

Stop! I scream. Stop, stop, please!

I wish I knew why I was so scared. She doesn't even look back as she slams the front door, and it makes me weak in where my knees used to be. I look down at the familiar steel pipes. I don't have legs. They're gone. That's why I was dancing. Trying to show her I could adjust, things were getting back to normal.

But they weren't. My mind's in a blender. My daughter never saw my steel legs, I'm sure of it. This is two memories competing, battling like rams for supremacy over a craggy ravine.

I lose my balance on the lip of the stairs. I swear I hear voices outside. I hear a guy propositioning her. She says No. A lot. I need to get out. Out. Follow.

And then the world flips and I'm drifting through space, watching the steps pitch in front of me, the bottom one rising up fast. If I break my neck in a dream, will I really die like they say? Falling and falling, and I hope it's true, I hope it's true.

Images skid across my mind. Carpet. Nosebleed. Front door. Pill after pill, bottle after bottle, nothing putting out the fire inside. Pain.

Get out. It's all I can do. Fuel first, stop the pain, save her. Get out. Find her. Make her safe.

XII

Well. That was pleasant.

My mouth is glued shut with dried saliva. I crank my way free from the blankets at the back of the van and crawl towards the front. It's a grey morning, the kind of early you can feel in your stomach. Nice and quiet here on the side of a transition road.

Shakes. Shakes and I are going to have a long talk. A long, long talk. And I'm not ready. I can't imagine three words together. Not a sentence. What the hell am I going to do, write out the questions for him? I bet he can't even read.

I'm out of the tree-lined roads and into the sprawling flatlands of the city's industrial quarter. Business hasn't been good here. Not since they shipped all the jobs overseas and built the nuclear power plant upstate. The city got blessed with a lot of large brick buildings full of equipment that nobody wanted to buy, in an area no one wanted to revitalize. The warehouse district.

Cops call this place the "Breeding Ground." From an airplane, I once saw the Breeding Ground as a bird sees it. A patch in the middle of green rolling suburbs, several miles wide. Like God reached down and pried off a chunk of the city with a spatula. Brown and grey and mud everywhere, the roads covered in veins of greenery that pushed up through asphalt that nobody drives on. It looked empty, like a museum dedicated to the failed effort of post-war optimism.

As close to a vacuum as you can get. No life but for the roaches. The few birds that stray out this way get jumped by the homeless, become a week's worth of meals. If Dr. Fortescu is the apex predator, the Breeding Ground is the primordial soup from which life springs.

I feel comfortable in the ugliness. This should be my front lawn, the only place I can feel part of society. But I don't. It's all bad memories. Nothing worth saving. I wish I could run a torch through the streets, watch it all turn to embers in one night. I'll have to settle for a piece at a time. Some people would call taking Shakes out a futile gesture, like weeding. Sure, other weeds will take Shakes's place, but I love knowing that he won't be on the lawn anymore.

I weave the van in between row after row of buildings, paying careful attention to the graffiti and territorial markings. The van has been pelted with a shoe and an empty can. Homeless people I didn't even see. The cave dwellers are trying to scare me. I got a little too close to their hovels, and they barked. They're lucky I don't have the time or bullets to waste barking back.

I turn a corner and the decay fades a bit. I'm in the territory of the drug cults. The center of the Breeding Ground is where the buildings haven't fallen apart so much. It's where rich people have invested their money in security systems and reinforced walls and barbed-wire fences. The untrained eye is probably already too nervous to pick up the tiny shifts in details. But it's there if you know where to look. The streets aren't clean, but they're unobstructed. The fences are solid. The buildings have bars over the windows.

The Cults have things to store, goods to move, none of it legal. Each building here is called a church, and each congregation is very protective of its parish. They tolerate their neighbors as much as possible. They have no patience for trespassers. The rest of the city treats the cults as no major problem. Out of sight, out of mind. But if a holy war were to break out here, the whole town would collapse.

The first building on the row has no sign, but I recognize the graffiti. Our Lady of the Punctured Vein. One of Dr. Robert's more famous cathedrals. This is not the place I'm looking for. Yet. I might return here, depending how my leads pan out. Or if my supplies get too low. There are guards posted at a small chainlink two-stage entrance. Junkies go through the first gate, wait in the holding area, show their money and try to get in. Nobody goes back out the same way they came in. You either get into the party or you get killed. The place I'm looking for isn't quite as welcoming as Our Lady of the Punctured Vein.

Three more churches and then I hit a left, down an alley where the buildings are tall enough to block out what's left of the grey daylight. The drawback here is that I can't back out of the alley if things get hairy. It's a straight drive through, which is how the architects planned it.

As I approach the gates, something stirs in me. Not fear. Hope? No. I don't know the right word to associate with it. Conflict. Part of me says get in, get out, get on with it. The other part wants to see how much medicine I can score. The only thing keeping me focused is confrontation.

The idea of talking to Shakes was starting to hold something for me. Some real promise. Aside from talking to Joe at the surplus store, I haven't had a real conversation with anyone. Not since the "accident". I'll try to savor this as much as I can.

The approach is ominous, up a ramp and into a stockyard where I can't see any people. The double row of spike strips on the ground ahead lets me know where to stop my van.

At the gate, I'm greeted with a 9mm barrel in my face and a guy at the back of my van trying to kick the door in. He tells me to step out. I lift my palms up and point down, mouthing the phrase "no legs" as best I can.

This is the first time the gunman gets a good look at me, and he wavers. I press the unlock button and the rear door flies open. There's cold steel pressing against the back of my head. I feel my toes curl, that's how good the phantom pain brought by the fear is.

"The fuck happened to you?" the thug asks.

I can't speak. Not yet. I point to a box on the front seat. Shotgun shells. The thug picks one up and looks at it. I motion to him impatiently to give it to me. After a brief look around to make sure I'm not packing a sawed-off, he relaxes.

"Not gonna do you much good without a fucking gun." He places the shells in my lap, taking careful time to brush his palm across my thigh. Fucking primate. Why must we touch to aid our understanding?

I ignore him and dig a key into the top of the shell and pour three ball bearings into my hand. I haven't been shot yet, so they're interested. I dig my finger in again and pull out some wadding, followed by some tiny blue pills.

The thug snatches it from my hand. He's about to pop one of them when I lay a hand on his wrist and point to the top of the pill. There's an inscription there, the two faces of Janus, with a scripted DRF underneath.

The thug catches his breath. I can see the rusty wheels in his head sparking into action. Why would such a powerful man use me as a courier? How could a lady with no legs gain access to a top-level guy like the Doctor?

I tap my wrist, times-a-wastin'. Shakes, I say. Which actually comes out sounding like: "Shhaykssss."

The thug outside stifles a laugh. I hope I only have to say it once. The inside man gets the idea. The lady is here on business from Fortescu. She needs to see Shakes. Nobody questions the word of God. The thugs clear the van in a matter of seconds. The gate starts to crank open. I'm putting the van into drive when one of them taps on the window. He motions with his gun for me to lower it.

"What happened to your legs?"

I tap my wrist again.

"Gate takes forty seconds to open. Come on, tell me a story. How'd you get the stumps?"

I think about it. I could mime an explosion with my hands. Or a hacksaw. This guy doesn't need to know my story. I say one word, the easiest one for me to form, and what my scrambled brain thinks is closest to the truth. "Bob," I tell him.

He, of course, misunderstands.

"God? Damn, God must hate you." The thugs rip into howls of laughter and a brief argument over whether I said "Bob", "Bomb", "God" or "Gun". Then one of them gets a nasally whine and starts slurring, saying "Shhaaayyykks, Shaaaykks" over and over to the delight of his Cro-Magnon friend.

I focus on the door. It really is slow. Plenty of time for thugs to fill an uninvited car with bullets. The drug cults can't be too careful. Other churches stick to their territory, but every once in a while, there are ambitious upstarts and cops who don't know well enough to ignore the laws.

Now the thug has added a limp to his performance, and he's drooling onto the ground and shaking his head like a bulldog, going "Shaaayyks, Shaaayks."

These two guys. I want to amend the list. I wish I was using some kind of bomb on Shakes. Could take the whole church down. But that would bring the worst kind of heat. Cops will hunt you down if you hurt one of their own, but for the most part, they're held back by the law, as much as they care about it. You piss off a criminal family and you'll be lucky to see another day, or even an hour, depending on the boss. And I know the deacons at the cults, the cardinals, those guys make an art of holding a grudge.

So I have to settle for hoping someone else does these guys in. They're still out there, laughing and joking. One of them, the guy who came in, talking about me. Something about feeling my stump.

"I got a stump for her," the other says.

Maybe I can hit them with my van on the way out. They're lost in a reverie of foul jokes. This is how they would talk about anybody. I shouldn't be so offended. Am I not getting fair and equal treatment here?

The gate is open. I think about it a second longer. I start to roll forward and then stop, motioning the two thugs over. They look up at me, waiting for some honest effort on my part to make them laugh.

"Prrsnnt," I say.

"Present?" one thug asks. They smile.

I reach into the shotgun shell and give them each two pills. Candy-colored and promising an escape to the nether reaches of their psyches.

"Frr brrk timmme," I tell them.

"Holy shit! Cross-top DXT! I think it's break time right now," the thigh-grabber shouts. They share a laugh.

I pull into the warehouse, hoping that they don't pop the pills until long after I'm gone. Sure, it's just rat poison, and not nearly enough to kill them. But a sick guard can still alert other people.

I make a note to thank Joe for his incredible foresight. He helped me plan this one, all the way down to hand-carving the pills to look like street goods. It helps that these two at the gates are obviously only employed to feed their habits. They're strung out and desperate for any kind of fix. They have no more perception of small detail. A true narcotics connoisseur would have spotted these pills as fakes a mile away.

The van's engine grows to a dull roar in the echo chamber of the deserted warehouse. The two men at the door fade into silhouettes of demons dancing.

I find a parking spot among a heap of trash bags about fifty feet from the door. I spend a minute or so strapping on my legs, pausing to run my hand over my thigh where the goon's hand had been.

That was the most contact I've had with a man since I became less than whole. I strap the legs on extra tight, the tiny pain driving away the little voices in my head.

You liked it didn't you?

Shut up.

Beggars can't be choosers.

I am not—

You could have killed that guy. But you didn't, because secretly...

Secretly nothing.

I pick up two crutches, the kind that slip over my forearms, and hook them on. Completely unnecessary, just a bit of camouflage. I'm out of the van, scuffing across the door, running my mental checklist, remembering my tools: poison pills, disguised as drugs, should get me through the door. Two knives strapped to my forearms, should get through a search if they let me lean on my crutches. And Joe's new toy, should give me plenty of enjoyment when I cut Shakes to ribbons.

Maybe you can get Shakes to cop a feel too. Hell, if he's high enough, he might try to steal third base...

I didn't like the touch. It made me sick. I didn't like it.

That much.

XIII

The inside of the church is far from immaculate. It's overrun with rust, broken bottles, broken bodies, the reek of the homeless and the strung out mingling with the smell of rotten food and soiled mattresses. What used to be offices on the side of the halls are just filthy pits now, bony bodies piled and slumped on the walls, heads twitching, eyes darting, overworked synapses and neurons firing and discharging. It should be nicer in Shakes's room. Have to go through Hell to get to Heaven, right?

The junkies on the floor are too burned out or high to take much note of my passing. Those that do see me freak out. It's either my face or the legs, I can't tell, but the sight of me is sending them on a bad trip.

At the end of the hallway, three hundred pounds of bald, bad attitude in filthy clothes, stands in front of a rusting metal spiral staircase. He's sweating, his shirt damp and looking like a map of a forest. Here are the green hills of his stomach. Further north, you can see the great lakes during flood season. They're spreading slowly. There's just my angry exhalations, and the echoes of his breathing down the corridor. He's not even really looking at me. He motions me up the stairs after giving me the once over. Not an elevator in the whole place. Great.

I guess it's too much to ask a drug dealer to be ADA-compliant. Now I've got to wind my way up a post-apocalypse circular staircase, each step only about a foot and a half wide. No room to swing my legs up sideways, and I don't trust the siderails enough to lean on them.

Puppy eyes do nothing to the man mountain. Even if the blob did offer me a piggy back, the stairs probably wouldn't take our combined weight. I'm not even sure they'll take mine.

The only option is to start climbing, so I do. Each six-inch rise feels like a small mountain. The goon at the foot of the stairs is breathing through his nose so hard it sounds like *he's* the one exerting himself. He reminds me of Frances. Frances would have volunteered to carry me.

Each move on my part sends the whole staircase wobbling. It makes little screeches like an old backyard swingset that's just a rusty husk. Support pipes below pop and crumble away with every step. This is the scariest thing I've done in a long time, and I recently shot a little girl on accident.

Shakes, thy church doth not tithe enough. Charge more for your shit, fix this place up. These are things I will not be saying to Shakes.

Halfway up, I catch a lucky break. Literally. The staircase has been bisected, replaced with a poorly welded ladder. I can climb the rest of the way. A good way to prime my arms for making the kill. But the dark cloud to my silver lining is – how am I going to get back down after I pull this off? Keep climbing. Figure out the exit plan when it's time to make an exit.

I'm greeted at the top of the stairs by a black, congealing stain on the floor that I hope is grease. I have no choice but to slide through it. My leg brace snags on the ledge, pulling it out of alignment, but I'm up. I roll onto my back for a moment to get my wind back. I close my eyes and feel the furnace of my rage reigniting, belching hot smoke like—that's not my imagination. I snap my eyes open as another wave of hot breath hits me, greeted by a face like a city roadmap, leathery brown, crisscrossed with deep wrinkles and puffy scars.

"Shit," he says.

"I was gonna say the same thing," I say, but he can't understand me.

He just stares, not offering to help me up. Even as I lift my torso slightly, he stays there, crouched over me. If I try to sit up, my face is going to head right for his. Don't want that.

I spin. He moves with me. I sigh and try rolling back the other way. He scurries alongside. I take the direct route and sit up. My face is about an inch from his before his breath beats me back down. I don't want to speak to this guy. Mostly because opening my mouth would let more of his smell in. I can feel the warmth of his crotch as he crouches lower.

He laughs. Would it alert anyone up here if I drove my thumb into this guy's throat? Not that it would help, since he's got a dog collar on. Odd fashion accessory. It takes out my first option. We've still got eyes, ears, and nose. Let's see what happens.

I roll again, just to move away from the edge. He climbs onto me. Little gobbets of phlegm patter my cheek. He doesn't seem like he's getting anything out of this. More like he's a big, overly friendly dog that wants to say hello. His pants are warm and wet. He leans in close to sniff me.

A three count. Just like shooting. Prep your weapon. Exhale slowly. Find your target: The nose.

Three.

Two.

One.

I swallow and lunge forward, biting down as hard as I can on the front of his nose. Just a quick snap. Holding on would make him hit me. A fast bite startles. It makes him protect himself, draw back. If I had legs, this would be the part where I kick him hard in the gut and then pounce on his skull. Instead I use my arms to crawl back from him to get a better look.

He cowers on a pile of dirty mattresses underneath a shattered window. His eyes water, burning with rage. His nose bleeds from three little moon-shaped cuts. I did good work. He lunges. Three inches from me, he comes to a dead stop and falls to the floor.

When he gets up again, gasping for breath and screaming in anger, I notice the collar has a chain attached to it, leading to a bracket in the wall.

"Shut up! Shutshutquiet!" *There's* a voice I recognize.

The little mongrel falls silent at the sound of it. I've managed to use the wall to pull myself back to my feet. A skinny man leans against the wall, almost indiscernible in the jumble of loose pipes and boards piled there. I hope he doesn't recognize me. My pants are draping as they should. I don't think he saw me stand up, so as far as he knows, I'm a normal girl with a limp on crutches.

"Pardon my dogdog. Who—who the fuck are—are you? Are."

I remain silent and stare at Shakes. This won't be a short conversation. We've got enough speech impediment stored up between us to last the rest of the year. I throw one of the hollowed-out shells at him. This one is special, painted sky blue with the good Doctor's logo stamped on the side. He pries the top and pours out three pills and a typed note. His eyes go wide.

"No I din't. Nonono. Supposed to befreefreefree..."

Now he's laughing. The mongrel by the wall starts to join in, which earns him a kick in the head. Shakes reads the note again. He turns to get it into better light. He barks a few more quick laughs and places the note in his pocket. He motions for me to follow him as he walks away.

It's when he's not standing still or leaning against something that his namesake becomes apparent. He moves like he's hooked up to a stuttering cattle prod.

I follow him through a series of rafters and catwalks, over the open production floor of his factory, where a large stained glass window hangs. Every drug cult has one. A way to identify themselves. It's usually a reproduction of what they put on their pills, something that's easy for spray painters to tag on buildings, a little logo they can hide on their "remanufactured" vehicles.

Shakes's design is sort of like a block-letter Japanese symbol that's fallen on its face. It's blue on an orange background.

Shakes takes me to what used to be the floor manager's office when this was still a factory. It's a small, glass-walled booth high above the production floor. You can see the chem labs down on one side and the sparks from the auto grinders on the other.

"You like—like the décor?"

I make a noise from my throat, something between indifference and slight interest.

"It's all me. Growing—I'm growing this bitch, you know? S'why you're here, yeah? I'm—yeah—getting' noticed up top? He'll take me back if you say...if you say, yeah, you tell Doc what you saw. Tell him I'm a hard worker—hardhard. But I'm not..." Shakes's eyes sweep around the room, "...stupid," he finishes.

The walls are coated with a parade of photographs. One section dedicated to newspaper ads for his cover businesses, the used-car dealers, the massage shops, the phone-sex lines.

Another wall is covered with a series of crayon drawings on construction paper. Little squiggly representations of pills and needles, arranged like math. Blue pill + (Vicodin) + Orange/Red (DXT) = 3 smiley faces. That sort of thing. A rating system, a how-to series of flash cards.

Behind his desk is the shrine. Victims and headlines. He's got crime-scene shots. Autopsy photos. Newspaper clippings of stories regarding the growing drug problem, mostly from his turf. There are obituaries, other stories detailing the short weeks before someone's death, when they entered witness protection or took out a restraining order.

There's one photo I can't take my eyes from, hard as I try. A woman standing in a doorway, her face in her hands, hair falling forward. A smile playing between her fingers. Did I really look so sexy?

Memories spark in the back of my brain, too quickly to stop or really pay attention. I get the snippets. Shakes in a white room, sitting near me. There's a circular saw just outside the frame of the picture, I remember that. It's... I also used to call it Mother's Little Helper.

This is all before the night the guy got burned in the alley. Way before that. Happy times when I wasn't so pleasant. Before I took a bottle to my jaw. Before I was taken apart with that same saw. I think it was that saw. I was beautiful. That was me before Shakes dropped the dime on me. It was something he said to Doctor Robert. I can't remember any details, and it kills me. I look at the picture, willing it to give me something.

Shakes stares. Have I been ogling my photo too long? He can't make the connection. I'm nothing like the woman in that picture. He keeps looking. For a long time. It's unbearable. I stare back. He's locked on me, his eyes like two black marbles. I want to kill him right now, but he knows something, and I need it. He sits on the edge of a rusty metal table and points at the spot next to him. I hobble over.

"I ain't stepped over no lines—stepped," he begins.

It's a question, not a statement. The fact that he said it means he has crossed a line, and he's worried that it's all over. He wants to impress the Doctor, obviously. But somewhere he was overzealous. Showing the right amount of ambition would bring a visit from the Doctor to discuss incorporation. Showing zeal would bring a final cease and desist notice.

He fidgets. Something on Shakes is always moving. His feet, his hands, his mouth. "What's he want?"

The longer I stay silent, the more frightened he's going to get. But I don't want him to go over the edge.

Read the note, I tell him.

"What?"

The note, read the note.

"What—what the fuck are—are you saying? Marblemouth you're a marblemouth!"

Before this day is over, I'm going to make him understand how hard it is to form certain consonants when part of your tongue is missing. I point to the note. He reads it again. No. He looks at it again.

"What's it say?"

He can't read. All he knows is Dr. Fortescu's symbol, stamped at the bottom of the note. The rest of it could say: "Shakes, you are responsible for the shambling mess you see before you and retribution has come upon ye." The note could have the lyrics to the theme song from *Three's Company*. It wouldn't matter.

This is horrible. Now I have to read the note out loud to him, which is going to take forever. It's a simple forgery, a request from the Doctor for information. "Caligula is becoming a pest, help us find him and you will be considered worthy to come back into the fold." That kind of thing. Ratting people out is what Shakes does best. This should be so easy for him.

The note also details a request to see what Shakes is holding in his inner sanctum, to see if his goods meet the Doctor's standard of quality. This means he has to take me to his private reserve vault, deep in the bowels of the building, where sound does not penetrate the walls. Where guards do not tread unless invited. Where a man could be strangled, stabbed, and tortured, and nobody would come to his aid. Where I could take my sweet time.

I'll have to send this in Morse code. Short sentences. Important words only. Pray he understands.

Doctor, I say. Doctor?

"I ain't stepped over no lines—lines. I been happy here—happy in—"

Shut up.

That's one phrase I've got a pretty good handle on. He quiets down.

Imagine having to give a speech with a huge chunk of uncooked steak in your mouth. Imagine trying to tell a story after a visit to the dentist, your face still numb from Novocain. This is where

I am. I stand in front of Shakes as calmly as possible, and I begin, using rudimentary sign language to make things clear:

"Dokkah Frtsku." Point to note. "Snt mmee to imvite you." Point to me, point to him, friendly. "You mmoove uht."Finger towards the ceiling. "Yourr cuhlt hss cuhlt tgever." Fingers interlaced, big smile, but not so big to gross him out. "Tllgll 'sboddern Dokkah. Helk Dokkah. Where Tllgllah? Chhllgllah? Haffa..."

I swallow. The front of my shirt coated in spit. My chin cooling off from the air conditioner breezing across the slime slick below my lip. What the fuck is a good sign for *Caligula*? This was supposed to be the moment of glory, the part where Clint Eastwood catches up to the bad guy, giving a righteous speech before blowing the idiot away.

Now it's the part where the girl has to be strong and not cry because she can't stand the sound of her own voice.

"I ain't stepped overoverover. IIII been here the whole time—whole."

He's not getting any of it. And he's really scared now. I can tell because his foot is snare drumming the floor tap-tap-tap-tap-tap-tap.

"Dokkah?"

"I stayed in my yard the whole time—whole. Gotta grow things, though. Times are—are tough with the recession people ain't buying like—people—they used to—"

How the fuck does Shakes know a word like recession?

"Dokkah imvite you. You n' Dokkah. T'gezher." I interlace my fingers gently again. Is he missing this? Does this motion also look like I'm saying the Doctor wants to squeeze him out or crush him? Frances would understand everything I was saying. Frances hangs on my every word. And Joe wouldn't even need words. For this idiot, I need a translator.

"Pahtnah," I say, extending my hand. He's got to get this one. I'm even giving him the submissive grip. My palm is up, fingers gently cupped, eyes more at the floor than his face. I've used this grip since I first learned how much it makes men feel at ease. I've used it since--

shit.

Shakes stares at me. I wipe the spit from my chin, my head turned slightly. I try to offer his my most polite smile. His eyes and mouth go comically round. Over his shoulder, I see myself reflected in a window. My hand over my mouth, covering the crazy quilt of scars that is my jaw. My head is turned down, so Shakes sees my good eye. It's all he needs. His eyes go the photo on the wall, then back to me.

The photo. Me. The photo.

He's not moving. He's got the pills back out, turning them over and over in his hand. Here is where an experienced professional would assess the situation, do a threat analysis, start picking options.

I don't have time for any of that shit. It's time for a balancing act. Measure once, cut twice. Or three or four times, depending on the sharpness of the blade. I raise my right pant leg and move a lever, releasing the shoe. Slowly, I slide it off, revealing the curved blade. Then I reach a little higher, hitting the release on the leg.

Shakes turns the pills over one last time, almost pops them, but stops. "Hey. Hey-hey-hey, Doctor F. wants to—to—Doctor—team up? Serious? All is f-f-f-fuck-forgiven?"

Shit. He was lost in his own little world. He hadn't even paid me any attention. And now, he finally notices me. "Fuck. Where—where the fuck is your leg?"

How do I play off having one leg and holding a razor sharp blade on a pole in my hand? I sweep the blade out hard across his face, spinning once and following through to hook his ankle, pulling back.

He yelps and drops to the floor, blood rushing through his fingers, as if pressing the ends of his tendon together would make it whole again. My hand is vise-tight over his mouth before a sound comes out. The cut I put on his forehead is superficial, but bleeding like crazy. I have to keep things on the ground now. I've only got one leg to stand on. If Shakes gets up, I'm dead.

"Tellidyoola," I say.

I hate talking. I really hate talking. I take it nice and slow, not caring how much spit gets in Shakes's ear.

"Calid...tellid..."

Shit.

This word should be easy. Reconstruction left me with a horrible underbite and what a speech therapist called "an inherent difficulty with plosives." This guy's name has none of the difficult sounds, and I'm still falling apart here.

"Calllli-guh-you-lah."

Shakes nods his head. I lift my hand a little. His machinery is working full swing down on the production floor, cars being stripped, sanded, painted over. Music blaring to keep the workers entertained. They're not going to hear. I just have to hope there are no scheduled breaks coming up.

"Caligula? You—you work for CalCalCal that pimp sent you here?"

"Noooo," I sneer. "Where izhee?"

"How—how the fuck should—know—I know?"

I slide my hand up, taking a grip on the blade just above the hook. I hold the end to the side of his head, grab his earlobe and ask him "where?" I press the blade into the bottom of his ear and the skin slices quick and soft like deli ham.

I have to clamp my hand down extra tight over his mouth for about three minutes. Enough time for Shakes to scream so much that he's hyperventilating.

"Terr nee where."

"Bitch!"

Why do men always pretend to be so tough at times like this? My required reading before coming here was a CIA manual about interrogation. Joe has ways to find these things. He's primed me with gentle prodding techniques honed in dozens of benevolent nations worldwide. This technique I'm using, Joe told me he learned it firsthand in a basement cell, probably in some foreign war.

I take two fingers and tug at the dangling hunk of Shakes's ear. It wobbles like a cherry-red gummy bear about to be torn in half. It's ugly and cruel. I almost feel bad doing it. Almost.

Look what you did to me. Look what your stupid mouth did. Look what happened when you ratted me out. I'm nothing now. I was pretty. I was a woman. Look at what you did to me, you filthy trash. My family. My life. Everything.

Why was I targeted? There is no such thing as random violence. Why me?

All of the things I wish I could be saying right now. The speech I had rehearsed. The pauses I would take. None of it matters. I realize now that none of it would have worked anyway, not even under the best circumstances. The most I could have hoped for was a recording of someone speaking my thoughts, something I could have played to him so he knew why he was going to die. I'll have to remember it for next time.

Instead, I have to let him die in ignorance. But first I need to know where Caligula is. Caligula will lead me to Delia Sugar, and so on and so forth.

"Hinter's District!"

Shakes screams it over and over again. It's muffled, but like Helen Keller, I feel the sounds in my palm. I wonder how long he's been screaming it. I was lost in a reverie. I bring my free hand up to my face, a bloody lump of cartilage with a diamond earring attached between thumb and forefinger. Guess I got carried away. But it did the job. I pocket the hunk of his ear and grab the other one.

"Widd who?" I ask.

"Nobody, nobody! He's keepin' his head downdowndown, so nobody don't take it off—off. He pushed some buttons—some. He crossed some lines—some. I stayed ininin my yard! You din't hafta do-do-do this!"

"You nyin?"

"No lie! Shit—lie—no!"

"Grrronka Gaadn...fffffur-ah-ka nnngg-aa—gn."

"Veronica—shit! Veronica—is this what this is?—I knew—I knew—when you said Doctor—I knew! Shit!"

"Where isshhhhee?"

Shakes goes quiet, lays there bleeding. So I repeat myself, leaning with the heel of my hand with all my weight on his crotch to help him focus.

"Veronica—Madden? Veronica...are you...?"

"Where...issshee? Terrl nggee whu oo ngo."

"I get it. Get. I understand what you're why you're you fucking bitch! What I think of her, like it's some test, I know she's evil evil evil."

That's pretty evil. Or it might be his speech impediment.

"Doctor says he wants peace but all this torture shit, torture ain't changed a thing thing. You bitch. Veronica Madden Madden Madden, where is she? Where is she, you ask, you don't know what you're, you're messing around marblemouth bitch. Looking for torture and that's all, hasn't changed, looking..."

I think Shakes is going into shock. Expected. I roll off of him. Before he can move I jam the blade into the back of his knee. Tendons cut on both legs, he doesn't know which way to roll. He's screaming a lot, and a little too loud, but I needed time to get back on one foot to put my other leg on. I strap it in and walk towards Shakes. His eyes are on my picture in the paper, a yellow, tattering scrap on the wall.

"It was business-business. They would have killed me—me—me if I didn't tell on you—tell. You weren't even supposed to make make make it out, and the Doc said he took care of it all that Mrs. Robinson Simon Garfunkel bullshit and you ain't changed, you ain't changed, you ain't changed..."

I walk up to him, my shoe alternating with the steel of the

exposed blade on my other foot hitting the floor. Thud-clank-thud-clank.

"I tried to—you weren't supposed to...but the kid...the kid—you were—but—"

I pause. The kid? Something about my daughter? But the machines are shutting down on the floor. It must be close to break time. I won't have time to finish this interview. Time to cut and run.

"Tha's nah nee," I tell him.

That's not me, I tell myself. The woman in that picture could never do this.

I plant my left leg on the floor by Shakes's shoulder and axe kick down with my right leg. The blood from his jugular paints most of the photos on the wall, but it misses mine. That sexy lady in the photo is still clean and pure.

Maybe the woman in the picture taught me to do this. Maybe I need to chase her down too.

Shakes shudders and convulses long past death. His body spasms and the air rushing past his vocal chords is enough to make it sounds like he's laughing at some private joke.

"Huh...huh...huh."

And the punchline is, he's not waking up. And the punchline is, I've just taken a life up close and personal. And the punchline is, the joke's on me. I scramble to a trashcan in the corner and heave my guts out. I'm crying. I hate myself for this. Through a scope, it's easy. I'm detached, far away. I can't smell that warm-blood smell. I don't have to watch them twitch.

I'm sticky. What the hell did I do to Shakes? What has Shakes done to me? Look what he's made of me. Look what I've become. I prod him with my foot, trying to get him to stop twitching. He won't.

But look at him, look at this factory. He kills people. Maybe not directly, but his drugs. He kills kids. My kid. Maybe. Not again. Never again.

Michael Paul Gonzalez

I kick him hard across the neck, and the blade digs in, sticking at the midpoint. He doesn't seem to notice. He's dead. Definitely dead. So why can't I stop kicking him? Why am I moving on to his arms, his legs, his stomach? Why am I decimating him?

He deserves this. An eye for an eye, and a full body mutilation for the loss of my life, my family. Serves him right. I step back to look at my handiwork and I have to laugh. Did I do this? Did I just grind a man into hamburger?

I can't even see my other life. This is life number three. I was someone else before the list. Then I was another woman entirely up until this moment. Now I'm a murderer. I'm not a vigilante. Killing is killing, I've done this before. It comes easily to me. I just have to close my eyes and think of something else.

Am I turning a page or just coming back home?

I can't care anymore. The *why* is no longer important. Just the *how*. Get it done. Sort out the pieces when it's all over. Now is not the time.

I pat Shake's body down, take the pills I find. I almost cry for joy when my fingers close on a tiny glass bottle. 40 ml. I could cry. No time to test it. I will need this tonight. Probably the whole thing, just to forget.

I snap my shoe back over the blade, noticing how much harder it is to do with the gummed remains of Shakes sticking up everything. I use the hem of his shirt, one of the only dry spots on his body, to wipe the blade down. I roll my pant leg over my leg, thanking the fates that the darkness in here will hide the splatter from anyone I pass.

From my back pocket I pull an olive laurel, Caligula's current signature piece, the kind of crown a Roman emperor would wear. This will let everyone know who decided to step up and take Shakes down. If Caligula tries to deny it, it would make him look weak. He'll have two choices: go public and take credit, which could get messy, or stay locked down and hide until the heat blows over and people figure out what really happened.

I lock the office door behind me, hanging Shakes's emblem on the door handle to signify he's deep into product testing and is not to be disturbed. That should keep most people away from his office for at least an hour, unless an emergency comes up.

I make my way down the hall. Ten yards past the circular staircase and around the corner is a perfectly useable straight staircase. It puts me at a T-intersection on the first floor around the corner from the door greeter. If I had time I'd kill that big bald sack of manure for making me take the hard way. Instead I stick to the shadows and give him the A-OK sign as I pass by.

"Seepin," I say, pointing up the stairs. "Tess croduck. L'il choo nuch." I mime sleeping with my hands under my cheek. The bald mountain can't stand my enthusiasm. I can tell he hates looking at me. He sits in a folding chair and goes back to studying the mold on the walls.

I make it to my van, take a minute to wipe as much blood off of my face as I can. Hope anyone left on site won't notice the new crimson pattern on my jacket. I drive out to the fence on the opposite side of the building, where I'm greeted by the same two thugs.

"Well, well. She's still alive. Boss musta liked what he saw."

I mime holding a car key by my temple, giving it a quick turn and rolling my eyes back. It's a different kind of language that Joe helped me with, one that the cults use in bars downtown to communicate across crowded rooms.

"He's on?" one of them asks.

"Like a RrrraceKah."

"I knew it!" the groper shouts. "High class V-8 shit. Boss is rolling in the big time now."

They both look at each other, fishing in their pockets for what's left of the pills I gave them earlier. Poison hasn't had time to work yet, or they just haven't noticed it. I reach into the glove box for the other shells, the hollowed-out greens. I dig out the pills. Shiny and pink, as friendly as a plastic egg on Easter. Dig in fellas.

"K6? Holy shit, we are movin' up, aren't we?"

The thugs wrestle to be the first to receive my generous bounty. I shake a few more out of the shell. "Frr yrr hahd wukk. Penty t'go roun'," I say, pouring the pills into their hands.

K6 is the latest designer drug to come out of the Doctor's lab. Very new, very chic, very hard to obtain. These guys have obviously never tried it, but they've heard the stories. The quick-dissolve gel-caps that release a jolt straight to your spine. K6 takes months of refinement in a special airtight lab and ingredients that are mostly imported or very difficult to make. I don't have that kind of time or those kind of resources.

My pills are homemade, and pretty damn potent. Pure lye coated with a thin layer of flour, followed by a glistening gelatin coating. Makes them go down easy. My pills are also very difficult to make. Lye and moisture don't mix well. The flakes will heat to over two hundred degrees when they come into contact with water. I'm not sure how it will react with stomach acid, and frankly I'm not going to be around to find out.

"Got any extra?" one asks.

I throw the rest of my painted poison into their palms.

"Go nutch," I tell them.

I never thought drug addiction would make me smile, but the sight of those two guards popping palmfuls of certain death is too good to resist.

I have thrown down the gauntlet and started a war. Sure, it was in Caligula's name, but what's the difference? There will be backstabbing, fighting, a power struggle. And while everyone fights, I will take care of business. Start with Hinter's District, where Shakes said I'd find Caligula. Get some info from the stacks downtown, a few more trips to Joe's to reload, and then it all ends. There are a lot of bridges between here and there. Ammunition to buy, weapons to conceal.

In my rearview mirror, the first thug falls down clutching his stomach. His friend bends to help when the cramps hit him, too. I accelerate, and I laugh and laugh, and I don't care how out of control my mouth is, how much of my spittle sprays the windows. I haven't been this happy for a long time.

Michael Paul Gonzalez

XIV

I've been sitting on the workshop table in Joe's place for a good forty-five minutes. He filled me in on the success of my courthouse delivery, how his client was very pleased with the product. I told him I didn't see any reports on shootings at the courthouse.

"Things happened that needed to happen. You did well," he said.

We moved on to other topics; local politics, weather, sports, killing. We've been talking about number six. Caligula, our city's answer to Archbishop Don "Magic" Juan. He runs drugs and whores all over the city and moonlights as a nationally-renowned Pick-Up Artist. He's not a pimp. He is *The Pimp*, author of two nationally published books, both bestsellers. His first effort, *Pimptastic*, was written while he was in his Franco-asshole phase, under the name Pompidou. Now he's moved on and become goth, calling himself Caligula, penning the number-one book, *Pimpin' on the Dark Side*. The man is pure sleaze any way you cut it. But man, is he connected.

Caligula is the man to go to for a good time. Not just for women. Big C is the central clearing house when it comes to vice. He sizes up his customers by their wallets, directs them to the appropriate drug cult, the brothel that fits their budget, the gambling garages and underground fight clubs where they can afford to lose.

Caligula is the emperor of the overstreets. He changes with the times, keeps his product fresh, his leads connected, and his women protected. He's in bed with the mayor, the governor, the chief of police, anyone who has power. Granted, Big C can't touch the heads of the drug cults. He has no power to intimidate syndicates or the families. But the everyday populace, he owns. Long as he keeps sharing, then those who are more powerful will continue to tolerate him.

I think the police tend to ignore his presence because he's consolidated so much of the prostitution industry. They only have to go after the fringe players while Caligula regulates his McBrothels. They would love it if the same thing could happen with the drug cults.

Joe's been working on my legs, patiently listening to my plans and filling me in on small details. He's polite enough not to interrupt, even though he seems a little agitated tonight, like he's got big news. So, as I wind up what should have been ten minutes of talk, he finally stops to take a break from grinding metal to offer his opinion.

"It's wonderful. You're doing great work. The Lord's work. He's going to smile down on you when it's all said and done, kiddo, you trust me."

"I chhst you conkleetee."

Joe taps the leg pipe he's working on gently, trying to get the joint to seat just so. "I can't tell you how proud you make me," he says, moving next to me. "You're an inspiration. Make a man want to pick up a rifle and stand a post. If you can do it, why can't I?"

I smile at him. Why not, indeed? I'm sure he's got plenty of axe to grind and plenty of people to use as grinders. I chuckle and ask him:

—Is this town big enough for two vigilantes?

"This town is big enough for anything. Think of what we could accomplish. Two cripples like us, nobody would see us coming."

I pause. I know what's coming here. I don't want to hurt his feelings, but he's crossing a line. My list is my list. My reasons are mine alone. Nobody else touches the list. And I don't move beyond the list unless it's necessary. I try to cut him off before he makes the

Michael Paul Gonzalez

offer.

—This is an angry woman thing, not a Batman and Robin thing.

He laughs. "I don't want to be your partner. Naw, I got things of my own to do, and I respect your work. I know I'm beating a dead horse here, but you gotta listen to me. I think the list is out of order. I think you need to hit the Doctor before you go after Hooded Jack. You know my clientele. I've been putting out feelers, seeing which way the wind blows..."

—We've been through this, I tell him

"I know, I know. But listen. The Doctor is primed to take a fall. He thinks he's untouchable. That's the best place for a target to be. Comfortable. What you did tonight is going to make it look like Caligula is playing for all the marbles. You knock him off next, and *hard*, and people will think that's the Doctor trying to keep things in balance. It'll also look like he's trying to shift the balance of power. Take him out when everything becomes pure chaos. Don't give him time to plan. Besides, Hooded Jack...well," and he gets close to me and lowers his voice, even though we're in a place where nobody could hear, "Hooded Jack has security like you wouldn't believe. If you give me time, I might be able to find a way in for you, make things easy. But trust me, you rush in there and they will deal with you. You take the Doctor out first and *everyone* will surface. That's a big power vacuum."

—The list is the list. The Doctor comes after Hooded Jack.

"Why?"

—I don't know why, but I know that's how it goes.

"Have it your way." And he smiles at me. No harm, no foul. Just a big, overprotective father figure. "But just... can I tell you what I'm thinking?"

I roll my eyes, not ready for another hard sell about why the list needs to change. But Joe is giving me everything I need to get the jobs done, so I might as well hear him out. I can tell he's dying to impress me with a new toy of some sort. I cock my head at him to let him know I'm listening.

"My grapevine tells me people out there aren't too happy with Caligula. It wasn't cops that found the olive branch at the scene of Shakes's murder. Not a word breathed to the press. But within three hours, everyone's looking for answers. The big dogs want to yank his chain, put him back in line. Maybe take him down for even *thinking* of going after a drug cult, no matter how small. You need to move fast, for two reasons. One: You don't want him finding any friendly ears. Everyone wants to know what he's up to. And I have it on good authority that Caligula is panicking. So, in the immortal words of Ricky Ricardo, Joo need to wax the motherfucker before he has a chance to 'splain."

Joe jogs across the room, starts throwing blankets and pipes off of a huge crate in the corner.

He shouts back over his shoulder. "Two: You need to destabilize the Breeding Ground. You need cops looking one way, higher-ups the other. You need everybody moving. Caligula is the keystone. See, what nobody wants right now is a war. Nobody's ready for it, and everyone's going to have to come out throwing punches. Shoot 'em all, let God sort 'em out, that kind of thing.

"Take Caligula's whole operation out, blame it on someone else, keep this ball rolling... You see where I'm going? Trouble is, everyone is too scared to take that first shot. But when it does happen, they'll all start killing each other off."

I've dreamed of that. The night would be truly wild. Complacency will die, the law of the jungle will return, and all of the hungry tigers out there will have to start fighting to figure out who's king. The cops will be busy. Overwhelmed. The drug cults will be forced to put extra effort into protecting their routes, and protecting their higher-ups. Everyone spread thin. Nobody moving. Fairy tales can come true.

Joe steals a glance over his shoulder and lowers his voice to a more conspiratorial tone. "I never rat on my customers. You know me, I'm loyal to a fault. But I'm going to give you some inside information. And only because I don't want to see you get hurt."

"It's..." Joe looks around one more time. "If Caligula's empire folds, and Delia Sugar has an agent on the scene, *and she will*, since Caligula keeps himself floating in whores, if he goes down, everyone will move towards her for answers. She'd be the only other known entity with a presence in his club. Everyone else on the fringes will get nervous. Develop itchy trigger fingers. Kill or be killed. And you get enough of that going, you're going to see the big players try to leave town. Dr. Robert will have to move to stay safe. Moving targets are harder for you, right?"

—I'm not changing the order!

"I know, I know. I'm not asking you...what I'm saying is, you need to do something so big that everybody is going to stop and take notice. Something huge. Something that tells everyone that leaving town could mean giving up everything to a new power player."

He looks truly excited now. I can see flames dancing in his eyes. I have visions of him fighting bravely overseas, pushing his men, maybe even burning down small villages for God and country. I love it.

"I was thinking this could be the thing you use to pin it on the Doctor, but it would work just as well coming from an unknown source. This is how you make people stop and look," he says, wheeling the crate over to me.

—You're going to hide their bodies in there?

Joe laughs, long and hard as he unlocks the crate and pops the lid open. There's a sheet of gray plastic stretched tightly over whatever's inside. He sees that I haven't quite gotten it, so he laughs even harder. "We light up the night."

My brain doesn't make the connection until he takes the palm of his hand and pushes on the plastic, leaving a perfect impression of his handprint.

Joe, you shall deliver me. The crate is at least four feet wide and three feet tall. And from the way Joe is laughing, I can tell that it's all full of the same thing. It's grey and plastic, alright. Pure C4.

"I trust you enough to let you know that this is partly for me, too. I owe Caligula. Long story, I'll tell you afterwards. I ever tell you I used to work UDT back in the day?"

Underwater Demolition Teams. About a million times.

Joe smiles. "You give me one night, I can get some players in there to rig the whole place up. You get out into the alley after taking care of Caligula. And I mean *out*, as far away as you can. Then his house falls. You get another notch on your revolver, I get to stretch my leg, make some fireworks, everybody wins."

I push myself off the table and into Joe's arms, hugging him hard. I hope he's not too startled, because I have no legs at the moment. Wouldn't want him to drop me. He hugs back and sets me down gently.

"Now what say you get out there and deliver us from evil, huh?"

Michael Paul Gonzalez

XV

Back to the library. So much to do and so little time. I'm making a point of being overprepared. Frances is puffing away somewhere in the basement, probably looking up "real neat" facts about historical data. This in between takes of the performance of his life. It is what I asked for, after all.

And he understood. It was a little refreshing to be able to look someone other than Joe in the eye and speak. I usually hate it, but after last night, it felt good. Frances listened, didn't try to finish my sentences for me...stared at my mouth a little too long, yeah, but he hung on every word.

His clumsy, creepy attempt at showing affection left a mark on me. Beggars really can't be choosers. Not that I'm begging. Frances is convinced there's something buried inside of me. Which, really is the same thing as something being missing. At this point I'm too exhausted to get angry at the whole thing.

Frances is just all right with me. I have him convinced that I'm taking an acting class through an extension at the university. Brave little me. Such courage to get up in front of all of those people. Putting myself on the line like that. What a load.

I have a monologue typed out. From a non-existent play called

"Bitsy Christ Light." The title makes no sense, so in an artistic way, I explained to Frances, it makes perfect sense. Especially when you examine the larger scope of the struggle that Bitsy must go through. It's a very touching play, I told him. This small naify-waify woman rises from an abusive relationship to confront the husband who so kept her oppressed for years and years. I typed most of this out, because I'm sure that saying "Bitsy" would mean spitting directly in his face, and I do need his help.

This monologue, it's from the part where Bitsy has her husband pinned to the living room floor and has a gun in his face, and she confronts him about everything he's done to ruin her life. He's been horrible to her, and she says she doesn't have to kill him to hurt him.

Frances knows I just can't memorize lines unless I hear them. And it would be a lot easier if I could hear them clearly. He didn't even question it. I can hear the echo of his voice rising up the open elevator shaft.

"No, Gavin, *you* are going to listen to *me*. There are things as a man you can't understand. Menstruation, Gavin, imagine it. Imagine!" I pray to God Frances isn't method acting down there.

There's some fluff at the beginning, but if I can pull off another act like I did at Shakes's place, make Caligula think I've been sent by the Doctor, then maybe I can get some intimidation going. Maybe he'll name names and places, tell me how to find other people to save his sorry ass. It's all there in my monologue.

While Sir Frances is going through multiple takes, I kill time by studying for the future, the ins and outs of St. Jude's Hospital. The doors, who installed them, how do they work in case of a fire? What kind of tile did they use on the floors? How many exits are there? Where are the metal detectors? The Doctor's office? Security shouldn't be hard. They'll be looking for gang bangers, dealers, the rough crowd. Crippled white chick? What's she going to do?

She's going to do a lot, that's what, and damn the media. I never got my ten minutes on the news when I was immolated, but now I own the first fifteen minutes of every broadcast. I'm jealous of me for finally getting the attention I deserve, because even now a man still gets the credit.

Another drug lord taken down. New leads in the Vasili slaying. Little Debbie clinging to life. No leads on the case, but witnesses reported a dark-skinned heavyset man running from the scene. An extra room at the hospital has been opened to hold all of the cards, flowers, and gifts from well-wishers. If stuffed animals could restore a child's health, Little Debbie would be immortal.

All of this because of me.

I shake my head and wonder what the other kids in the sick ward think of this. Those other sad sacks that were Wednesday's Child, or Tuesday's Special Focus, or a previous cause that only got five minutes before sports. I feel for you, kids.

I glance over to the table on my right, where my list, crumpling and fraying and sweat-stained and blurred, sits. It reads:

10. ~~Vasili~~

9. ~~Susan Schrader~~

8. ~~Grace Brooks – need camo webbing and paper bags~~. SLOPPY BITCH!

7. ~~Shakes – maybe sooner~~ Learn restraint.

6. Caligula – Familiar address?

5. Delia Sugar – News story p7 linked to Shakes now

4. Hooded Jack (?) – could be driver – shipping a lot – wharfs?

3. Dr. Robert Fortescu – could afford black car – leaving town soon – hurry

2. Veronica Madden – vehicle? –

1. ??? – How do you know someone's here? *Because there's always a number one.*

I have to stash it fast when little ripples form in my water bottle, announcing the imminent arrival of Francasaurus Rex.

"This play is pretty good. Gritty, you know? I like it a lot. It's good. I mean really good." Frances must have guessed that I wrote it. He's panting a little. Maybe his heart is racing for my approval. Maybe he just took the stairs too fast. "I really like the part at the end. It's, uh...it's neat."

Christ Frances, you work in a library. There are dictionaries here. A thesaurus right there by your desk. Come on! *Neat.*

"Hey, did you see the latest victim on the news? I know you're into that true crime stuff."

Oh, Frances.

"That drug-cult guy? Boy, somebody messed him up."

Let's not discuss this.

"They say it was a ritual slaying, the way his legs were mutilated."

Ritual slaying? There's a new one. Can we talk about something else?

"And you know the weirdest thing? It happened at one of those buildings you were looking at the other day. Remember when you got those blueprints?"

This is a road Frances shouldn't travel. I point to the tape recorder in his hand.

"Oh. You want to hear? Should I leave? It's kind of embarrassing to hear my own—"

For a moment I hear the distorted sounds of double Frances as I hit play. The real Frances stops talking after a bit, so I can hear the recording of the important questions.

"Menstruation, Gavin, imagine it. Imagine! I know about her, Gavin." And here I wrote in a long pause, for dramatic effect, "Why so quiet? Delia's angry. She's going to eat you alive, and I think I'll let her. Unless you start talking. It's her or me, what's your decision? Because if you're scared of her, you should be god-damned terrified of me. Tell me what you know about Jack. And Delia. Now!" There's a pause, then, "What, you want coffee? Coffee, Gavin? Yeah, you think.

You know...I. I tried to. You know. Gavin, motherfucker!"

I hit stop. Frances handled my tribute to Mamet at the end quite nicely. A bit melodramatic. Some stress on the wrong syllables. And he completely ignored most of my stage directions. But, you take what you can get.

Here are some of the difficulties inherent in my plan. I have to make Caligula believe this is a message from the Doctor or one of his very close associates. Which means we can't have any business about menstruation slipping out. I plan to break the tape recorder when I'm done. He only needs to hear it once.

There's a bit of a wildcard with Joe's side project, blowing up the building. But Joe said that he'd give me plenty of time to vacate. If Joe says it's safe, it's safe.

Anyone who survives the explosion is going to see me leave. So I'll be wearing something purple, Delia Sugar's color. Delia will get the blame, and nobody is calm enough right now to ask questions. Instant gang war, just add water. I just have to hope Caligula doesn't ask questions.

I check the windows outside. There's a hint of rain. My arm and my left hip were nagging at me on the way into the library, so I had to take a detour and get needle-focused. Now my eyes are getting blurry. Nap's coming and I don't have time to get outside. I should chase Frances out of here before I depart on my side trip...

I think he's gone...

I think he's re-shelving...

Or maybe he's staring at me and waiting and breathing...

Looking at me like I'm going to explode and he's not half wrong and...

There's going to be a lot of innocents on the way to Caligula. A lot of Little Debbies. I don't think I have enough Clearwater to make it okay.

I hope Joe built my running legs good and strong. They're

going to go through Hell.

XVI

I don't know if precocious is a word that can be used once your child passes a certain age, but my daughter never lost that nature. It's the only word I can use to describe her. Right now, she's on the other side of her bedroom door sitting against it with her back so I can't get in. The soft muffled thump of her head bouncing against the door every three seconds or so, angry teenager Morse code.

"Go away."

Thump.

Don't do that, I tell her.

Thump.

"You're a nutbag," she replies.

Thump.

I tell her it isn't nice to call me names. Like she would care. We used to have the most amazing relationship. Not one of those "like sisters" or "best friends" things you see in Hollywood movies. I wasn't a cool mom. I was a good mom. A great mom.

Somewhere along the way, she turned on me, and I don't know why. She didn't show any of the signs that usually precede this kind of rebellion on TV specials. No black clothes. No heavy eye makeup. No dating pasty stick-thin boys.

So what did I do?

You come out of there, I sing-song.

"Or what?" she screams.

I don't know, I coo. I've got a gun-hee-hee-hee.

What a joker I am. But she falls dead silent. You can feel the seriousness descend into the room. I have to look down and check my hands and make sure that I don't actually have a gun.

I don't, but I look away and check again just to make sure.

What did I do? I ask.

"My nose is bleeding, you fuck. There are better ways to say no..."

My attention is drawn by a noise at the far end of the hall. Kind of a tic-tic-tic. A sharp noise, like a stone being skipped down an empty high school hallway.

I follow the noise. Every step away from her bedroom makes it grow louder. Now someone is striking that stone on the dinner table. Behind me, the bedroom door creaks open. I spin around in time to see my daughter's head duck back in. Her face looked like a bad painting, pale-skin skies over a crimson sunset. The door slams.

I keep following the noise.

"Fucking psycho!" she screams.

I stumble forward at the sharpness of her voice.

Nobody's going to hurt you. Nobody's ever going to hurt you again, I tell her.

At the end of the hall, in front of the basement door, the noise is steady, a hollow tick-tocking. I descend into blackness. I try the light switch three steps down, but it doesn't work.

I make it to the dusty floor by feel alone. The noise surrounds me, a shuffling sound punctuated every half second or so with a hollow knock. I try to think like an intruder. If I was going to hide, where would I go?

Tap. Tap. A sharp noise. Then another noise, a muted golf clap kind of thing.

I take one step forward and the light kicks on above me. I'm blinded. The fluorescents just took a while to warm up. There's enough wattage to light every last recess in the room.

My eyes blur. Movement all around me. The walls ripple. I blink once, twice, and my vision clears. I swallow a startled yelp. I look down. I still have my legs, but now I can't feel them.

All around me, lining every wall, a series of rolling coat racks stands edge to edge. The more I turn, the more there are, until they surround me. The contents of each rack alternates. One is filled with prosthetic legs of all sizes, some broken and bent. The next rack has legs with primitive joints that are visible like an action figure, others coated in latex, realistic to the last detail. The next is simple steel pipes, the next polymer, then PVC, space-age futuristic comfort cruising machines.

Some of the racks drip red. Some of them have chains attached to the coat rack crossbars, meathooks at the end dug into the sawed-off stumps of real thighs. Real legs, severed, blasted, torn, shredded. They twitch, and each twitch sets off a chain reaction, a nasty Newton's Cradle, one leg bumping another, swish-swish. Equal and opposite reaction, swish-swish. Until it gets to the end of the rack, where the next set of legs, the synthetic ones, carry the motion, and it's swish-swish-click-click. Tap tap. Golf Clap. Ever so light and airy.

Tap-tap-click-click-swish-swish, and I'm going to suffocate down here.

And a man's voice says: "You did this to yourself. First do no harm."

At the top of the stairs the silhouette hovers, and it comes for me. And this time I can't wake up.

No, I scream. No, no, no, and I'm pulling my hair out like a bad actress in a seventies movie. The door slams with such incredible force that some of the legs fall from the racks, and the legs I'm standing on, the beautiful, curvy, sweet, supple legs, they snap like twigs, and down I go into a pile of metal, blood, flesh, dust, and plastic.

There's another man, his slumped body near me in the pile of debris. He reaches out for me with one hand, or maybe he died that way since he's not moving, a glint of light playing off the ring on his finger. His fingertips brush mine, then he fades into blackness.

I float out of myself, see my body on the floor, everything fading away, swallowed by the linoleum, until it's just me, staring up, empty and dead-eyed. Legless.

I'm somewhere else. An alley. Ambulances are coming and it can't be good.

I blink and the room looks like white, sterile, sanitary. Just for a second. Then it's empty, black and dusty. I pull myself across the floor, towards the stairs, past two artificial legs and a set of crutches.

Through the open door at the top of the stairs she says, "Fucking bitch. Leave me alone! Bitch."

And I answer, my voice weak:

I'll save you. I'm coming to save you.

Nobody's going to hurt you ever again.

Ever.

If it's the last thing I do, I'll see to it.

Michael Paul Gonzalez

XVII

Nobody's ever going to hurt you again.

I don't remember shooting up, barely remember the library, but here I am. Shit. I still hear her voice echoing down the hallway. What happened? The dashboard clock tells me it's late afternoon. Of course, according to the dash clock, it's always late afternoon. One look outside confirms it. I lost a whole day.

My van starts a little rough, but I coax it into motion and make my way down the road for my ten o'clock meeting, ready or not here it comes. By the time I've rolled a couple of blocks, the bottle loses its pull on me. The little demon inside my head curls up for a nap. Fine by me.

Those bitter memories from last night are like a vise on my brain, tightening with every mile I move closer to my destination. Some of that was real. Some of that happened. Maybe all of it. The legs. All of those legs and limbs, dismembered parts floating just below the surface of the black pond in my memory. I'm responsible for them.

The buildings on either side of the street manifest those ghosts. Disembodied legs and breasts and asses painted on signs to advertise good times. The Red Light district. This is the only other area of the city that the law never seems to notice. The police have a plan, and for the most part, it works. Keep crime "legal" in these designated areas, and you can spend more time and less money policing the lower crime areas. Less stress and work for the cops, happier citizens, everything is good. There's the standard raid every month or so, a big bust that hits all the news outlets, someone gets hauled off or taken down, usually a two-bit player who was ripe for a fall anyway. The citizens see their tax dollars at work, lament the state of humanity, and return to their sitcoms.

Part of me enjoys the idea of Red Light. There's something about the lure of it, I guess. Seeing broken boys and girls making a living the easy way by taking it the hard way. Going to the back-alley heroin clubs where everybody knows your vein. Or maybe it's because this is the last step, the closest we all come to being like animals, hunting for food and sex. Not all of the ladies and gents here are hookers. Some are sex addicts, some are drug addicts, some are just crazy. You can buy and sell anything in Red Light.

I pass by a corner grocery store, its insides dark and mysterious, the silhouettes of two women move behind the glass. Another jolt hits me. This intersection. Something about that man in the alley from my dream, and this intersection. I was following him. I don't know what I mixed last night, booze or pills or needles, but it's not letting go easy.

His car. What was it about this corner and his car? Waiting for the light to roll from red to green, I get flashes of a night.

A hooker. I was stuck in traffic. She leaned into a window, swaying her hips a little as she talked. I followed the car. Angry? Watched it from a block away until they were done. When they finished, I saw her head bounce off the inside of the passenger-side window. Then the door opened, and she flew out, landing in a heap on the sidewalk.

Busted her nose on the concrete. Sprang up to her feet, quick like a rabbit, but she couldn't stand. Dazed. She screamed at the car, and it sped off. She stepped in front of me before I could follow him. Put her hands on my car, drops of blood spattering down, turning my hood into a slutty Pollack. She was skinny, shaking from cold or withdrawal, staring at me with big Chihuahua eyes. Told me to leave him alone. Wasn't worth it. Said he wasn't paying out. Not taking, not giving. Then she just smiled a bloody smile, a mix of blackened gums and bloody lumps of bad teeth. She walked away like nothing happened. If I couldn't catch him, then it would be her. I chased her to the end of the block.

Green light. A woman staggers across the intersection, towing a shopping cart impossibly laden with cans and bottles. Teetering, like they're all going to...

Tumble down. Twice. She couldn't walk straight. When I caught up to her, she turned and spat a bloody streak across my shirt. Go home, she said. For my own good. Told me I should have my pimp take care of it if I had a beef. And that set me off. Whatever was left in me that was proper and dignified...

I punched her, hard enough to drop her, a little Rorschach of blood popping from the back of her head across the concrete. Her cheek, the one I didn't hit, was marked with a square purple bruise, the kind only a ring could make. A ring I knew.

Then, a chunk of brick sailed by my head. Her street sisters, coming to the rescue. I ran back to my car, pulled into traffic, and felt completely lost. I made it three blocks before I had to stop. My eyes blurred. Couldn't pull over. Frozen in the middle of the road for ten minutes. Heedless to the horns blaring behind me, the angry pedestrians and horny johns tapping on my windshield. Horns so loud I can hear them...

Because I can hear them. A routine patrol by some rookie cop who drew the short straw. He's behind my van. He honks, then gets on the PA and tells me to keep moving. Wouldn't hit the sirens because even cops don't want much attention down here. I comply, moving on, frustrated, chasing that broken string of memory.

There is no such thing as a bad part of town. There are two worlds. One where people were lucky enough to find themselves enslaved by jobs, bills, families, anything to take their mind off of the decay that surrounds them. Any pointless task that can be marketed, polished, and sold to give someone a feeling of hope, progress, meaning in their life. And then, there's the feudal society that opened my eyes and made me aware of life, true life, every reeking, lurking, disgusting nook and cranny of it. Where people have to move, have to struggle or die.

Some people can quote you song lyrics like nobody's business. Me, I can tell you the safest spots to score a hit or get serviced, and in Red Light, I've done neither. I think.

That Chihuahua girl. She probably had a life once, too. Before some awful change brought her here and she started over. Her face floats through my mind, the thick scab on her lower lip where her tooth had bitten through from the fall. The Chihuahua girl belonged to a loose-knit cabal of women of the night who congregated at the city cemetery before hitting the streets. The graveyard was an old, slumping sinkhole of wet mud and scrubby grass that was built God-knows-when before the settlers came. It's full of crypts and graves, and is home to *the* Mistress of the Night, one Delia Sugar.

Delia is a bit too eccentric for a madam, if you ask me. She's Nigerian I think. You should see her come out at night, striding the tops of decrepit tombs and cisterns and fountains, prowling above her flock, moving like a ripple against the night sky. Her flock is something to behold as well. Each with a bright purple accent somewhere on their body to mark them as one of hers. Hair dye. Sashes. Pants, shirts, bras, whatever.

Nobody messes with Delia's children. And what a family they are. Skinny little boys whose ribs stretch through their too-pale skin. Knock-kneed Goth queens and toothless middle-aged heroin addicts. Black, yellow, brown, red, a regular rainbow coalition. The cheapest lays in town, all of them. Homeless and jobless and devoted entirely to the continuation and elevation of their holy mother Delia.

Delia provides. Delia finds them clothes, and food, and warm spots to sleep, and drugs, whatever they'd like. All they have to do is obey her. She tells them who their jobs will be. They don't ask questions. If there haven't been enough reservations made on the evening, she'll send them out into the city proper for some random coupling. Free samples, she calls it. Drawing in new business.

They never see a penny of it. They just go back to her. Easiest life there could be. You do your job, and you get exactly what is promised to you, and really, excluding societal norms, what's wrong with that?

Chihuahua girl worked for Delia. But she's not why Delia's on the list. I wonder if she's still alive, or if she had a kid, or maybe gained a pound or five. Does she still have what's left of her teeth?

It's driving me crazy, darting at my mind like a mosquito. I close my eyes for a brief moment, because I know this is important. It's on the tip of my tongue. Delia. There is something important about Delia. I don't want to rush Caligula, because this plan is important, but Delia will have answers.

"HEY LOOK—!!"

My eyes snap open at the sound of the shout, and I get a split-second view of a stick-like woman with ratty purple hair just before she makes a sickening kettle-drum thud on the hood of my van. My front tires hop as they roll over her body, and I manage to slam the brakes hard enough to avoid running her over with the back wheels.

I should call Joe, tell him I might run late for that ten o'clock. I hope he knows to hold off on the fireworks at Caligula's. Maybe he'll come looking for me.

Did I just kill my Chihuahua girl? It doesn't bother me as much as the fact that I'm in the middle of Red Light and I've run over one of the queen's daughters.

PART TWO

A Change of Plans...

XVIII

Nobody on the street seems to have noticed my faux pas. Below my van, above the ticking of the engine cooling, there's frantic scratching like a puppy anxious to get outside. Or a skinny crank whore getting burned by a hot exhaust pipe. I open the door and see one long leg angling out from under the van, clad in a black-and-white-striped legging. Now I know how Dorothy felt.

Over the tick-tick-tick of my cooling engine, she laughs. She shifts and screams. It turns into a high-pitched whine, and then she swallows hard and starts laughing again. She's pulled herself out from under the van, sort of. Her upper body is coming, but her leg has stayed in the same position. I must have powdered her hip. I try to tell myself it's her fault for being so damned malnourished. Drink some milk, and maybe it would have just been a deep bruise.

"Oh shit..." she says, pulling herself out a little further so she can see up into the van. "I'm gonna tell..."

I've got the door open, looking her right in the face, all puffed on one side. I don't think it's Chihuahua girl, but I'm a little teary. Running wouldn't be the swiftest plan right now, but it's all I've got. There are people approaching the van. All of them look concerned, angry, afraid. All of them clad in purple.

Not one of them seems to care about the crushed woman. They see my face and they think *I've* been mangled in the accident. Even when they're next to my van, almost standing on top of her, they take little notice of her yelps. One of them finally shuffles through the crowd and grabs her wrists, bracing their legs. She's chanting a litany of *NoNoNoNoNoNo* at them, which turns into a banshee scream that threatens to shatter storefront windows. Screaming and metal creaking, gravel sliding, blood lubricating, boots dragging hollow on the road. Broken legs dangling and twisting and bleeding and burning.

I wish I could feel what she feels right now.

"Savor it," I mumble, but I know she can't hear me.

My eardrums pop and my head snaps forward. I'm in a clean room, my legs dangling like the whore's, blood...telling me I'm going to lose them. Nothing can be done. It's the only way. Where's my voice? I want to scream, but I can't. I won't let myself.

Another pop, the pressure in my head dissipates. I don't resist when the crowd pulls me away from the van. Now isn't the time for the Bruce Lee routine. Not that I could fight this many people. I dart my hand into my coat pocket and seize the list, the only evidence on me, and I start to eat it as fast as I can. The paper tastes horrible, sweat and mildew and brass.

Then my mouth is full of fingers, people are prying at my face, trying to stop me from chewing. One of them latches onto the corner sticking out of my mouth, tears it free. I swallow and choke, and they keep trying to hook fingers in and scoop out paper until I open my mouth wide, sticking out my shredded lumpy tongue, laughing.

I wonder what's on the corner they saved. I hope I swallowed the right people.

They lay me out on some outstretched coats, a makeshift gurney. I lock eyes again with the broken whore. I want to kill her. She's ruined the timing. The stupid little bitch. Joe's a professional. He's going to stick to his plans. If Big C's club blows tonight, if he dies, I will have nothing to do with it. I will have no answers and no leads. You take one piece out of the puzzle and the whole thing is worthless.

They're going to take me to Delia, or else they would have killed me. They're going to put her right in my lap, and I can't kill her. I can't do this out of order. Caligula has to die first. Chaos in the streets in a matter of hours.

Killing Delia brings chaos, makes everyone think there's an underworld war in full effect, but it lacks a story arc. There's no purpose, no aim. Drugs are the fuel of the underworld economy, not sex. Delia gives to everyone, Caligula deals and networks selectively. Killing him sends a message. Killing her *after* him makes her look like collateral damage and keeps me moving.

I watch my van shrinking in the distance, still in the middle of the road. This is the sad part of the movie where the cowgirl is separated from her horse, where it's lost to the fates. Will they kill it? Quarter it? Will it somehow survive? They didn't even close the door. Anybody could walk in there, and with a little bit of nosing around, come across my arsenal. One of my legs fell off in the accident. All of my weapons are in the back.

I feel like such a pussy. Two of them toss the broken girl in the back of my van and move it off into a side street. We turn a corner and they raise me up, past the cracked façade of the cemetery. My heart is a strange electrical lump spasming in my ribcage, that kind of sickening heartbreak normally reserved for teenagers on the verge of a breakup.

I had plans. This can't be finished. Not yet.

The inside of the cemetery is warm, glowing in pockets from the sparse fires that Delia's children keep burning. We wind our way through some skinny side paths and towards an Italian mausoleum. Down through an open door at the foot of a sunken staircase. Very Indiana Jones. I'm carted through and set down on a large velvet pillow, crusted and stained with God knows what.

I roll over and see a pair of bare feet, the ankles loaded with huge beaded bracelets. Remarkably clean.

"Mrs. Robinson!" she exclaims. "My, my. It has been *too* long." Her syrupy drawl makes me want to sleep. Her lower legs are wrapped in thin strips of purple fabric. The rest of her is a combination of glitz and garishness. It doesn't matter how nice your clothes are if you have to live in a graveyard.

It's her. I can feel what's left of my lower jaw trembling. I need to take this woman's life. My hands are like two caged dogs begging to be let loose, to tear her throat and to plant the seeds of my thumbnails deep in the soil of her rich, brown eyes.

"How have you been?" she coos to me.

Fine, I reply. Twice. Then another time, and then she understands.

"Oh, Mrs. Robinson...you have such a gift for conversation. I had almost forgotten your melodious voice."

How does she know my name? Even though it's *not* my name, how does she know?

Her smile is amazingly white, and in it I see the thread of memory. I've met her before. We've had dealings.

She pulls a huge book from beneath a cushion and shuffles over to me. She's wiry. Skin so dark, she sits next to me like my shadow come to life. Caresses my left thigh. I feel like I'm about to die. Why did I write her name at number six?

Delia runs her hand along my jaw. She traces the odd shape of my lips two or three times before opening the book on her lap. In a strange way, it feels like a mother/daughter kind of thing.

"It's always so nice when family can get back together," she says. "Even the black sheep."

Inside the book are carefully arranged newsclippings. Random pieces about Delia and her children, her philanthropic efforts, her less legal activities. Then she turns the page and I choke. I literally heave and swallow and I can't breathe. It's me. It's that same picture from Shakes's office. Smiling, sexy me.

"Come on, honey, breathe. Oh..." Delia is up and looking for tissue.

There's a picture of me walking. Walking on firm, curvy

beautiful...

Delia comes back.

"Here," she shoves tissues under my nose. I try to turn the page, but Delia stops me. "You are like a bad penny, Mrs. Robinson. Red Light always brings so much trouble for you, and yet here you are, playing the hapless moth."

I motion for a pencil and paper, but she shakes her head. "Take your time."

So I start to tell her the best story I can think of. That I'm tired of being lonely. That it's not easy being a paraplegic, and that I have needs, and what better place than here, where no one judges... but she's shaking her head.

"Don't lie to Delia. Sugar, Delia can't abide liars. Why don't you start with that night above Vincenzo's?"

Vincenzo's. They've been shut down ever since I popped Vasili's head like a party balloon.

"I have friends and connections here in Red Light. They're dying. Their connections are dying. People in the Breeding Ground are dying. I trace those lines, because it's my business to know things, and I know all of those lines point back to you. And now, you've come into my backyard and tried to kill one of my children. Two and two, two and two..."

No, I shake my head. Accident, I say. But she's not having any of it.

"The city's about to be cut up four ways, there's only so much territory to go around and too many people angling for a piece. And word's been getting around about some ambitious little business person clearing room on the corporate ladder. Vasili. Shakes. All of these are your work?"

She holds up the tiny scrap of paper they salvaged from my mouth. I'm digesting the rest of the list. I can start it again, not a problem. But she doesn't know that I'm coming for her.

"Before I find out what you know, I need to know what you

remember. Do you remember me? Speak up, now. Tell me what you're up to. You're straining some very delicate relationships. For the love of God, you're in going to shift the balance of power back to the police. Do I need to tell you how frightening that will be?"

I try not to let my face show any concern.

"You have no idea what I'm talking about, do you?"

I nod, try to look hopeful, innocent, wrong girl, wrong girl, wrong—

Delia shrieks with laughter. She's literally rolling on the floor, patting her stomach. I start to relax when she springs. She draws a knife from her belt and pounces on my chest, pinning me down. The tip of the knife prods my cheeks, draws circles around the scar on my lower jaw, pokes like a needle at my throat. Her face is a death mask, the black pools of her eyes reflecting my frightened face in stereo. Her mouth breaks into a wide smile, brilliant and dazzling and deadly.

"Look at your face! I just can't bring myself to do it. Memories, memories. The little thorn in my side. If I can't pluck you out, I'll just have to make some use of you. So start over again. Tell me every detail. Every single thing. Who else have you killed?"

So I do. Delia has to send for water four times. She has to order two towels so I can keep my chin dry. She runs out of tissues because I keep breaking down every five minutes from exhaustion or embarrassment, I can't tell.

The whole time I talk, she moves around the tiny crypt, collecting vials and papers. She takes some dried leaves out of a mesh sack. There's a stench in the air, a bitter chemical tang. She sprinkles some powder on the leaves and rolls a cigarette.

As I finish telling the story of my slice-and-dice on Shakes, she's using an eyedropper to put more fluid on the cigarette. She runs her fingers through my hair. I ask her what she knows about the Doctor.

"You know how Robert and I are. Fighting one minute, friendly the next. I stay out of his way, he ignores me."

What about Hooded Jack? What about Veronica, I mumble.

"Hmm?" Delia looks puzzled.

So I repeat myself. Again and again until she gets it. What about Veronica Madden? Where is she? What do you know about Veronica Madden?

"This is too good to be true."

I can't tell if she's paid attention to anything I said. She holds the cigarette between steepled fingers, smiling at me. Change of subject time, I guess.

"Well. I suppose I haven't seen her in quite some time. Maybe she's moved on to bigger and better things. Maybe she's dead. Pardon my language, but she really fucked you over, didn't she?"

I ask her why she calls me Mrs. Robinson. She laughs and points at the picture in the paper.

"You had...an accident. A quite famous one, but the papers didn't get the story quite right. They were fed half-truths and red herrings. You were a Jane Doe. But they called you Mrs. Robinson, because you were unresponsive in the hospital until a certain song came on the radio. I thought the whole thing was ridiculous."

She sidles up next to me. "I want to pick your brain, and there are two ways to do it. One is pleasant, the other is not. Let's try the pleasant way first." She waggles the cigarette.

I hope she's not going to do what I think.

"We're going to dive. You'll love this. And I think I will too. If you don't give me the answers I need, we'll explore again. But the tools will be sharper. Rustier. And the path to your memories will start... here."

She gives a quick stab of the tip of her knife into the top of my thigh stump, an electric jolt that immolates the hollows of my bones from my hips to my shoulders before disappearing.

"I'm very good with a blade. I'm even better with this." Delia lights the cigarette, and the smell is like nothing I've ever known. I notice she was careful not to take a pull. Whatever's on there is going to be more potent than Clearwater. She won't have to cut my head open. It'll burst on its own.

"Sweet Death," she smiles at me. "It has many names. Wet. The club kids call it Sherm-2. Illy-Dozer. Such stupid names for something so poetic and amazing." She turns serious. "Ready?"

I nod. What else can I do?

"We'll start easy. Who was supposed to be next?"

I run through the list in my mind. Who the hell was the next target? And should I pick them? Or would it be better to go to the top of the list since she's looking to make a power grab? I decide to go with honesty.

"Caligula?" she repeats. "Interesting. I had plans for him myself. And then who?"

You don't want to know why? I ask.

"No. Who was next?"

Was it Hooded Jack or the Doctor? I don't remember...

"Were you coming for me?"

No, I shake my head. In that friendly, retarded-puppy-dog kind of way. Oh, no Miss Delia, I could never harm you never. The things you can say without saying a word.

"Were you coming to collect me?"

Her eyes are so deep and honest, lit silver by the reflected light of the blade resting near her hip. I can't help myself. Maybe it's the second-hand smoke coming off the cigarette. I nod.

Delia has an oxygen tank, I don't know where she got it, the mouthpiece pulled tight over her face. Her eyes are starting to get bloodshot, pupils dilating, tearing up. Her eyelids flutter, she draws a deep breath.

"Clean air for me. Smoke for you until you clear the air."

She reaches under the mask with a square of paper. She darts her tongue out to show it to me, a small black snake head darting out of a hole in the ether.

"Are you ready to give me the truth?"

I think I smile at her, but I can't feel my face.

She smiles. "Mrs. Robinson, are you trying to seduce me?"

She jerks the mask aside and kisses me, forcing her tongue into my mouth. If I didn't have the huge gap in my lower teeth, I could bite her, I could make her sorry. But now all I can do is whimper. She licks at the roof of my mouth a few times. It feels like a drill boring into my palette, then my mouth is melting.

Her saliva stings like acid. Then it tastes like honey. She jerks back from me, collapsing to the floor, pressing the mask over her mouth and inhaling. Her mouth disappears as her breath fogs on the mask. The room swims in smoke from the cigarette, and whatever she just dropped on me is kicking hard. Colors dance between the smoke plumes. Whatever is in the air around me, I need it inside of me.

"Sweet Death," she says, holding out the cigarette, and I take a drag because it's all I can do.

I can't feel my arms. I can't feel my legs. I sit back.

"We're going to learn a few things tonight. Relax."

I want to tell her to go to hell but—

XIX

I'm spinning around inside of a circus tent made of stone. The floor is black and icy. Whatever this shit is, it's way better than the filth I was taking from the bottle. A light shines from above, and the floor ripples into a different picture. An alley.

A voice.

"There was a woman once who loved her husband very much. She followed him to the ends of the earth. To his very end. Later, there was another woman who thought that man would be the answer to all of her questions. Neither of the ladies got what they wanted. This isn't the truth, but it's as close as you'll get."

"The wife watched him keep late hours with his job. Truly dangerous work, but selfless, and for the good of the community. It was a case of not being able to see the forest for the trees. The very problems he went out to solve were festering under his own roof. They thought they had an arrangement. Good cop, bad cop. He was both, because he knew who she was and he let her get away with murder. He had a moral code he was following, the thought that if he worked hard to clean up everything else, it would wash the blood from her hands and the guilt from his conscience. He tried so hard. She watched him sink into his work for months and months, and tried to pick up the pieces when he came back to her between assignments.

If you break something enough, sooner or later the pieces never fit back together."

The whole thing swims in front of me on the floor. Bad trip in Panavision. A woman, sort of a version of me, but with legs, and she's yelling at this guy in a living room, and he's yelling back. I don't know why I don't remember any of this.

"He can't quit. There's something of an addiction in it for him. The rush he gets. Someone else in the underworld got their hooks into him. He made a connection he shouldn't have made, but he wanted to pay the house off, wanted to make sure his wife had nice things. It wasn't a matter of saying no. It was succeed or die. She didn't like that he'd gone behind her back. A line was crossed. Soon enough, they hated each other, and that made their love even stronger. They had to stay together for the child…"

The dream-me pulls out a little black box, shoving it under the guy's nose, pointing up the stairs, and he bats it away.

"She couldn't see the forest either. The problems she insisted that she had under control were seeping around the house. Infecting the only other person she cared about. She knew the danger this new deal could mean for her daughter. The woman had been the gatekeeper of her home, making sure the forces of darkness couldn't arrive uninvited. He rhusband had blown a hole in that wall of protection by dealing with the wrong people."

There's a sickening pause. When she's not talking, the whole room glides and swirls. Hot smoke cascades into my lungs, melts my stomach, puddles my organs against my spine. I want her to keep talking. So I answer.

"You goddih rrrigh."

"The night it ended, do you remember? She goes to a bar. She sees her husband in a booth across the way with someone on each arm. Both of them in purple. My children. Clarabelle and Jillian, two of my finest."

This, I remember perfectly. One woman dressed in nothing more than a fishnet bodystocking, and the other wearing tall boots and a leather coat. The clarity of this memory almost pains me.

"Clarabelle was a good man."

My mental picture adjusts without a hitch. The fishnet lady is gone, replaced by a skinny thug in a jean jacket and short-shorts with fishnet stockings. This seems just as true, if not more so.

"Oh, her anger. The last straw. She was ready to break bones. Little did she realize, her hard-working husband, he was just in the middle of something. For all of the trouble he'd invited into their lives, he was doing his damnedest to resolve the problems. Call it pride or hubris, but even had she known what he was there to try to do, the only real solution would require violence and blood. She could have been such a help there, but he was never the type to ask for help, which is how these situations always start."

When he was at work, he was gone. His body came home every night, but his mind was somewhere else. He would leave at odd hours. He would come home in shock, pale as a sheet, and tell me nothing. And he would never touch me. Not even a kiss. Even when I grabbed him, that last night, and forced him to kiss me, he gave back all the passion of a baloney sandwich. That's the part that finally drove me over the edge. Wasn't it? Shouldn't I be paying attention? Was I the violent woman?

"Mrs. Robinson came in wearing white. She was that type. Not that she wanted to embody purity, but because she loved the way it stained when things took a turn. Clarabelle didn't know this. He thought wearing white meant she worked for Doctor Robert. Mrs. Robinson made a beeline for her husband. Clarabelle moved on her. I would have stopped him if I could. But circumstances had me watching from the shadows. To my relief, an angry little Frenchman in a black striped sweater intervened."

This part I definitely remember. He stank of cheap wine and clove cigarettes. A walking cliché, no matter his fancies.

"Caligula. Although back then, he was Pompidou. Bestselling author, self-made paper tycoon."

Pompidou wouldn't let me get near them. He tried to calm

me, said we should have a drink. And then he touched me. That's the last part I remember.

"My children should never have attacked. They don't draw blood unless that's what the customer pays for. Or to defend me. They saw white and they attacked."

I was ten feet away from the table when Pompidou grabbed me. He grabbed my hair and yanked...

"Pompidou dragged Mrs. Robinson halfway across that bar, and her husband could only watch. He wasn't worried for her safety, but his own. A box had been opened that should have remained closed. Pandora's wrath. The idiot hadn't realized who she really was. She cracked Pompidou's ribs. Battered his face. Folded him over a table so hard, the inside of his spine must have bruised..."

I remember watching the air go out of him. That confused, angry puckered face he made. I almost laughed. Then came another noise, breaking glass.

"Clarabelle thought the whole deal had gone south at this point. He smashed a bottle in half. Mrs. Robinson tried to fight him. Her husband hadn't moved a muscle the whole time. He just looked at her. Could she read his eyes, do you think? Did she know what was going through his head?"

I remember that punk Clarabelle yanking my hair down quickly. I always kept my hair tied back and tucked away for this very reason. I was angry when I went in there. I was hasty. He pulled my face toward the floor by a fistful of my ponytail and then he threw this weird uppercut. I saw a jagged brown circle of glass coming at my face and I tried to pull back.

"By this time, even the folks at the bar were concerned. Seeing a woman with half a bottle sticking out of her lower jaw could melt the hardest heart, I suppose. They tried to help, but she refused. At this point, Mrs. Robinson was in shock. White hot rage that had nowhere to go, because her brain couldn't register what happened. She followed Clarabelle out into the street. And do you remember what happened next?"

No. No, I shake my head. No, I say out loud. No. No. No.

I don't know if I'm mourning this memory or if I just don't remember. Am I repressing again? Do I want to know this? I don't want to know anything. I only want to know steel and bullets and blood and vengeance.

"You remember nothing?"

No.

"Good."

And the circus tent goes black.

When I wake up, I'm back in my van, safe and warm. My neck stings. With my eyes closed, I run a finger along my lower jaw. The skin is wrinkled and scored. Rough. But I think I can feel the ring of tissue the bottle left. There's some dead skin on one of the scars and for second it feels like a piece of the label on the bottle, a remnant resurfaced.

I check myself out in the mirror, hating the way my mouth looks. There's too much damage there for just a bottle. But still... unmistakably there on my neck, a perfect circle. I must have gone to a crappy doctor. A professional wouldn't have left a scar. Or maybe there wasn't time between that night and the explosion to fix me. I remember that picture from Shakes's office, how I couldn't see my chin. I wonder now, when they took that picture, was I being vain, covering up my disfigurement?

The memory of the scar, that's all I have. I know there was a story there. I know I learned something from Delia, but it's all gone. Like a salvia divinorum trip, Delia had gotten me high, I'd seen the face of God, read the universe like a book, and when the high washed out of me, so did all of the knowledge.

My neck looks like it has a small boil on it, an angry red dome of skin with a small dark dot in the center. A spider bite? A bad syringe job?

Where did the scar come from?

Some things in my van have been moved. There are some large bags in the back, a suitcase or two, and my weapons stash. There's a little parchment scroll wrapped around some dried twigs and two purple roses sitting on the dashboard:

Mrs. Robinson,

I am so pleased to have had the opportunity to meet you again. If the sun is just setting, then Sweet Death didn't keep you down for long. We gave you a shot of Morning Sunshine to help perk you up. You're quite resilient! Would you please do me a favor of favors and pay a visit to Caligula? He should be at his club underneath Satan's Inkwell. He'll probably be going into hiding soon, so haste! He'll no doubt be delighted to see you. Don't tell him your name, Mrs. Robinson. See if he can guess!

The doorman owes me a favor. He'll be looking out for you. I've left you some clothes in the back. Perhaps seeing you again will be too much for Caligula's poor heart to take and he'll perish at your loveliness. The Doctor is quite close with Caligula. I think it's a partnership that would be better dissolved. I'll be waiting for you on the other side with more of the truth.

D-

Great. So now I'm off on a choose-your-own-adventure. Looking out the window, three of Delia's children mill around the streetlamps. She's a smart one. This whole run will keep me inside of Red Light. So my choice is to either buck her orders and die, or do what I want to do anyway and nail big C. Call me selfish, but I don't like others sharing in this.

I'm on auto-pilot, winding down the streets of Red Light, pulling through alleys and backlots until I see the spot I'm looking for. It's a long, wet alley that shrinks the farther it goes. I pull the van over by a dumpster, far enough back that the goons milling by the entrance don't really pay me much mind. I climb over the seat to the back of the van and open the suitcase that Delia left for me.

Should I laugh or scream? What the hell am I looking at? It's like a tangled ball of twine, sort of like what Christmas lights look like when they're unpacked the next year. I'm supposed to wear this? Why? And how?

I'm not doing this. Not her way.

I strap my legs on and get my kill case ready. Delia has been very careful to select my tools for me. No guns, nothing that would allow me to hustle away from her watchdogs. She's given me three options.

1.   A high E string from a grand piano tied at either end to two sticks. Not quite a professional quality garrote, but it will strangle just the same.

2.   A knife. Quick and easy, but very messy, and definitely a last resort.

3.   The ultimate Red Light accessory: the junkie's bandolier. It's a little crisscross strap that goes around my chest and is loaded down with syringes. These are famous at parties thrown by the bigger cults. They usually have some busty young girl fresh from farm country walking around wearing only the strap. People can fondle her, grope her, and take a little hit with them.

Caligula's parties typically cater to the more bizarre crowd, so the only attention I'll be getting is as one of the staff. But my bandolier is special. Three syringes are filled with botulinum toxin A, stolen from a dermatologist's office. The most lethal toxin known to mankind available at a high cost to the general public for shooting into their faces. And it doesn't even get them high. Well, not physically, anyway. The rest of the needles have Delia's special blend, so I'm sure to be popular in there.

I'll be the happy sample girl at the supermarket. Someone wants to get high, and I think there will be a lot of takers in this place, they'll be all over me. I just have to make sure they get the right samples. Most of the needles will get them floating. The special ones will stop their hearts. Or get rid of crow's feet and forehead lines if they shoot up in the right spots.

She's given me no long-range weapons. Meaning when I'm done with this, I pretty much have to walk back into her arms, because I won't be able to fight my way out of Red Light.

As I finish hiding these things away, I feel a tap on my shoulder. I strike, bringing my elbow up and connecting with something that makes a hollow *tok* sound, like a little gourd. It's only when the street punk hits the ground that I notice he's wearing purple. He's not alone.

Two girls, twins I think, are standing a few feet back.

"Whadja do that for?"

I point at the thug, then motion with my arm. *Look around you, moron. It's not safe here.*

"Put the outfit on. You have to. Delia says."

Have you seen the outfit, I ask.

They stare at me. I'm not going to say it again. They click switchblades in stereo. Debate my case or put the stupid outfit on? I head back into the van as they pick their unconscious mate up from the asphalt.

I unravel the little fabric ball. It's all chainlinks and metal loops and fasteners and black vinyl. Which are the sleeves and which are the legs?

The material is surprisingly stretchy, and covers more than I thought it would. My legs look ridiculous. I look like an old dockhouse with seaweed clinging to the supports. A means to an end, I think. A small movement forward is still progress, even if I look like a fool. I step out of the van and one of the twins starts to make a remark, but I cut her off with a look.

The only good thing about the outfit is how easily it lets me hide my tools. The knife is on my left leg, invisible in the dangling fabric against the metal pole. The piano wire is the same on the other leg.

I hobble down the alley towards the little sunken entrance, a wave of nostalgia rolling over me. Little silvery ghosts of Delia's story flash at me. There's the big hole in the wall where I collapsed in the rain after something or other happened. I know it's just one dark blotch of shadow among many, but I swear I see my silhouette there, burned in like some day-after Hiroshima victim.

There's the dumpster where I collapsed, a dark stain congealed on the street right at the corner of the bin. It could be my blood. It hasn't been that long. Maybe the rain hasn't washed it away. Maybe the rain couldn't do it.

The memories of my drug trip push through my mind like tide through pier pilings. Clarabelle. I was horribly disfigured by a man named Clarabelle. If Delia's telling me the truth, that is. She's the only one filling in the blanks right now, so she may as well be right.

Mrs. Robinson. Just by knowing that's a lie, I'm closer to knowing my real name. I hope Jesus loves me more than I will know.

"Walk!" One of Delia's kids shouts at me from the end of the alley, shaking me out of my reverie. There's at least three of them back there. Delia's knows things I need to know and she's willing to share, for a price. She knows she can string me out. Or maybe she's going to kill me when this job ends. Two can play that game.

The air bleeds dim neon purple, the glow of the sign in the window of Satan's Inkwell paints the word TATTOO in reverse across scattered puddles. This isn't the kind of place cheeky college kids come to raise their coolness quotient. It's pretty serious. They only do work in black or dark green. Not my business tonight.

I bypass the tattoo shop entrance and make the hard turn down a staircase that cuts parallel to the building. Step by step, ever so carefully, rocking side to side like a child's bop bag. I almost trip over the bouncer on his stool at the landing, a look of sheer terror on his face. He's never seen anything like me. His hand twitches, alternately reaching for a walkie-talkie or his pepper spray, I can't tell.

"What are *you*?" he asks, then hastens to add, "...doing here?"

For a second, it almost sounds like he knows me. But that pause gave it away. *What* am I? Typical. I set my teeth and prepare to speak as best as I can.

"Prrty grrl. Frrm Geelia."

Maybe this guy's used to having a conversation over loud music, but he actually understands me and motions me in. I stare at him. I love him. Someone I can talk to, communicate.

"Move it, party girl. First shift just left, and we got hungry customers inside," he growls.

The bar is so dark inside that it's like stepping into a void. Colors swim dull and wavy at the edge of my vision. Red lights sweep the bar. Bodies swimming against bodies, orgies in the corners, tripkids on the floor. Nobody in here is level. Nobody but me.

I remove a purple sash from my belt and wrap it around the lower half of my face. I step next to a kid on the floor sitting crosslegged and he looks me up and down three times. He slowly pokes a finger out towards my leg. His finger goes through the mesh of the pant leg and into the air in front of my pole. In this light, it must look like my legs are invisible. The kid starts screaming, convulsing on the floor. He backpedals into a throng of dancers who angrily push him aside.

I feel like I'm still walking inside of Delia's trip. There's the booth at the back, a big circular table lined with velvet. That was where he was sitting. My husband. I had a husband. Or maybe I still do. Seeing it tears off the emotional scab. It's bleeding fresh now, and I no longer have the strength to walk. I'm just standing, standing. Junkies and tripkids massage my breasts, drawing needles off of my bandolier and kissing my shoulders in tribute.

A young girl, probably no more than fourteen, tries to grab one of the Botox needles. I seize her wrist. She stares at me, ready for trouble. The easy way out would be breaking her fingers and shoving her along, but I have to blend in until my target presents himself. I lead her hand to my breast, where I plant it firmly, suggesting she should squeeze. She does, and reaches for one of the "safe" needles.

One of the party lights washes over her face, and it changes.

My daughter. She's not my daughter. But she could be. I can't let her do this. She's too young and too pure. She can't be the next Little Debbie, fighting for life in a hospital bed. I make a move to kiss her, pulling down the scarf from my face, tongue-lump flickering, and it does the job. She squirms away, trying to look apologetic, trying to look like she wasn't going for a free score. I know she'll find a hit somewhere else in the next ten minutes, but at least it won't have come from me.

One shadow in the corner of the room nods its head at me. It congeals into a man in a trench coat.

"Chuck told me there was something weird at the door I should check out. What an understatement."

I smile at him. I feel like I've seen him before somewhere, but I'm not sure where. Something about that buried rage in his eyes is familiar.

"He said you're here from Delia. What do you have for me?"

Nothing, I shake my head.

"Straight for the boss then?"

I nod.

"Follow me."

We make our way to the bar, crossing behind it into a small anteroom. He opens another door that turns out to be a service elevator, smiling at me.

We descend into darkness, and he warns me, "Caligula's gonna love those fucking legs. I hope you've got some energy tonight."

Time for the ampu-tease...

The doors open onto an expansive chamber that was once an old subway station, built sometime before World War II and sealed off shortly after. The tiles are pristine. The light fixtures from an era when people were respectful and wouldn't steal things that weren't bolted down or scrawl all over them with paint markers. Everything is draped in velvet, lined in satin, there are about a million candles burning.

Goth is just a way for boring people to seem interesting.

This is the great chamber of Caligula. We go down a set of steps that lead to the old tracks, dusty and unused. The place still smells like an underground station, musty air and axle grease fighting to beat back the smell of stale urine. In the shadows ahead, there's a writhing mass on the floor. It looks like a nest full of giant baby mice, all pink and squirming. Women. Big C. His misogyny hasn't aged well.

I wish I could throw some witty banter around with my guide. He introduced himself on the ride down as Nova, saying it with the sort of half shrug that suggested the name was assigned to him. Nova stops by a dais holding an ornate bell about fifty feet from the mass of humanity on the tracks ahead.

When Nova rings it, all of the women stop moving, and slowly ooze away, like water scattering from a drop of oil. They form a circle, completely nude, sitting, lounging, smiling their drugged-out smiles. It looks like a Hendrix album cover down here. And there in the center, fully clothed, is Caligula himself.

"Who rings for me?" he demands, his voice echoing off of the walls.

What is this, Dungeons and Dragons?

He stands up, and I must say, he cuts quite an impressive figure. He's wearing a puffy shirt, tight leather pants, knee-high boots, his hair pulled back into a thick braided tail. Every bad Goth cliché rolled into one. I'm sure when I get closer I'll see that he's filed his canine teeth to sharp points. He strides forward laying a gentle hand on the occasional naked woman's head.

Nova goes forward to meet him and I'm forced to wait in the half light and dripping silence. They converse for a few moments, then come back towards me.

It strikes me that Caligula might tend to remember a girl like me. He was there when I got the scar on my jaw. I'll have to hope he doesn't ask me to remove the scarf. I start to run a finger along the edge of a syringe. Maybe I can get him to shoot up quickly. But I need to get this shot into his chest or his mouth, or a major vein. Then I'll be contending with Nova and the harpies. I'd like a few answers while I'm down here, but Delia took away my tape recorder with Frances's monologue. If Caligula knows anything about where the Doctor is or why I hate him so much, I'll have to find it out the hard way.

Big C strides up to me, that kind of kicky, overconfident walk usually reserved for men with mullets and fast cars. At ten feet away it becomes obvious he's bombed out of his mind. There are red marks all over his neck, big splotchy purple finger prints.

"You've interrupted us," he tells me. "We were riding the ridge of life and death. Finding out if love lies beyond the plane of oxygen and vacuum." He traces a finger around his throat. "It's hard to return to the place you've taken us from. But Nova rang the bell, so this must be important. He tells me you've come from Ms. Sugar."

I nod, trying to strike a pose somewhere between indifference and mock-theatricality.

He eyes what's left of my bandolier. "All for me? This is quite an offering."

Oh yes, I nod. As long as I don't move around too much, I don't think he'll notice my legs. I have to try to walk behind him so he can't see my wobbling gait. He stalks back towards his pit of women, waving for me to follow. As I move forward I try to check the girls, see if anyone is hiding a weapon or ready to strike. They barely note my passing.

"Ladies, I have business," Caligula says as he stalks through the girls towards a makeshift altar near the bricked-over tunnel mouth.

Most of the women are panting, a few coughing. All of their throats are red, some with the faint outline of a handprint or little crescent moon cuts where fingernails dug in.

"Asphyxiation," Nova offers as he walks at my shoulder. "They do this about once a month. Take adrenaline, speed, anything to get their hearts pumping. Then they roll around on the floor choking each other. Supposedly the point before blackout is the most amazing high, second only to the shot they get when they huff pure oxygen afterwards." He jerks a thumb at a bookcase near a column, its shelves loaded with tiny personal oxygen tanks.

I look at Nova. If I had much of a jaw left, it would be slack, I'm sure.

"Anhedonia's a hell of a thing," he says.

We're track-level, and Caligula has mounted a throne at the end of the line, looming over us. On the passenger platform above his seat is a luxurious four-poster bed. Oxygen tanks of all sizes surround him, like a monstrous subterranean pipe organ. He snaps his fingers and the gaggle of naked chicks disperses, some of them climbing the platform and going behind the veil on the bed, others fading into the shadows. One of his hands rests on a glass-knobbed cane, his fingers tapping impatiently. Then he says something that lets me know he's completely out of his gourd.

"You're very attractive. Beautiful, I'd say. You have a…darkness."

He thinks I'm a street whore. I would be insulted, but at least it gets me close to my goal. I wanted to use the Tox on him, but his little kink has given me a better idea.

"Thirteen concubines and now, a walking sampler. Delia must truly want something special from me. Come to me," he motions with his finger.

I start towards his little throne, but I'm never going to make those narrow steps. I hesitate, shuffling a little and trying to look coquettish, as it seems a Goth thing to do. When Caligula whips a .45 out from the side of his throne, I know my ruse isn't working.

"Up here. Now," he demands, his whole Prince-of-Darkness routine flickering for just a moment.

So I try. I can't really bend at the knee, and there's no handrail. I'm in deep trouble. Apparently these negotiations aren't the friendly kind. He's unbuckling his belt with one hand and cocking the gun with the other.

I fall forward slightly, catching myself on the stairs with my hands. I'll crawl up to him, and I'll try to look sexy the whole time. I figure it'll pacify his bullshit dominant alpha thing. It's definitely got his interest, as he's lowered the gun. One step at a time, closer to thee, Big C, so that I may choke the life from you.

It's around the third step that I realize my worst enemy in the room is not Caligula, not the naked harem back there, but my stupid, strappy pants. They've snagged on something. I can't shake them loose. I can't cut them loose because drawing my knife would look more than a bit threatening. I lower my body down and try a different angle. It only succeeds in pulling my leg off slightly. I knew I should have had Joe remold the cups on these legs. I think I've lost weight. I should have put an extra sock over my thigh.

Big C looks thoroughly unimpressed now. "You're killing the mood, sweetness."

I pull harder, and the worst happens. The leg goes right off. At first it's not noticeable, the webbing of the pantleg is holding it on, but then it rolls sickly to one side and proceeds in the opposite direction down the staircase. No more knife.

Caligula sets his gun down and stands up. I look back over my shoulder. If Nova is still in the room, he's off in one of the shadowy recesses somewhere. Nobody has shouted yet or called for help, so I guess I'm all right for the time being.

"How exquisite," Caligula says, touching his chest lightly. "Ladies...my concubines, come look at this."

Four heads peek out from the bed at strange angles, and the ladies glide back onto the platform, wrapped in sheets. Somebody gasps. Most of them look sick.

Caligula crawls down the steps towards me, like a deranged spider. He cups my chin in his hand. "You've made me elated again. You've taken my breath away. We've met before..."

My mind spins. I need to get some space between me and Caligula. Find some shadows, don't let him get a good look. His concubines slowly descend, all pale and gossamer. The romance of the picture is spoiled by the finer details: track marks, greenish skin, rotting teeth and superficial scars. They surround me and carry me the rest of the way up the stairs, leaving my leg behind.

"I didn't think the rumors were true..." he says.

They set me at the foot of Big C's throne, while he moves down to the floor and picks up my leg. At first, he hefts it like a golf club, swinging it slowly, watching the foot react. He slowly unlaces the shoe, his eyes never leave mine. The other women are enthralled.

I don't know if it's the shadows or the mood or the placebo effect, but my phantoms are starting again. Caligula has a hand clamped around the ankle of my leg, and I can feel it in the air before me. I watch the shoe loosen and slide off, revealing the flat metal paddle foot, and I swear I feel the breeze between my toes.

Caligula is probably one of the more repulsive men I've ever seen, but I have to admit it, I'm a little turned on right now.

If I can keep his eyes on my legs, maybe he won't linger on my face. I keep my eyes on his and move my hand down to my other leg, slowly undoing one of the straps, tracing my fingers around the cup. Big C catches his breath again.

"Both of them? My, my my..."

The women crouch closer to me, hands reaching for my body. They grab needles off of my chest, and I don't even care which is which. There's only me and Big C right now.

He strokes the steel pole that makes up my calf, standing there below me, and I feel it. I feel it all. I want it in stereo. I yank the straps on my other leg and send it sailing down to him. I spread the stumps of my thighs wide and lean forward, not in a sluttish way, only to tell him I want more.

He obliges, picking up my other leg. He starts to move up the steps, staring at my thighs.

"Let me touch them."

They're always so fascinated by the remnants. Physical touch is the last thing I want now. I'm somewhere else, I'm wondering how much farther he can take me with my legs in his hands. I lean back and shake my head, sliding my thighs closed.

"Mmooor," I mumble.

He gets it. He moves around behind me, setting one leg on each side of me. I watch his fingers trace my big rubber knees, my skinny alloy calves, the complex ankle joints, the composite "tendon" attaching thigh joint to calf.

His concubines scatter to the four winds. They're off getting buzzed, and perhaps two of them are now in full cardiac arrest from the Tox. Big C rubs up against my back, his chest caressing my shoulders, his hands still working my legs. I reach up for him over my head and draw him close.

He leans into me, bringing his face close to my ear. He kisses me lightly on my neck, where the skin is fairly thick and unresponsive. I embrace him tightly, so tightly that I can feel sweat starting to pour from his body. I feel his heart begin to thunder in his chest.

His fingers trace my ears, my cheeks, my jawline. And they pause ever so slightly on the circular scar underneath, just long enough for me to feel that spark of recognition. Shit. I was lost in the moment.

His embrace doesn't change, but I feel his body cool slightly, tensing. "I thought you died a long, long time ago. It was you. It's been you this whole time, hasn't it?" he whispers.

I shrug, better to feign ignorance.

"You've been taking everyone out. You framed me for Shakes's murder..."

Shit, I don't want to talk business now, I was just getting into this. But he's still all over me.

"Wann yrrr hellp," I tell him. "Wann ngo werrz Grronka Ngaggn...fffffffrrronka..."

"Veronica? You want to know where Veronica Madden is? Do you think I'm stupid?"

I play it dumb.

"Veronica Madden is a bitch," he says, tugging the hair near the nape of my neck. "Veronica Madden is a leftover whore. She's worthless. Atrocious. I wish to God I'd never met the woman."

The back of my head is hot, burning as he twists my hair. I feel like the skin is going to tear off, then he slackens, breathing near me. "What the fuck is wrong with you?" He moves back a little. I still feel the heat radiating from him.

"You're working with Delia, trying to take what I've made. But you can't have it. You could have gone after anyone else, but you chose me. You can't have what I've made."

He snaps his fingers, and something rustles on the bed. A sharp intake of breath, cut off, strangled. Gasping. There's a pause, long enough that I realize I'm holding my breath, too. Waiting to hear a sound.

Click.

Caligula snaps his fingers again. There's a tidal wave of gasping, intake, breath, hanging on to life. His concubines are choking each other on command. "That's power. That's what I have, and that's what I'm not giving up. God, your legs are exquisite."

Frankly, I'm barely listening to his speech. I feel his fingers dancing on the insides of my knees, his hand occasionally brushing my inner thigh.

"I told you before that a girl has no place doing man's work. But you just...keep...coming...back. No more, no more, no more. You knew me as a Frenchman, a politician, a power grabber. Now I am power. Now I am action. Would you like to see *this* man work, girl? I'm going to send you to hell, but I want to send you there happy..."

His tongue dances up and down my neck, and I've never wanted anyone so much in my life. Stronger than my need to feel him is my need to feel him die. I reach up behind my head again, pulling him in closer.

"Say you're sorry, say you're sorry..." His hands knead my flesh. "I'm gonna kill you. I want to hear you say it. Earn my pity."

I pass the handles of the garrote from hand to hand behind his head and pull down and in, cutting off his air supply. He can't scream. He can't breathe. He can't do anything now but die for me.

I'm have screaming, half panting. The ladies around us probably think he's giving me the greatest orgasm, and in a way they're right. My brain screams at me, for God's sake let loose, that's a man dying in your hands. Instead I just crank tighter. Isn't this supposed to get easier each time? Am I not the angel of righteousness?

If I have to choose between answers to my questions or finishing my list, it's going to be the latter. A job has been written and it must be done.

He wanted an apology? I want an apology. It's all I've ever wanted. Shakes, Grace Brooks, someone, anyone, to just say sorry and mean it. Not "business is business." Not "you were in the wrong place at the wrong time." Not "what could I have done?" Just a genuine, heartfelt apology for what's happened to me. Instead, I get atonement, because I can't ask for anything else. Atonement doesn't take words.

I feel dampness on my cheeks. I tell myself it's his sweat, his spittle. It's not my tears. It's not me crying because I haven't had my perfect moment of revenge. It's not sadness that his knowledge about my past is gone. It's certainly not the end of this sensual contact. No, never.

A gasp floats from the edge of the platform. Then a startled shriek, followed by panting. I try to twist around so that I can see. One of the breathless whores rises above the edge of the platform and dives for me.

She hits the tracks in front of me, pulling herself along the rough ground, reaching for me. A needle dangles from her arm. The botulinum. She chokes and wheezes and half-screams, convulsing. Caligula's dead weight sinks into my back. He's not struggling. His heart is done. He's done. I release the garrote and he crumples to the floor behind me.

I suppose I could find symbolism here as I sit broken on dead-end train tracks, a dead pimp behind me and a dying hooker in front of me. Like the spirit of vengeance that I am, I turn and vomit onto the floor. Two by my own hands. I swear I'm going back to sniping.

Nova drops down onto the tracks and walks toward me, one hand reaching to his belt, drawing out a gleaming revolver. I have nothing. No mobility. I can't scamper to the bed on my hands, I certainly can't go down the steps.

He raises his arm up, and I wait for the explosion, the muffled pop that will signal the end of my game. The air behind me grows warm, and my head is jerked back and slammed to the floor. Caligula, his face almost purple, his boot holding down my hair on the floor.

"Too much," he hisses. "You turn me on too much. Steal oxygen. Whore!" His fingers scramble at his neck. "You're gonna say sorry... say sorry..."

"Futch yuuu!" I scream. It's all I can think to say.

His hand clutches at the garrote, buried deep in the skin of his neck. He finds one handle, then unwraps the wire, and his neck starts bleeding, a neat little red line all the way around. It looks like someone has cut his head off and set it back neatly on his neck. His breathing sickens me, a harsh raspy intake followed by a whistling exhalation.

He draws his hand back and smashes me across the face. The softness of it startles him. There are missing chunks of bone that surprise his fist, soft spots where he was expecting resistance. None of this lessens the fact that it hurts like hell.

He coughs and bends down, retrieving his cane, still standing on my hair. Shrieking, he raises the cane above his head, ready to hit one out of the park. My last thought is a worry about my hair, if he's pulling it out at the root, if I'm going to look worse than I already do.

I look at him because I want to see what raw hatred looks like, so that I may know myself before I die. I want to know how he does it with such abandon. His eyes are wide and dark, black pits surrounded by bloodshot yellow. I'm reflected in stereo, warped, crying, broken, and wasted. He snarls and his hand plunges down.

"I'll tell you about Veroni--"

Caligula's face breaks into shards of bone and gristle as he flies backwards and crashes across his bed. The reverberations of a gunshot bounce off the walls for what feels like forever, vibrating, hollow, reverent as church bells.

The list has not been broken. I choked Caligula out. I don't know what rose up. Maybe my hatred wasn't enough to kill him, but he's dead now. And I didn't do it. And it really doesn't feel all that bad.

I pull myself up to a seated position to see Nova, cool as a cucumber, literally blowing the smoke from his gun barrel. He smiles at me as he pulls a purple kerchief from his pocket.

"Welcome to the club," he says, tossing me the bandanna. I stare at it in my lap, the repeated white paisley pattern reminding me of the endlessness, the trap, the vicious cycle.

"You just started a war big enough to burn this city to the ground. Congratulations. Now get your legs on and let's go."

You think you know someone and they just turn out to be full of surprises. I wasn't expecting Nova to decorate the basement chamber with Caligula's brains. His name, as it turns out, is Trevor, and he's a fairly gruff fellow, Delia's inside man on the job. We're at the base of the stairs leading up to the club.

The concubines mill about, examining the walls or their fingers, or anything that moves and streaks across their clouded vision. I expected some kind of retaliation. Pleasuring Caligula was their job. The job's dead. They move on.

While I strap on my legs, one of them approaches me and asks if she can have more drugs. I said I was out. She points at one of the Botulinum victims and demands some of what she'd had.

"It killed her," I say, startled at how well I'm able to speak. Maybe getting punched in the face helps my impediment? "Her heart 'sploded. Drown in her'own glug."

The whore pauses, taking in the form of her dead, bony friend on the tracks. "Still, it's not fair."

Trevor asks a few times if he can help with the legs, but I decline. We go through the usual pleasantries of him trying to talk to me, me staying silent, him resorting to sign language as if that might help me talk, and finally, silence punctuated by nervous mutterings on his part when he becomes too uncomfortable. His upper lip is coated in a thin sheen of sweat and he's bouncing on the balls of his feet. I should ask him what he's on, but speaking would get us nowhere.

One thing that's nice about my condition: people tend to tell me the truth. Silence makes most people uncomfortable. They'll talk just to hear themselves, but after a while, the absence of noise is too much, they'll tell me anything I want to hear, just to get a word, a mutter, a drooling noise of recognition.

"Times are changing," Trevor says, stopping at the edge of the tracks, where the ornate bell he rang still sits on the stand. "This gang-war stuff is bullshit. Everyone's in the mayor's pocket, and he's in the Doctor's pocket. Et fucking cetera. It's all about a show of support so that the impoverished areas of town can be squashed, ground out, and reborn as multi-use live-work bullshit. It's a land grab. So now all of the old crime families, the drug cults, the slum runners, everyone who had done such a good job leaving each other alone, they're all rallying for power. Less territory to share, means less revenue for the small fish. It's all or nothing."

Trevor lifts the bell. He gives it to me to hold. "What's your beef, anyway? Who do you work for?" He doesn't wait for an answer. "You work for Delia now, no shit. That's the only right answer."

Savior or not, Trevor is inching his way out of my heart minute by minute. Just another guy who obviously wants nothing to do with me.

He pulls a small pack out of his pocket. Semtex explosive. A timer.

"No evidence this way," Trevor smiles, noting my look of concern.

Which reminds me...

"Weee shhd gleeeg," I say.

"I'm taking out the whole basement. Leave nothing behind. You see anything you want here, you better be ready to carry it out."

I slow down, choose my words carefully. "Whole buirrrdnng 'sgonn glo... 'splode. We godd go." I motion urgently to the door.

"Keep your legs on, sweetheart. I know what I'm doing here. This isn't enough to take the building down," Trevor says. "I've rigged this thing up to a little oxygen canister. We're gonna toss this into Caligula's stash of oxygen, and when it goes, there'll be a blaze so big, it could only have been an accident."

I shrug. Explaining that Joe already has the whole building rigged would just rain on his parade. Trevor seems like the angry ex-military type to me. He's not going to listen to a woman. The bell shakes in my hands as he finishes what he's doing.

"You better be able to run. And you better keep your shit together when we get back to Delia. I'm already tired of pulling your ass out of the fire. Think you can get out on your own in five minutes?"

I'm already moving, leaving the bell in his hands and jetting for the exit. It's almost twelve, and Joe loves symbolism. After midnight, he's gonna bring the whole house down.

I wish this was like a movie, where I'd hear a beep. And another. Rythmic. Pulsing. Like a heartbeat. A metronome. Something counting time. But in the real world noisy bombs attract attention and nobody has time for that. Trevor's about to make his own little supernova down here, that'll be plenty loud.

Caligula will be dead and buried, the whole bar reduced to rubble, and it kind of breaks my heart. Strange time to get nostalgic, I know, but I was born here. The person I am now wouldn't exist but for this horrible place. If it's going to be immolated, I should be the one doing it. Not Joe, not Nova.

This is the place where I lost everything I used to own, everything that used to mean something. I wanted time upstairs to look around, to take in the chairs, the stools, to shake loose the memories that are bucking against the gates of my new brain.

And what I want most of all is to sit in that dark booth in the corner, maybe have a drink, and if I could make it last long enough, or maybe if the right song came on or the right mix of people were standing there, *he'd come out of the shadows...*

"Move!" Trevor shouts behind me as we head up the stairs.

He'd melt out of the darkness, approach the booth and sit. He'd put his hand on my knee, and even though it was fake, he wouldn't pull back. He'd take my face in his hands, not in any form of grotesque fascination, but in genuine love. He would cry at the loss of the face he knew, but he would draw close to me, and draw me out of myself. The world would be ours again.

And for him, I'd have the patience to speak, or write, or do whatever it is that would let me communicate with him. I know he'd listen. He'd pretend not to see me drool, he'd find an imaginary spot to examine on his pant leg when my face got too contorted as I tried to form those three clichéd words I most want to tell him. Then I could tell him I'm sorry, that we should have a second chance. Sometimes, you can never apologize enough...

"Sticklegs, we got to go!"

Trevor yanks at my collar. He passes me and pulls me up, over the bodies of the concubines, all of them too dazed to notice us. I waddle as fast as I can, but my feet are dragging. Somehow, I'm catching each of these girls, looking at them eye to eye, seeing inside of them. What brought them to this point was just a long string of mistakes and wrong turns. And what's going to kill them is me.

What killed him is me.

They're going to die here in the sub-basement and it's my fault.

He died here, in the alley, and it's my fault.

I want answers for them, answers for me, and before my brain can sink into any of it, I'm lifted up and away. Trevor kicks and elbows his way up the stairs, through the crowd, rushing us out the door. He sets me down in the alleyway. We stare at each other for just a second.

I feel the beginning of a laugh coming, the sheer lack of understanding finally just pushing me too far. I look down the alley, the intersection just a dark shadowy patch with a thin light wavering above. I remember his shadow there. And then flames erased it all.

Huge flames and pain and all of it my fault.

I'm crying as Trevor tugs me towards the mouth of the alley, where a shadow really does lurk, a figure so much like his that I can't bear to get closer.

The ground beneath us buckles. Then we hear the screams begin in the basement as secondary pops go up. Flames burst through the windows. Cracks form in the alley floor. People are clambering over each other, killing each other to escape certain death in the club.

Trevor lets out a whoop as he drags me towards that shadow, the tall man, and his face slowly resolves. It's just the punk whose nose I squashed earlier. His chicky friend waves us towards my van, our only route of escape.

We jump in as all of the sound drains out of the alley, the air sucking back before a silent shockwave hits the van, slamming it against the alley wall. I hear the first part of the explosion, and then my hearing goes out. Everyone else in the van has their mouths open wide, tendons straining in their necks. I lip-read Trevor asking "what the fuck?" and looking out the window as the entire building is rocked by charge after charge of Joe's C4.

The building folds in on itself as each floor falls—whuff, whuff, whuff—on the one below it. A land grab. A re-zoning project. My vengeance has been co-opted into a suburban expansion plan.

Trevor pins me in my seat, knife to my throat, and I lip read: "Who did this?"

I decide a lie might help me here. If I'm stuck working for Delia, I can nudge things in favor of my list. Hooded Jack, I tell him, and I can't tell if he understands. He blinks twice, then stares at me as if his brain is rebooting. He nods, keeping an angry eye on me.

As the smoke rises from the alley, we pull into traffic, and right on cue, right as the another tear leaves my eye, the sky breaks and the rain comes down.

XXIII

I'm led back to the underground crypt, where Delia waits with two more blotter squares dangling neatly from two huge cups of tea. I said nothing else in the van. Trevor pushed the knife against my cheek hard enough to draw blood. He pulled the bully act on Delia's kids in the van too. Pointing fingers at everyone, trying to find the traitor in his midst. He's bursting at the seams to throw some accusations in front of the boss lady. Delia sees the look of concern on his face, but he's still respectful enough not to speak until spoken to.

"Did you find what you were looking for?" she asks me.

I meet her eyes, something like jealousy and anger and resentment and thanks bubbling inside of me. She motions me to sit, and I do.

"Did it feel good? Do you remember now?"

Can't hear, I tell her, but it's a lie. Below a strange warping hum and a high-pitched whistling noise, I hear her just fine.

Trevor leans forward like a second grader urging *pick me, pick me*. Delia takes no notice of him. She opens a small wooden box and draws out another Sweet Death cigarette.

"Trevor, I can see you're dying to tell me all about the bar exploding. Believe me, I'm aware. Everyone in the city is aware. The Puerto Rican families in Corazon Negro are organizing. We've got gangs ready to push in here that haven't been interested in Red Light for years. Did I not ask for restraint?"

His face goes slack. "You think I did that? I knew what I was doing. I built IEDs for the fuckin' Navy for—"

"Mrs. Robinson, what the fuck happened?" She pushes one cup of tea closer to me. "Drink."

What the Hell, it's been a long night, and this tea smells pretty good. Delia smiles warmly.

"You're dismissed, Trevor."

He opens his mouth, then stops. He's boiling. I think he genuinely wants to kill me. He leaves, kicking over several candles on the way out. "Goddamn clusterfuck! I followed orders..."

"He's quite passionate. I admire that in him." Delia shakes her head. "It's a city of wonders we live in, Mrs. Robinson. It is simply impossible to think that something can't happen here. You think there couldn't be a civil war. There will be. You think it wouldn't be because of a cripple. But I do wonder. I do much wonder if a cripple didn't bring down the house of Caligula."

She pauses, sips her tea and raises her eyebrows at me. This is worse than outright anger. This is the kind of treatment only a furious mother could give to her child. I actually want her to punish me at this point. I hate this waiting.

"We came across a list while you were in the bar. Found it in the back of your van. Care to explain?"

She hands me the battered piece of light blue paper. It was the sheet just underneath the one I wrote on. My heavy-handed penmanship left a perfect indentation on this page, an invisible carbon copy. She taps at her name with a pen. I'll be damned.

"Number five?" she asks, but I barely hear her.

I snatch the pen and paper from her hand. The room goes

dark for me. There's only me and the list, and order from chaos. I scribble some notes on auto pilot, fixing the mistakes, filling in the blanks, trying to make it all look right again. My book of names, in ink, indelible.

Now my list looks like this:

10. ~~Vasili~~

9. ~~Susan Schrader~~

8. ~~Grace Brooks – need camo webbing and paper bags.~~ SLOPPY BITCH!

7. ~~Shakes – maybe sooner~~ overboard, but fun.

6. ~~Caligula – Familiar address?~~ sicksicksicksick

5. Delia Sugar – I'M NOT SORRY. I'LL FIND A WAY

4. Hooded Jack - NEXT

3. Dr. Robert Fortescu – took her heart. I want his in return.

2. Veronica Madden –

1. Fuck if I know.

Really fucked this one up, didn't you?

Shut up.

Look at Delia there. You have a pen in your hand, a pen can stab.

She knows something.

You'll figure it out on your own.

Shut up!

I feel Delia's hand gently stop my pen and the room comes back into focus. She takes the list back and reads it over, clucking slightly.

"Hooded Jack. He's had it in for Caligula for a long time. Are you working for him? You seem like his type."

I shrug.

"This needs to finish, Mrs. Robinson. I'm only telling you this because I care."

I start to write on the paper—*I've been trying to fig—*

Her hand stops me again. Her fingers guide my chin up until our eyes meet.

"Time is all I have. Speak to me."

I shake my head. Of all the things she could ask.

"You won't leave this room until you do."

Fine with me, I stare at her.

"You won't get any further answers," she says, holding the blotters.

Good, throw them away. I don't care.

Then she has a match in one hand and the scrapbook in the other. Her rough thumbnail digs into the match head, ready to flick down and blaze it. And the book is open in the other hand, a picture of me attached to a long news article. I think it's me. It's a fuzzy shot of a lady in a hospital bed. And on the facing page, there's me in what must be an older picture, walking, a hand reaching into the frame from the right side to hold my hand. A slender arm, young, graceful, it has to be her, it has to be... And she flicks the page back and forth ever so briefly, holding the match close, too close.

"Speak."

I look at her again. I don't want to drool, I don't want to look soft and useless. She moves the scrapbook, and underneath is my small tape recorder.

"And what about this gem?"

She hits play, and here comes Frances.

"...Delia's angry. She's going to eat you alive, and I think I'll let her. Unless you start talking. It's her or me, what's your decision? Because if you're scared of her, you should be god-damned terrified of me. Tell me what you know about Jack. And Delia. Now... What, you want coffee? Coffee, Gavin? Yeah, you think. You know...I. I tried to. You know. Gavin, motherfucker!"

Frances is going way over the top, in a way that would make the most zealous community college actor tell him to back off a bit. Hearing his voice gives me a twinge of pain.

Delia hits the stop button. She lowers the matchstick, dead and black now, but I can't relax. She looks at me like a toy collector gazing on her prize possession.

"You wrote that?"

I nod.

"Amazing," she says. "Say the name. Gavin." She pauses, her thumb working the cover of the matchbook open and closed.

"Nnng...mm...nnngagddn."

"Mmm," she smiles. "That's what I thought. It's why I love theater, Mrs. Robinson. What is said in between the lines, what is shown without speaking. Why did you choose that name? Do you know?"

I shake my head.

"Speak!" she barks, raising another matchstick up. Her thumbnail makes a quick *snak* sound, followed by the sputter of flame.

"Nno!" I say, and she lowers the match. Telegraph it. Just say the important words, breathe deep, stop to swallow when the saliva builds up. I've done this before.

"Mrs. Robinson, you made a concerted effort to implicate me in a gang war. I must say it's hurt me tremendously."

She smiles, her teeth so bright in here, her eyes so grey, swimming in dull yellow seas.

"Did you write what's on this tape? Did you tell someone what to say?"

"Bofe."

"Why that name?"

"Nnngmmaaggvvn? Don' know why. Ffffrrgggeddn egryshing. Annn jssst let me rrrrrriiite. Let me rrrrr—"

"No."

Damn, she's enjoying this too much.

"I rrrremmber splloshun. N dee arlley. Mann in ny deams, res is a buur—bluur. Msff Robnnhhon—no culoo. Why you caww ne tha."

"Well, what a wonderful place to start."

She opens the book and turns the pages until she settles on something she likes. She holds it out for me. A newspaper article, just a small page-six kind of thing. Violence in this town is not front-page news until it's spectacular or widespread. There's that fuzzy shot, me on a gurney by an ambulance. I think it's me. It's distant, three paramedics looking nervously over their shoulders, expecting some random lunatic to shoot them. EMTs in this city have a very high mortality rate. Junkies love to kill them. Their wagons are a treasure trove. The sheets are soaked in blood, so much that it looks like there's shiny vinyl on top of me. There's my leg dangling, but the angle is almost impossible, like Chihuahua Girl under my van. My face is turned toward the camera, the bottom half coated in blood. Eyes wide open, but unseeing. The title underneath says LONE SURVIVOR. The rest is torn away.

I laugh. Just a little. God bless me please. This is like opening a photo album to some long-forgotten memory of childhood, something so cherished that when you see it your heart leaps and your mind curses you for ever having forgotten. I was Mrs. Robinson. I had a fake name.

Delia is all sympathy. "I know it hurts to remember these things...but we must. Because the more you see, the more you'll understand. I'm your friend. I'm on your side, and always have been.

You know your real name, don't you?"

No, I shake my head. And even if I did, I wouldn't tell her. "Onee geemuns whahn nee—ree maim. Fa powrr."

I write it for her: Only demons want your real name. For power.

"Bet you wish you'd have thought about all of that long before you met the Doctor."

I stare at her, waiting for the other shoe to drop.

"I'm going to give it all back to you."

Break my head open like a piggy bank, pick out the pieces you need. Give me something, anything.

"You'll want the Doctor dead. Hooded Jack dead. And more than anything, you'll want Veronica Madden dead. Maybe me too. That's my bargain, you spare me. I'm giving you everything you want. I'm your friend. Always have been..."

The demon of my addiction hisses in my ear, words cold as an icepick. *No. You came down off the mountain and bore that list to the people of this city, and its word is law.*

The bottle is fighting for control over me now, when I'm this close to remembering, this close to sanity. So we'll bend the rules, Mrs. Robinson and I. We'll start to find side exits, doors, ways out. Because the truth is, I want to take that blotter. I want Sweet Death. There are answers in there. She could kill me while I'm high and I wouldn't care. She could be lying to me, and I wouldn't care if I had something resembling a truth. Knowing my name, or anyone in my family, well that would be a peach. As long as I died with details.

So I put on a show for her. A little shaky hand, some more tears, a couple of moosey howls thrown in. I'm too frail. Too, too frail. I pat the book, making my fingers too weak to even grasp a page. I need the book, I need the knowledge.

"We'll just have to bury that nasty person you've become and get some answers. Hold out your tongue."

I push my tongue out, noticing the slight way she recoils at the sight of the mangled red lump. Thinking of it, what it must look like, all of the concerns about Shakes and Big C wash out of me. What was I doing on that gurney in the picture? What are those EMTs so scared of? I want to hear more.

She sets the little square down, gently, like a snowflake on my tongue. I feel it start to dissolve, making my lips go salty and cold. Her fingers race towards my mouth, a lit cigarette between them, and I take a pull, a huge pull, rushing into the darkness, running towards my former self.

And then I disappear.

XXIV

Welcome back to the show.

Freefalling inside of that big, black, empty silken tent, the floor swims in purple light, rippling and shiny. I land ankle deep in it, whatever it is. It's cool on my feet. If I can feel that, then I have legs. Whatever Delia refined in Sweet Death, it's some good shit.

"Where did we leave off? Your tragic night at the bar... How do you feel?"

I lay down in the coolness of the water, float in it, stare at the ceiling as it pulses and sags and drips. It flips and bends and then the bar resolves above me. Nice third-person perspective. There I am, leggy me, and there's Caligula grabbing my arm. Dream-me's eyes are locked onto my husband, sitting there in the booth with other people. He's humiliated that I'm here, and he won't acknowledge me.

The picture starts moving in slow motion. Caligula's grip tightens. My hands drive into his chest. Clarabelle, the skinny boy who was sitting next to my husband, comes at me with the bottle. His hand drags across a table top and there's a little brown shimmer as the bottle breaks in half.

And there's me, staring at the bottle for a split second before I realize he intends to cut me. Me, just looking at my husband. Our marriage had to count for something. Surely he didn't want me to get hurt. He should protect me—he's a cop. My husband was a cop? Why didn't I catch that last time?

"Your husband refined you. You knew how to fight, he helped you learn how to fight smart. You were decent with a gun at close range, but he showed you how to fire a gun, a rifle, a semi-automatic. You used to go to the gun club together. I know these things because I was your friend before, and I still am. It was your little romantic getaway, every weekend that he was free...free from what, Mrs. Robinson, do you remember?"

To protect and serve. To betray and destroy. The picture freezes, the bottle inches from my face, my husband in the corner, and his eyes darting like frightened mice. That was his version of crying.

"To help you would be to blow his cover, and neither of you would have made it out of that bar alive. To sit back and remain undercover meant watching his wife getting murdered before him. What to do, what to do..."

The doors that barred those memories had been welded shut. The wrenching scream as they flew open echoed around the room, inside of my head, through my body.

Watching myself on the ceiling, getting stabbed by Clarabelle. In a snap, my husband moves, charging towards me, eyes filled with anger. Too slow to stop that bottle from coming into my jaw. The picture explodes into a white haze as the bottle penetrates my skin.

When the flare dies down, he's chasing someone out the door. Or is someone chasing him? He's running. A woman approaches me. It's Delia Sugar, and I can't tell if this is her interfering in my dream or if this really happened. I lay in a cooling puddle of my own blood, strangely tingly on my skin.

"The Doctor's here," she says. "You should have left when you had the chance. You don't want to see what happens next."

Two of her assistants drag me towards a back door, but I shake them off and stagger to follow my husband, everyone in the bar staring at me.

Michael Paul Gonzalez

"I quit," I mutter at them. I chant it, quietly, slurred, bleeding as I totter through the bar, everyone looking at me like I could fall over dead at any second. I wish there was a mirror. What would I have looked like with that bottle lodged in my chin?

"You were one of the baddest ladies underground. A lot of people held grudges against you. But you managed to keep that all separate from your real life, you had managed to shield your daughter from it all," Delia, from outside my mind, I hear her. I did most of my work while she was away at school. I think. What did I do? What's Delia getting at? "And what will they all do now that they know you're a policeman's wife?"

I hated it. I hated all of it. His job was the other woman in our relationship. I had to find a way to get close. I hated going to the range, I hate the smell of gun oil. Hand-to-hand training was sometimes the only touching we would do for weeks.

Maybe it's why I hate sniping. The feel of the rifle. The voice I hear in my head telling me to exhale slowly, to squeeze, not pull.

"Mrs. Robinson? Did you love him?"

That night was the last we were together. And it was my fault. That much I remember. He died because of me. I'd come there to quit everything. Doctor Robert was going to make an example of me. My husband was trying to buy me time to get out. I was never supposed to show up there.

"Oh, but look at your face, Mrs. Robinson! Let me get a tissue..."

The whole tent smears and circles, swishes and resolves like a kaleidoscope. I think Delia's patting my cheeks dry out there. The room swims with images of our past.

He was gone six days a week. Most days he'd be out at the crack of dawn, and if I was lucky, home in time for supper. He saw undercover as his ticket up. It wasn't supposed to last forever. Just a year or two, then the promotion would come.

I'm not the patient type. There's only so long you can count your shoe collection, arrange flowers, find new ways to decorate.

Once your daughter grows up, that is.

Once she grows up and figures out how things work. When he's bringing his "work" home with him, and I catch her in the basement experimenting with needles, rolling paper, whatever he skimmed that week. And I catch her making phone calls to the Doctor. But maybe she was--

"Why did you follow him?" Delia asks out there.

"I wanted to save him." I actually spoke that, and I'm surprised to hear the clarity of my voice. "With everything that was happening, I just wanted a chance, a second chance, but I couldn't get that because of the Doctor. I don't know why my husband...why Gavin...why there wasn't a way out of...I don't know what he was tied up with. I wanted my family back."

"Gavin. There's that name again. You're throwing walls up. He was lured into the criminal underworld. He lost his perspective. Who do you think brought him there?"

"Yes...he got caught up...everything...easy money, I remember, easy, and he was working for the Doctor... We had a nice house, a family and a nice house. It was nice," why am I talking like Frances? "I decorated. I kept it clean. We had a basement. We had a second floor. It was..."

"Those first few years, you were able to overlook what your husband did when he left, because you were comfortable. You were convinced that he was making the city a better place."

"He was."

"He was making your life better because he worked for me."

"When did he meet you?"

A pause, barely perceptible, but long enough that it seems she's having trouble remembering. "He was part of a bust on one of my East Side operations. I made a bargain with him." Or maybe she's making up her answer.

"He never stopped talking about you. These wonderful stories he would tell me, how he was doing this for your own good. And one day you happened upon us. You came home early from your work. Do you remember?"

Everything is hazy at this point. Maybe she's feeding me lines, maybe the drug is too strong. All I do is listen.

"I promised you I'd keep you all safe, as long as he helped to keep me safe until he moved on from undercover work. We all need help sometimes."

There's a vague picture of this on the ceiling, the three of us in the kitchen, but it looks wrong, as if someone has clipped our photos from separate places and pasted them there.

There's a strange pressure on my ears. Delia must be doing something to me out there in the waking world.

"Do you remember the night your daughter had the unfortunate pleasure of meeting Doctor Robert Fortescu? The monster. You obviously remember what he did to you..."

I see him again, holding the jar, the cold grey heart floating inside, the threat to come for me.

"Do you know what he does in his medical practice downtown? When people go under? Men do such strange things to feel powerful. Is he the type of man you'd make a deal with?"

You don't make friends with monsters. They find you, they destroy you. There's no order to any of it. They want what they want.

"You worked for him."

If you say so.

"When that became untenable, you told him you were leaving. You said it was inviting trouble into your life, that your daughter was going down a bad path. He said you could leave, and he set a price. Her heart. Remember?"

Sort of.

"You had a plan to get her to safety and get out of town. That's all this has ever been about. I tried to help you save her. This is how it all began, that night in Pompidou's bar. You were going to tell him that you were leaving town. Your husband was going to be the distraction. And then you found out that your husband was in on the whole thing. He was pimping out your daughter. Your flesh and blood."

I don't know why, but I think she's lying.

"All so he could stay in the Doctor's good graces."

I don't know *how* I know she's wrong, but she is.

"She was right there in that back room, the little girl with raccoon eyes and bruised thighs."

Why would he have chosen to save *me*, then? Why pull his badge when he knew it would mean his death?

"I think we should work together, you and I. From now on. Join my family. The world out there doesn't want you. You're half a woman! Here, you'd have meaning and purpose."

No – I hear myself say. The List.

"The list is almost done, Mrs. Robinson. You'll have your chance to see Doctor Robert. I understand some debts always need to be repaid. This isn't a choice. I'm the only one that has need of you now, and if you don't do what I ask, then I'll have no need of you. And what then? Join my family."

My brain goes purple as a huge wave of pressure billows across my psyche, painting the insides of my eyes in kaleidoscope colors and bathing the world in pungent smoke. She's really cranking it up out there with the sweet death. Most people would probably have broken by now, done whatever she asked. I don't think she realizes who she's dealing with. She'll need heavier drugs to break me. I'm the Keith Richards of the underworld.

"Remember your daughter," she says. "Remember your husband! How he bled, how he broke, just because he carried a badge, just because he tried to save you. He kept silent until they poured the gasoline on him. And it was that split second before they lit him up that—"

Michael Paul Gonzalez

"Shut up."

"Just say yes to me. You want the Doctor? Or do you want death? I was there, Mrs. Robinson. I was in that bar, that same bar where he kept your daughter chained in the back, where man after man after man would pay a fee to get thirty seconds of magic with her. All night. That's what Doctor Robert did to you. He took everything, and then he took it again, then he took some more."

Hold the phone here... I see this snippet unfolding, a dark corner of the bar, a long line of men waiting by a faded green door. Delia standing next to me, telling me it's too late, that I should leave. But I feel an insistent buzz in the back of my head that my daughter is in a safe house. I was about to leave town. I wasn't here to rescue her. I was here to make a statement. And Delia was there, laughing. She's taking money from the men, her children are working security on that green door.

She's lying.

It wasn't my daughter back there, but it was someone's kid. Some poor girl who made some horrible life choices, who just wanted love or guidance or a safe place, and Delia gave them the worst deal imaginable.

"I swear to God, I don't want to kill you, Mrs. Robinson, but for you to ignore your daughter—"

And suddenly, Delia is screaming.

I feel like I'm floating to the top of a tar-filled pool, breaking into the light as Delia's screams get louder, popping my ears, ringing like fire alarms.

A hummingbird flutters at my wrist, turning into an angry wasp stinging, then sharp snake teeth clamping down. My eyes snap open.

It's Delia, clawing at my wrist, my hand clutching a pen which I've managed to drive into her chest just below her left clavicle.

She's laying there, shaking like a puppet, blood jetting from her neck, rattling on the floor like a skeleton in a whoreskin suit.

"It was," she says, and then she breathes out *ooooo*, a horrible death rattle. She coughs. "Veronica. Veronica, it was always... Veronica...you don't..."

She falls silent. Not dead, because the blood is still pumping out of her in slowing waves. I can count her remaining minutes on one hand. At times like this, I'm glad I can't talk. I wouldn't know what to say.

Trevor explodes into the room, followed closely by a few of Delia's kids. He lifts me off of her with one hand, tossing me across the room like a pillow. I land gracelessly on my hip, tumbling like a broken hubcap until I crash upside down into the wall.

I guess saying sorry would be out of the question.

The whole scene unfolds in front of me upside-down. Trevor trying to staunch the blood pouring from Delia. She's doing this weird kind of inhale-scream thing. I don't think I punctured any organs. She might even live. Fucking baby.

By the time I've turned everything right side up again, Delia is near death and two of her kids have my arms stretched out, pinning me against the wall. Sweet Death still hangs on me like a morning fog. Trevor stalks over to me and bends close to my face. He casts dark glances at my two captors and they release me and move away. He's so close I can feel his breath on my ear.

"Two inches lower and it would have been her heart, fuckup," he whispers. "We're getting you out of here."

While I process this, he stands up, draws his fist back, and punches me square in the nose. Little lights explode behind my eyelids and my face feels like it's riding a wave every time my heart beats.

"Mrs. Sugar," Trevor asks, "are you all right?"

Delia doesn't answer. Through my flashing stars, I see her eyes burning in the darkened corner like an angry rat. Trevor moves to help her. To my amazement, she shakes him off and stands up. She hobbles over to me, blood-wet shirt soaked to her skin, so tight I can count her shining brown ribs.

"Gather the children," she wheezes. She runs a finger through her blood and smears it across my forehead. She turns to Trevor. "Make it bad. Make it hurt."

The skin on my cheek feels like it's filling with marshmallows. I think my eye might swell shut. Whatever punishment is coming my way, it couldn't hurt much worse than Trevor's punch. Delia collapses as more of her kids storm into the room, ready to tear me apart.

They lift me, two kids on either side of my body, draping my arms over their shoulders. Like they're trying to help me walk off a drink or two, and now we're headed for the stairs, climbing, climbing.

Behind me, Trevor calls to them, "Nobody else touches her. She's fucking mine."

And then we're upstairs. The grounds surrounding Delia's quarters are Standing Room Only. Two huge groups of night kids with a skinny path up the middle, leading to my van. My last ticket out.

Trevor comes out, and clambers to the top of a tall crypt, holding court over everyone. He points to himself three times as he says. "Judge. Jury. Executioner. Any objections?"

The crowd is silent. He'd make a pretty solid 80s B-movie henchmen.

Trevor leaps down and grabs me by the front of my jacket, hauling me up above his head. "Court is in session!"

The crowd screams in approval. He pulls me down so my face is close to his, nose-to-nose. Beneath their roar, I can barely hear him.

"This is going to hurt. A lot. I think I can get us out, but I can't make any promises. I should leave you for dead, but orders are orders."

The last of the Sweet Death in my system washes away in a burst of adrenaline. Trevor leans close to my ear again, and there's a little tremble in his voice.

"Sorry about this."

He tosses me toward the van. I barely get my hands up in time, but everything still hurts, cement and broken asphalt and pebbles and scrub weed sanding my face and thighs and any other exposed skin. This stupid strappy outfit Delia made me wear does nothing to protect me.

I skip out of the lot and careen into a little cement cross, cracking it with the force of impact. Trevor stalks towards me, and we have a little non-verbal conversation that goes something like:

—What the fuck?

—I said I was sorry.

—Again, what the fuck?

Trevor jumps into the air and stomps down hard on my right thigh. It looks vicious, and hurts, but it also feels like he pulled it a little. I think he's taking it easy on me when he pulls me up by the hair. I flail my arms, looking for anything to take the weight off my scalp. He draws back a fist. The crowd goes crazy. Then, just as suddenly, they fall silent. So he drops me.

One little knock-kneed paleface has clambered from the underground tomb, cradling Delia's body. She looks brittle as onion paper. She's bled out. The girl slowly stalks across the cemetery, all of the kids hanging their heads. She lays Delia inside of a small fenced-in plot.

Delia's hand twitches, lifts up once, trembling. She lowers her hand to her side and her eyes drift skyward.

"I have been with you for over a year now," Trevor shouts. "There ain't a soul here Delia trusts more. If this is her night to leave, I'll be damned if it happens before she sees justice."

"Delia," they say in unison, low and sustained, almost like a sung prayer.

"Who helps you? Who feeds you?" Trevor asks.

"Delia," they chant again.

"What's our word for mother? What's our word for queen?"

"Delia." The name comes like a war cry, like a plea for my blood.

Delia's mouth trembles. Her face contorts, and she draws one final breath. Every element of the cemetery respects the moment. The wind stops blowing, nothing moves as she exhales. "Blood for blood."

And oh, the moaning, the crying, the demands for my head. *I almost want me to get punished now.*

Trevor shouts, "Blood for blood. Let's drive!"

The crowd becomes a single living organism, emitting a wail like nothing I've ever heard. You'd think some teen pop idol just happened by. "This van brought us to her. This van will take her out."

The crowd gasps. I mean, as a whole, they audibly gasp. They're chanting as one.

"Crush...crush...CRUSH!"

Trevor points at the van and says, "Ropes." He lifts his right hand and says, "Helmet." He lifts his left hand and says, "Mouthpiece."

"We are the power in this city!" he shouts, ringing clear above the roar of the crowd, "Everyone else...bugs on our windshield. We're the survivors!"

The crowd goes wild. Two happy little drugged-out onlookers approach Trevor, handing him a black crash helmet and a mouthpiece. I guess they've done this little ceremony before. That explains the excitement.

Trevor raises the helmet in a salute to Delia. "For you, Delia. For you."

Her dying eyes are shiny wet with tears of pride and joy.

As he bites down on the mouthpiece, two more little drug monkeys race out of the crowd and grab my arms. Two more are going to work on the front of my van, busting out the windshield with crowbars. The safety glass doesn't shatter, but eventually buckles and folds like a heavy sheet of plastic. They rip it from the frame. Trevor climbs into the van and they shut the door, anchoring two lengths of rope to each side of the windshield frame.

I'm hoisted onto the grille of my van, arms spread. I'm too confused to fight, and what good would it do me now? Trevor may have beaten the shit out of me, but he also said he was sorry, so he's pretty much my only ticket out of here. If he's not trying to kill me.

They tie my wrists tight to each rope, and I'm crucified on the front of my EconoVan. I see where this is going.

Trevor starts the van. The vibration on my back is oddly relaxing. The hot air blowing across the radiator feels like the breath of a dragon waiting to eat me alive. The headlights click on and Delia is painted pearly white there on the ground. The kids line up before her, dropping flowers, needles, rolling papers onto her, making her pyre.

After paying tribute, each kid walks up to the front of the van and shouts a request to Trevor.

"Start with the cemetery gates," one screams.

"Take her straight down McCallister into the freeway underpass!"

"Pain. I want pain!" This last kid's eyes are big and bulgy in a Mommy Dearest sort of way. He slugs me in the stomach as hard as he can, which isn't hard at all. I sell it like he crushed my spine. Might as well give him some satisfaction.

The cemetery gates, two big slabs of wrought iron. They stand alone, the wall long ago crumbled to nothing. They're just a non-functional monument to the city's past at this point. Well, tonight they're a set of goalposts, and I'm the football. The freeway underpass lies beyond, then a wall of solid cement. My van, a battering ram. And me, soon to be a moth on the radiator.

All of the children lock eyes onto me, angry and upset as Trevor backs the van up. He turns in a wide arc, and my body pendulums a little on the grille. My wrists hurt like hell, hands tingling. I hope this is over soon. The engine gutters and roars, and the gates in the distance race towards me. Wind whips at my face, my cheeks ballooning out. I'd scream, but the van's already doing that for me.

All I can do is admire the history. The ancient nubs of tombstones worn to almost nothing, blurring by. The historic iron gates, an effort to placate the history buffs of our fair city. Frances taught me this back when I was studying. Poor Frances. He's going to be all alone now. I'll miss him.

Trevor guns the engine, and my vision turns blurry as the van vibrates and rumbles, picking up speed towards the gate. The wind tears at my eyes and I have to squint to see my death coming, but I will watch it. I don't want to miss this.

I recognize the whine of third gear. We're probably doing around forty now, across ground that's pockmarked and bumpy, full or rocks and holes and dead people. The gates are flimsy iron. They'll bust pretty fast when I hit them. That big chain and lock might hold though. That could be bad. If I'm lucky, one of the spokes in the fence will lance through my eye and I won't have to watch the rest of the show.

Time really does contract in moments of stress. I hate this.

I really have to pee. I don't know how long I've been holding it, but it feels like days. Hitting those gates isn't going to help. Then again, all of this jostling isn't doing wonders.

Adrenaline and fear keep all of my important muscles clenched, which is good. My body hasn't given up yet. It will relax when it knows the moment is about to come.

Ten yards from the gate, we rumble up and to the right, avoiding our target and bouncing over some large cement grave markers. If I had legs, they'd be getting cracked pretty good right now. Instead, I'm flapping against the front of my van like a cheap air

Michael Paul Gonzalez

freshener on a rearview mirror.

Trevor is screaming, not angry defiance, more of a yee-haw kind of thing. The van slams hard down into a rain ditch, blasting my back as we jerk onto the sidewalk. When we make the final jump from curb to road, I hit the van so hard I feel the grille plate crack and fall away. The hot breath from the radiator intensifies.

Trevor shouts at me, "We're not out of this yet!"

"Thank you for trying," I say, soft and low.

I'm fascinated by the city as it speeds by me. I feel like I'm flying. Lights blur through the tears in my eyes. My face has gone completely numb, and my wrists feel like they're being dipped in acid. My arms are pulled so tight that my chest is constricting and I'm having trouble breathing. I have no way to shift my weight, no legs to take pressure off. I'm going out like Jesus. Closer to thee, my Lord.

Behind us, the growl of motorcycles. Not racing bikes. Sound more like chopped bobbers. I wonder what color they are?

The more the feeling drains from my body, the more my brain begins to pulse. Images flash by me with each streetlight. Every turn we make sends memories pouring through my body.

The wind is gone. The pain is gone. Feeling is gone. The city disappears. I'm lost in my quasi-past.

Delia's story replays in my head, my brain shaking out the nuggets of truth from the silt of shitty water she dumped in there. My husband was a cop. Crooked as hell. Gavin? I don't know if that's his name. He taught me to fight because he wanted me to be able to protect myself and my family. Taught me to shoot. That part was a lie. I've always known how to shoot, fight and kill. I was better at it than he was from the day we met. I taught him. And our daughter...she got into something bad, she got tangled with the Doctor... And I know they killed him. Why can't I see her face?

My face grows cold from wind-whipped tears, as Trevor swerves the van in and out of oncoming traffic. Gunshots pop from the driver's-side window. This all sounds very exciting. I hope he's winning.

A sickening screech, then a hollow scraping noise. Trevor slams on the brakes. A motorcycle skids past us, the rider following a split second later. Trevor cranks the van hard to the left and we gun down a side street, racing out of Red Light and into the city proper.

Another motorcycle screams behind us, the headlight pushing its way forward next to the van. More muffled pops, my poor van cracking and breaking as bullets riddle the chassis. She's going out like a champ. Trevor yanks us hard left again and we're up on the sidewalk. Motorcycle tires screech as the rider tries to brake, but it's too late. Trevor scrapes him off against an abandoned storefront. We rumble down the sidewalk, taking out a newspaper machine which I narrowly dodge. He hops the curb again and we're back out in the street.

The spires of tall buildings surrounding the library grow closer. I wonder if Frances is in there doing more research for me. I want to go back to the library. I want to read again, and plan, and make lists and diagrams. This all looked so much better on paper. It's all out of control now. I just want to be able to place my hands on something and make it work the way it's supposed to.

Another bike rips by, centering in front of us, weaving side to side. There are two riders. What's left of my hearing disintegrates as Trevor fires shots over my head, never taking his foot off the gas.

The biker eludes Trevor's fire while his Bitch Seat Rider tries desperately to light a rag that's been stuffed into a bottle. It catches, big time. A huge flame jets from his hand and he turns back to look at us.

The buildings coast by. The streetlights flicker and grow dark. The smell of the rancid waters tells me we're near the wharf. A drop of water hits my face and for a second I mistake it for sea spray. But it's just rain. Bitch Seat is waiting for a moment when the bike is steady, waiting for his chance to throw. The flame dances and streaks across the road, bobbing with the bike. We're chasing a dragon.

The waves of heat roll and bounce like Gavin when they lit him up. He didn't make it far. He didn't do that Hollywood stuntman firedance thing where they stagger around with their arms up. It was panicky. He lost control. He was trying to run, trying to roll, trying to slap out the flames all at the same time. Screaming, and all I could do was watch. I wanted to burn with him. Embrace him and end it all, but it was over so fast. And there was still her, my daughter, alone. A thunderstorm broke, putting him out in seconds. He was dead long before that.

We're about to get toasted. We'll never get enough speed to ram the bike, and Trevor hasn't fired a shot off in a while. What's he waiting for?

I see it before they do.

A roadblock at the head of the dock warehouses. Two beat-up old trucks, homemade gray-and-blue camo paintjobs. Through the netting on the back, I spy some heavy artillery poking right at us. Even with the wind screaming at my face, my eyes are open wide. The firing squad or the fire. And it looks like it'll be both.

A muzzle flare from the truck ahead paints the streets white before I hear the shot. The biker takes evasive action, swerving hard to the right. His passenger lets the Molotov cocktail go with a hook shot. It arc's at me, looping for my head like it's guided by wire. I try to dip as Trevor slams on the brakes, resigning myself to the fact that something on me is going to melt soon.

The backs of both bikers ripple and explode as bullets punch through them. They fall and flip, sliding away from us. The men who were lined up near the trucks run towards us, only a few yards away.

The bottle is getting lower, and for a second I think I'm safe. It's going to be too low.

I'm wrong.

It shatters on the bumper below me, sending the contents splattering over the face of the van. Liquid becomes fire in the blink of an eye. My brain sends two messages: BREATH and SCREAM. I find I can do neither. All I am is pain, skin crackling away, one raw wound, trying to open my eyes against the flames. Because I know if I do I'll see Gavin waiting for me. Why was Delia so hung up on his name?

The van jerks to a stop and the men charge toward us, one of them drawing a knife. Trevor slaps his jacket over me, trying to put out the flames. I think he's just fanning them.

Then, I'm surrounded by men, all of them beating at me with their jackets and shirts. I feel the tension on my wrists release, and I'm tossed to the ground. Rain pelts my back. My arms have no feeling and my legs feel like they're still on fire, all the way to my toes. For once, I don't want my phantom pains.

Everyone's talking at once.

"She's out! She's out!"

"She okay?"

"Her legs were...uh...well, you know."

"Let's get her back to the docks."

I burned. Just like my husband. I came out on the other side. Not reforged, just melted. Not ready to finish my job. But I'll be damned if I don't. He screamed for me. He called my name. I couldn't even make a peep. What does that say about him? Or me?

I don't know if it's exhaustion or shock or hyperventilation from taking my first breaths in a few minutes, but I'm well on the verge of a blackout. One of the men says Jack is waiting for me.

If I can find a way to move again, they're all dead.

#

My first hour here has been an education. Hooded Jack is the name of the group, and not the name of one man. I was excited at first, thinking I was being taken to *the* Hooded Jack. They took me back to a makeshift gurney set up inside of an empty shipping container. A man greeted me there, sitting in a rickety chair and smiling up at me. He introduced himself as Jack. Then he told the two men who brought me in, Jack and Jack, that they could leave and bring Jack back to the trailer.

I asked to see Hooded Jack three times, and after the man in the chair stopped laughing, he explained the whole situation. I suppose it's a crafty little way to make sure that the head of the snake is less likely to be blown off.

I wonder what they're calling me out there. Jill?

The only one not being called Jack is Trevor, and at the very least he owes me an explanation. After calling for him three or four times, Jack-in-the-chair tells me Trevor's being debriefed, and won't be with us anytime soon. Once he's back in uniform, he'll be Jack, too. Apparently Hooded Jack likes to put people in deep cover to get information. Jack tells me they have eyes everywhere, that their organization has people working code-word secret missions, that any knowledge of these spies, if caught, would be fully denied by Hooded

Jack. It's a regular Area 51 out here.

All of the guys running around, the ones in short sleeves anyway, have black bands covering their left forearms. On these bands are simple white stripes denoting rank. For instance, Jack-in-the-chair is carrying two bars and a Red Cross. Even if I had the strength to fight him, I wouldn't. The Doctor of my enemy is my friend, or something like that. My arms feel like wet noodles and my legs feel badly sunburned. I really want a change of clothes. I smell like a combination of burnt socks and rotten barbeque.

Dr. Jack gives me a thorough medical examination and finds me to be "pretty banged up" but otherwise okay. The official word? Road rash. Bruises. Cuts, scrapes. Nothing broken.

The burns on my leg are superficial. Any longer under the fire and we might have had a problem. I still can't curl the fingers on my right hand tightly.

Dr. Jack has a pretty decent bedside manner. He gives me a blanket and an IV drip, but I wouldn't trust him to work on a hangnail once I get mobile again. I know how these operations work. Someone wins you over and then the heavies come in.

Status check.

My wrists are raw and my arms are shaky. It'll be a while before I can shoot a gun. My van is trashed. My list is gone. I'm completely cut off. I'm not sure if I'll get to kill another soul. But I'm alive, the proverbial bad penny, just like Delia said.

I don't need the list anymore. I need to figure out who's in charge here and how I can kill them, even if it means killing everyone. Then find Doctor Robert, then Veronica Madden. Or was it the other way around? Blood is blood, who cares? My stomach is a roiling pool of acid. I want to lash out and kill every single person on the wharfs right now. The curtain to the tent parts, and a man walks in. I just need to find a way to start again. I need another benefactor. If I could get a call out to Joe, he'd find a way to help me out of this. He wants the list done as badly as I do.

Two hard raps on the side of the container wall, and ten the whole thing shifts around as a bunch of guys in blackout body armor clamber in.

"You must be Jack," I say to the one in front. They're fully masked, so I have no idea if that got a chuckle.

"Tie her up."

Guess not.

Maybe he didn't understand me. Maybe he's not in the mood for jokes. Two Jacks-in-the-back push past him and roll me onto my stomach, binding my arms tight behind my back, taking little mind that my wrists have already taken a beating tonight. They lift me unceremoniously into a shopping cart. And we're off.

I lean back and watch the purple-stained sky dance across the gaps in between the dock houses and storage buildings, a reflection of the oil-stained water below. I bet sunrises here are great.

Ahead, a giant warehouse door slides open. The entrance is black, a large void waiting to swallow us whole. As the front of the shopping cart crosses the threshold, a single floodlight comes on in the center of the cavernous space. Shapes beyond the light, partially obscured by the dancing dust motes. Eyes on me. Just a single pair, two dirty nickels in the darkness. The two Jacks stop my cart in the center of the spotlight and back away.

A voice speaks in the gloom and shadows, "Hoods," followed by the soft rustling sound of cotton sliding over skin. Now it feels like there's more eyes on me. A lot more.

"Lights."

The warehouse snaps into painful halogen clarity, and I'm surrounded by men sitting on crates, men standing in the corner cleaning guns, men crouched and watching me, snipers on the crossbeams, hooded men everywhere. Some are in ski masks, others in pillowcases, Mexican wrestling masks, some in what look like mummy wraps. They're just chatting each other up, having a good ol' time at the club, like every day is half-woman-in-a-shopping cart day.

"Turn her," says the voice from behind me.

The cart rumbles over the rough warehouse floor, as they turn me to face three more hooded men. The one on the left sways a little, and I think he's the one. I don't know why. He looks the least conspicuous of anyone in the room. He's not as big. His balaclava isn't clean. His clothes are non-descript. The black band on his forearm has no designation of rank, maybe that's it.

I can't see his eyes. He's wearing amber shooter's glasses under his mask. He regards me for a moment and asks me if I killed Delia Sugar. Something is weird about his voice. It changes every time he speaks. Sometimes it's deeper, sometimes rougher, but never constant.

I shake my head and shrug my shoulders, figuring that's about the best answer I can give regarding Ms. Sugar. He's not having it.

"Is she dead?"

Before I can answer, the hooded guy on the left steps forwards and from his voice, I know it's Trevor. "Everything happened too fast. I wasn't able to take vitals. But she looked dead enough."

"We don't assess victory on assumptions. Why didn't you finish the job?"

"My mission was to see that the package was removed safely. Nothing compromises the mission," Trevor pauses, then adds, "Sir."

"Were you not driving the van?" the leader growls.

"Yeah, but—"

The man on the leader's other side slaps the back of Trevor's head. "Protocol!"

"My name is *Sir*, not 'yeah, but.' We're not in the field. We're at home, and at home rank is respected. You could have run Delia over on your way out. You could have fired a shot. You could have—"

"We were under fire. I was protecting the package! Sir."

"The other half of your mission related to targets of opportunity."

"She's dead," Trevor says.

"Confirmed kills are the only thing I want to hear about. If I have to send someone to dig her up to make sure--"

"She'sss gheg," I say. It silences him. I can't tell if he's taking in the info, trying to figure out what I said, or a little of both.

"Later," the leader says, and that's enough for TrevorJack to know he's been dismissed. A lot of the guys in the group shake their heads.

"I suppose you're wondering why you're here," the leader asks me.

I shrug and look around as if to say the thought had occurred to me.

"Do you know Hooded Jack?"

There's obviously no right answer here, so I stay silent.

"Does the name Veronica Madden mean anything to you?"

I wish it did. I keep playing bemused statue.

"Do you know who I am?"

I give him my best stare, which doesn't seem to do much. He holds his hand out and a captain draws a gun from his belt and chambers a round. He hands it to the leader.

"You want to kill me? Was I next?" the leader asks.

He walks toward me. Slowly. I think he's a bit older because he swaggers a little, like most aging guys do when their knees go bad. He presses the gun to my temple.

"Was I next?"

I'm not giving him anything.

"Do you want to kill Hooded Jack?"

He jams the gun a little harder against my temple. I am stone. He lowers the gun and spins it in his palm, extending it to me. He takes a step back.

The leader offers me a smile and cocks his head. "Go ahead. Shoot."

I've never been one to look a gift horse in the mouth. I bring the pistol up quickly in a standard police grip. Hooded Jack's hands go up and he rests them on his head. None of the other men in the room make a move.

"Good," he says. "How brave are you? Brave enough to kill me? You won't leave this warehouse alive. Would it be worth it? If I told you I knew who you were before and who you are now, would you still want me dead?"

I draw in a deep breath. Hold it. Exhale slowly. How would he even know there was a before? My brain says I can find a way out of this, but my body says it's tired. Tired of the drugs, the painkillers, the murders. Tired of continuing. Tired of violence, tired of drawing breath. Maybe knowing isn't worth it. My finger moves on its own, squeezing.

What about the others? I hesitate. I need to get out of here. I just need to find a way out, get some rest, maybe just one more shot to get me through, but this is about justice, it's...

"COME ON!" Hooded Jack barks.

My finger declares independence from my body, sealing my fate. The trigger slides nicely, the pressure grows. I reach the crucial point, the trigger resisting as much as it will before delivering the goods. Nobody on the floor draws a gun to stop me. They don't need to. I'm sure I'm sitting dead red for snipers in the rafters.

Now or never. My work on the list will stop here. If this is the main guy in Hooded Jack and not a decoy trying to test me, it'll still count as progress. Six out of ten ain't bad.

Click.

There's a dead silence, wavering under the thunderous current of my heart beating. I think everyone else can hear it too. The fucker set me up. The gun wasn't loaded.

"Good," he laughs. "Good, good. I was afraid after all of this, you'd be ready to give it up."

His hands, still resting on his head, grasp the top of his hood and pull. He lowers his face, and pulls off his glasses, then stands up nice and straight to look me in the eye.

It defies logic. It's impossible.

Click.

Click click click.

My finger keeps going on the trigger. I'm removed. Floating. I feel tears on my face. Feel the gun in my hand. Feel it without feeling anything at all.

"That's good, sweetheart, that's the fire we need. We've got a big week coming. You need to detox, and then we'll talk."

And with that, Hooded Jack turns his back and limps away. The old guy swagger. A walk that I've seen a million times before. A walk that you can only get with artificial legs.

Click click click click.

My finger won't stop, and my voice ringing off of the warehouse walls as I bawl his name like a child, and the sound comes out of my mouth perfectly.

Joe...

Joe...

Joe...

I've only felt pain like this once before in my life, and then, I was in a hospital bed with a button for morphine any time I wanted it. Now, I'm crumpled in a shopping cart in a warehouse that stinks of industrial grease. Dignified me, in so much pain my body can't even register it.

After Joe left the room, the others filed out a few at a time. Alone in the dark, thinking how much this should hurt, and feeling only the steady pulse of blood in my forehead and neck. Ten minutes in the blackness with nothing but my thoughts is enough to make my brain wash out with the tide. I feel the shopping cart biting into my ass, poking my back, the rusty rails itching against my hands. Did he say detox? Is that what's happening now?

Joe, my supposed bigger brother, father figure, whatever. He lied to me, said supported my cause. What does he know? He said he cared about what I was doing. I guess that wasn't a lie. He was number three. How could he not care?

The last guy out of the room told me that Hooded Jack cares about its soldiers. It wants everyone clean. I know that's a lie. Joe doesn't care. He saw the track marks on my arm when we used to meet, and never said a word.

Michael Paul Gonzalez

These questions and accusations and thoughts and ideas and pain and yearning and sweat and shit...it's enough to drown me. It's not the drugs, it's not coming down. This is the last support beam under my mind finally giving way. This is the weight of the world becoming too much. This is the realization that trying to put order to things is useless. Trying is just busy work to keep us occupied until we die.

Then the feedback starts.

A noise that sounds like a faint whistle, a hiss on the verge of nothingness. A bathroom faucet left open just enough to let a thin stream of water out. The pitch changes and it vibrates up and down, growing louder until it's the sound of a TV test pattern.

And it grows. And grows. The sustained scream of screeching tires. An electric guitar whistling a note that would make Hendrix cry, turned way past eleven. A jet engine three feet away getting ready for takeoff. Every damned soul in Hell screaming in my face.

My body starts melting through the holes in the shopping cart. Oozing down onto the floor, and I feel the metal scrape and pick at my flesh on the way through. Bile fills my mouth and every muscle in my body cramps, releasing long enough to let me draw breath before they seize again. I need a hit. Clearwater. Sweet Death. Morphine. Rubbing Alcohol.

I need something now. Something something something! My brain bucks like a car battery in winter struggling to fire an engine. Everything shakes and burns. I want to kill someone now. That would take the edge off. I want to bite throats of every last Jack here, watch the blood soak through the hoods, chew their faces until they don't needs masks to stay anonymous.

Everything grows still, and in the blackness above me pale figures light up on the rafters, one by one, staring down at me. If I close my eyes, their faces jump uncomfortably close, hungry eyes, leering mouths, glowing on the insides of my eyelids. As long as I don't blink they stay on the rafters.

Vasili is the first among them to speak.

"You are lucky shot," he says in his thick accent, miming a pistol. "Made me spit out piece of my spine. You feel better about things now? You know that I deserve what I got, but you don't know why. Very Eastern European justice." He laughs.

Grace Brooks, arms folded, scarf tied around her head, wedged into a corner on a beam. "What did I do?" she asks. "I don't even know you. I've never seen you before in my life. What did I do? What did my daughter do? How is she?"

When I open my mouth to reply, a thick geyser vomits forth. Black gold. Texas tea. It bubbles and pops on the floor, smooth and shiny, the surface pearlescent like an oil slick. Mouth shut, eyes open. The only way out is through.

Caligula looks satisfied with his lack of being. Paler and whiter than ever, he's still trying to play that street pimp. "Your daughter...'swhat this was all about, right? You want answers? I ain't givin' you shit. Still nothing better than a whore to me. She wanted what she wanted and I gave it. S'what I do. I don't know what the Doctor saw in you. Why he chose you. I'll take you now. You need someone, and you know nobody gonna take you. I know a lot of people that want to go stumpy. And they would pay big. That's as close to love as you're gonna get..."

Shakes totters next to Susan Schrader. Somewhere below, reflected in whatever I just puked up, Gavin's face.

"Thethethe fuck. I tole you I din't do nothin' do. Shitfuck. Din't do nothin'. Your girlgirlgirl came to me. Me. I din't make her do nothin'. She wanted it and more and more and more."

"I'm not sorry," Susan says, throwing a glance at Gavin.

"What's your name?" I try to whisper at him.

His is the only face that doesn't get closer when I blink. The room is a vacuum, no sound, no light but what their bodies cast. I blink and they all scream. Not a scream like they're trying to scare me. It's an eternal thing, the sound they didn't get to make when I took their lives.

Charles Baldacci shakes his head at me. "She was selling to

Michael Paul Gonzalez

me. Not the other way around. She sold to me. You never think of them as people, you know. Never see them as...feeling...I got feelings too..."

I don't berate them, because I don't want to validate their existence. I want them to go away.

Wonder what Delia put in the drugs. Why isn't she up there? Pity. I was hoping she'd come finish her thought about Veronica...

Grace Brooks tumbles from the rafters and falls with a wet *slap* next to my shopping cart. The detached part of my brain wonders if it's me or her screaming. She's writhing and boneless, pure agony ad incorporeal meat. My body moves on its own, pushing hard against the sides of the cart, vaulting up and out onto the floor. Crawling with my arms towards the door.

Joe, I scream.

Gavin.

Anyone.

Grace Brooks pulls herself along next to me as I race for the door. She tries to speak, but every time her mouth opens, a gush of blood pours out. Little flaps of skin float on the tide, each one like the face of Little Debbie. Grace's head wobbles, the severed tendons visible in her neck through the puckered exit wound. I did that. I did it. I can't crawl away fast enough. She's there, and I have to look at her.

By the time I get to the door, my palms are raw and bloody. The front of my body feels sanded by the rough floor. I bang on the door and scream for help, and a voice yells back at me.

"Shut up."

Not a man's voice, not a Jack. A young girl.

"Stay in there," she says. "Stay in there and rot, you bitch!"

I hear my voice ask for help, pathetic and cracking. Just some water, I try to say. Just something, just help.

When I close my eyes, I see a basement. Just for a flash. A

stool lit by a thin shaft of sunlight fighting its way through the grime on the window.

When I blink again, it's the warehouse. The voice on the other side of the door says, "I called the cops."

Why, I ask.

"Fuck you, Mom," the voice says. "Rot. You open that door and I'll kick your head in, I swear."

Mom? Instead of fainting, or screaming, my brain thinks: When did my daughter become a member of Hooded Jack? And I remember this, sitting in the basement, coming down like this. The last good thing my daughter tried to do before she gave up on me. She didn't give up. She couldn't beat me so she joined me. I remember this much. I was coming down, and she was supposed to flush everything, and instead, when she got to the last vial, she took a little taste...and...

She...

She can't be out there now. But even still, I can't stop myself from talking to her.

"I love you."

"We'll see," she says.

Then a seizure of biblical proportions takes my body, and I bounce across the floor like water on a hot wok. My head bounces off of the concrete a few times, and soon enough, I've fish-flopped all the way back to the shopping cart.

All of my targets standing above me on the ground. Circling my body. Dripping on me. Shakes with his limp from where I ankled him, his body like freshly shredded beef. Vasili with his open skull. Caligula and his blue strangled face and cut throat. Charles Baldacci, the middle of his face missing, like a cyclops with a blown-out vagina for an eye. Grace Brooks with her long-distance tracheotomy. Susan Schrader, her guts hanging out. They look at me with something close to pity, bordering on anger. High above me on the rafter, Gavin appears and looks down at me.

Then he falls, and the last thing I see is his face, contorted, mouth open and teeth glaring, rocketing straight at me, and if this were slow we would kiss. But it's not. When he hits me it's going to hurt.

He's darkness, just the darkness of my past, something I let out a long time ago, struggling, clawing to get back into my body. Maybe it never left me.

And I can't help but thinking I deserve whatever pain he gives me.

"Hell of a ride, huh?"

The voice comes from a hundred miles away or just over my shoulder, I don't know. When I open my eyes, light rips into my head hard enough that the muscles in my calves cramp. My teeth clench and my breath comes ragged. Someone's pouring little drops of water onto my lips like they do in the movies when you've been rescued from the desert.

It's when the cramps relax that I remember that I don't have legs. A wet washcloth presses over my eyes and I crack them open. Even here, in the cool damp darkness, the light hurts. Maybe I'm blind now. Maybe my eyes exploded.

"Took me three days to come down off that shit. You broke my record, did it in two. Know what they put in there?"

"Whrrs mm dogga?" I whisper.

The person draws in a breath. "Where's...?"

"Dogga," I whisper. "Dogga," I yelp. I heard her voice. I heard her voice.

This last part I spoke, so I know he couldn't understand.

"I don't know," says the voice, and I don't know if he's talking about her or just saying he can't understand me. It could be Joe out there, but I don't have the strength to look.

More water is offered, and I swallow as fast as I can. Something small and solid bounces off my teeth, lands in my mouth, and my next swallow hurts bad, like I took down a wooden building block. More water follows, and my body is on autopilot, taking it in, making my raw throat crack like a mud flat.

Water drips down my temples, carving fresh tracks through my skin. Like a fool, I keep trying to look around. The colors swim and dance and move from side to side, bleeding away in a fresh blast of light every time I blink. Greens and purples and oranges slide across my vision. Burned retinas make all the colors shift and swim and mutate, and I wonder if I'm still flying. A cramping pain stitches up my side, my body crying out to get high again.

"Formaldehyde," the voice breaks the silence. "We knew she was giving you Sweet Death. A combo platter. Marijuana and PCP soaked in formaldehyde. Delia throws a couple of other little treats on there too, we don't know what. Psilocybin, maybe? Salvia Divinorum? Opens your brain up. Makes you highly suggestible. If someone's guiding your trip, you'll see whatever they tell you to see. There was nothing our agent could do to help you."

Somewhere, a switch in the back of my brain kicks over and a little engine turns on, draining all of the heat and pain from my head.

"I gave you some Vicodin. Just promise me you won't sue if this fucks you up even worse." He laughs at his little joke.

I try to sit up and promptly vomit onto my chest. He rolls me over to keep my face sideways until the heaves stop.

"Guess we're not out of the woods yet," he says. "Looks like the pill came back up, too. This is going to be rough for you."

Somewhere in the distance I hear the echo of a girl's voice.

***

No more visions. No more dead bodies. Just me, lying on

top of a hill in the desert, watching the clouds fly by in fast forward, watching the sun jump up to high noon and stay. Baking me. Cooking me alive. To call me dehydrated would be an understatement. I'm powdered. I'm dry papyrus. There's no blood left in my vessels, just a long series of windswept, echoing tunnels.

I have legs. I have legs! I lift them up a fraction, a hair's width, and I feel my heel make contact with the floor, feel it in my jaw. My tongue is perfect. My mouth is there. If I could move my arms I could feel my hairline. But I can't because I'm empty.

I'm the ant on the sidewalk and God is up there with his magnifying glass. My stomach starts to smolder, then smoke. I raise my head just in time to see it burst into flame. Gavin pounces on me, out of nowhere, gripping my shoulders and screaming my name, and he's aflame too. We lock eyes, his tears the only moisture in the world, his face cracking like a barbecued hog. I explode with him, mix with the sand, become dust, every particle of me knows only pain. When the sun sets, the wind scatters me, and I lose myself in the breeze.

***

The room is black. My headache is gone. My body feels stiff and sore. Someone is sitting on the ground next to me.

"I think we can move you out today," he says. He strokes my hair once, the way a father would touch his daughter. "I've got a lot to tell you."

The room is bisected. To my left, the warehouse looms dark and empty. To my right, a small white room, no more than fourteen feet wide. Clean and white and devoid of smells and sounds. There's a man on either side of me, sitting in identical poses. In the white room, it's a doctor, but I can't see his face. In the warehouse, it's Hooded Jack, but his face is in shadow, too.

I hear them shift and get up. The doctor glides, making no sound. But Hooded Jack, when he walks, I can hear the spring mechanism in his leg click and straighten. I can't find my voice to call his name.

"Your legs are just across the room. You put 'em on when you feel like it. Come find me. All of the boys know where I am."

He looks at me for a minute, then shakes his head and walks out.

An IV is rigged up to my right arm, a little bottle of Vicodin by my side. My arms feel like Styrofoam, and my hands are numb. My fingers open like the claw machine at an rcade, slow and imprecise, but I manage to wrestle the bottle into submission. I pop a vike, close my eyes and wait. The pain I feel now is miniscule, but I want it all gone, I want a clear head before I stand again.

When I roll over to look at the white room, it's gone, and the other half of the warehouse is back.

***

It's high noon outside and the warehouse is hot as hell. It doesn't hurt to look around anymore. There's dried blood on the floor, probably some vomit and other things I'd rather not think about. My rusty shopping cart on its side. Faint white shapes ghosting in my peripheral vision, up there on the rafters.

I armwalk across the room to my legs. It takes me a minute to get them on properly. I've wasted away here. The thigh cups are loose, sliding enough that I have to cinch the buckles extra tight. There's a black cloth tied to my left leg. I pick it off and unroll it. It's one of the armbands of Hooded Jack, marked for sergeant. A decent starting offer, but I'm not wearing it.

When I feel comfortable enough, like I could run if needed, I check the rafters. Empty. The dead have left me.

I look through the big square of light on the wall, out into the open sun and the heat. Men at work, only now none of them are dressed in drab. Nobody sports an armband. They're all normal-looking dockworkers for some front company. They wear identical smocks, the same jackets and boots. Joe's military influence in everyday working life.

One of them gives a shrill whistle that could stop a hundred New York cabs. "She's up!" he shouts.

The other men give me a quick look and redouble their efforts, polishing and moving and cutting and loading. One of the workers hustles in and hands me a note. He notices the armband I'm clutching, takes a second to count the stripes, then decides I'm not worth saluting. He gives me a friendly nod instead and runs back to work.

The paper is tiny, plain old lined notebook paper, every other word in someone else's handwriting. Definitely Joe's style. Wouldn't want anyone tracing him.

Moving my eyes takes effort. So does blinking, breathing, thinking. If this is being clean, I don't like it. The fact that I'm still alive means one of two things: Joe has a guilty conscience and he doesn't think I'm a threat, or he needs something from me. Or a little of both.

Mrs. Robinson,

Promise not to kill me and I'll explain everything.

Joe's idea of humor.

Details will be shared in person.

I look around the warehouse for a toy. A pipe. A screwdriver. Any kind of offensive weapon. No luck. I kick at the dirt and it hits me. My legs. The release button near my shoe. I hit it and the shoe springs off. The blade is still there, tinged brown with Shakes's blood. I hustle the shoe back on before anyone sees me.

I walk through the doorway into the light and TrevorJack is there to greet me, head freshly shaved. He walks with his chin up, chest puffed out. And I laugh. He asks me what's so funny and I laugh harder. He's the guy from the courthouse, the angry American with a pocket knife. TrevorJack's in the Army now, always has been. Good for him.

He falls a half step behind me. "Here's the important nickel tour," he growls. "Look up. Two crane towers for moving cargo. Snipers on both with a full field of vision. Outdoors, you'll have one of them watching you at all times. Indoors, I'm your shadow. We're a half mile from the nearest facility exit, and there are over four hundred of us on base at any given time. You can't get out. So for your sake, keep the shoe on. I helped him make that leg."

I set my jaw and walk a little faster, think a little harder. I can still do this.

"Don't know what the big deal is about you," his voice is low, he knows he's breaking protocol, "but I've been undercover in Delia's yard for over a year. Deep cover stuff. I had the whole thing worked. There was shit about to go down like you wouldn't believe. I would have been the linchpin to bring it all down. Put Hooded Jack over the top. But somehow, you were deemed more important. I had to pull your ass out of the fire. I wish to God I could throw you back in. You've been nothing but dead weight so far. I don't like anything about you. Not your face. Not your legs. Not your helpless cripple routine."

Walk faster, I say.

TrevorJack moves closer and asks me to repeat myself. For an answer, I flick my thumb into his throat, just enough to set him coughing.

You like me better now? I ask.

We make the rest of the trip in silence.

Amid hacking and coughing and deadly glances, TrevorJack leads me to a small shack out on the pier. It doesn't seem like Joe's M.O. It's a little too out in the open. Two sentinels on either side work extra hard to look like dockworkers taking a smoke break. I can see a bulge in their pants, and not the fun kind. Concealed holsters. 9mm Glocks, most likely. A nice, reliable, easily acquired piece.

They straighten up when they see us approach, one of them giving two sharp knocks on the door. The other motions for us to halt, gives me the once over before patting me down. He takes extra time around my hips and waist, probably making sure that all of those buckles and straps aren't hiding any nasty surprises. Nice to see that Joe's trust for me only extends so far. The sentry works quickly with the gear, loosening the buckles. I feel my thighs sliding inside of the cup, getting raw. I wish I had some socks to take the burn off.

"Legs off, Jack's orders," he tells me. "Need a hand down?"

I twist past him and brace against the wall, lowering myself. My legs roll away to either side. Guess Joe wants a captive audience.

The sentry leans back towards a small window in the door and says, "clear." This guy obviously watches a lot of war movies.

The door swings open and TrevorJack turns sharply on his

heel, motioning for me to enter. The sentry on the left shakes his head. "This ain't the Air Farce, moron. Chain of command, yes. Protocol, no. Who you tryin' to impress anyway?"

TrevorJack deflates, tries to strike a casual pose by leaning against the wall.

"You're not standing post with us either, knob," the other sentry says. "Think you're hot shit since you got back from Delia's?"

"Haul your pencil-necked, pasty ass out of here," the other sentry barks, swinging a kick at Trevor's ass.

—Why don't you stop wagging your dicks around long enough for me to get by? I ask.

This of course, gets nothing but blank stares from all present. TrevorJack finds a spot on his shoe to examine for a while. Then, realizing that there's more of me to see down here, he pretends to bird-watch.

From inside the shack, Joe says, "She's right. You should know better than to have a pissing contest in front of a lady. We're all Hooded Jack. He's back in the fold, so ease up on him unless I tell you not to." TrevorJack relaxes at this, some of his bluster coming back. Then Joe tells me, "Come in and shut the door behind you."

"Should we carry her in?" the sentry asks.

—Not unless you want your eyes scratched out, you no-dicked shit-swallowing pus-eating maggot, I say, batting my eyelashes.

After a beat, Joe says, "There's a true soldier. Come in."

I do as I'm told, not even looking back to see how the man-fest resolves itself.

"Got a lot of retired military working for me. You know, pension isn't what it should be. Problem is, they keep those natural divisions going. I tried to fix it by dividing them in two: Street ops and water ops, Army and Navy. Didn't help. But it did foster competition, so I know they'll bust their asses trying to prove who's best, and Hooded Jack reaps the rewards. Some of the Navy guys decided to specialize. I have a couple of old SEALs out there, some Rangers too.

They're my hard hitters. Long as they don't fall apart or kill each other, I'm happy. You want a cushion?"

I shake my head, trying to subtly scan the room for two things: weapons and a way out. Being on the docks like this, I suppose I could try swimming down the coast to make my getaway. I haven't--

"Stop looking around like that. You ain't Steve McQueen, and you ain't escaping." There's no threat in Joe's voice. He moves closer to me and leans back against his desk. "Prisoners try to escape. You're a guest. Just not the kind of guest that can come and go as she pleases. But let's keep it easy, right?"

A cramp hits my stomach and I flop to my left a bit. Joe doesn't move.

"Did you take your Vicodin?"

I nod.

He shakes his head. "Delia really goatfucked you with that Sweet Death. You can come down from it, but you never get over it. You have to find substitutes. Like it or not, you're a junkie now. Welcome to the club."

He offers me a pill, pale orange, hash mark in the middle. Probably a mild sedative or painkiller. I'm not taking it.

"We found some vials of Clearwater in your bag. How long you been on that?"

I shake my head.

—It was for a kill I was setting up, I say. Was gonna take Shakes out with an OD, that was the original plan.

"I used to count the track marks on your thighs when I fit your legs. Quit lying."

—Better than the morphine they gave me at the hospital. When did you start caring?

"You never told me you had a problem. Anything you don't tell me isn't my business."

—You never told me you were Hooded Jack.

"Anything I don't tell you isn't your business."

—You're still on my list. Why?

Joe goes back to his desk and pulls out a small box. I recognize it. A little cardboard pencil box, the decorations long since worn off. He doesn't need to open it for me to know that inside are three lengths of surgical tubing, two old dull glass syringes, and three vials of Clearwater, probably evaporated. There'll be a fine residue of coke dust at the bottom, a blackened spoon with some heroin tar on it, my family photo taped to the inside of the lid. I used to keep it in my desk. Along with...no clue.

—I gave that to you...

"I know, I was there."

—At...the funeral?

"What funeral?"

—My husband's... Gavin's...

"Your husband? Let's not talk about him. He's half the reason you're in the shape you are."

My heart stops. —Was Dr. Robert my husband?

This sets Joe off like a powder keg. I've never seen him laugh like this, long and hard, his face turning almost purple.

"No...Jesus no. You're scrambled. We could sell your brain at Denny's with a side of bacon and toast."

—What happened to me?

"Do you remember what was in that red case you used to have? The one I tore apart to make a gun case for you?"

—I barely remember the fucking case. It was scuffed up. Beat up, ugly, tough leather. Like me. It's the only reason I hung on to it.

Joe sets the box in front of me and opens the lid, and everything inside has changed. No residue, no dust, no vials, tubes, nothing but a small stack of photos and some papers, neatly folded and clipped together. I burst into tears. It's one thing when the people you're trying to kill lie to you, but it's something else when you can't trust your own brain.

"That was your daughter's."

I don't know what's in my head now, but I can't call them memories. They're not lies. Hints, clues, re-enactments, hallucinations, maybe there's not a word for it. The Germans would have a word for it. They have a word for everything.

Joe shuffles away from me and smiles. "You know what my job used to be in the Navy? I was the guy you never wanted to meet, the guy in charge of DBT. Dastardly, Bastardly Things. I'm about a thousand miles from innocent. I paid for my mistakes. You saw to that. You were the queen of DBT."

—It doesn't make sense. None of it. We used to... I mean, you took care of me, you made my legs, you helped me...

"I helped *me*, too. This friendly chit-chat bullshit...it's not gonna last, all right?"

—I don't know what you're talking about.

"We used to work together, back before we worked together. You fucked me over once. Never again. I've been helping you as long as I have because you were angry and spitting bullets. I had some work I needed done, so I pointed those bullets at some of my enemies."

Is he saying the list isn't even my list? Can I not trust anything?

"We're going to reach an understanding before you go on your merry way."

—But you helped me...you're like a father to me, Joe, fuck! I just want to know who I am...what I am...what have I done? What have I been doing?

"You remember when you first came to my shop? I mean the very first time. Someone tipped you off that I was a good connection for guns. I thought you'd stalked me, tracked me down, ready to put one between my eyes. I was ready to kill you on the spot. Soon as I figured out your brains were mush, I had to make some decisions. But then you started talking about your plans. Showed me the list, which, except for slot number four, has been a tremendous boon to the business of Hooded Jack. Do you remember the first list you showed me? I was number ten. You were supposed to get me first. I helped point you away from Hooded Jack for two reasons. One, I like breathing. Two, you never would have survived the attempt. I've had someone near you every step of the way to make sure you got the job done. Cars on the street. Roosters on their perches, all to see if you still had your old charms. And you lost them all. Not even a hint of your former self. My guys threatened, you hid. They banged up your equipment, you took cover. And rubber bullets? You should have known that's the kind of shit that would come back to bite you. I needed to make sure that you weren't who you used to be. You were trying to protect innocent people. You changed."

My hands tremble, my gut heaves, beyond tears. It's a primal call. Only two things that can fill this void. Since I can't kill Joe, it's got to be Clearwater. Withdrawal, Hell, this is death if I don't get something in my veins soon. Sweet Death, Clearwater, morphine, rubbing alcohol, I don't care.

"Even now," Joe says, "I look at you, and I feel it. I saved your daughter, and in return," he taps his false leg, "you 'helped' me. Took it easy. So this is me taking it easy on you. You don't deserve even the sliver of knowledge I'm giving you today. Take those letters out of the box."

I'm curled on the floor like a puppy that's been kicked around. Joe's not hitting me, but he might as well be. He pushes the box closer, and I cradle it, run my fingers over the lid, around the corners. It's maddening because it should feel familiar, but it doesn't. It was hers. I know it belonged to her only because Joe said so, and my brain tells me so. I know what was in it, but I don't *remember*. I don't feel it. It's so plain, so worn down, the outlines of stickers she put on there, but they're long since scraped away, gummed over, ghosts of her childhood.

I open the lid, stare at the stack of papers. Unfold the top sheet. It's ordered, small typeface covers only the top left corner. This list was made on at least three different typewriters, so I know Joe did it.

10. ~~Vasili~~

9. ~~Susan Schrader~~

8. ~~Grace Brooks~~

7. ~~Shakes~~

6. ~~Caligula~~

5. ~~Delia Sugar~~

4. ████████ *I don't belong here.*

3. Dr. Robert Fortescu *Finish this.*

2. ████████████ ---- *already gone*

1. *Focus on what you know.*

At the bottom of the stack of papers is another small scrap, this one yellow and brittle as a dried leaf. I had mistaken it for the lining of the box peeling away.

"Read it," Joe says.

He takes it out and unfolds it carefully. The paper breaks anyway, and Joe has to lay it out in front of me in quadrants. It's a half-page of handwritten script, smudged and fading, written in a hurry. It's slashed with black bars redacting information like a classified government document, and taped to the bottom is a photo of me in a hospital bed. Tubes going everywhere. My head covered in bandages. The back of the photo says, "Jack, Sorry about that. One for you, two for her! Truce! —D.R.F."

"That was sent to me after you left the first time," he says. "That's what Dr. Robert did to you. And this," he taps his leg, "is what he did to me when he found out I tried to help your daughter. You remember something else on your own, fine, but I ain't telling you shit."

—What else was in this box? I ask.

"You get the answers I give you," Joe says. "You can read what's declassified. Work for everything else."

Great. G.I. Joe is in full battle dress. So I read it, hoping that there will be something inside, some small detail, that kicks my brain over so that who I am now can finally meet who I used to be, and we can catch up on old times.

***

July 13, ██ *–* ██████████ *Veronica Madden is a monster. It's all gone to shit. Susan* ████████████ *tried to* ████████████ *my life,* ██ ██████ *coming back. Veronica finds me, walking home from school, she threatens me,* ███████████████████████ *I believe the stories. What the fuck do you say* fucked up serial killer?

It has to stop. Someone has to stop it. ██████████████ ████████ *if you're reading this, then I'm probably dead or near to it. She's going to track me down.* █████████████ ██████ *the police can't help. Veronica and the Doctor own them. I have to leave what I know where someone will find it.*

██████████████████████████████████ ████████████ *everywhere* ████████████████ *were bodies or kills. If I die, ask one of my friends what my favorite book was. Find the book in the library, and you'll find the answers.*

She always takes trophies. ████ *helpless.* ████████ *mother* ███████████████████████████ *is going to* ██ *save me.*

The last time ████████████████████████ ██████ *told me there was nowhere I could go.*

I needed help. HELP.

She said she'd protect me--

***

The paper is torn away below that line. When I look up, Joe says, "You gave that to me the night your daughter died. That's the truth. Those were her last words. You asked me to protect her and I tried."

It makes me feel warm and fuzzy inside. Tears crest in my eyes. I pray with every fiber of my being that this thing rolling inside of my head is a genuine memory. My daughter was looking for help. She had nobody else to turn to, and I tried my damndest to answer the call. And still she died. And look what became of me. It doesn't feel like penance. I can't find her grave because I don't know her name or how she died or when. But I tried to stop it. Sometimes you can never apologize enough.

"Sometimes you get stuck, and you need help. Something so bad, you'll turn anywhere you can." Joe's finger traces the ridge of the leg socket, and I can't tell if he's lost in thought or if he's talking about me. "You're the only one that can get close to Doctor Robert. The only one he'd possibly let back inside, even if it it's just to see you die. That's the only thing stopping me from killing you right now, because I actually think you can do it. I'm gonna let you walk, just so I can see him die. My dogs will be on your heels. We'll just be giving you a healthy head start. You have to find him and kill him before my crew kills you."

—Why did you mark it out? What does it say?

"You don't get all of the answers—"

—What does it say? What the fuck do you want from me?

"Dr. Robert is still alive..."

—I don't care anymore.

Joe shakes his head. I armwalk closer to him and repeat myself, swinging a punch at his good leg and miss by a mile. He smiles at me and I scream, something primal, fierce.

Pathetic.

"You burning?"

I nod.

Joe reaches into one of the many pockets on his pants and pulls out a small glass jar. From his jacket pocket he pulls a syringe. "I'll let you get off the compound in one piece. Once you get out, you start running and don't look back. You find the Doctor and you take care of him. He dies, you live. I see you again, you're dead."

—Why did Dr. Robert steal my daughter's heart? Why did I kill Vasili? Why did I kill anyone? Who am I, Joe, who am I?

He slaps at my arm, trying to raise a vein. He pushes the syringe through the little rubber stopper on top, and two small drops of Clearwater squirt out and run down the side of the bottle. My old friend, crying to see me. Scolding me like I was a toddler who got away at the toy store.

—What about Veronica Madden?

"Dr. Robert Fortescu took your daughter's heart and showed it to you just before he tried to take yours. He orchestrated the entire night of your husband's death. I have given you one final chance to right that wrong, and you're here fucking around hoping to kill someone who was a bit player in your shit show."

I see my daughter's face, I hear her voice, and it hurts because I don't remember her. Really remember. Who she was, what she meant. What anything means. It just hurts.

And the Doctor is going to feel it. And Veronica. Hurting them won't bring my daughter back, but it will make me feel better. And that's all I want.

When I blink, images bombard me: the Doctor waving that jar in front of my face. Losing my legs, real. Watching my husband burn, no clue. Watching my daughter die... I don't know how it happened, but I was there. I couldn't stop it. Nobody's asking questions about her, why isn't anybody...

I close my eyes as the needle breaks my skin and the temperature in the room drops fifteen degrees and my head empties and my pain stops and I can finally

---

Breathe.

And focus.

Michael Paul Gonzalez

Close by...

    —What did you do to her?

Echoing, somewhere, I'm in a big room...

    —Jesus Christ, I didn't think someone could bleed that much.

    —Get her up to Op-06, I have plans.

    —They're going to need a shop vac to pick up what's left of that Baldacci guy. Cops are all over this thing...

    —You don't tell anyone she's here. You didn't see anything.

    —What do you mean?

And then they're whispering.

—I mean you were not in this room. This never happened. *She* doesn't exist. *She* is not a patient here.

—For my own good, right?

—You have the right idea. Would you like to join her?

…

—Then I suggest you toddle on. You know what they say about finding good help, Veronica…

And then a noise, a whining. Something tearing the air.

Shaking.

Screaming.

Cutting.

Changing...

Erasing...

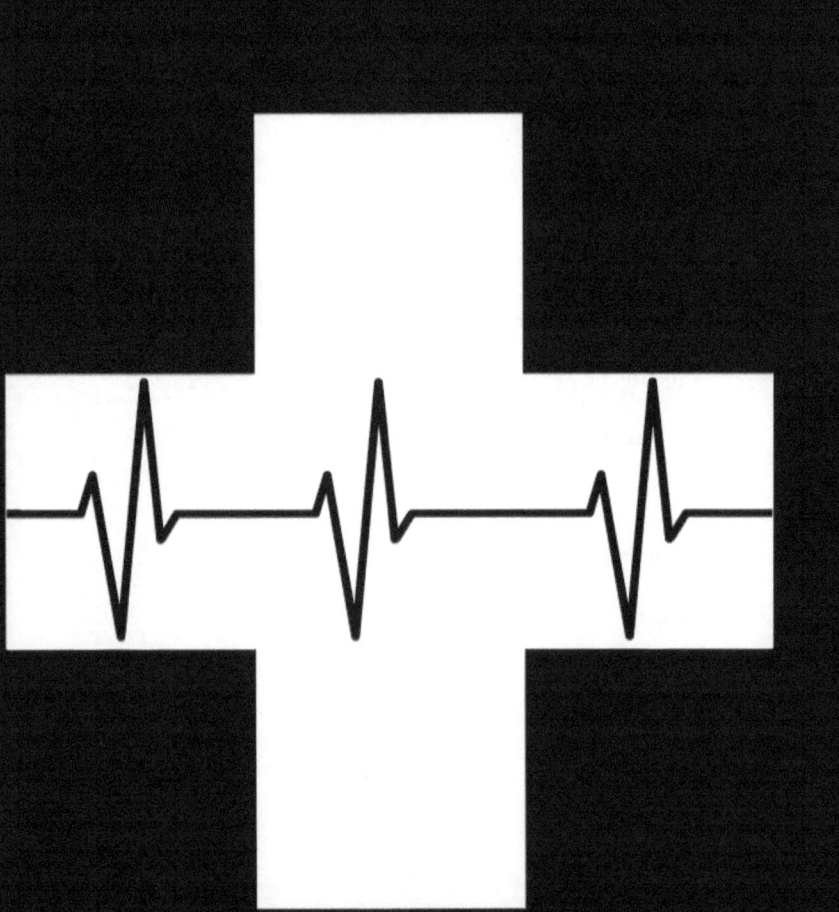

PART THREE

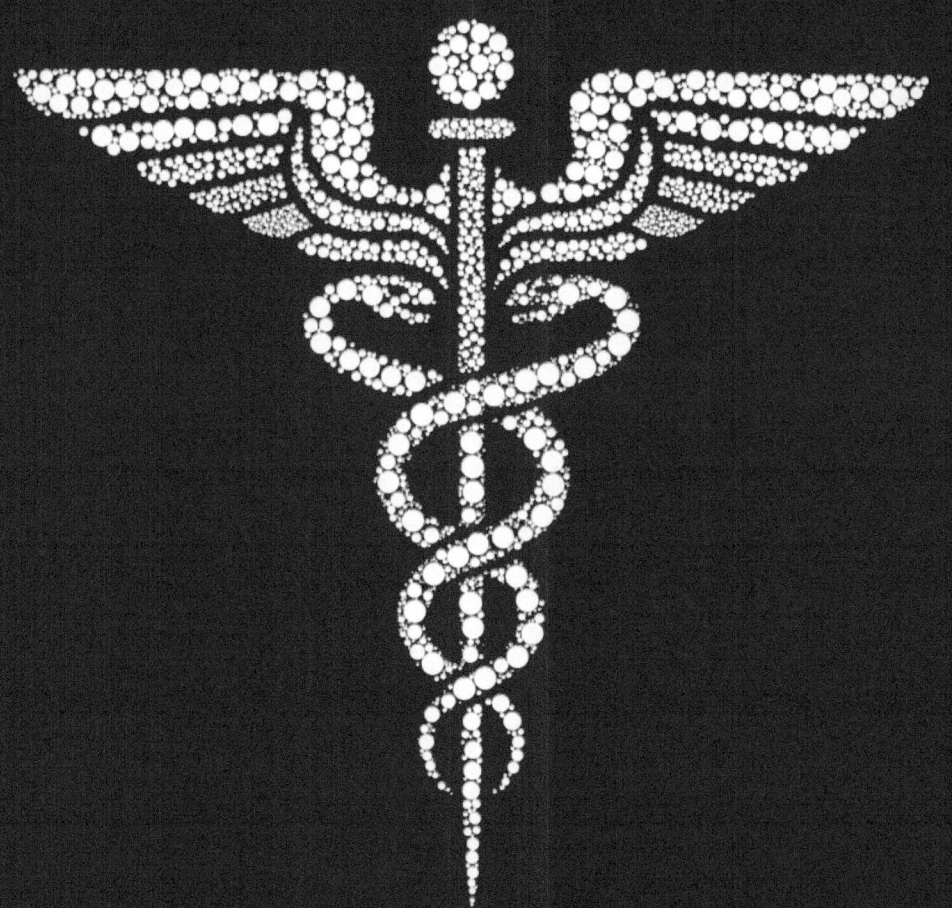

Doctor Robert
and
Veronica

I have a list of ten people who must die. It's all I have. My daughter is dead. My husband is dead. My daughter had something to do with Dr. Robert. These facts do not seem to be in dispute. Joe still needs to die. It can wait.

My current situation comes to me in segments. It was dark outside, now it's light. I'm sitting down, a breeze on my face because my van has no windshield. I'm on the driver's side. The van's moving. They fixed my van? The steering wheel jerks a little and my right hand slaps instinctively for the brake. I find it, and I get the van over to the curb as easily as I can.

Breathe. Focus and breathe.

I have to keep moving. I don't know if Joe set me in here and sent me rolling or if I've been coming in and out. But I remember his chest-thumping, knuckle-dragger macho bullshit. Dogs on my heels. Was I really there? Did I get that close to him? I have to drive. The whole city is after me, swarming me, pushing me towards the Doctor but I don't know if I want to go.

My vision is Vaseline-smeared, blurry, bleeding, distorted. I should park the van and find a different ride. I can't pull over because I might have a tail. The mirrors are all busted off the van from the chase through the city, so I have no way to tell who's back there.

I have to keep the speed slow. Have to find more Clearwater. Have to find the Doctor. Veronica. Hooded Jack. Number one.

I feel like I'm in the passenger seat watching myself sobbing big, slimy tears. I want my husband. Or my daughter. Someone to hold me. Something normal. It doesn't have to be right, just normal. But I'm too far gone, destroyed, hacked, slashed, wilted and withered like a dead flower—

Frances!

I just need to talk to Frances. No research bullshit, just to talk, like he always wanted. I'll tell him everything about me being a radiant flower and he'll wrap me up in a big, fat, greasy, sweaty hug. Bury me in his folds; smother me in his body odor. Contact. I just need one fucking piece of contact.

I pull away from the curb, waiting for a rifle crack, waiting to feel my head explode.

I'm going to the library. I don't want to be a murderer anymore. I don't want to know anything, no more discoveries. I want to be in a place where everything is order, linear, numbered, safe, quiet.

I blink, a half a mile gone, and I don't remember any of it. Is it raining or am I crying again? I rub my thumb against my scarred jaw every few seconds, just for proof. Just so I know who I am.

The library is up ahead, parking lot empty. Yellow lights on the outside struggle against the encroaching night gloom. I pull the van into my favorite corner, a handicapped spot near the door, covered on one side by shrubbery and around a corner from the main entrance. I feel a couple of drops of rain on my shoulder as I make my way through the doors.

There he is, behind the counter. Frances. My Frances. This would be the part of the movie where they cue the music. My heart melts. He's got his broad back to me as he files away a couple of papers. I do my usual, sauntering up to the counter and tapping twice lightly with the palm of my hand.

Michael Paul Gonzalez

He starts, that little jolt of tension running through his body like he's trying hard not to wet his pants. I know Frances has been excited to see me before, but never like this. I can't help it; I stretch my arms towards him. I think I'm crying. I must look slobbering drunk. He won't look at me. Something's up. He looks guilty.

"We're closing up," he says, avoiding eye contact.

He spins on his heel and walks to the far side of the counter, pulling up the partition and trying to make his way to the back room. His cheeks glow bright red. I can feel the heat of embarrassment coming off of him.

"Hey," I say, knowing it's one of my best words, and since it's one of the few I've ever said to him.

The sound of my voice is enough to get him to stop. His hands scramble in his pocket like a terrier chasing a rat down a hole. Racing for his keys. Eyes looking anywhere but at me.

"I wann you gee ngai frreeen. Fansss." I want you to be my friend. Me from a week ago would punch me now. Blubbering, simpering, mess of a--

"I can't help you anymore," he answers. "You should go."

"I ngeee yah heeerlk. Yurrall I gah ngow. I wann all skahk." I don't care if I sound like a drooling maniac. My last friend in the world is turning his back on me. Well, close to friend. Whatever. This hurts.

"Clees."

"I know who you are," Frances says, finally finding his key. "I know what you did."

He wrenches it in the doorknob, turning hard, trying to open the door repeatedly before the lock even trips. The glass vibrates with each attempted thrust, and finally, he coordinates key and knob and makes it through. I've had enough time to get over to him. He hears me coming and tries to shut the door, but I get my leg in the way. The door slams on my metal knee joint. I grab it and say, "Ow!"

Which is enough to make Frances feel like shit. He opens the door, and he's stuck. Should he help me? Should he close the door while he has the chance? His chivalry wins out. He takes a hesitant step into the room, and I grab a fistful of his shirt, leaning back and dragging him down to the floor.

—Who am I then, Frances, you fat fuck? Huh? Who? I'm your friend. You're my only fucking friend in the world and I hate your guts. You don't know the first fucking thing about me!

Which comes out unintelligible, coating his face in spit.

—I'll tell you who I am. I'm a woman at the end of her rope. I'm a woman who wants revenge for something, but I don't know what, who wants to make amends with her daughter, but I don't remember who she was, who wants to die to be with her husband, but live to punish his killers. I'm also a woman, Frances, you moron, with no knees. No knee joints means no *ow!* I'm full of shit! I'm a lowly piece of sewer scum and you *still* don't deserve me—

I go on like this for a bit. Frances starts screaming for help. But, like he said, it's close to closing. There's maybe a couple of homeless people in here, nobody who will hear or care. I locked the door behind me on the way in, just like Frances showed me for my late-night study sessions. Good ol' Mrs. Robinson, the hard-working student. Least Frances could do to help her out, right?

"You kill people. You kill people!"

Frances is hysterical. So I slap him. It's enough to jolt me back to my senses. I'm losing it. It feels so strange to think it, even stranger to know it in my bones, but there it is. I am going crazy. It's not a notion. Not drug related, not anything. I pull back, trying to raise up so I can get onto my feet. I feel a stiffening lump in Frances's pants. Are panic boners a thing? I rock forward and slap him again before rolling off.

Watching Frances try to stand up is like watching a baby horse take its first steps. A very large horse, but nonetheless...

—What do you know about it, Frances?

Frances isn't talking. He's going into shock. His eyes scrunch up, his body is tense, as if he's expecting me to take him down on the spot.

It's late, he's been working hard, he's tired. Jesus, how the hell could I get all of that across to him? I speak slowly, and I'm pretty proud, because the words come out coherently:

"I'm nah gunn herr you."

At this, Frances squeals a little and pushes further back into the wall, as if he hopes to fade through the plaster.

"Fannssess," I try again. "Errfnng's fokk ukk. Donno wuss wonng wiff ngee."

"I saw you on the news. Coming out of the garage."

"Whukarajj?"

"You're on the ten o'clock news because you were at the garage the night Susan Schrader got killed."

I slump to the floor. "I wuzz in ngaygerhoog, reesrk, rikeoo seg."

"One of the people you shot, she started talking in the hospital today. About someone with no legs. The cops think it's a man...but it was you, wasn't it? You researched the garage where she was shot. You researched the soccer field where Grace Brooks died. Am I going to jail?"

Rubber bullets. Like Joe said, the kind of thing that comes back to bite you in the ass. And they had surveillance on the sidewalk outside the building. Nothing I could do about it.

Frances's bottom lip is moving like a jackhammer, and I don't know what to say to make it better. How do I explain that I'm a hero? How do I tell him that I'm doing the right thing?

"Are you going to kill me?" Frances asks.

I stare at him. "Ngo. Why wuh I?"

"I always thought you were so nice. I used to take care of you when you fell asleep in here, made sure nobody bothered you."

"I ngee yurr hewllk." I'm kneading the front of Frances's shirt with one fist, tugging at him. He's got to make this right because I don't know what to do anymore.

"You should go," he whispers.

I start to cry. I try to hug him, dig my fingers into his fleshy shoulders, pull him close, but he scrambles away.

"911," he says.

"Ngo, don' goo dat, Fanns. I ngee you gee my frenn. I ngee you—"

"I called when I saw you walk in. They're offering a reward. They weren't...I mean, it's not that I think you're guilty, but, if you were, I mean...please leave. Please just go before they get here."

My knees go weak. What a fantastic sensation. I stumble back into a chair, the weight of my false legs jerking me around as they splay out before me. I don't have the strength to stand anymore.

"Rewarrh?" I whisper.

"I don't want any trouble. I don't even want the money, I just don't want you here. Go now. Maybe they won't find you..."

"You wahn Rewarrh? You gig ngee uk frr a fugkn..."

My arms fold around my middle, and I feel a lump in my stomach. Hardened steel. For a moment I think my heart has turned to stone, sinking fast. But it's my gun. I stay doubled over as my fingers close around the grip.

Frances paces in small circles, watching the windows, looking for flashing lights and sirens, and I know he's going to have a long wait because I know this town. Informant calls get investigated during the day while the vermin sleep. Nobody's coming for him.

My arm goes up faster than a hockey goalie making a save. Gun leveled, right at Frances's big water buffalo skull.

"No...oh no, what are you doing, why why why?" Frances's face is blackberry jello, deep purple, quivering.

Michael Paul Gonzalez

He sold me out for a shitty 1-800-TIPS reward.

I hate him.

I love him for helping me.

These decisions can be so hard.

Frances, his eyes are big, black watery blobs, face flushed, lips quivering like freshly unearthed worms. He's already given up.

I take aim at the side of his head.

I hear a voice, and I know it's me, saying "Frances wouldn't say anything. He wouldn't rat us out to anyone."

And I reply, "You know it's not true."

Maybe he'll die of a heart attack before I have to make the decision. I want to tell Frances that this will be okay. That this way, nothing will hurt him. People are following me, bad people, and they'll hurt him. This way, he'll be safe, and there won't be anybody to run from. People should have more control over who hurts them.

"Leave," I hear myself say. I don't know if I'm talking to him or me.

Frances hasn't done a damn thing wrong, probably not in his entire life. As much of a slob as he is, being annoying is not a crime. His heavy breathing hasn't changed my life for the worse. And yet. And yet...

I leap over to him, jamming the barrel of the gun into the side of his head hard enough to draw blood. My hands are on the gun, steadying it. Rock solid. He's shaking, crawling on the floor, looking for his glasses.

Please don't try to put this moment in focus, Frances. Just close your eyes and resolve to try harder next time. Hold your breath like I'm doing. Exhale and let go. Exhale as I squeeze and don't pull.

My eyes close and then open. Sight. Acquire. I feel the massive weight of the gun buck in my hands.

My mind is at the edge of an ocean, and I only hear the

breakers and the gulls. He was scared, sure, but nobody can hurt him now. I've given him all the protection I could. I did everything I could. The right thing. And on the edge of consciousness, I hear my voice, laughing, saying, "Good girl...good girl."

I did the right thing. Ask me again in five minutes, in three hours, in a month, a year, whatever. I'll say it again: I did the right thing. We should all be so lucky to meet Death and see a friendly face under the hood. Maybe Frances spent his last minutes asking himself why I would do such a thing. Maybe he was glad it was me and not someone else. That'll work.

I'm too scared to move, expecting the police, or Hooded Jack, or someone to come bursting through the door and pepper me with bullets. It doesn't happen. I'm laying across Frances's body, rocking back and forth, looking at the ceiling. Like relaxing on a big, dying, bleeding cow waiting to become a leather sofa.

My face is wet, but I don't feel the crying. The stink of his blood and the gunpowder is like smelling salts, jolting me. I breathe it deeper, get my nose right in that crater and take a good, long pull. I want to feel something. It's only when Frances starts his death twitch that that I finally get up. His mouth opens and closes softly, and I swear he's saying,

"Neat. Neat. Neat."

I don't remember how I got to the parking lot.

I yank open the side of my van and crawl onto the back seat.

Maybe I'm screaming, maybe I'm not. The gunshot is still echoing in my skull.

Fifteen minutes ago, Frances was alive. Always there for me, always ready to grab a map or a picture, anything for me. Delicate flower. I hit the driver's side window with my hand, shout, open and slam the door. Eventually, my hand starts to hurt. Now I can hear myself, hear that I'm screaming and crying, asking why Frances had to die, and I still can't feel it. The answer is, I'll never know the answer. None of it makes sense anymore. People get mixed up in things, and they don't even realize it, and there's only one way out. Getting up, going to work every day, doing the right thing, that's not the kind of thing you do and live to tell about anyway.

Time to drive. Rolling over the armrest between the two front seats, I spot it on the floor. It looks like an old straw, chewed up and folded. But it's salvation. A hypodermic. Used, obviously, but there's something in there, a drop or two, and anything is better than nothing. I pull it from the floor, tendrils of congealed soda syrup and God knows what else trailing behind, primordial. My Excalibur. The needle is blackened, sterilized over a lighter once, maybe more. The tube's not bent up too bad. The plunger looks like it'll last at least one more use.

But where to deliver?

Such a small portion, it needs to go into the bloodstream quickly, needs to go right to the heart or right to the head. I clench the syringe in my teeth as I loosen my belt, tasting old ashtray and rotten caramel, asphalt and beer. And then I realize I don't need my belt.

I simply need to change direction. Turn the needle inward. Lift up what's left of my tongue and probe in the dark, hope I find that fat juicy vein. I scrape under my tongue lightly, a certain tenderness will tell me I've reached the right spot.

The first two tries don't feel right. Flaring pain, burning, but it doesn't feel like a vein. But the third time, as they say...and when the plunger goes down, I forget what they say. My mouth is all spark and fire, my teeth are aluminum grinding together, my gums drip acid.

My tongue swells, but that plunger isn't down all the way yet.

Every drop. I want it all. It hurts because I haven't tried hard enough. It's painful because I haven't earned my salvation. It feels like there's a marble under my tongue-skin, an insect's egg, a scarab. I fold in on myself, my brain exploding into nothingness. Everything is blue sky, crisp woods. There's a sound outside, dim and distant like the call of birds in the treetops. A fluttering of wings. Or is it clapping? Or is it three street soldiers slapping on the back window of the van, pulling the door open, shouting to one another?

Shadows rise above me like mountains, moving, jostling, reaching for me. Weaving in between them, like a ribbon of light, like an aurora, I see a girl. The way her hair is pulled back. The shape of her ear, her jawline. My jawline. Well, the one I used to have. She turns around to me, and says, "I'm not here."

I've been looking for her for so long. I was supposed to save her, and here she is, my daughter, my… my…little ███.

God, I can't even remember her name. Even now, starting at her, staring at whatever this is. She's not there. She's there. She's not a little girl anymore. She's a teenager. That age where you love them and can't stand them. The roommate who contributes nothing and is still your everything.

"Straighten up, you bitch. He took my heart," ███ adds. "And thanks for trying to 'save' me."

She scrambles over the headrest and latches onto my chest, pries at my mouth, claws at my eyes, and the burning in my head is out of control now. I bite down hard and feel the syringe still in my mouth, the needle still jammed firmly under-tongue, blood, lightning, the plastic slowly weakening, giving way, the taste of what's left inside adding to the blaze.

"Swallow it," ███ says.

She hits my stomach, pries at my legs, dancing through my muffled screams are echoes of a voice saying something about cardiac arrest. Someone else says seizure. Someone else says I'm faking.

I open my eyes and I'm in my van, which is now wrapped around a light pole in a neighborhood I don't recognize, and there are men surrounding me.

██ crawls down my body, punching and prying, pushing a hand up my pantleg, digging into my thighs, forcing herself up and through, first just a finger, and then her hand. The whole time I'm crying, begging, *I brought you into this world, I brought you in, and why are you doing this?* Then she's climbing up and up, a reverse breech birth, my body spasms again and again, and I want to check for blood, but there's no sense in it.

██'s gone. She's gone. Back from whence she came. Is this withdrawals? An overdose? A psychotic break?

A chorus of voices surround me, a religious experience, all of them shouting, Jesus Christ, Jesus Christ! The world spins, my head snaps around and I vomit blood.

One of the men has me down, loosening my shirt. Tapping my cheek. Trying to keep me conscious. The sky turns dark, and it looks like rain again. Thunder claps, five solid, ground-shattering explosions, and the first few warm drops hit my cheek. Then it stops. The thunder rings off of the streets, like the fading echo of several handguns going off at the same time. Rough hands haul me up and toss me across the back seat of someone else's car.

Faces swim across my vision like melting candles. They're kids. All of them up there, high-school delinquent joyriders. The one staring at me looks a little panicked. He slaps me.

"You're making this difficult," he says.

"You better not die," another voice calls. "Do not let her fucking die in my car!"

"You got a fucking set of heart paddles in the trunk?"

"Don't get smart with me, asshole!"

"What the fuck am I supposed to do?"

"We coulda called 911, you know!"

"We just smoked 911. Mission is paramount. Jack wants her delivered to the Doctor."

Through slitted eyelids, I see the boy next to me, his cheeks splashed red, genuine concern in his eyes. I start to rock in and out of waking consciousness, as the boys try to stay cool, even going so far as to talk about chicks and cars and useless, trivial shit... Every few minutes someone nudges me, says to keep an eye on me, don't let me die, whatever.

Then I'm floating up and up, holding against gravity, hard to breathe. My face starts slamming into something soft, rhythmically. Something bony jabbing into my stomach – a shoulder? I'm being carried. We jog for a few minutes until I'm thrown down on a bench. No, a gurney.

A sea of faces. I'm propped up, pushed away from the boys who watch me fade down the hall. We stop in a small room. Everything is too bright in here. I hear a man muttering to himself, dialing a phone. There's a pause.

"Sharon. You know the Doc always told us to keep an eye out for his prize? His... his fucking *prize*, Sharon. I got a lady here. No legs. Ugly as fuck. I think she's the one. Call him now. Tell him there's not much time. I'm getting her up to O-Six."

Back down the hall, back out the door, past the boys again, their faces puzzled. One of them asks where we're going. The man tells them I have to be transferred to a different facility. But I know what's happening.

We're heading back to the Doctor, and there's nothing I can do. I have no legs and I must run. I have no jaw and I must scream. I have no weapons and I must kill.

My heart is slowing down. When I blink under the harsh lights, my eyelids go translucent, I see my blood flowing, little rivers slowly stalling and drying out. Then I'm in the hollow dark of the tent again, drifting past Delia Sugar, past Joe, and my water breaks.

There are burning cramps, horrible prolonged strains, and something moves inside of me. My lower body is exploding. Something's coming out, and there's no way I can do this, no way to deliver whatever it is.

My stomach distends, stretches, my pelvis cracks, my thighs spasm out sideways, and still the pain won't stop. Even here, in my unconscious, I have to close my eyes against the pain. A balloon full of rusty nails, a salt-covered gunny sack of razor blades. Doesn't quite do the pain justice, but it begins to give an idea. There's one last swelling, one huge jolt, and it feels like everything inside of me is broken and burned.

I open my eyes and her silhouette fades into a slit of light on the wall. She spins, staggers and falls. She's saying she's my daughter, it's me ███, it's me mom, please...

On another plane of reality, someone grabs my face, performing mouth to mouth. Shouting that we need to put on some speed and get to the Doctor.

Behind my daughter, I see another slumped form, one I can't quite make out. She's telling me I don't understand anything about the Doctor. She hates me. I understand.

They're out there fighting for my life.

My daughter takes a step towards me, and suddenly she's in my arms. I hold her, tell her everything's going to be okay. Nobody's going to hurt her again. It's better this way, because she won't feel any more pain. I'll make it better. I'll make it all better. She doesn't have to haunt me. Just go away. Just go.

And she does, dissolving through my fingers, letting out one short, sharp scream before leaving me alone in the dark.

Michael Paul Gonzalez

XXXII

I wake up in a clean white room. I think it's a men's room. I'm on a job. I don't have any legs. I'm here to kill someone. I'm pretty sure. I'm sitting on a toilet dressed in full field gear, a heavy flak jacket making it difficult to balance. I lower myself to the floor.

Everything is spotless and pristine. Three stalls down, a pair of feet, pants rumpled around the ankles. I think that's my target, so I should probably just kill them. I reach up to my shoulder, fingers finding a carbon blade, light and lethal. I slither slowly across the floor, towards the shoes. My other hand moves to my shoulder strap, pulls out a Glock-9, and I keep belly crawling, never breaking stride.

Simple plan. I don't know if this guy's expecting me. So I'll slide in hard on my back, a quick stab through the foot as a distraction, then a shot straight through the bottom of the jaw. Job done.

He can't be expecting me, because nobody takes a dump this way. He's not moving at all. Not a top-tap, no breathing, no grunting. No smell. I'm right outside the door. I inhale, hold, visualize the plan, keep my breath held. No noise to give me away.

I move. My wrist snaps up and back, driving the blade clean through the right shoe. If he screams, I don't hear it over the rustle and clank of my equipment as I slide in to deliver the death blow. The gun is up, clean and straight, and my finger squeezes and the shot takes out my hearing. I close my eyes, waiting for a body to slump down onto me, or blood. I get a light dusting of plaster instead. Did I miss?

There's nobody up there. Nothing in this stall but an empty set of prosthetic legs, my knife planted into one shoe like it's claiming the land for my country. I pull myself into the stall completely. Someone had to have heard that. I'm compromised. They're all onto me now. They'll be here soon.

I'm dead. I'm dead. I'm dead.

I need to hide. Might as well go up. Problem. How to climb up onto a toilet that has no lid? The little horseshoe seat isn't sturdy enough to use for leverage. I could just pull myself up, but I don't think I could balance on the lip of the toilet very well.

I've got to get a little wet, I guess. I hook my fingers around the cold porcelain, pull myself up, and the little electronic eye on the wall triggers. The toilet flushes. I watch the vortex of water swell and disappear.

Mrs. Robinson, this is your life.

Just a little higher...my hand slips and plunges into the cold, murky water, but at least the bowl looks pretty clean. I jam a finger, but it's not my shooting hand. It takes everything I have to spin around and keep my balance on the seat, and there, just inside the stall door, is my daughter.

"Mom, you're a mess," she says.

My synapses take a five-second vacation, except for my left hand, which grabs at the air in front of me. She fades away, but I see her smile a few times when I blink.

I bat at my pockets, finding a bent-up, faded syringe, toothmarks in the middle. No good. I look between my legs, into the toilet. It's clean and clear. The faint smell of chemical. Maybe it's Clearwater. Maybe. I'm not about to drink toilet water to find out. With my daughter standing there staring at me from the inside of my eyelids, it doesn't seem like such a bad thing.

Michael Paul Gonzalez

All I can do is wait. And wait.

Finally, she fades completely, her features swimming up and over my eyes, recessing back into my brain. A reminder. Sometimes you just need a reminder to keep you moving. The bathroom light pulses fluorescent to red-purple to blue-green, a kaleidoscope of colors in rhythm with my heart. Someone stops outside the door.

Cramps bend me in half and I flop down from the toilet, hard to the cold tile floor, twitching. My legs are on fire, a twisting pain, wooden stakes pushing through fresh, fleshy soil. I look down to see two freshly sprouted legs, pink and rough and shiny, like something a starfish would grow after losing a fight. I feel my face, all putty and cold cream.

I try to stand up, but the new legs are made of jelly. They melt through the floor and I slide down until what's left of me makes contact. The bathroom door opens and a man dressed in medical scrubs enters. He's faceless, literally, just a big, misshapen lump above the collar. I drag myself out of the stall and into a corner, pressed in hard, kicking a warning with phantom feet. The man moves another step closer to me. The mirrors here run floor to ceiling, playing our little dance in stereo. Seeing our frozen reflection, we look like something you could pick up from any hack artist, some anguished coffee house soul by the beach. Half a woman cowering in the corner, a faceless man menacing her.

I punch at the air, feel it resisting against me, hear it shatter like glass.

I frisk myself looking for anything, some way to keep fighting. Where did my gun go? Where was that knife? I paddle across the tile and yank the knife out of the prosthetic foot, holding it before me. My last line of defense.

My head still buzzes. The colors in the bathroom follow the sound of the dying fluorescent light by the door. A faint hum, whining up and down, the light makes everything excruciating.

"We'll have you back soon," he says, his voice high and lilting in the black fog. Then his face resolves, and I've seen him somewhere before, but I can't remember. A little blurry circle floats in front of his face, like he didn't give the camera crew permission to use his likeness.

He makes a move towards me, and he says, "Stay with us," he says. "Veronica and the Doctor. So much to do, so much to discuss," looking right at him, his mouth is still, phasing in and out of vision.

When he takes a step towards me, I flinch, except it wasn't the man in front of me. It was the one next to me. In the mirror. I blink.

The mirror is lying to me. I don't see me. There's a girl holding something, a shard of broken glass, her hand wrapped in a towel. She's crouched in the corner, pale and green, one knee bent up in front of her. In front of this girl, there's an orderly. The whole room is tiny lime-colored tile, floor to ceiling, three toilet stalls, this girl, and the orderly.

I look in front of me. It's Doctor Robert Fortescu. When he moves, the orderly in the mirror moves too. When I draw back from him, raising the knife higher, the girl in the mirror slams back against the wall and copies me.

This is why they tell kids not to do drugs.

"How did you get out of your room?"

And then the Doctor, under his breath, says, "Fucking junkies. Look what they've done to you."

The orderly says, "Nobody needs to get hurt. Put it down. We can't have you running around."

And Doctor F says, "People always try to convince themselves that higher price doesn't mean higher quality. And they're wrong. You will tell me who gave this to you. Later?"

My head swims with insects, hundreds of tiny pinprick legs moving across my forehead like an expressway. In the mirror, the pale girl tugs hard at her hair, eyes bugged out, the veins in her neck and head pulsing like worms beneath soil. She lowers her knife a fraction, and the orderly takes a step forward, so I raise my knife again. And the girl in the corner holds out her jagged glass knife.

Michael Paul Gonzalez

I've had enough. I drive the heel of my hand into the mirror, spiderwebbing the bottom corner of the little hospital scene. The orderly is still there in the reflection, and Dr. Robert is still here on my side, but at least I don't have to look at the girl anymore. I only see her legs and hands at the fringes of the cracks. So of course she starts screaming.

Doctor Robert reaches a hand into his pocket slowly. "Quiet now," he whispers.

I close my mouth and the girl in the mirror stops screaming too. The orderly says, "Did you take your meds?"

In the cracked glass, three or four reflections of myself, my face beet red, my shoulders heaving from breathing hard. I think that's me.

"Murk," the Doctor says, "is what piss poor white trash make in their trailer house bathtubs. Knockoff Clearwater. There's no real way to tell the difference between my products and the counterfeiters', not taste, smell, texture, buzz. But my merchandise has no withdrawal symptoms. I have long-term customers. Nobody else does, because nobody else cares."

Even though the Doctor is three feet away from me, I feel his hands on my arms, my neck.

"Was it Delia Sugar who gave this to you? You may never recover... But fret not, for it will not go unpunished."

My heart pounds so hard that it feels like someone's kicking the side of my head. The room swings with every heartbeat. There's a pain in rhythm with my pulse. I realize I'm hitting my head on the wall, and it hurts, but I don't stop. In the mirror, the girl is on her hands and knees, using her head as a battering ram, trying to break through into my skull. Trying to make a connection.

"Horrible withdrawal symptoms. Paralysis. Hallucinations. Extreme mood swings. Unchecked aggression. Delusions of grandeur. False memories. Stroke. Irritable bowels, the list goes on."

In the background, in the mirror, the orderly calls for help on his radio.

"This," the Doctor continues, "is going to sting a little bit."

He withdraws his hand from his coat pocket holding a syringe wrapped in sterile paper, and a long needle. A looooooong, cavity-piercing needle. Between his pinky and ring fingers is a small ampoule with clear liquid inside.

I see the shape of the girl behind the crack in the mirror, her feet flailing, her voice racked by sobs like a whale trying to sing out of water.

My head lolls forward. My knife is on the floor in front of me. I don't remember dropping it. The Doctor takes the opportunity to jab the needle into the side of my neck and push the plunger in. It's so long it feels like it's traveled up my carotid artery into my head. I feel the tip scraping the edge of my spinal column.

"I never forgot you," he breathes into me. "First do no harm. But second…"

My eyelids flutter as the color in the room races through the visible spectrum. Before my vision goes, the pair in the mirror is joined by two burly men in brown uniforms, security. They rush the girl.

Everything goes white. The light at the end of my tunnel.

The security guards saying, "Calm down. Stop fighting us. Relax…"

The girl screams, "I killed Charles Baldacci! I killed Susan Schrader! I killed Grace Brooks! Justice! Justice!"

And then I'm gone.

***

I remember happier times, when my family was…

I really don't remember anything from the good days. Nothing anymore. The days with my daughter, bonding over a…a what? I've been telling myself the whole time that all of this was for her. She's been all that's kept me going. But I haven't really thought about her.

Charles Baldacci was guilty. What did he do to ██? What the fuck is my daughter's name? Why wasn't he on the list if he was guilty?

Damn. Damn. Damn.

I'm only able to turn my head slightly to the side, and even then, my vision isn't clear enough to see anything beyond the spiderwebbed crack I made in the mirror. Still in the bathroom. But maybe it's not a bathroom. Maybe those are other hospital beds and not stalls. Maybe those are IV stands, not antique water tanks.

Two feet move in the mirror. Above the paper slippers, a pair of knobby ankles and some basic hospital pajamas. It's me. My name is fill-in-the-blank, and I am an addict. She, me, crouches down and puts her hand up to the cracked glass. Her eyes are filmy, faraway and lost.

"Remember this?" she asks.

Her face isn't very clear, but even so, her jaw is scarred, her hairline is jagged. I'm afraid to answer or ask any questions. Whatever's holding this vision together could shatter and blow away.

She runs her hand across her face, feels her hairline, mutters, "Ashes to ashes..."

She holds a little card in her hand, a picture of a man on it with a hazy border. Done in simple black and white, two dates at the bottom, beginning and end. In between the years, there's his name, or it should be there, but I only see ██████████. So maybe his name isn't Gavin after all.

"Charles did it," she sings. "Charles Baldacci took everything away. He got what he deserved. Not my fault. Not my fault."

"Doctor Robert said he could save her," she mumbles.

A muffled voice calls from her side, in the hall, "Calm down."

"I never touched her!" she screams in reply. "I was there, you weren't there, you sanctimonious..."

"Stop it!" the voice screams.

She slumps to the floor, next to me in the mirror, her voice barely audible. "Baldacci did it! Not me. Not me?"

That is me in withdrawal, coming out of something, sweating toxins with every pore, my skin sallow and rubbery. And this is me in some strange room, my skin pasty, the last remnants of whatever the Doctor gave me binding to my system. Or are we in the same place? Is the mirror simply a membrane separating two single-celled organisms the verge of merging?

I think my eyes have dilated. If this mirror was working properly, I'd see two deep black pits in my skull, swallowing every drop of light.

Her head rocks forward and she spews a litany of half-spoken words that I can't understand. But in the hall, her hall, there are more voices.

"Any change in her condition?"

"She's got a lot left in her system."

"Has he decided yet?"

"He has what he needs. He's going to operate tonight."

At this, the girl's head snaps up.

"No!" she barks.

And I mean *barks*. Over and over, and then she starts throwing herself into the mirror, near my face. I try to scramble away, but my arms only flop around, boneless, striking the glass in the same spot she does, so I can't tell if the new cracks are from me or her. She's kicking hard. Keys rattle in the door, hers or mine I can't tell, someone fumbling to get inside.

"Orderly! Orderly!" a voice shouts in her hallway.

She parrots it with each kick, *orderly!*

The door opens, and a man in a pale-brown uniform skids in. The glass bows out above me with every kick the girl lands. If she's trying to get out, she'll have to hurry. Security will be on her in three steps. She spins and throws a table at the guard, then takes off full tilt for the wall. Straight at me.

She jumps, the soles of both of her feet racing toward my face. They hit the wall, the mirror, and explode through. The glass holds, but reality shatters for a moment and she's broken in. Her legs bicycle in the air until the security guard seizes her shoulder. A split second later, her legs, the legs in the bathroom with me, bend backwards above the knee with a vicious *snap*. They land in my lap, cleanly severed, no blood. In the mirror, a shape fills the doorway, a tall man in a long white coat. I know him. He preps a needle. Charges at the girl, telling security to hold her down. I swear the Doctor is smiling. And then the light becomes too much and I have to squeeze my eyes tight.

When I look again, the mirror shows an orderly row of stalls, or beds, and where the girl's legs - my old legs - would have landed, are my legs. My metal replacements.

A clean room is just a space waiting for a mess to be made.

XXXIII

Saint Something-or-Other.

Saint Jude's?

That'll work for now. Saint Jude's Hospital for lost causes. Or rehabilitation. A turn-of-the-other-century brick-and-mortar monstrosity that health officials gave up on long ago. This was where poor people came for government-funded treatment. Very little regulation and no oversight. It was closed as a public medical facility in the late 1980s, then sat vacant until the city started using it as a drug treatment triage center. It became easier to throw junkies into locked cinderblock rooms and let them out after a week than to jail them. The police department also started using it off-the-books to hold low-level criminals and suspects. One day, in an election year - surely a coincidence – concerns were raised about public safety and human rights, and the whole facility got shut down.

The empty facility was eventually bought by an investment group, which was made of one person: Dr. Robert. Now he had a way to launder his money and widen the scope of his operations. It sits on the fringe of the Breeding Ground, ostensibly a warehouse for medical equipment storage. Those are the lower floors. Nobody asks about the upper floors, where Dr. Robert still checks in select clientele. This is where I've woken up.

My lips are gummed together, and I've got cottonmouth. But I know this is real now. Call me Alice, because I've come through the other side of the looking glass. Who says drug-induced hallucinations can't be helpful? Withdrawals have gone and my veins are scrubbed painfully clean. Everything started and ended here. My second life. My daughter's life. I used to bring people here. These walls are like frosted glass doors to me, and I can see the shapes of memory lurking on the other side.

Everything swims in blue-green light and my mouth tastes like burnt metal. My thighs drum fast on the floor, hands clutching at nothing. Something seizes my neck and flips me over, ramming my head against the ground, picking me up, doing it again.

Oh, it's just me.

I'm having a seizure. It feels good, another affirmation that I'm alive. Footsteps pounding across tile, some shouting, and then someone pushing their knee down hard into my chest, holding down my arms, trying to hold my head still.

A few more jolts and I'm done. Every heartbeat feels like a small explosion in my temples. My blood travels in long slow waves from my heart through my chest, up my neck, into my head, down into my hands, feet that don't exist. Rusty water sloshing through empty pipes that have outlived their usefulness.

Someone is asking me if I'm okay.

An orderly moves in, pushes back the men who were holding me down. One of them helps me sit up as the others escort everyone out.

"Fuckin' junkies..."

"I think she's awake..."

"Who gives a shit, she can't understand me..."

"Tell him if he wants to see her, he better hurry. She ain't gonna last..."

"He told us to keep her alive. That's our job."

Their voices fade down the hall, and my eyelids are pulled back, my mouth swabbed, my wrists plugged into an IV. Clean needle. But my veins are like overcooked pasta, big, fat, floppy and ready to break apart.

Alone again, in a paper gown, defenseless. The door to the room is remains open. What little sound is in my room washes out the door, trickling through the empty halls. When there's nothing, when it's so quiet that I can't even hear my heart beating, his footsteps approach.

He turns the corner, a vision in white. Crisp white pants, white vest and jacket, white latex gloves, white outdoor coat, white hair, white beard. Always so sterile.

I try not to give him the pleasure of seeing that I'm scared shitless, but the smile on his face tells me he knows. He's the kind of guy that always knows.

"How's my favorite patient?" Dr. Robert asks.

I say nothing.

"I'm off duty, business to take care of in the city, but I thought I'd come say hello... Same room, you know," he says, looking around. "It's been repainted since your last visit. We had trouble getting the bloodstains out."

He reaches into one of the big pockets on the outside of his coat.

"I brought you a note," he says, moving to the far side of the room. "I'm going to set it on this table over here, and when you're well enough, you come and read it."

He starts to walk away, then stops and goes back to the note. He pulls something small and white from his pocket, holds it up. It's rounded, triangular.

"Remember this? I got the idea from a little boutique store by the highway in the desert. They tumble rocks, polish them, engrave inspirational words on them. I think they're intended for those suburbanite Zen gardens. Who knows? But, I do like the idea. This one says *Motivation*." He sets it on top of the note. "I have another just like it holding some things down on my desk. It says *Retribution*."

I start to ask him what his plans are, but I don't want to give him the satisfaction of hearing my voice.

"I almost forgot," he adds, moving quickly to my IV.

When he gets close, my hands jerk up, and I can't tell whether it's to protect myself or attack him. I'll never know, because my wrists are restrained to the bed frame. The Doctor looks at this and smiles.

"Wouldn't want you to hurt yourself," he grins. "I'm sure your stomach is just burning right now, your muscles probably feel dry as jerky. I'll take care of that."

He pulls a small syringe from his pocket and adds it to the IV pickup tube.

"A little Clearwater to ease your suffering. Pure, by the way. I've added a few new ingredients. I usually don't do market focus groups, but do let me know how you like it. Your dreams should be quite pleasant. I'll have the restraints removed while you're out."

He goes to the doorway, stopping by the little table with the note. "Don't rush things. Last time you were here, you wound up hurting your knee," and he taps the paperweight for emphasis.

He looks at me, no smile, just a blank predator's stare, for a good minute. He wants to make sure I understand. That's my kneecap on the table. He has the other one in his office. He keeps trophies. I just barely notice that he has a necklace on underneath his collar, small white stones strung together. Those could be my toes.

He leaves, and the noise slowly trickles back into the room, hospital sounds, intercoms, squeaky shoes on the floor...lights buzzing...heart beating...sheets moving like rip-stop nylon like...light forcing its way into my eyes and blinding me from...

Nothing.

***

There's a battered sign at my feet, a little hand-embroidered thing. It says:

"Declare the past, diagnose the present, foretell the future; practice these acts. As to diseases, make a habit of two things—to help, or at least to do no harm. — Epidemics, I, xi."

I step over it carefully, through a doorframe, and into a dusky room with boarded windows. A table sits at the far end, chipped pressboard top and shiny steel legs, with a woman lying on the top. I think she's naked, but she's covered in a blanket, and she's in pain. The Doctor hovers around the table, still dressed in white, but now he's not as clean. He looks at me, tells me, "You're not too late."

I don't feel any fear as I approach him. I'm not sure who the woman on the table is, but she's definitely pregnant. Her wrists are bound by nylon cord that's stretched under the table, her legs are chained down.

Fortescu pulls out a wicked-looking jigsaw, shows it to the lady. "I sedated her so we wouldn't have to deal with the screams. But look at her, you can still see it in her eyes..."

He strokes the woman's forehead, smooths her hair back. "Don't worry," he tells her, "you'll get to see your baby before you die. Better early than never, right?"

He moves the saw close to her belly, pushing the tip in ever so slightly, and the woman's body goes rigid, convulses. Her eyelids flutter, and then she's gone.

He throws the saw down to the floor. "Damn it! Almost had it that time." He removes his surgical gloves and tosses them on the woman's face. He checks her pulse. "Heart attack. I wish I'd have had the stethoscope on her. To hear that explosion!" He laughs, his eyes are wild, "How's the father?"

"Dead," I hear myself reply. I pull a small camera from my pocket. "I got some real Kodak moments. I'll have Shakes make some prints. You want matte or glossy?"

I can't believe any of this could have happened, but part of me knows it did. Part of me knows I was there.

Michael Paul Gonzalez

Interrogating. Asking questions. It's one of the things I used to be good at. I could make anyone talk, given the right tools. Joe was right when he called me the queen of DBT.

"Smile," I tell the Doctor, and he wipes a hand through his hair, leaving a blood smear on his forehead. He poses above the remnants of the mother on the table, the valiant hunter, and I snap away.

We share a laugh.

"Burn that print," he says.

"Of course."

And the room fades to dark, lights flashing red to black, which I know is the blood flowing behind my eyes. I'm still alive. I'm just out of it. Just a sidetrack, a temporary thing.

When the lights come back, I'm in a different room, everything orange, the furniture, the light bulbs. Two men sit on one side of a big orange transparent plastic desk, and the Doctor sits on the other. One of the men is in a form-fitting tailored suit, and I recognize him as Big C, in his Pompidou phase. The Doctor looks resplendent now, his white suit reflecting the light, making him look like the Sun King of the Underworld.

Making a deal, carving things up. Parts of the city go to different people. I've walked into the middle of this meeting, and the men aren't too happy about it. Pompidou throws a fit, screaming, pounding the table, his accent difficult to decipher. In his novel, he called this kind of talk "FauxFrench," which is what he used when talking to the media. "HoFrench" was for the girls. I remember all of this because I had a run-in with Pompidou, tried to discuss his politics in the un-friendliest terms possible. Neither of us enjoyed it much, he less than me.

His right arm sports a cast wrapped in purple velvet. The one he called his "pimp hand" for "keepin' them in line." I ask him how it's healing and he sneers at me. I tell him he should call it his bitch hand, because he hits like a bitch. He's up and out of the chair, going into his suit pocket for a gun, but the Doctor stops him with a simple gesture.

Fortescu asks me to wait in the hall. Private meeting, he says. He smiles too politely, in a way that tells me perhaps I was the topic of *conversation. The kind of look your boss gives you when he knows you only have a week left before he fires you. He asks me again to wait in the hall, then goes on talking with Pompidou, which means he's no longer speaking to me.*

I step back, sinking into the wall, plush orange velvet. I rock back on my heels. The fabric turns liquid, viscous, sucking at me, pulling me in, embracing me...

***

I break the surface of a still pool. Cold air on my face. Above me, a negative night sky, bright white with black dots where stars should be. It's a tile ceiling. Lights blazing on me from two directions, and I can't see anyone else in the room, just silhouettes.

"We must keep you clean," a voice, the Doctor. "Bedsores, infection, all common problems."

I'm determined to keep my silence until speaking can gain me something. Right now, I'm not sure. There are questions I could ask, should ask. Something in me knows the Doctor, knows he's waiting to hear something, the wrong thing. Right for me, wrong for him, or vice versa.

"Your face is still dirty," he says, approaching me.

His fingers splay and rest on my forehead, thumb just under my nose. He pushes down and I submerge. I didn't have time to draw a full breath. My body's in panic mode. When I thrash, I feel my arms tied to the sides of the tub overhead, my waist anchored to the tub floor.

I don't think the Doctor wants me dead. Not yet. But he's not letting me up. He wants something from me.

I'm drowning, have been for months now, probably years. Soaked, always soaked because the rain never stops.

Blood vessels burst in my right eye. My chest spasms, my lungs push out old air, desperate for something to keep me going. Anything.

Above, I feel an IV needle inserted into my wrist, something dripping in, my body going ice cold. Muscles screaming, my body going hypoxic. Stealing oxygen.

My heart slows, beats grow heavy like a series of slamming doors, the lights going out after the crew has cleaned up and everyone's gone home.

Maybe I'm still underwater, maybe they've pulled me out.

"I just don't have the heart for this anymore. What shall I do with you?"

Picture my brain as a structure, a Japanese paper house. Four separate rooms. I can build more if I need them, and I can visit whichever I please.

Room one: my body. My organs strewn about, connected to the whole structure, plugged in, fully powered. Make sure things stay this way.

Room two: all mirrors. There's too many of me here, but I can bend them, rearrange them until I recognize the person I see. There's fewer mirrors now than earlier in the week. The floor is strewn with broken bits, and I realize I've been looking down at the shards instead of inward at the whole glass.

Room three: a library. Books line the walls. No Frances here. I know these books, the stories of my life. I'm writing them. Every time I learn something I can add to these books. I can go back and re-read, edit. Make everything make sense. I just need to get them off the shelf.

Room four: a window. I look out onto the real world, where the Doctor is with my physical self. He's got me on a drip, gives me drugs to keep my motor running, then pulls the rug out, lets me start to crumple. He can probably keep this up for days before my body gives out.

Out there, he's talking to me about all of the things I've done right. Thanking me for what I did to Vasili. He was afraid he was going to have to farm the work out. But, he says, I am ever his trooper. Most people, when they get fired, they move on, find new things to do with their lives.

"I'm not done yet," I tell him, and strangely enough, he gets it on the first try.

"Oh, I hope not," he says. "For once, I'd like to be proved wrong. My guess is, there's a limit to what the human heart can take. A little string tying emotions directly to vital functions. You wind the string too tight, it snaps, and that's that. I want to find out if it's possible to kill someone by breaking their heart."

"Sure," I tell him. "Why not?" I add. Then, "What the hell are you talking about, anyway?"

I retreat behind the glass, listening to his voice, slightly muffled, his lips moving just out of sync with his speech.

"I want to walk you back through the halls of your mind."

"Is this about my daughter?"

"This is about a lot of things."

I look out from the room in my mind, forehead pressed against the glass. I decide to rise for another question. The window sloughs like water, my face just breaking the surface.

"What about Veronica Madden?" I ask.

"That's funny," he says, then pauses. "I thought I was asking the questions here. She'll be along."

He draws a needle from the table next to my bed, and I feel the walls in all four of my rooms buckle. My little house is about to implode. He pushes the tip into the IV chamber, then pulls it back out without pushing the syringe.

"I don't think the gentle approach is doing you much good,"

he says. "Let's be direct."

Something hard and cold bites into the side of my neck, and the rooms in my house wring around each other, trapping me inside, looking out of fractured glass into the physical world. The Doctor withdraws his needle, and everything I am drains out.

***

This is not quite hypnotic suggestion, not quite dream study. I don't know how the Doctor is doing this. Not quite pulling strings. Just directing my mind to drive as he sees fit, but it's all real.

First meeting:

It comes in flashes. I'm set up on a high building, gripping the gutter with my right hand, rifle braced against my shoulder. A little puff of air, the gun hardly jolts, and a tranquilizer dart slams into the base of Joe's neck. He slumps over. I shimmy down the building.

Inside. I haul Joe up onto a table. Jam a stick wrapped with twine into his mouth. Slap him awake. Drop my toolkit onto the floor next to him, find an outlet, get to work. I haul out a circular saw, an acetylene torch, a leather belt, chains, cuffs.

I run the chains under the desk, spread eagle him and clamp him in. I wrap the belt around his leg and crank down hard, and Joe gets uncomfortable, even through the drug-induced haze. He wakes up when I plug in the saw and give it a good rip. Just the hum of that steel blade in the air. His eyes go wide as saucers.

"Jesus, no," he says. Or tries to say, but the stuck muffles his speech.

"Housecall," I say. "You've been a naughty boy and the Doctor is not happy."

I let the saw rip. These were the kinds of things that were best to do in one clean stroke, like killing your dog after he's gone rabid. Don't spend time dwelling on it, just do what has to be done.

It's astounding the amount of blood that spurts from his leg. His femur is tough, and the saw jams at least three times before the cut goes through. I throw the saw down and get to work with the acetylene torch, my cauterizer.

"It smells like a fucking barbeque in here," I tell him. I give him a shot of morphine, just to unclench his heart. Keep him on this side of consciousness. Let him feel the hurt.

By this point he's bitten through his gag. He's on the edge of shock, and he's muttering, almost to himself.

"Whatever you think I did to the Doctor, what he's doing to you is ten times worse," he slurs.

"This isn't going to save your life. The leg was just part one. For him. Next one's for me, payback for the bullet you put in my shoulder."

"She came here once, you know? Looking to score, throwing your name around like it should mean something."

"Who?"

"Your little girl," he smiles.

That's enough to stop me.

"What do you know about it?" I ask. They all talk, they always do. Even in a state like this, just to stop you. Anything to save what little you leave them. I'm here to kill him, not to listen, but I haven't seen ▮▮▮ for days, which partly explains my mood.

"She works nights at Pompidou's. You know that? You know the Doctor sends her there, right?"

"Are you lying to me?"

"If I'm lyin', I'm dyin'... well..."

I'm supposed to take some parts of Joe back to the Doctor tonight. This was Doctor Robert's first attempt at seizing power in the Breeding Ground.

Even though it means I'll probably suffer the same fate as Joe, I need to know. ▮▮▮ is so distant, so gone, and this... if I could fix this... take back what was mine. Even though I'm a monster, I'm a mother too. The thought of Pompidou and my daughter. The Doctor and my daughter. Betrayal like this is unacceptable.

"If you're lying I swear to God I'll come back here and make a fucking jigsaw puzzle out of you."

He's passed out. It was an empty threat anyway. I didn't expect him to survive the night, let alone live to fight another day. Just in case, I pick his cell phone from his pocket and speed dial the last number he called, figuring it had to be one of his guys.

"He's bleeding," I say into the phone. "Working late is a bitch."

I uncuff his ankle, pick up his leg, lug it over my shoulder like a softball bat.

I wonder what I ever did with that thing, anyway?

Second Meeting:

Joe's workshop, tucked into a corner. I still have my legs. Joe is down one, hobbling on a metal pole. I'm leaning back against the wall, watching him work, loading clips, checking sights, preparing.

"This is fucked," he says. "I should kill you."

"Likewise," I reply. "We're both being thoroughly unprofessional here."

"So?" His fingers are a little unsteady, fumbling with the last of the rounds he's pushing into a banana clip.

My fingers drum on a little box next to me. I hand it to him. "This is why you should trust me."

It's the little pencil box. He opens it, pulls out a picture. "This your girl?" he asks.

"She was four there. Happier times, and all of that bullshit."

I sift through some of the other photos in the box. Show him playful pics of the Doctor and I dissecting informants, torturing the wives of heavy hitters, making our presence felt. He could turn this evidence over to federal authorities, the news media, knock Doctor Robert from his perch with one shot. But what I care about the most are her pictures.

"I'm giving her to you. I know what I did to you is fucked up, and I don't expect you to forgive that easily, but don't take it out on her. I'm trading Doctor Robert's life for hers. Here's the address. Get her out of there, get her back here. If I make it out of this, I'll disappear with her. If I'm not back here by morning, send her somewhere safe."

"You trust me?"

"Would you trust me if I didn't give you this?"

"I still don't trust you."

"You retain the right to kill her if I don't come back. Or, you could give her that box, the money that's in there, and get her on a bus out of town."

"She got family somewhere?"

"Anywhere's better than here. She's a smart kid. Keep the Doctor's men away from Pompidou's. Keep her safe. Then we're Even-Stevens."

"Bullshit. You still have both of your legs. We're a long, slow boat ride from even."

"You're still breathing and your organs are intact. Besides, if this works out, the Doctor will be dead. There always has to be a king of the hill."

"Or queen?"

"I'm tired of it. I'll be on that bus with my daughter tonight if it all goes right. And then it's Hail to the New King, baby."

"And if it goes sideways," he says, "you'll be dead."

"Or worse."

***

I think they're moving my gurney.

I want that box back. Photos. I kept trophies, too. But my boss just happened to be a high-profile medical professional in the city, and I never burned a single print. Frugal me, I always saved for rainy days.

My heart skips and stutters, purple lightning blossoms behind my eyelids. The Doctor's voice echoes around me, consuming me. My pupils dilate and vibrate with each noise he makes. His voice is my entire existence.

"When you wake up, I simply must show you these EKG readings. Fascinating. I think we're getting closer. Building some good crests. We'll see if we can't crank it up... Where to go next... Vasili made sense. Shakes. Caligula. Hooded Jack. But Susan Schrader and Grace Brooks? You take things so personally..."

I feel my bed incline, folding me in half, sitting me up. The Doctor is at the foot of the bed, holding a mirror. Even by my own standards, I look atrocious. My right eye is a mess, my pupil deep violet in a sea of crimson red. My skin is yellow, my cheeks sallow, and I may have lost another tooth.

"We'll build to your daughter," he says. "This is a gauntlet. A little taste now, see if you can take it."

A single tear rolls down my cheek at the same moment my left nostril begins to bleed. The front of my hospital gown is crusted with food or vomit or both.

I wonder if he knew these things about me before my life disappeared. Maybe I'm talking in my sleep. Maybe he doesn't know anything. It's just me versus my brain. A gauntlet.

He leans the mirror forward, making my reflection sink into the bed at my feet. "I'm getting bored," he says.

***

"I'm getting bored," my daughter says. "We never do anything fun."

We're sitting in the parking garage of Susan Schrader's office building.

"I can't exactly take you to the mall and movies," I tell her.

A car pulls up across the lot.

"He's here," my daughter says.

Michael Paul Gonzalez

"Two weeks?" I ask.

"Can we skip it this next time?"

And my heart breaks.

"Why?"

"It's almost prom. I should be hanging out with my friends, not in some shitty apartment...no offense."

"Two weeks," I say, and it's not a request.

I stare at her, and she has no answer. She steps out of the van and jogs across the lot to the other car. The man inside give me an imitation of a friendly wave.

So that's how it is now.

Far away, I hear her voice say, "Hi, Dad."

And my heart breaks again. Something falls out of her backpack as she climbs into his car. I try to call out to her, but they pull off quickly, not even a glance back.

I get out and walk across the lot, trying to watch their car as it enters traffic. They're in there, talking, laughing, having the time of their lives. I'm a speck in their rearview mirror.

I get to the parking spot, catch a faint whiff of his cologne, fooling myself that I hate the smell. At first, I think she dropped a pencil box, but the shape is wrong. It's a little pill box. I open it, and what's left of my heart turns to powder and blows away.

A syringe. A tube. Two small vials. Three orange pills in a little baggie, the face of Janus neatly imprinted on top. It can be such a joy to discover what has truly made you angry.

I hop back into my van, slam it into drive, and redline it for the hospital.

***

"This is very serious indeed," Dr. Robert tells me.

This is still from before. I have my legs, and I'm boiling mad. I've just spent the last twenty minutes telling him what my daughter's been doing with his product. I want names. I want his sales force lined up against a wall. I want blood.

And all he's giving me is his ten-thousand-watt smile.

"Get him in here," I shout.

"He stopped her from buying some very bad product. You know he wouldn't force her to do anything untoward. Heaven knows he has enough girls to keep him entertained—"

"I can find him," and I start to leave. "He's dead."

"No. I don't think I can give my blessing on such a thing. Besides, she's not yours anymore. You're divorced now. Single. Move on. Live it up."

"I don't need your blessing."

"I believe Adam and Eve said the same thing and look at what happened to them..."

"You wouldn't understand," I say.

And he touches my cheek. I'm boiling. I draw a gun from my waistband and pistol whip his ribs. I raise the gun up, ready to smash his face.

"Cracked rib? You can still be seen in public with that," I tell him. "Leave her alone. Get her out of this. Or else I give the media something to talk about."

"Good help is hard to find. You have been more than good help to me, and that's all that's keeping you alive now. You need to leave before I change my mind."

I use my free hand to smack his ear. His hair goes wild, white shoots standing up everywhere. "I'm done," I tell him.

"Yes, indeed," he replies.

"This is all done," I tell him.

"I'll only ask you once to reconsider. And of course, you will

Michael Paul Gonzalez

have to pay your pound of flesh."

I spit in his face.

"Oh, say it isn't so," he sneers.

I walk out of his office. I'm dead. Rule number one is never cross the boss. The Doctor never forgets a slight. If I stop now, go back, let him take a finger or a toe, he might consider us even.

But it's my daughter. It's him or me. By quitting, I've issued a silent challenge. The part of the movie where one cowboy tells the other the town ain't big enough for the two of them.

I storm from the hospital, stopping only to yank a directory from a phone booth. This has to happen fast. I check the address for Surplus Military Warehouse. My second stop. First I have to go to the police.

***

"Sometimes I wonder what's in that pretty little head of yours," he says. "Sometimes I'm tempted to have a look."

The Doctor lays scalpels in order on my lap, small to extra-large. I'm restrained.

"This is all about remembering," he says. "Even for those who never forget, a memory can grow dull, lose its sheen. Sometimes we need a sharp reminder."

Before I know it, he's got a small blade jabbed hard into the bottom of my right thigh, drawing circles.

"Do you remember this? Stay with it. Feel it. This can't kill you. I can't kill you. You know what it's going to take. You know..."

And my screams echo and fade off of the tile walls, reminding me of a time in an alley when sirens came. When I was sitting in the rain, the weight of something awful on my shoulders. I needed help, and maybe the police could have helped. But they didn't get there first. It was an ambulance.

They cleaned up the scene. Baldacci. The Junkie. Me. All of us in the back of the van, riding to the hospital on the last night of my last life. This is what memory feels like. This is the beginning of what I've been fighting for. I'm ready to give up.

Sometimes when she'd get to her bedroom, she'd slam the door so hard that the whole house shook. When I would go knock on the door, she would say something like "Visiting hours are over," and I would leave, tail between my legs.

So what made this time different? Why did I stay? Because the Doctor was going to make an example out of me, which meant he would make an example out of her.

"You're not supposed to be here. You're lucky Dad's at work, or he'd — "

"Something bad is going to happen tonight. If you're not going to come with me, you have to promise me you'll go somewhere. There's a safe place where people will watch you--"

She tells me to fuck off.

"Then don't open the door for anyone. I'll see if I can have someone come here for you."

She tells me to fuck off, and I can feel the acid from her voice spray across my mind.

"I have a gun," I tell her. "For you. If you're going to stay here. It'll be here, just outside the door."

Then her door flies open so hard the report of it against the wall makes me think the gun misfired. She blows past me down the stairs, tossing a litany of curses over her shoulder.

I don't understand.

I'm not a good mother.

I don't care about her.

If I did...

If I did...

Her right arm swung heavy with the gun, how she picked it up that fast, I'll never know. Her eyes tell me she doesn't want to shoot me, but her body is rigid. I made a move for her, from the top of the stairs. Her arm came up and her finger squeezed. I knew the safety was on, but still I ducked. And slipped. And tumbled down the staircase. I rolled over in time to hear the door hammer closed, heavy and hollow.

Later, I paid a visit to Joe, Jack, whatever. Because someone had to protect her if I couldn't. And the only person I could trust was someone I'd once tried to kill.

Before that meeting, I had to take the direct heat off of her. That meant a meeting with Pompidou.

***

"No amount of sorry weel 'elp you," Pompidou frogs at me. "You are, how you say, screwed, non?"

"Cut the Frenchie shit. I'm not here to apologize to you. And I'm not trying to tell the Doctor sorry either. We're going to come to an understanding."

"Ze semm way you try to understand weeth moi?"

"It's not like I tore your arm off. Stop whining."

"What em I supposed to tell eem?"

"I'm the one that's kept his closet clean these past few years. If he lets me walk, I'll promise not to talk about him, about you, about anyone. It's in your best interest to help me. If he disagrees, things will get violent."

"Ah, non."

"Ah oui, French Crepe. You tell him you're handing me over. You leave my daughter out of it. He'll come for me, she'll get out of town, and that's it."

"Zat's eet? You'll be dead."

"One of us will. You just stay out of the way when the bullets start flying, maybe you'll get to move up the food chain, huh? Tonight. You name the place and I'll be there."

"Midnight under Satan's Inkwell." His accent is gone now. "This will never work, you know."

"What's the worst he could do?"

***

The last drive to Red Light.

My ex-husband was an undercover cop, and I knew he was working this district. I needed his help for this. Not that I expected him to take the risk, but if there was ever a reason for him to be on my side, it had to be his daughter. This meant an ungodly amount of apologizing on my part.

The Chihuahua girl is in the car. His car. And I know what's happening in there. I see how he treats her, how he smashes her head against the window when she either won't leave or asks for more money. He dumps her on the sidewalk, and I want to chase him down. But Chihuahua girl is in my way, grabbing at me. I ask her if she knows where he was headed. When she doesn't comply, I hit her.

Beat her.

Punish her for my mistakes. She grabs for me and I hold her forearms, tearing long, nasty gashes with my fingernails. She jabs me in the eye with her thumb and it makes me fight harder. I only stop when Delia's other kids come to her rescue. I didn't want to do this over the phone. I wanted to say this to his face. I wanted to see if there was still some caring in there. For me, the family.

Instead, I drive lazy circles around Red Light, trying to remember his beeper number, then dialing it again and again until my phone almost runs out of power.

When he calls back, I tell him we need to meet at Satan's Inkwell, half an hour before midnight. He knows what's going to happen. He tells me I should just take ███ and get out of town.

I tell him Doctor Robert, inadvertently or not, tried to get ███ hooked on drugs. He took something from me, from her. Is that not enough to get my husband to act? Nothing could stop me from making this meeting. After tonight she's safe, and one way or another I'm out of your life. He's trying to kill her. We have to get her out. Gavin asks if I know what this could do to him.

I hang up.

***

Feels like my right eye is gone, the socket stuffed with wet gauze. Everything below my neck is fuzzy static. It's going to be a long-distance call trying to talk my hands into doing anything. The Doctor is at the foot of my bed, surrounded by some of his "orderlies" and "nurses", street dealers, dressed in white, as is his standard. They examine a chart; he's teaching them about injection points. One of the nurses notices me, silently touches Dr. Robert's arm to let him know I'm awake.

"That'll be all," he says, and they filter out until it's just me, him, and one nurse.

Her body is hazy and bright, like a soft-focus scene from a '50s romance. Shirtsleeves rolled up to her elbows. Matching sets of four angry cuts run the length of each of her forearms, puckered and red. Thick black stitches stop the flesh on her arms from unraveling in the breeze. Her fingers dance over a small pouch on her belt. Too small for a gun, but there must be something in there she's dying to try on me. Her exalted position, being the only one left, leads me to one natural conclusion.

"Orientation and training," he says. "I cater to a higher class, so those that sell for me must be able to instruct clientele on the most efficacious injection techniques. Different sites, different highs. Nobody else gets to see you. Just like last time. But this time, I'm not letting you go."

I raise a hand to my face, surprised that he's given me this much range of motion, but everything tingles. Not pain, not pleasure, just discomfort, panicked nerve endings sending out distress signals that nobody's answering.

"How's your memory? Seeing things nice and clear in there?" he asks.

I don't answer. I worked for these memories, not him. I refuse to believe--

"Things blurry out here? Your eye was terribly infected. Veronica..." and he reaches his hand out and she comes forward, opening the pouch, giving him a bottle of eye wash. I feel artificial tears, cold and sterile, pouring into my skull in my good eye. "Let's get you good and strong, make sure that heart of yours is healthy and pumping. See how tough it is. Today, if you tolerate your injection, I may let you move around, get a little exercise. Supervised, of course."

Ever the humanitarian.

This is the part of the movie where the lady loses all hope. I'm too weak to kill myself, I have no legs, only the reassurance that I may know what it all means just before the Doctor kills me. And what will I have gained?

The Doctor fills an eye cup with a faint blue liquid from a different container. When he lifts the patch from my eye, I see nothing, no light, no shape. There's a vague smell of sweat and something else. He flips the cup quickly, the liquid swirling down into the toilet-dead socket. It goes down like an ice-cold steel rod into soft mud. I hiss.

"My, my!" the Doctor exclaims. "That worked better than I hoped."

I close my good eye and colors explode inside my head. It feels like what's left of my bad eye is circling the drain, ready to drop through the hole and push its way into my brain. All I can do is hurt. I can follow that pain, chase it until it tells me something.

***

Satan's Inkwell is busy with drunken twentysomethings, lost and looking for an excuse to do something bad. They're too busy with their own games to notice me. But the players notice. The connected men who line the shadowy walls, ring the pool table, they all stop what they're doing when I enter. Just long enough to look me over. They know why I'm here, and they're trying to size up the situation, see where they should place their bets.

I'm not giving them much to look at. I've got a simple white dress on, a little clingy, but it's the best way for them to think I'm not packing anything. Why bother? I knew it would be impossible to fight my way out of this.

In the back corner of the club, there's a booth, slightly elevated, out of sight. The side walls are one-way glass, so whoever sits there can see the whole club without being bothered. Not whoever. The Doctor. He's the only one who sits there.

As I approach his table, a hand reaches from the shadows and pulls me to the side. I feel a whisper in my ear before I really see her.

"Dear, you shouldn't have come tonight."

I look at Delia's face, ancient and ageless, smooth as burnished leather.

"Let this go. You won't leave here alive. Let him have her, and at least you both live."

I try to push past her, but she stops me again. Her eyes dart quickly to a door at the back of the room. There's a short line of men waiting. The door opens and two guys walk out, refusing to make eye contact with anyone. They look guilty. And sated.

"He'll have her working that shift every night for the next year. Probably make you watch for a week before he kills you. And then he'll finish her off. Think."

Michael Paul Gonzalez

"Not gonna happen," I say.

"Yes, I heard you enlisted Hooded Jack to keep her safe."

"What do you know about it?"

"You were looking for a way out? This is it. Make a deal with him. He keeps your daughter, alive, and you leave town."

"That can't happen anymore."

"You're opening the cage of something that will eat you alive. Nobody stands up to the Doctor. It isn't done."

"Everything's impossible until it isn't." I push her aside, making my way deeper into the room.

Pompidou stands up from his booth near the corner, the whole room goes on edge. His stupid little striped sweater, his stupid tight pants. He moves right next to me, places an arm gently on my waist as if to dance.

"Ah can mek zees all go away..."

I try to move away, but he counters, stays with me step for step.

"Zere is no reason we cannot all coexzeest--"

He whimpers when I lock his wrist discreetly with my thumb and forefinger and twist. A hiccup now and I could shatter some bones. "English," I say.

"Bitch!" he hisses. "Fine. For all anyone knows, this could be a big misunderstanding. You could be here to visit the Doctor. You make a deal. He told me you wouldn't even have to apologize. Nobody rocks the boat, we go back to square one..."

"Do you think he's watching us now?" I ask, knowing the answer.

My right hand pistons into Pompidou's chest, driving the wind from him, crumpling him to the floor. "I'm not here to make deals. I'm here to buy time and die."

Across the way, my ex-husband is just sitting there watching. He wasn't here to help me. He's pissed I'm here, but he's afraid to make a move yet. He doesn't know what I have planned. Or he just thinks the Doctor is going to snuff me out without so much a wink in his direction. No way he's ready to commit suicide by pulling that badge, ready to take a beating so that I can have a few extra seconds, some time, any time, to get this done. Which is just fine with me. Except...

Behind me, the smash of a glass bottle, Clarabelle making his move. I lock eyes with my husband...ex-husband, and he smiles. His eyes are hollow, the eyes of a corpse.

Just before Clarabelle connects and drives the half-bottle into the soft underside of my jaw, I manage to scream, "He's a cop! This is a raid!" while pointing at him. His hands go up and he tries to shrink into his coat.

Everything blooms into searing white before fading down to red, and I'm running for the door, pushing my way into the alley where everyone is already at work on my ex-husband. Pounding, kicking, pouring gasoline. Guess they found his badge after a not-so-gentle frisking. Complete and utter chaos, because if there's one thing that would draw more heat than a turncoat, it was a cop.

This is the kind of fight where an ambitious young thug could slip a knife into the Doctor just to have a story to tell. That's all I wanted. I just wasn't counting in getting my face rearranged by Clara-fucking-belle.

I'm feeling the beginnings of a full-grade concussion coming on, trying to work my mouth to scream, hampered by the cone of glass planted there. So much blood on me. My husband looks like a side of beef at the butchers, stripped and bloody. I don't feel too bad.

The Doctor's car is across the way, men circling defensively, trying to hold a corridor open in the swelling mass of humanity so the Doctor can get to his car and get out safely. That was my window. That was my chance and it's disappearing.

I stumble, fall, flail. Men surround me, ready to destroy me for the Doctor. And then the fireball goes up. My husband roasting alive, screaming, burning hot enough to consume the bloodlust. Everyone stops to watch him burn. Some cheer, others move to put him out and are beaten back.

His voice lingers, still screaming, echoing off the walls behind me.

Calling my name.

Veronica.

Veronica.

Veronica.

My name is

***

"Madden," I hear it in my mind, not a whisper, not a cry. A relative coming home. An old hope chest reopened.

This is exactly what the Doctor was waiting for. He smiles, his eyes watery and bright, arms extended to me.

"So nice to have you back, Mrs. Madden."

My ex-husband's name was Madden. Not Gavin. Frances just misunderstood. I misunderstood. I hid the truth from myself.

Why would I put myself on the list before the Doctor?

"How do you feel?" The Doctor sits at the foot of my bed, his hand lightly caressing my left thigh stump.

"What did you see? I'm happy to verify everything for you."

I try to talk, but my mouth is gummed closed. My face feels like a cheap latex Halloween mask.

"You were the first person to ever stand up to me. What I did, it wasn't because of you. It was for them. So they would know never to cross me. You made people question if it was possible to take me down. They had to be reminded who I am."

He takes out a vial of Clearwater and preps a needle.

"You know I could never let you go. I could never leave you

alone out there in the world."

I wonder if I've been here the whole time, walking the list to get back to my name. Maybe I never left the hospital. Maybe I've never killed a soul. My legs are gone, my body is wasted, my family destroyed, and it can't just be because of drugs, it can't just be a flashback or a hallucination.

It's not.

There's something more to this.

Something bigger than just

The drug.

The Doctor drives it home into my inner thigh, and I get an instant jolt.

"Hooded Jack made his peace with me. He got your daughter to a safe house. I convinced him he needed to give me the address. That's why he's on your list. He was supposed to help you and he failed. Back wen things were still great between you and I, one of your jobs was taking his leg as an apology after he slighted me. Even after that, he *still* wanted to help you. He's that rare breed of honorable crook. But you? You have been belligerent to the end. I don't want to kill you, I just want your penance. In another lifetime, I took your legs. I took your face. But I'm still angry. I need to get this out of my system. Sometimes you can never apologize enough."

His fingers trace over my thigh, and I don't know if he's talking about him or me.

Maybe you don't need all of the answers to your questions. Maybe you only need to know one thing and then you can die happy.

My name is Veronica Madden. I will die full of questions. About Mrs. Robinson. About my daughter. About Veronica Madden.

Whatever the Doctor gave me burns through my leg. It's swollen and black and purple, and I think they'll have to amputate again to save me. Cut away more. Remove another piece and divine me from my innards, show me who I am.

I fall in and out of consciousness, blowing through the history of my life like a runaway train through a terminal at the subway station. Just little glances.

***

Sitting in a hospital room on a gurney, coated in blood, unsure of what happened or who I am.

The Doctor in the corner with an orderly having a conversation.

The orderly rocks back and forth, staring at me. "What did you do to her?"

The Doctor doesn't answer. He regards his tools on the table.

The orderly looks for any excuse to leave, but he knows he can't go without the Doctor's blessing. "Jesus Christ, I didn't think someone could bleed that much."

The Doctor turns, gives a quick nod to my left. "Get her up to Op-06, I have plans."

I can't really move my head. My neck is fully restrained, but in my peripheral vision, there's another gurney, painted red, glistening.

"They're going to need a shop vac to pick up what's left of that Baldacci guy. Cops are all over this thing..."

Fortescu stops the orderly, pins him to the wall and lightly presses a surgical knife into his throat. "You don't tell anyone she's here. You didn't see anything."

"What do you mean?"

Their voices go low. We must be in a fairly public room. The Doctor runs the knife along one of the orderly's sideburns, shearing it off neatly.

"I mean you were not in this room. This never happened." He rubs thumb and forefinger together in front of the orderly, curly hairs raining down. He nods at the other gurney, "She doesn't exist." He gestures to me with the knife, "She is not a patient here."

"I was on a long lunch. Wasn't even here."

"You have the right idea." The orderly doesn't move. Fortescu leans back, rests heavy on the gurney. "Would you like to join her?"

The orderly can't stop staring at me, what's left of me. He looks back at the Doctor and shakes his head. He bows. He lowers his head and stares at the floor.

"Then I suggest you toddle on."

The Doctor approaches, hollow footsteps echoing around the room. He wheels a small table, so much equipment I have no idea what he has in mind. We were a team. I whisper that to him, but my mouth doesn't move, so it comes out as a defeated sigh. He's the last hope I have to stay alive. All of this blood I must have lost.

"You know what they say about finding good help, Veronica..."
He touches my cheek.

My skin feels thick and cold and dull. I'm drugged to the gills.
His mouth moves and I can hear his words coming slow and steady, out
of sync...

"I don't trust him to stay quiet, do you? No. I'll take care of
him. Later, of course. I'll be too tired by the time we finish. Now let's
talk. You know the rules. First, do no harm. That's rule one, and you've
done so much harm these past few days. You questioned me. You tried
to walk out. To stand on your own. I cannot accept it. I assume you'll
understand if I refuse to accept any further apology. Sometimes, you
can never apologize enough. This is a request from Hooded Jack. We've
made amends. He wanted to be here for this. Even-Stevens, he said."

Then a scream like ten thousand demons, all the souls in Hell,
my voice joining them. Flecks of blood and flesh spatter the Doctor's
face, and I'm dimly aware of heavy vibration on my left leg.

A cool breeze. My foot is falling asleep. Just falling asleep.

And the Doctor holds up his bone saw. He raises it to his mouth,
blows on it, smiles at me and shakes his head.

"We'll have to get you to the ER after this. I hope they can save
you. I really hope they keep you alive, because I'm still so very, very
upset."

He pulls the trigger on the saw and the screaming starts again.

Wiggle your toes, I tell myself. Shake your foot.

Wake it up.

Pins and needles, pins and needles...

***

I wake up. They've moved me to a recovery room. My legs are
throbbing. Itching. Burning. The skin feels like it's all gone dry, peeling
off, stripped away. I've got hoses and tubes stuck in every part of my
body.

The Doctor sits at the foot of my bed. He knows I'm awake. Something is wrong with this picture, the way he's sitting. Draped across the foot of my bed like that. I should feel him on top of my calves.

He smiles as he sees my eyes dance around, watches my brain work. "She's almost got it...almost."

It's when I try to sit up that I realize my legs are gone. I try to let out a scream, but my throat is dry, my jaw feels like it's been bandaged shut.

"The thought sparks in the brain, the synapses fire, electricity dancing across neurons, firing down neural pathways from the brain down the spinal cord, a sonar ping from on high doing a status check, and the answer comes back: something's fucked up here."

He cackles.

"You are one tough patient. A fighter. When I finished removing your other leg, I tried to start on your face. I was going to hold the trigger on the saw, just let it bounce there and see what gravity did. Make some ground chuck. But then I thought about everything we've been through together, everything we've done. You've made me a sentimental wreck. When I thought of all the time we spent together, I stopped...well, almost stopped. I got a pretty good rip in. And I thought... wouldn't it be fun to see the pretty thing suffer? Wouldn't it be interesting to see if she will choke on her own vanity at the sight of herself?"

He runs his fingers across my face, but I don't feel it. He must be caressing bandages, gauze, plaster. "Wait until you see what you have to live with." He reaches down to my left thigh, and it feels like he's reached inside my body to squeeze bone, pluck tendon.

"Sometimes, you can never apologize enough." His face is beet red, veins throbbing in his neck and forehead. I can't make a sound. I can only ride the pain.

He holds up a little remote control that's attached to my bed, presents it like a waiter with a wine bottle. "Morphine?" he asks. "A very good blend."

I nod my head and he pushes the button. I want to kill myself for bending to him. It doesn't stop hurting, but the feeling changes.

Michael Paul Gonzalez

Diminishes. I pull further away.

Doctor Robert produces a syringe from his pocket and gives me an injection. "That's the good medicine," he says. "I want you better so I can hear you apologize again. And again. This is going to take quite some time."

When Clearwater hits my veins, my legs turn cool blue and the room becomes a refrigerator. At that moment, even with the man who tried to kill me sitting on my bed where my legs used to be, even in a hospital where I didn't know what would happen next, where my daughter was, knew nothing of the list or the killing that was about to start, everything was okay.

This is the moment tactical explosions went off in my head. This was the start of everything disappearing. The ashes scattering.

"You're famous now. The papers know you're here, thanks to Orderly Johnson. You remember, the squeamish fellow I had to chase away? He was concerned my treatment of you was less than ethical. He talks when he drinks. Shame. Pity he's no longer around to meet the press. I spoke to them instead. You're a Jane Doe, rescued from the scene of that horrible fire at Satan's Inkwell. The reporter wanted a name, something catchy for his story. I decided on Mrs. Robinson. After all, to survive trauma like yours, someone on high must be looking out for you. Jesus loves you more than you will know, all that. You used to laugh at my jokes. So stone-faced now. Or is that just the sedative? Anyway, I'm the lead doctor in a fight to save your life, a hero to the city. You've turned me into a humanitarian, Mrs. Robinson, and I can't thank you enough."

***

I wake up. The Doctor has moved me to a recovery room and my head is throbbing. Visions dance through my head of the dark time at the hospital. What could have been weeks, months. The Doctor nursing me back to health. Teaching me how to walk on false legs. Pumping me full of drugs and parading me in front of the media, smiling, taking it all in.

I push it back. The past is gone. Nothing else matters but now.

Now I won't be Mrs. Robinson. Now I won't have a saving grace. The Doctor is going to kill me, and I can accept it. I just need to find a way to take him with me.

I could sit here and convalesce, draw connections, see how the list was just my mind's way of walking me through a series of events. Nobody had to die, really. I just wanted them dead. Wanted them to suffer for what happened to me and my daughter. All of this is Doctor Robert pulling the strings. Without even trying, he got me to wipe out most of his competition.

There are two shapes at the end of my bed, two men in uniform, talking. Their mouths move but I can't hear anything. Two orderlies, one in white, the other in black. Their pale skin shines green under the fluorescent light. I can tell by the bulge at the white one's hip, he's concealing a gun. The other I'm not so sure about. I'm watching a changing of the guard. Looks like I'll be stuck with the friend of the NRA.

The man in black turns to the other one, asks him a question. It must be a joke of some kind at my expense, because the white guy grabs his crotch, shakes it at me as they both burst into laughter.

The door closes, and we're alone. He starts towards my bed, and comes up short when he sees my eyes are open. He mouths the question: *Awake?*

I blink. He takes this as the cue to remove his pants. He's skinny, his body has the lean look of a long-term user. Around his right thigh is a leather belt, three hypodermics tied to his leg.

The door's locked, his mouth says. *We're all alone. The Doctor told me I could take a break with you.* The sound is far away, muffled, like he's talking to me through a pillow. *He said this would help you remember the last time...*

There's an IV leading into my arm, the last remnants of the pickup tube empty. The orderly takes a needle off of his thigh strap and flicks it a couple of times, then puts the whole dose into his quad. He pulls another needle off and injects the rest of it into my IV.

These are the rules the Doctor gave me, I lip read. *Told me I*

Michael Paul Gonzalez

could do anything I wanted, long as you were out of it. But I want you lit. I want you to feel this. You on, honey? You on?

He climbs onto the bed, pulls the blanket back and his hands are all over my thighs. The good part of this is that Clearwater makes you numb at first. Maybe I won't feel him on top of me. I'll still have to see him groaning and grunting, still smell his sweat. He's having a hard time getting the flagpole to rise. That'll buy me a little time. Even if he gets it up, I won't feel a thing.

Could he really be this stupid? Doesn't he know the rush that comes with Clearwater? What it does to muscles, to focus, to rage? Is my demon also my deliverance?

I feel everything. Each individual thread in his tattered sweater as it chafes against my stomach. Each hair on his leg stabbing into my thigh, his hands like sandpaper on my breasts, my face, my neck.

He pulls back and asks me if I'm having fun. Keeps fumbling with his junk. It hasn't started yet.

I blink. Squeeze my fists, surprised by the strength I feel. A jolt of focus, riding the rapids. My favorite part of any high. I feel like I could lift a car.

Aside from the IV in my arm, nothing tethers me to the bed. I'll probably only get one shot at this. He wants a ride, I'll give him one.

I slowly loop my arms underneath his, rubbing his back. I don't want him to notice until it's too late. He's bouncing around like a rabbit on crack, trying to get it up and get it in and failing, every nerve in my body on fire and screaming.

But I focus. I exhale. I spot my target.

Embrace me, my sweet embraceable you.

He notices my neck has gone stiff, my body is rigid as a plank.

You coming? I see him ask.

His face is inches from mine, and I take my moment.

Sight-acquire-fire.

Or in this case, headbutt. I drive my head forward as hard as I can into the bridge of his nose. Then I loop my arms over his shoulders, clasping my hands at his neck, a reverse full-nelson choke. My thumb and forefinger pinch together on his windpipe while I use my hands to push back. Whatever I've got in my IV, I want more of it.

He stands up from the bed, taking me with him, the drug giving him the same rush of strength that I have. But I don't let go. My advantage is, I can still breathe. His heart thunders like mine, but I get oxygen to feed the fire while his suffocates. *Now* he's hard, I can feel his manhood poking at my thigh as I hang off his neck, probably turning as purple as his face. He wanted *la petite mort* and I gave him the *grosse*.

His body shudders, and I feel him explode on my leg, pulsing, emptying. His knees go weak and he slumps forward. He died happy. I feel my gorge rise and instead of fighting it, lose whatever was left in my stomach all over his face. Neither of us is leaving this room dignified, but every indignity buys me a few more minutes of life.

Clock's ticking on this high. This is all I get.

After he twitches a couple more times, I feel safe enough to release my chokehold. But not safe enough to be alone with him. I pull myself to the foot of the bed where he left his clothes. His belt. Walkie-talkie. Wallet.

Gun.

A beautiful little Glock-9, smooth action, fully loaded. I can't waste a shot on him. But I can sure as hell cave his skull in.

I slide back over to him on the floor. He's dead. Not even twitching. Crumpled on the floor with a wilted boner. Not good enough.

I pop the clip out of the gun. Wouldn't want to risk an accidental shot. I flip the pistol and bring the butt down on the side of his head, hard enough to shatter his cheek. I relocate the bridge of his nose into his right eye socket. Crack his jaw. And his ribs. And the rest of his nose. I hammer at him until his upper lip tears loose, until his front teeth smash and pile and jut at strange ankles into what's left of his nostrils, until his skull looks like the world's worst dip bowl.

I'm covered in his blood. I can't hear. Blind in one eye. No legs. Knocking on the door to drug-induced heart failure.

But I have a gun now.

Paging Doctor Fortescu.

Doctor Fortescu to recovery, stat.

XXXVII

My final ambush. I doubt I'll get out of this alive, so there's no worry about subtlety and no fear of failure. Thank God I don't have legs. All of the mirrors are eye-level and I'm way down here. Seeing myself now would probably break me.

The orderly still has one needle strapped to his thigh. All of my organs are boiling in oil, my heart is collapsing, and it's only going to get worse. One last jumpstart to carry me through when this one winds down. I need to find the Doctor.

Belly crawling, can't put the gun away. I have to be ready to fire. The fact that nobody has charged into the room has me nervous. It's really hard to slither through a pool of blood. I leave streaks and smudges on the floor, dark red speckled with black. A little death angel.

I'm right back where I started. Legless, crawling and hanging on for dear life. This happened before. The Doctor had me propped up in a room the first time, using me as a pincushion, lending me to his faithful soldiers. And I broke away into the rain somehow. I found a van that was handicapable, somehow. Somehow is beginning to seem like the work of the Doctor. Like I have been led along this path the whole time.

But now, the list is done. It's just me and ten rounds. I crack the door open and close my eye. A hunter can't rely on sight alone. What does it sound like out there? Cold. Quiet. An overwhelming silence, the kind you only hear in empty places.

I open my eye. I've been moved to a different building. This isn't medical storage. This is a hospital. Active, abandoned, I can't tell.

I inch through the door, checking both sides of the hallway carefully. No motion. There are doors at either end with small rectangular windows. If I keep to the corners, nobody should notice me. The hall is lined with rooms just like mine, and I can't help but wonder who else is here. What did they do? Are they still saying sorry to the Doctor?

Another couple of slithers and I'm in the corner at the other end of the hallway. The window here shows more light than the other side. I lean back, my heart hiccupping in my chest. I take a deep breath and mutter a prayer that everything holds together until I meet Doctor Robert again. Nobody punishes a patient without the Doctor's permission. His workers know better than to go rogue. He's around, just need to figure out where.

I reach up to the door handle, moving slowly, keeping my gun ready. I crack the door and look through, seeing another hallway, this one carpeted. That's gonna chafe. Doors line the side I can see. I'll assume the other half of the hall looks the same way. Ambush city.

I rock forward on my hands and push back hard, exploding through the door, landing on my back, sweeping the area and rolling as I go. When I'm satisfied it's empty I stop to catch my breath. If Doctor Robert is more than two hundred feet from here, getting to him will probably kill me.

Breathe. Slow down and listen. Try to read the signs on the doors. Hard to do with one eye. Where would he be? It's late, there's a test running. He's trying to kill me, seeing how much I can take. Any good scientist would want to know the results.

My muscles cramp every time I try to move. I can barely lift my arms without fire radiating down my spine and through my fingers. I check the clip on the gun. Let the mountain come to Moses.

I hold my breath against the pain and raise the gun to the ceiling, firing a single shot.

The entire left side of my body goes numb, refuses to move. I flop to the floor, cracking my head on the wall on the way down. I can't tell if I'm holding my breath or if I just can't breathe. I should feel my heart pounding, see the blood moving, but there's nothing.

The engine has seized.

My right arm feels weak, too, but it's searching for that needle. My last hope. Everything swims in lightning-bright purples and blues. The trail of blood I've left behind me glows like the bridge to Valhalla. My brain stutters, the floor changing from carpet to alley road and back. Voices ring in my head, screaming, shouting, calling for blood.

I blink, and in the alley before me I see a broken bottle. I grab it.

I blink, and on the carpet at my left thigh is the syringe. I grab it.

I can barely push hard enough to break the skin of my leg. I lean on the plunger with everything I've got. Watch the pea under my skin turn into a marble, into a rock. Try to massage it. Tell myself that the drug doesn't need my blood to travel.

I try to pull myself up, clutching furniture, doorknobs, anything. Somewhere along the way, I catch a red handle.

I blink, and I'm in the alley. It's raining.

I blink, and I'm in the hallway, hanging onto the fire alarm, and it's raining.

I flop forward.

***

She's a speck at the end of the alley. From here, she could be just another woman on her way home, just another hooker on the street looking for work. She fades into the haze of the rain, and I don't recognize her shape anymore. She shimmers, turns and disappears, and I let the high wash over me.

Michael Paul Gonzalez

Sorry, I whisper, lost in the rain.

I pull myself to my feet. I have feet here? Stagger around in the rain. Dance like no one is watching. Clearwater is amazing. I could do anything. Be anything. So could she. I have to find her. Three blocks later, I do.

I see her in an alley, feel the heat of anger in my cheeks. I told her not to do this. I warned her. She's there, leaning against the wall, dancing with someone.

This is the answer? This is where it started?

I push forward in the shadows, drawing my gun. Trash everywhere. My foot catches something, sending it clattering across the alley. I crouch low. She takes a minute to look around, decides it was probably a rat, goes back to her conversation. I get up slowly, my hand so tight on my pistol that I can feel my pulse in my palm.

Why was I here?

He moves around the corner next to her, forty-something, balding, laughing his pudgy laugh. I don't recognize him. But I recognize what's in his hand. Surgical tubing, a vial between his ring and middle finger. He shakes it at her and smiles.

And she kisses him.

Her delicate little face, not even a woman yet, she presses her lips to his greasy, jowly face and keeps it there. She wants what he's got.

Behind them, an unmarked town car, passenger door wide open. They've got a spectator. A little Russian weasel wheelman. Vasili.

She takes the needle from Baldacci, starts tying the tube around her arm. I forget her for a second, wanting a hit of what she has.

But she's my daughter. She's more important than erasing my pain. She has the needle at the crook of her elbow, and it's enough for me. I see the rest of her life, a series of these men and these alleys, doing anything she can to get what she wants. She could have had more. She should have had more. This man will be the first in a long line of misery for her.

Unless I do something.

I can do something.

I charge them, gun leveled, his fat face in line with the barrel. I'm too excited to do it right. I don't squeeze, I pull.

The shot misses. Or maybe it goes right where I wanted it to.

She spins around, a neat little pirouette, slumps to the alley floor clutching what's left of her arm. He doesn't even turn to see where the shot came from, just starts running. I breathe, focus, squeeze, still running.

The car peels out, door flapping in the breeze. I have to choose – the moving target or the easy one?

I focus on Baldacci instead. One pop and the back of his thigh ripples, a dark stain spreading on his khaki pants. He collapses, and I'm on top of him, demanding his name.

Charles, he says. Baldacci. She wanted to party, he says, are you a cop?

There's a wailing behind me, bouncing off the walls. Not sirens. It's her. Crying.

She's crying, and he has to suffer.

I don't know her I swear, got nothing to do with her, he says. You got a beef with her, go ahead and take care of it. I just came here on referral.

His lower lip trembles. He raises his arms up to show he means no harm, and his sleeve rolls back. He's wearing a black armband, one lonely stripe showing him to be little more than cannon fodder for Hooded Jack.

I heard she was the best, he says. Don't kill me, he warbles.

What are you, he asks, her mother?

Michael Paul Gonzalez

I jam the gun barrel into his mouth hard enough to shatter teeth. And then, I pull. Two quick shots. He twitches once and he's gone. But it's not enough for me. I hammer him again and again, erasing his face, showing the world how ugly he is.

Stop, she screams behind me, and I do.

I slump over, my fingers tracing over the gun, my eyes glazed and wandering.

Why would you do this? What would make you do this? You were supposed to get out. They were supposed to get you out.

She's not listening to me. Or maybe she just can't understand. I push the needle under her nose.

You want a whole life of fucking men in back alleys for this shit? You know where this will get you?

She gasps and squeezes what's left of her arm, her elbow ripped open like a piñata, little more than gristle and tendons holding it together. A beautiful Rorschach spreads down the side of her shirt.

The needle in my hand still has some liquid. It can stop her crying. That's all I've ever wanted since day one, since minute zero, just to stop her crying, keep her happy.

I inject into her neck, trying to find the quickest way to make her feel good again, and it works. Her crying stops, becomes a brief whimper, and then she's almost sleeping.

My hand on that needle. My thumb on the plunger. I damned her.

I put it there.

This is what she has in store for the rest of her life.

Me.

She deserves better.

She deserves no pain. She deserves no suffering. A quick, simple, clean...

Shot.

She's laying sprawled across the ground, a dark black hole in her forehead, her eyes somewhere else. She's gone. She's free from pain. She'll never suffer again.

It's easy to do what you think you can't. You just close your eyes and think of other things.

I'll take it all on for her. I'll suffer three times for every pain she's ever felt. I scream so hard, hard enough to powder brick, to split the sky. I started this. Veronica Madden, me, I killed her. I'm number one. I should be. But everyone else has to go first. From the doctor to the dealer to the pimp to the madame to the divorce lawyer to the delivery men. Scorched earth.

Sirens echo off the walls, ambulances. I fall to the ground, cover my head as the rain puddles around me, filling with the blood of Charles Baldacci, my daughter, my tears.

Just one ambulance. Black and blue, followed closely by that same towncar. Vasili – what kind of doublecross was he running? Escorting for Hooded Jack, ratting me out to the Doctor's men?

You think you know yourself, and you turn out to be full of surprises. You see an event from far enough away to finally see everything, and you realize maybe, just maybe you were wrong. Maybe there is no list, no conspiracy, no crazy hitwoman. Maybe there was just a criminal and an addict who didn't want her daughter going down the same road, so she did the only thing she could. To try to make a difference. To stop her life from being pointless.

Whoops.

This should have ended here. The list never should have started.

I try to turn the gun on myself, but men pour out of the ambulance, piling on top of me.

This is the bitch he's been looking for, they say.

We've got to get her back to the Doctor.

Michael Paul Gonzalez

Time to say sorry, bitch.

Lightning breaks the sky, and my heart stops.

***

Lightning hits my body, and my heart has started again. The drug is working, for how long, I don't know.

The hallway is still empty. This is near the top floor of the hospital. I remember because they brought me here before. This was where the Doctor began the process of my apology, taking my legs.

Eight rounds left. All I need is one.

I deserve the bullet more than he does. Seven for him, one for me. Whatever it takes.

I don't regret what I did.

It's better to be hurt by someone you know.

Security still hasn't shown since I put a round in the ceiling. I pull myself back where I cam from, pull on the handle once, rock back, and roll through the opening. There's a nurse just inside the door, kneeling over the bloodstain in the doorway.

My nurse with her cold, sweet smile. Her gouged forearms. Her scars will be the last remembrance of the night I clung to life. Footsteps pounding up the hall, and I know that the Doctor will be coming, and he'll have help. This would be too exciting for him to miss. My heart misfires like an old dirtbike. I'm out of needles, out of ideas.

I just need to see his face. Just need to breathe long enough for one exhale, one squeeze.

Thunder builds in the hallway, a stampede, shaking the walls, vibrating the floor. The Doctor bursts in wild-eyed, all in white, white hair perfectly combed. His two eyes burn into my single good one.

"My God you did it... you really did it. Just like the last time. Your heart is so strong... I should have known it wouldn't break. What is it inside of you?" If his mouth is moving, I can't tell.

Two men rush up behind him, security guards, guns drawn. The room folds in on itself, my vision stretches and snaps back to normal.

"What the hell happened here?" the Doctor asks, and he truly doesn't seem to know.

The nurse says something to Doctor Robert in reply, but it sounds like one low bass rumble. Shoot them all. I have enough ammunition to take care of the whole mess. I slump back against the wall.

"How did she get out?" the Doctor fusses. "What happened here? Mrs. Madden? Mrs. Madden, are you all right? Can you hear me?"

I get it. He's acting. This is the part of the movie where the bad guy tries to play innocent. I want a happy ending. I want my actions to mean something. The guards seem hesitant to approach me.

"The blood...the blood, I saw it and I called...I don't know how she got out..." Now the nurse's speech hits me, delayed and late, a Doppler ripple tearing through her gravelly sound.

"Look what he did to me," I say. And of course they don't understand. They don't register. "Look what I've become."

I lift my right arm, feel the blood sluicing through my veins so loose and free, nothing driving it, nothing sustaining my motion. Hope is all I have now. The Clearwater isn't working, neither is my heart. But my right arm moves. Raises. Holds up the gun, matte grey and deadly, and I see it, feel it, know it's real. Know that I'm not the crazy one. This is the summit. It's still conquering Everest if you die on the peak, right?

"Help me now..."

The security guards advance on me, two stepping, shouting for me to lower the gun. The nurse curls into a little fetal ball, her butt straining out the fabric of her pants, the bright white such an easy target. Bright white like the Doctor.

An easier target.

The guards are on either side of him, ready to fire, and he's slack, arms at his sides. I pray for telepathy, bellow my thoughts to the security guards. Have some decency! Read my face! Leave and tell the outside world what's happening here. Media reports, news stories, something, just five minutes...the Terror at the Trauma Center. Hell's Hospital. Carnage in the Care Unit. Someone just has to say something. Make someone care. Put it on paper. Make it organized, make it stick. Build a list. Order, order. They are statues, great iron things ready to kill me.

As my brain scrambles to eat up the last of the good oxygen fogging in my skull, the world becomes sharper. I see reflections of myself in Doctor Robert's eyes. In his left, I'm whole and angelic, sickly green, cowering in the corner with a knife made out of a shard of mirror.

Who I was.

In his right eye, I'm legless, destroyed, bandaged and bloody, gripping a 9mm handgun.

Who I am.

The bloodstain on the carpet takes me to the truth. I killed my daughter. I started this whole thing because I wouldn't give her up. Because I loved her then and still do now, mistakes and all.

It's all I have, so I have to run with it.

The sky has finally cleared, and for a crazy lady with a pistol, it has made my life's work a mess. Now my list reads:

11. Charles Baldacci – used my daughter when he should have been saving her

10. Vasili – turned his back on Hooded Jack, delivered my daughter to a john

9. Susan Schrader – divorce attorney

8. Grace Brooks – my daughter hated her TV show

7. Shakes – gave her drugs

6. Caligula – tried to pimp her out

5. Delia Sugar – bargained my daughter for my life

4. Hooded Jack – lied to me

3. Dr. Robert Fortescu – I quit.

2. Veronica Madden – look in the mirror.

1. Mrs. Robinson – All my fault.

The guards have their guns leveled on me. And I can't tell if they're orderlies, or feds, or cops, or my inner demons. I'm not seeing in color anymore. One of them barks for me to drop it, but I can't. Because this has to end. Even if it's just in my mind, even if none of this ever happened, he stole my daughter's heart, and I can't let it slide.

They tell me if I don't drop it now, I'm dead. They tell me it doesn't have to end this way.

So I bring the gun up, and everyone makes a move on me.

What the Hell.

This isn't the kind of thing you live to tell about anyway.

So I exhale.

And squeeze.

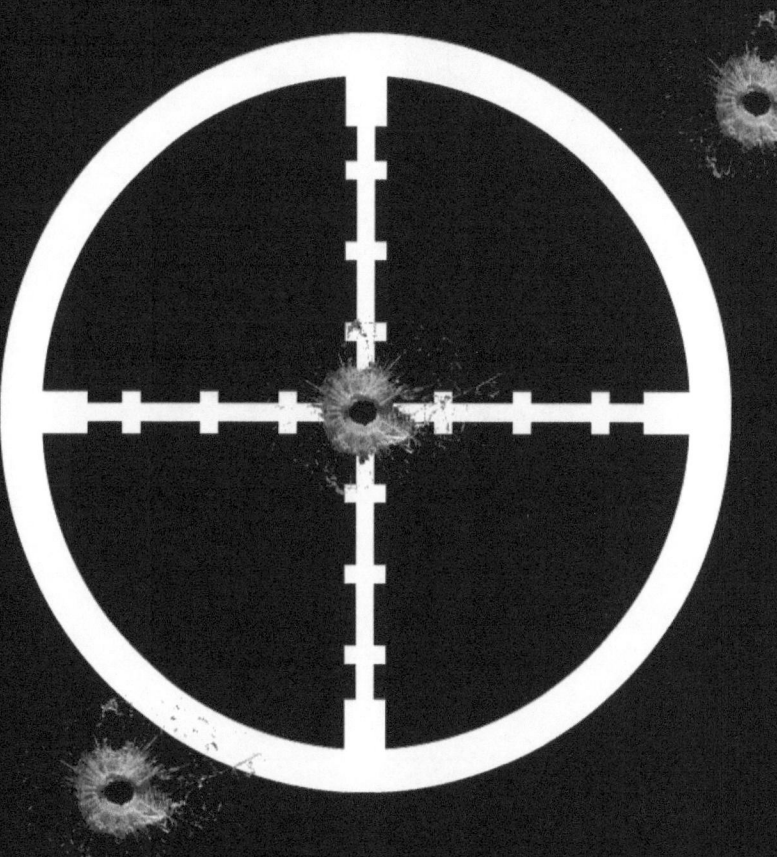

www.ingramcontent.com/pod-product-compliance
Lightning Source LLC
Chambersburg PA
CBHW020232180626
46810CB00006B/2159